THE GENESIS ALLEGORY

Alex P. Berg

BATDOG PRESS
KNOXVILLE, TN

Batdog Press
www.batdogpress.com

Publisher's Note: This is a work of fiction. Names, characters, places, and incidents portrayed in this novel are a product of the author's imagination.

Editor: John Jarrold
Cover Art: Damon Za
Book Layout: ©2013 BookDesignTemplates.com

The Genesis Allegory/ Alex P. Berg — 1st ed.
ISBN 978-1-942274-01-8

CHAPTER ONE

The Proposal

Mycah pulled a pocket watch from his vest pocket. 7:45. At least fifteen more minutes before everyone would start to arrive.

"Anxious, much?"

Mycah looked up at Jerud. "I'm fine. Why do you ask?"

Jerud gave a throaty chuckle. "Well, I'm still on my first mug of ale, and that's the third time you've checked your precious watch. Give it some time, lad. They'll be here."

Mycah raked a hand through his wavy locks. "They'd better be punctual. In our business punctuality matters. A minute early or late and mistakes get made."

"Yeah, but this ain't a job," said Jerud. "Like I said. They'll be here. Just pour yourself a mug and relax."

"And what do you mean by 'precious watch?' You're darn right this watch is precious. It's a precision timing device acquired from the finest watchsmith in all of Guildean."

Another throaty chuckle emanated from Jerud. "Acquired. Yeah. That's one way to put it."

Mycah drew his fingers instinctively across the gilded watch chain. How could Jerud be so relaxed? When they were on a job anxiety fled Mycah like a fickle breeze. That was one of the reasons he was so good at what he did. Jittery fingers led to mistakes, and mistakes could cost lives— or at least ruin them. But here he sat alone with Jerud in a private room at a supper club, and his nerves threatened to unravel him. Of all the things to be anxious about, speaking to a crowd of associates should be the least of his worries. But the job was big, and the pitch needed to be good. Perfect, even.

"I'm going to stretch my legs," said Mycah. "Maybe check on the wine situation. Wouldn't want parched throats once people start to show."

"Suit yourself." Jerud drew a draught from his mug. "I'll hold down the fort."

"I know my throat's already a little scratchy, what with the cigar smoke seeping in from upstairs. Maybe I'll get some tea too. A nice chamomile. Honestly, I'm not sure why you picked this place, Jerud. I think—"

"Mycah? *Go.* I'll be here. Go get some fresh air and come back when you're ready. Just try not to get in Marta's hair, alright?"

"Gotcha. Going."

Mycah stood and headed up the spiral stairs to the kitchen. Despite his complaints to Jerud, The Black Swan suited their needs quite well. The meeting room was hidden underground, secluded in the basement next to the wine cellar. The only entrance lay in the kitchen, tucked away behind the ovens where the pantry should be. An alternate escape route would've been nice, but Mycah suspected the worst danger he might encounter tonight would be a random drunk looking for the way out to the loo.

Privacy and security weren't the only reasons to have picked The Black Swan for the evening's meeting. The food wasn't bad, either. A host of delicious smells greeted Mycah as he reached the top of the stairs—slow-cooked meats, fresh herbs, and oven roasted root vegetables. Fat sizzled over a fire, and hot oil popped angrily as it assaulted a chicken cutlet.

Mycah drew in the scents and sounds as he cracked the door. Something sweet wafted past his nostrils. He glanced at the oven. Pies bubbled merrily within, but whether they were meat or apple he couldn't tell. He'd have to ask Marta for some regardless of the filling. The meat and cheese trays she'd brought down to the private room wouldn't satisfy the guests once they got a whiff of the pies.

Mycah spotted Marta at the front of the kitchen, emptying out mugs into the sink. "Marta! A minute, if you please."

Marta owned and operated the Swan, an establishment of dubious legality that offered varied services to distinguishing patrons with coin to spare. Wishing for a night of wine and song? The common room featured music nightly, often showcasing severely underrated performers. Needed a place to rest one's head after a day's travels? The Black Swan offered that too, as well as company for the bed for the right price. Everything at the Swan operated discreetly, something Mycah could very much appreciate.

"Great." Marta rolled her eyes. "Now what?"

Mycah tried to look hurt. "C'mon Marta, I—"

"Don't bat those pretty blue eyes at me. Spill it. What do you want?"

"Marta, your pies are like honey, and I am but a fly."

Marta gave him a look. "Excuse me?"

Mycah cleared his throat. "Never mind. Any chance we could get some of those pastries in the private room? Not to mention more wine. And tea. I want to make sure the guests are comfortable."

Marta shook her head. "You didn't think I'd forgotten about you? The pies'll be ready in two ticks. I'll have Kat bring a couple trays down. One for your guests and another for Jerud. Lord knows he could eat a whole tray by himself. Though he should give them to you instead. You're skin and bones, child."

Mycah pulled back as Marta tried to pinch him. "I'm not skinny. I'm wiry. Nothing but lean muscle here."

He patted his biceps.

"Right. Anyway, I'll have Kat bring a flagon of wine and a pot of tea. I've got some water boiling over the fire. Won't be long."

Marta had a firm demeanor about her without being harsh. Pester most innkeeps for food and chances were they'd start throwing their bulk around and waving a spoon in your face, crying about how busy they were. Not Marta. She merely said what she meant and people listened. Her haunting beauty probably had something to do with that last part.

"You have my thanks, Marta," said Mycah.

"I'd rather have your coin. I granted Jerud the private room, but the food and drink don't come cheap." Marta hustled away to gather more empty mugs.

Mycah played with a few lonely coins in his vest pocket. Coin, indeed. Well, there would be more than enough of that to go around if everything worked as planned.

Mycah checked his pocket watch again. Still just 7:52. Looking to kill some time, he meandered out of the kitchen and toward the common room to see what the night's entertainment could offer.

Black drapes hung heavily over the entrance. Mycah pushed through them and immediately paused, blinking several times to adjust his eyes to the oppressive darkness. The room stretched amply for such a modest establishment—it was big enough to sit a hundred men at least—yet just two lanterns hanging at the sides of a hemispherical stage added their flickering light to the space.

A slender dark haired woman in a fitted, sweeping dress stood at the center of the stage. She sang softly while an older gentleman crouching on a stool at the back plucked at a mandolin. Bodies filled a good half of the tables despite the early hour, and the patrons listened in rapt attention. Barely a sound could be heard over the soulful melody of the songstress and her minstrel.

Mycah took a seat at a secluded bench near the back wall and removed a small knife from his vest pocket. Deftly, he began to twirl it over the fingers of his right hand.

Twirl, pluck, twirl, pluck, twirl, pluck.

It was a simple trick, one he'd learned when he was just a snot-faced urchin stealing coins from unsuspecting pockets, but it helped soothe his nerves.

Let the mind relax and let the fingers do the work.

Over and up and around the side of his fingers spun the knife, then back on top.

Twirl, pluck.

Once in a groove, Mycah could keep the motion flowing effortlessly for hours. He found it was the best way to help him collect his thoughts. Performing simple repetitive motions and letting the mind wander was the key to working through any hitch, nerves or otherwise.

The warm notes of the soothing ballad washed over him as his fingers danced with the blade. The young woman sang of solemn things. Of broken hearts and loves lost. Of long nights and cold winters. Of youths squandered and wasted away. She seemed far too young to know such aches so intimately, yet Mycah could commiserate. He'd shared his own giant's share of hardship in roughly as few years as the songstress had.

Leaning against the wall, Mycah rested his eyelids and let the pacific waves of music carry him to a place of serenity, like a raft slowly drifting out upon a calm sea. After a mere moment and yet an eternity at the same time, the music faded and a warm round of applause filled the common room. Mycah opened his eyes and felt for his watch. Had it been only one song, or perhaps more?

He checked the time. 8:35. Blast! The guests had probably arrived by now. He needed to return to Jerud immediately.

Working his way around the whistling and clapping patrons—when had the common room filled up, anyway?—Mycah pushed through the black-as-night curtains. The glare and din of the kitchen assaulted him with a veritable circus of activity. Steeling himself against the noise, he hurried down the back steps and into the subdued arms of the basement suite.

Several of the guests had arrived but thankfully not all. The burly Wenton twins, Ben and Bill, joked and snorted while the falsely unassuming Evelyn Sharpe cleaned her fingernails with a knife meant for shucking oysters. Rickety Jim, the finest masquerader east of the Snowfells, helped himself to a slice of meat pie and a glass of cabernet, and Two-foot Pete laughed uproariously alongside Jerud—regaled by the big man with a tale of the glory days, no doubt.

The two made quite the pair. Lumbering Jerud, who could choke out a hog with a single arm and eat the entire beast for a snack afterward, and lanky Two-foot Pete, owner of the most acute pair of ears of any man he'd ever met and the silliest nickname to boot. Seriously, what kind of name was Two-foot Pete? Everyone had two feet. If he'd lost a leg, One-Foot Pete would've made sense, but Two? Mycah didn't get it. He'd have to ask Jerud about it some day.

"Mycah," Pete hollered, waving for him to come over. "How ya been, lad? It's been at least, oh, whawouldcha say... five years since I saw ya? Ya was a good hand shorter back 'en 'an y'are now, I'd reckon."

"True," said Jerud. "But he'd probably be a hand and a half shorter and ten hands deep in the earth now if I hadn't found him."

Jerud made a hacking motion at his throat while sticking out his tongue and rolling his eyes. His antics elicited another rollicking laugh out of Pete.

"Hey, Pete. How you doing?" said Mycah. "I see you're already enjoying the refreshments. Make yourself comfy. We'll get started soon."

While the two old friends joked and shared tales, Mycah maneuvered over to the serving platters to help himself to a slice of the meat pie. His stomach growled as he cut himself a thick wedge that overflowed with cubed lamb, carrots, parsnips, and potatoes. There wasn't any apple pie in sight, so perhaps his nose had deceived him.

Barely had he made a dent in the slice than another pair of individuals sauntered down the stairs. First came the Red Lady—dressed modestly by her standards in a fitted deep crimson dress with a high neckline and long sleeves. Auburn hair cascaded over her shoulders and down the front of her gown in loose waves, caressing her prudently concealed but ample bosom. Mycah found himself a little short of breath. Rumor had it she'd once swayed a high-ranking member of the merchant council to sell his entire estate to buy her a ruby necklace grand enough to match her own beauty, but rumors were often exaggerated. If true, she wasn't wearing the necklace tonight. No matter. Her heaving bust drew no shortage of leering eyes on its own merits.

Just after her came Thomas Flynn, a wizened old man who some called the Count of Contraptions. If you needed something made, a gadget of any sort, he was your man. Jerud had worked with him a few times long ago. He'd related a story to Mycah of when the old man fashioned a serviceable musket out of a lead pipe, a nail, a piece of twine, and a potato. The tale sounded implausible, but Mycah didn't have any reason to doubt Jerud. Where they'd obtained black powder for the musket however was another question entirely. If old Tom Flynn were clever enough to manufacture that out of such simple ingredients, he'd be the wealthiest man in all of Guildean.

The two new arrivals began making the rounds, introducing themselves to those they hadn't met and sharing pleasantries with the rest. Mycah's stomach growled again, and he realized the majority of his pie still lay uneaten. With forced leisure, he consumed the remainder of the slice slowly and waited for the last guest to arrive. Part of him wanted to wolf it down and go back for seconds, but the last thing Mycah needed was a stomach ache before his big speech.

Take it slow and keep away from the spirits. You'll need a clear head for what's to come.

At nearly 9:00 by Mycah's watch, the last guest descended into the common room. Rayven. The nickname stemmed from his appearance. Arrow-straight, jet-black hair fell to just below his collarbone, and the entirety of his garb from boots to coat blended into the shadows, dull of sheen and midnight black. A yew bow peeked over his shoulder along with a quiver of arrows fletched with feathers plucked from the same bird from which he drew his moniker. His gaunt cheeks and chalky skin created a sense of hunger about him. Not like a man who was in desperate need of a meal, but more like a serpent coiled and ready to strike. Avoiding the others, he glided to the back of the room. Neglecting the refreshments, he sat down and propped up his boots on a chair in front of him.

Mycah knew nearly all the others from previous jobs, and those he didn't have experience with Jerud did. But

Rayven was a relative unknown. Scuttlebutt painted him as the best of the best. A jack-of-all-trades who could get things done and disappear at a moment's notice. Inviting him to the meeting was a calculated risk, but Mycah needed someone of Rayven's talents. He'd just have to keep a keen eye on him down the stretch.

Mycah noticed Jerud eyeing him from the front of the room. The nerves that beset him earlier were gone, replaced instead with a burning desire to plunge into the grandest exploit of his young career. Mycah gave Jerud a nod. It was time. Jerud, lifting his bulk from his seat, gathered everyone's attention with his booming voice.

"Ladies, gentlemen, friends, and esteemed guests. Thank you for joining us this evening. I hope you've enjoyed the fine delicacies provided here tonight—the Lord knows I've eaten more than my fair share." Jerud patted his considerable girth, eliciting a ripple of laughter from the guests. "But as you may have surmised, there's more to this gathering than free food and ale. For more, I'll pass you over to my dear friend and partner in crime, Mycah Cuthbert."

Mycah rose from his seat and sidled across the room to join Jerud at the front. Mycah felt the weight of nine sets of eyes fixed upon him, boring into him with their curiosity. Quickly, before losing his nerve, he dove in.

"You're all here," Mycah said, "because you're among the very best at what you do. Thieves, con men, grifters, charlatans, frauds, and shysters of all types are gathered here tonight for one reason and one reason only. We all share a common bond. An intense distaste for honest work and an itching desire to liberate items from their rightful owners.

"I've gathered you tonight because I have a vision. A vision of a heist so grand that no fewer than the ten of us gathered here tonight could possibly pull it off. It won't be easy. Not by any stretch of the imagination. But I know what you're all capable of, and I know we can accomplish what I have in mind.

"Now what I'm about to propose is both extremely lucrative and extremely dangerous. So far no one here is committed to anything. If any of you feel unsure or uneasy about what I might divulge, please help yourselves to another glass of wine or a mug of ale before you head on up the stairs. For everyone else, I'll need a nod of acknowledgement to let me know you're in."

The moment of truth had arrived. If anyone left, at best everything would be delayed while he and Jerud looked for replacements. At worst, his plans would die in a fire. Mycah held his breath as he glanced around the room, ticking off the seconds in his head as he made eye contact with each and every individual. Despite a couple shared glances between a few of those gathered, not a person left their seat. Soon everyone gave him a nod. Except...

Rayven stuck a solitary finger into the air and cleared his throat, causing everyone to turn back and spare him a glance. The man truly blended into the shadows. Mycah had forgotten he was there.

"The bounty. How much?"

"Ahh," said Rickety Jim, nodding thoughtfully. "Good point. What's the take? If we're to risk our necks, I'd be nice to know what we're getting in for, Mycah."

Mycah exhaled. He'd anticipated the question, and he hoped the answer would be enough to tempt those still perched upon the fence of indecision.

"The job'll net us five thousand guilders. Gold."

A fair few eyebrows raised amongst the guests.

"Apiece."

Several people gasped quietly. Rickety Jim let out a high-pitched whistle.

"Well then," Jim said. "I'm in. You bet I am."

"So what about you, Rayven?" asked Mycah. "You in?"

Rayven raised his eyes from the floor and held Mycah's gaze for a few precious seconds. Mycah could feel the tension in the room building like a roiling thunderhead. A small fortune in gold hinged on one man's response. Eventually, Rayven gave a curt nod before dropping his eyes to inspect his fingernails.

"Well," said the Red Lady in a silky voice. "I suppose it's settled. So for that much gold, what in the world are we pilfering? Are we to coax the sacred vestments off the Archbishop himself? Don't think I won't try..."

Mycah joined in a round of laughter with the others at the thought of the Red Lady seducing the Archbishop of Guildean.

"No," he said as the laughter died down. "But you're closer than you think. We're going to steal the Staff of the Vernal Equinox from the Stormqueen."

Stunned silence filled the private room.

"Um... was that a joke?" asked one of the Wenton brothers.

"No. I'm serious," replied Mycah.

Simultaneously, everyone erupted into a fit of questions and exclamations.

"Are you crazy!" said Rickety Jim, jumping out of his seat.

"You've got to be joking," said Evelyn as she stabbed a table with her knife.

Tom Flynn shook his head. "This is a bad idea. Very bad."

"Everyone, calm down!" bellowed Jerud over the clamor, standing and waving his arms in appeal. "The lad's not mad. Listen to him before you string him up by his thumbs. I think you'll all find there's a fair amount of merit in his plan."

As the uproar subsided, Mycah gave Jerud a thankful glance. He'd long ago lost count of how many times the big fellow had sprung him from a jam.

"Alright," said Mycah. "Might as well get right to it. This is how I envision it all happening."

The beginning of the pitch came easiest. Mycah had practiced it a dozen times at least. First he related an overview of his plan, but then he delved into specifics. How individuals would be sorted into teams. What ruses each team would perform and for what purpose. Mycah talked about routes of entry, timings, and fail-safes in case anything went awry. Once he got started, the words surged out of him like floodwater from a broken levee. He presented maps and schematics—architectural drawings of the Stormqueen's palace and the surrounding city. People asked questions, shared input, pointed out minute details that would either ensure success or doom them to failure.

As the night wore on, Mycah saw the tension drain out of the faces around him. Grim half-frowns turned into eager smirks, and twinkles lit up gleaming eyes. Those who just hours before had viewed him as little more than a talented youth mentored under Jerud's wing now nodded at his words with a measure of respect.

With the lanterns burning low and the proposal fully revealed, the participants agreed upon a time and date for their next meeting and began to retire for the night one by one. Two-Foot Pete headed up the stairs last, leaving Mycah and Jerud alone in the basement surrounded by empty chairs, bottles, and the remnants of Marta's meat pies.

Mycah, free of the burden of delivering his proposal, poured himself a glass of wine. He joined Jerud, who'd melted into the folds of the couch.

"So," said Mycah. "What do you think, old man? How'd I do? Are we actually going to be able to pull this off?"

Jerud blinked eyelids heavy with sleep. "You want the honest answer, lad?"

"Of course."

"Well... I'm impressed. Went better than in practice. You gave them no alternative but to believe in your plan. And in you. Heck, even I believe in you now."

Mycah raised an inquisitive eyebrow. "What do you mean 'even you' believe in me? You've always believed."

"Of course I did, lad," said Jerud. "Of course I did. But now that everyone else is on board, well... now I really believe. Come on. Don't give me that look."

Mycah couldn't help but grin.

"Come on," said Jerud, stifling a yawn. "Let's get some rest. We've got a lot of work to do."

CHAPTER TWO

Watch and Wait

Mycah pulled away from the eyepiece of his spyglass and massaged his right temple. When he was just a naïve rapscallion, he never envisioned one of the physical perils of being a professional thief would include eyestrain, and yet every job involved a hundred times more surveillance than honest-to-goodness action. Performing a stakeout was one thing, but spyglasses always gave Mycah headaches after prolonged use.

Stiff legs were another of the understated dangers of surveillance. Mycah stood, bent over to stretch his hamstrings, and began to pace around the suite. The Red Lady, or Red as they'd all started to call her, had used her feminine wiles to convince the desk clerk at The Ptarmigan to allow them the use of the hotel's fifth-story penthouse suite for a full week. While the accommodations were luxurious, they were irrelevant for Mycah's purposes. The appeal of the penthouse was its view.

Across the street from the Ptarmigan stretched the palatial estate of the Stormqueen, the most majestic, awe-inspiring residence Mycah had ever laid eyes on. The walls

15

surrounding the grounds spanned no less than five city blocks on the east side and eight blocks on the north and south. From the primary gates on the eastern side of the complex, a paved path of polished granite meandered around lush flower beds, porcelain fountains, and manicured topiary gardens overflowing with caricatures of everything from stallions and eagles to griffins and dragons. One small patch of holly shrubs had been clipped to resemble a pack of horrible monsters of nightmare with razor-sharp talons and swollen eyes at the ends of long dangling stalks.

Like a river, the path snaked about the grounds until it emptied into a massive plaza. At least two thousand revelers could fit in the square, and surely that many or more would be present at the Rite of Spring festival five nights hence. At the center of the plaza, however, stood the piece de résistance—a massive fountain of the Stormqueen raising a knobby staff to the heavens while water rained out around her into a shallow pool beneath.

At the center of the grounds loomed the Stormpalace, a massive edifice that dwarfed every other building in the city except for the Grand Cathedral of Guildean. Marble pillars flanked the entryway, and several stories above a balcony perfect for public addresses overlooked the square. Windows stretched as far as the eye could see, lingering alongside gilded parapets and hand-carved gargoyle rainspouts. Given it's exterior, Mycah salivated at what wealth must hide within the palace's walls.

Mycah peered back into the spyglass toward the western entrance of the estate, the 'business end' as he called it. Every estate, no matter how grand, possessed a business end. A place where deliveries could be made and workers could enter and exit without sullying the majesty of the rest of the grounds. While the grandeur of the eastern half of the palace was appealing, Mycah only needed familiarize himself with the western entrance intimately.

A quick rap at the door preceded the entrance of Jerud and one of the Wentons. Was that Bill, or Ben? Mycah could never tell the two apart. Jerud stripped off his overcoat and threw it on the back of a chair before taking a seat next to Mycah.

"Well, we've got the pastry cart," said Jerud. "We stashed it in the lockup over on Southwick."

"Good," said Mycah. "Any issues?"

"Nope," said Jerud. "Everything went just as planned. The driver's route led him right into our accident. You should've seen it. Me and Bill was going at it, yelling and cursing at each other. He hopped out and tried to get us to calm down. By the time he'd broken us up, Ben had made clean off with his cart."

Jerud broke out in a wide grin. "Oh Mycah, you should've seen the look on his face when he realized his cart was gone. It was priceless. Lord Almighty! It was all I could do not to bust out laughing."

Jerud started to laugh, and soon his entire belly shook with his mirth. Tears formed at the corners of his eyes. As his laughter subsided, Jerud pulled a kerchief from his pocket and dried his cheeks. A look of soberness spread across his face.

"Ahh... He'll probably lose his job because of us. Poor bastard..."

"Yeah, probably." Mycah clapped his hand on Jerud's shoulder. "Try not to dwell on it, big guy."

"I know." Jerud sighed. "I just don't like it when some innocent fool gets hurt. What if he had a family? Like the palace guard who we liquored up and stole all his clothes. You think Rain's gonna take it easy on him for being such an idiot? I bet he got canned, too. What if he had a wife and kids?"

Mycah shrugged. "You know as well as I do we needed a Stormguard's uniform to use as a template, and that was the easiest way to get one. Look, when you steal things someone's going to get hurt. It's inevitable. You don't seem too bent out of shape about stealing from the Stormqueen."

"Yeah, but the Stormqueen's not gonna be living on the street after we take her staff. Which reminds me—" Jerud lowered his voice. "Are you sure you want to go through with this, lad? Stealing from a Stormqueen? It's not the smartest move in the world you know?"

"Oh come on, Jerud," said Mycah. "We've been through this."

"I'm just saying—she's got powerful magic, lad! She's bound to have laid some serious magical traps all over that staff. It might be cursed."

Mycah pressed his fingers to his temple. "Jerud, it's not going to be cursed. I doubt she's ever considered the possibility anyone might try to steal it."

"Just because no one's ever tried doesn't mean—"

"Jerud, curses are the last thing you should be concerned about. Worry about the Stormguards catching us or someone screwing up or about the people we've hurt along the way. But please, not curses."

Jerud grumbled. "Great, now you've got me worried about that guard again. And curses to boot. Bah! I should pray. Maybe the Lord'll have answers for me. You certainly don't."

Jerud made the Lord's cross with his thumb and forefinger across his forehead and chest, lowered his head, and stared at his thumbs.

Mycah regarded Jerud with a pang in his heart. Underneath Jerud's gruff exterior thrived a caring, nurturing, and extremely pious soul. Mycah sometimes wondered how Jerud had fallen into his profession, but he was glad he had. If not for Jerud's fatherly instincts, Mycah would most likely be missing a hand or rotting away in a dungeon somewhere.

Mycah sighed. He never felt like he was any good at reassuring Jerud when he had a crisis of confidence. How could he be? Mycah, despite his undeniable talent, sometimes questioned his life choices as well. The pastry delivery man, the palace guard—they were just the most recent victims of his grandiose plans. How many lives would he trample on his quest for riches? Mycah kept telling himself this job, whichever he currently pursed, would be his last. But it never was.

Staring out the window toward the Stormqueen's plaza, Mycah couldn't help but wonder about the ramifications of stealing the Staff of the Vernal Equinox. Every year on the morn of the first day of spring, a throng would gather at the plaza, bringing offerings of seeds, ale, and honey. They'd prostrate themselves before the might of the Stormqueen, begging for her to banish the cold winds of winter and call forth the warm rays and gentle rains of spring. And every year at noon, as the church bells of the Grand Cathedral knelled out a twelfth toll, a hush would descend over the gathered masses. Stormqueen Rain, clothed from head to toe in deep blue, flowing robes, would appear on the balcony with her equinoctial staff held reverently at her side. Mycah could remember it clearly, as if it were a few years past when he'd attended the celebration himself for the first time.

"Children of the earth," Rain proclaimed in a voice that carried effortlessly across her estate and into the surrounding streets. "I see you here bowed before me in supplication. I see the offerings you have brought before you, the fruits of your labors, the gifts of the earth. I hear the grumbling of your bellies as your larders run low, and I feel the weight of your need. I hear your plea! Let winter end, and spring renew!"

Rain extended her left hand into the chill winter air, fingers waving ever so slightly. The crowd held its breath. A gentle breeze lifted the folds of her robe. First just the sleeves, then the fabric around her legs as the breeze grew stronger. The dull winter sky began to darken, clouds gathering and swirling high above the palace. Just a handful at first, but within minutes heavy gray thunderheads covered the sky. The breeze strengthened, whipping around the Stormqueen with unseen vigor. Rain thrust the staff high overhead, and thunder pealed from the Heavens. Not once or twice but over and over, relentlessly booming as if to proclaim the sheer might of the Stormqueen.

As suddenly as it began the booming disappeared, re-placed instead with the gentle patter of raindrops on streets and rooftops across the city. Every year the rains would last for a full week, after which the skies would clear, carrying with them the life-bringing warmth of sun.

Mycah's concern was with the power of the equinoctial staff itself. The intermediary he worked with had indicated his client wanted the staff and nothing else, and clearly the client was willing to pay quite handsomely for it. But did the staff control the weather, or did the Stormqueen do that herself? Could she craft another if the staff was lost? And if the staff were stolen, would the spring rains still come? Or would winter reign eternal? The possibility was sobering.

Another question nagged at him. Who was his mystery client? Mycah had long since learned doing business face to face with clients only led to problems. If the client and the thief didn't know each other's identities it made life much easier after a job was completed, which was why Mycah always used an intermediary who held funds from clients in escrow until completion of a heist. Nonetheless, he couldn't help but wonder who could be both wealthy and motivated enough to commission the theft of the staff.

Guildean was an independent city-state. A local council comprised of merchants, a few elected officials, and the head of the city watch enacted laws and levied taxes to fund civic improvements and pay the police force, but as a general rule the government kept its fingers as free of dirt as possible. The members of the merchant council pushed for minimal interference in their businesses, and more often than not the city's elected officials rested in the pockets of the merchants. The city was largely left to function to its own devices.

That meant the only entities possessing any real power in Guildean were the Church and the Stormqueen. An uneasy alliance existed between them—the Church made no secret of the fact that they denounced the Stormqueen and her heathen magics—but both powers seemed content enough to maintain the status quo. Though they each employed small standing armies, they'd never done more than send verbal jabs at each other, at least during Mycah's lifetime. But now someone was making an obvious power grab in going after the Stormqueen's staff. The Church condemned all forms of mysticism outright, so it seemed unlikely they'd want anything to do with one of the Stormqueen's artifacts. But if not the Church, then who?

Perhaps one of the other Stormqueens had dreams of swelling her own influence at the expense of Rain's. Mycah had never left Guildean, but he knew from travelers' stories that Rain was one of four. The other Stormqueens—Zephyr, Typhoon, and Howl—lived in cities far to the north, east, and south, and just as Rain's duty was to usher in the spring, each other Stormqueen was tasked with initiating a season as well. Mycah could only imagine there must be some animosity between the enchantresses. Whoever was in charge of marshaling the winds of winter couldn't have been nearly as popular as Rain.

Perhaps the financier was someone from Rain's past—someone who held a grudge against her and wished to disgrace her in the eyes of the public. But the populace depended upon spring rains to bring about a bounteous harvest. They worshiped Rain almost as a god. If anything, the loss of the staff would create social unrest. Whoever the mystery client was, he or she must surely stand to benefit from such turmoil.

The creak of the suite's front door brought Mycah out of his reverie. Tom Flynn strode in looking pleased. He pulled up a seat next to the window.

"You're looking chipper," Mycah said.

"I continue to surprise myself, you know," Tom preened. "I always knew I had a knack for machinery, but I never knew I was such an artist."

"What are you talking about?" Jerud asked.

"The dining cart," said Tom. "That was right up my alley. And the collapsible guard hats? Those were a stroke of genius. But the cake? You two are going to love it. It's gorgeous. You'd never know I didn't go to pastry school."

"I don't think they have pastry schools," said Jerud. "Cooking schools, sure, but pastry?"

"Don't ruin my moment, oaf." Tom leered at the big fellow.

"What about that special charcoal you promised us?" asked Mycah. "Is it ready yet? We're going to need enough to heat that whole palace for two days seeing as they're not taking any deliveries the morning of the festival."

"I've got Evelyn and Two-foot Pete working on it," said Tom. "It's a lot of work, but they'll get it done in time. They're resourceful."

"Good," said Mycah. "We can't afford any screw-ups. Anything looks like it's falling behind schedule, you let me know alright?"

Tom and Jerud both nodded.

Peering around the room, Mycah spotted the Wenton brother that had arrived with Jerud propped up on a sofa in the corner cleaning his fingernails. Just as he was about to ask him a question, he thought better of it and turned to Jerud.

"Hey, Jerud... is that Bill?"

"What? No lad, that's Ben," Jerud said. "Can't you tell the two apart?"

"No. You can?" asked Mycah.

"Of course, they look completely different. Back me up, Tom.".

"I'm with Jerud on this one, son," said Tom. "I'm not sure they're even twins. Maybe twins from a different mother..."

Twins from a different mother? What did that mean? Mycah shook his head and turned toward Ben.

"Hey, uh, Ben," Mycah said. "Go fetch Rayven for me. Tell him we're going to need to try on a few articles of clothing. And find a decent tailor while you're at it. I think we might need one."

"Sure thing," said the Wenton. He hopped off the couch and hustled out the door.

Turning back to the window, Mycah bent back down and pressed his eye to the spyglass. The Winter's End ball, held annually on the eve of the rite of spring, was five nights away. Five nights remained until the biggest night of Mycah's life.

CHAPTER THREE

The Snag

The pastry cart clattered over the cobblestones. Dusk's wan rays trickled over the rooftops, barely providing any light, but the moons were out in force. Lunaris, the greater, was waxing gibbous, while the lesser moons Cheru and Ubim shone with an intense vigor. Though some merchants still hawked their wares in the early evening, the majority of the thoroughfare lay empty. Most patrons had opted to do their day's shopping early to avoid the chill bite of the night air.

Mycah, dressed in a double-breasted chef's coat and pressed pants of pristine white, gritted his teeth against the cool breeze. He wished for a heavy woolen overcoat and a pair of warm gloves, or better yet, a warm fire by which to warm his backside. Hands gripping the reins, he urged the old sorrel-colored mares around a corner with a gentle tug.

"You ready for this?" Mycah asked.

Rayven, seated next to him on the cart, looked completely transformed in his own chef's garb of pure white. A light dusting of flour decorated his pale hands, and his jet black hair hid in a bun underneath a tall chef's toque. Other than his decidedly unconvincing slim physique, he looked every bit the part of a renowned pastry chef. Rayven raised a silent eyebrow in response to Mycah's question, his dark steely eyes answering for him.

"Just figured I'd ask," Mycah said. "I haven't heard a peep out of you in ages."

Rayven took his time in responding. "I dislike surrendering my bow."

Mycah too felt a little naked without his usual arsenal of carefully concealed weapons—a knife at each side, another in his vest pocket, and his most prized possession, a small single-shot derringer tucked away in his boot. Mycah had been loath to leave it behind, but his surveillance indicated they'd be thoroughly searched.

"Just think," Mycah said with a forced grin. "If this comes down to battle, we're as good as dead anyway."

Rayven elected not to respond.

Mycah urged the mares over a bridge that spanned Guildean's aqueduct. The city planners had been smart in keeping the aqueduct system primarily underground—it resulted in much less refuse and human waste being dumped into the water—but due to the lay of the city the waterway occasionally popped aboveground. The bridge spit them onto Solomon Way where greater traffic, both human and equine, greeted them. After a few minutes of travel along the avenue, bright lanterns atop the walls of the Stormqueen's estate flared into view. Mycah pulled out his pocket watch. Satisfied with the time, he tucked it away within his coat.

"Alright. Let's do this," said Mycah. He cracked the reins to the mares to hurry their pace.

Mycah drove the cart several more blocks alongside the estate's wall until he approached a gated guardhouse to his right. He reined in the horses and called down to a pair of guards stationed at the gates.

"Good eve', sirs." Mycah tipped his toque to the guardsmen. "We're here to deliver the cake for the queen's jubilee."

"Papers?" asked the head guardsman.

Rayven removed a folded envelope from his coat pocket that he handed to the sentry. The watchman unfolded it and extracted a letter written in a tight script. A flowing signature and an official seal adorned its base. As the guardsman read, he motioned his partner to the back of the cart.

Two more sentries stood at attention atop the walls, long-barreled muskets held erectly at their sides. Clad in fitted ultramarine frock coats with yellow sashes and tall, leathery top hats—also dyed a deep blue—the Stormguards eyed Mycah and Rayven alertly. After a perfunctory check in the back of the pastry cart, the guardsman hopped out and nodded to his partner at the gate.

"Alright, everything checks out." The head guardsman handed the papers back to Rayven. "Report at the loading entrance."

Another Stormguard approached from the inside of the gate. After removing a fat key from the side of his frock coat, he unlocked the gate and waved them through. With a quick flick of the reins, the cart lurched forward through the gateway and down a paved path leading to the back of the palace. Compared to the majestic gardens adorning the front entrance, the path in back felt downright workman-like. Lonely trimmed hedges hugged the track with only a lily pad-filled koi pond nearby to keep them company.

Urging the horses along the path, Mycah brought the cart to a paved circular expanse nestled at the base of the palace. Two more uniformed Stormguards, similarly garbed to those on the exterior walls but armed with sabers and hand cannons, ushered them in and showed them where to park. After a thorough pat down by the Stormguards to check for contraband, Mycah and Rayven climbed to the back of the pastry cart and set down the liftgate. Carefully the pair rolled out a dining cart carrying their prized possession and maneuvered it up to the entrance to the palatial residence. A well-dressed steward greeted them.

"Truly magnificent," said the steward as he admired the meticulously piped swirls that adorned all five layers of the grand cake. "The level of detail Chef Remmie incorporates into these cakes year after year continues to impress. I only wish he were here for me to give him my thanks."

Mycah tipped his hat. "Regrettably, Chef Remmie is far too busy crafting confections for his clientele to partake in deliveries. I'll pass along your sentiments. He'll be humbled by your praise."

"Well let's bring it in to the kitchen, shall we?" said the steward. "You haven't been here before, have you? No, I think not. I'm sure I'd remember if you had. Follow me, I'll show you the way."

The steward motioned to a guard to open the gate. He ushered them inside, walking briskly through the high-ceilinged entranceway and into a long, brightly lit corridor.

"I'll appreciate a modicum of haste, if possible," noted the steward. "As you can well imagine, we're extremely busy tonight in preparation of the grand ball, and a host of other measures require my attention."

He led them around corners and through vaulted corridors, passing storerooms filled with assortments of dry foodstuffs, cured meats, and jars of undistinguishable perishables. Servants in navy blue uniforms passed by carrying sacks of grains and haunches of lamb, barely sparing the trio and their grandiose cake a second glance. Eventually, they arrived at a pair of heavy double doors, which the steward propped open to allow Mycah and Rayven to roll in the cart.

Despite having studied the architectural schematics for the palace, Mycah was impressed by the sheer size of the kitchens. Ovens occupied one full side of the cavern, while chopping and carving stations on the other side rubbed shoulders against ingredient racks overflowing with multicolored spices, fragrant herbs, fresh vegetables and cured meats. Grills and spits squatted along an invisible line dividing the kitchen. Cooks and assistants buzzed about dicing, chopping, sautéing, braising, and flambéing. Lording over the worker bees was the queen—a heavyset woman barking orders and instructions out as she inspected each station. Mycah couldn't see any waving of wooden spoons coming from her direction, yet he was sure if the right piece of cutlery presented itself this woman would wield it with reckless abandon.

More impressive than the size of the kitchen was its cleanliness, and yet not a single kitchen scullion could be seen shoveling ash or scrubbing chimneys. Lucky for them, they didn't have to. Directly below the kitchen, a boiler room generated heat and steam and piped it throughout the palace. From the furnaces, specially designed flues funneled radiant heat up from the fires into the kitchen's ovens and grills, and vents above the grills directed smoke outside. It all worked flawlessly.

Mycah barely suppressed a smile. At least, it worked flawlessly under normal circumstances.

"Hurry now," said the steward. "The cold storage locker's at the end of the kitchen. Just around the corner."

Many wealthy residences housed small iceboxes in the cellar, but the winter's ice only lasted a few months into spring, necessitating traditional means of food preservation for the remainder of the year. The Stormqueen, however, operated a full walk-in cold cellar year round. Mycah supposed that for someone who could command violent storms of sleet and ice keeping a storage locker cold could be accomplished with a simple snap of her fingers.

With the steward clearing a path through the throng of cooks, Rayven and Mycah pushed the cart forward. As they neared the first grill, Mycah scratched the nape of his neck and palmed a small, flat pouch hidden under his collar. Two chefs stood at the grill, basting racks of succulent lamb chops with a syrupy glaze. Subtly, Mycah shifted his end of the cart, bumping one of the cooks in the small of his back as he turned one of the racks.

The chef cried out. "Argh, watch where you're—"

"Terribly sorry, sir," said Mycah. He rested his right hand upon the chef's shoulder in commiseration while with his left he slid the pouch between the bars of the cooking grate and into the flue. He continued after the cart, following the steward, but as they neared the other end of the kitchen voices from behind cried out.

"Good Lord!" said the steward as he turned to see the source of the commotion.

Thick, black, acrid smoke roiled out of the lamb-laden grill and poured into the kitchen like a rotten fog. With it came a pungent aroma of burnt hair and sulfur. Scullions flapped kitchen towels while cooks scrambled desperately trying to transfer the meat to serving trays.

"You can find your way out?" asked the steward.

Mycah and Rayven nodded.

"Good. The cold locker's out the door and to the right. What a disaster!"

As the steward hurried off, Mycah and Rayven pushed the cake out of the madness of the kitchen and into the locker, leaving the door cracked behind them for light.

"Two minutes. Go." Mycah began to tick the seconds down in his head.

Together, Mycah and Rayven dug their fingers under the bottom layer of the cake and lifted in unison revealing a hollow frame with a tightly packed bundle nestled in the center. Setting the cake down on the floor, Mycah ripped into the bundle and tossed a packet of clothes into Rayven's outstretched hands. Quickly he tore off his chef's coat and pants and threw on the clothes enclosed in his packet: a white collared shirt, ultramarine trousers, an ultramarine frock coat with a yellow sash, and sturdy, well oiled boots.

The guardsman's tall hats had initially posed a problem, but Tom had engineered a mechanism that allowed them to collapse into flat disks. Mycah removed his pancake-like hat from the bottom of the frame and flipped a lever on the inner brim, causing the top of the hat to spring outward with a twang.

The clock in Mycah's head completed its first full revolution. "One minute..."

Rayven had already finished dressing into his Stormguard's costume and was unscrewing the caps off the corners of the dining cart. Mycah pocketed a small set of lock picks from his bundle and gathered the discarded chef's garb. After retrieving his prized pocket watch, he shoved the clothing into the castoff packets. Meanwhile, Rayven extracted saber blades and sheaths from the hollow tubes that comprised the cart. Having replaced the newly filled packets back into the frame, Mycah helped snap hilts onto the bare blades.

"Thirty seconds," Mycah said tersely.

Mycah quickly belted on the saber and reached into the hollow frame for the last piece of the guard's outfit—a pair of perfectly replicated hand cannons, one of which he pitched to Rayven. Looping the cannon into a circlet at the side of his belt, Mycah joined Rayven in lifting the cake mold off the floor and back onto the hollow base. As he left, he cast a hurried glance around the locker to confirm that nothing was out of place.

Chaos still reigned in the kitchen as thick smoke boiled out the grill Mycah had tampered with as well as two others and half a wall's worth of ovens. Tom had drilled into Mycah that once the pouch came into contact with the specially prepared charcoal burning in the boiler room below they'd have at best two and a half minutes before the smoke began to clear. But Tom had sold himself short. The acrid smoke showed no signs of abating. With the distraction still firmly in place, Mycah and Rayven purposefully strode off in the opposite direction.

Both of them had committed the palace's plans to memory. They marched silently through corridors and breezeways until, after several twists and turns, the palace spit them out into a massive foyer featuring two curved stairways leading to the Stormqueen's private chambers. Atop the stairway flanking a pair of polished oaken doors towered two hulking giants, dressed similarly to the rest of the queen's guard but with a pair of golden sashes running down each shoulder rather than one.

Despite their costumes, there'd be no getting past Rain's private guard. They were quite familiar with everyone authorized to enter the private sanctum. Instead, Mycah turned away from the stairway and to his left, where he and Rayven descended a much smaller spiral staircase leading to the palace bowels. The stairs led down two stories. At the stair's exit, Mycah held up his hand to stop Rayven and checked his watch.

"Wait," said Mycah, tucking the watch back into his coat pocket.

After a few moments, the sound of footsteps rose and fell—a night's sentry making his rounds. Once the footfalls had faded, Mycah popped out from the stairwell and headed into a dimly lit corridor, counting the doors until he reached the third on the left. Mycah tested the door handle. Locked as expected. From his pant pocket he drew forth a key, placed it into the lock and turned. He heard a reassuring click.

"Thanks, Red," said Mycah.

Not only had the Red Lady coaxed guards' routes and timings out of a love-struck young watchman, she'd snagged his keys and slipped them to Rickety Jim for an impression while she whispered sweet nothings into his ear. And as Jim told it, the guard had been stone-cold sober the entire time! Of course, Red could probably coax a mother hen into giving up her own chicks for nothing more than a kiss. Well perhaps not a hen, but a rooster for sure.

Mycah and Rayven snuck into the room and quietly closed the door. Mycah squinted in the darkness. The lanterns had been turned down as low as they would go to conserve fuel. Rayven liberated one of them from a wall sconce and adjusted the wick, sending light shooting through the room. Carts filled with clean linens sat parked next to bright copper washbasins. Spigots promising hot water from the boiler room protruded out from the walls, while steam seeped in through vents up high. The whole room smelled of tallow perfume, and the lye in the air made his throat itch. Thankfully, the room was deserted, since all the servants were otherwise occupied preparing for the grand ball later in the eve. Rayven motioned toward the opposing wall where carts filled with soiled clothes and bed sheets lay underneath the openings of numerous laundry chutes.

Mycah tapped on the chute smack dab in the middle of the bunch. "This is the one." He peered up into the darkness. "It's going to be tight. We'll need to strip down."

Mycah unbuckled his belt and hid it underneath a pile of linens in the cart adjacent to his chute. He stuffed his heavy frock coat and top hat in beside it. Chances were no one would enter the laundry room tonight, but force of habit kept him from leaving anything within the reach of prying eyes.

Rayven gestured toward the chute. "Youth before beauty."

"Hey, a joke," said Mycah. "I was beginning to think you were made of granite. C'mon, give me a lift."

Mycah pinched his shoulders and tucked his arms in close. Cupping his hands, Rayven boosted him into the chute. Once inside, Mycah could barely move his arms, but by wiggling his body back and forth he slowly weaseled his way upward. After raising himself a body length, he called down.

"Can you get in on your own?"

"I'm resourceful. I'll manage."

Rayven spoke the truth, but his varied skill set wasn't the main reason Mycah had chosen him to accompany him on the night's adventure. He was the only one other than himself who'd be able to fit in the chute. Well— besides Red of course. But her bosom would've made maneuvering in the chute difficult, to say the least.

As Rayven entered the chute, the darkness grew more oppressive. Bit by bit, Mycah wormed his way up. After several minutes of climbing, he couldn't see the hands in front of his face.

"How you doing down there, sunshine?" Mycah asked.

"Simply radiant."

Mycah rolled his eyes. Coaxing conversation out of Rayven was like trying to squeeze milk from a cat. It only poured out in tiny driblets. If Jerud's personality were anything like Rayven's, Mycah would've divorced him long ago. Unfortunately, trying to fit Jerud's expansive paunch into the laundry shoot would have been like trying to fit a fully-grown hog into a single sausage casing.

Eventually, a dim glow appeared at the top of the chute.

"We're close," Mycah said. "I can see the entrance hatch ahead."

Pulling himself up the last few feet to the opening, Mycah snaked a hand upward and silently cracked open the hatch. The room was dimly lit, but Mycah could make out the hems of lavish gowns, chemises, and dresses of every cut and color. For someone who only appeared in public wearing flowing robes, Rain's closet certainly contained a remarkable variety of clothing. Sensing the coast to be clear, Mycah pulled the hatch back only to find it opened halfway before bumping into the back of the laundry chute.

"Damn... I can't open the hatch all the way. I don't think I can squirm through."

"Then *force* it open." Rayven sounded irritated.

Mycah felt along the top of the chute. Soon his fingers found where two bolts held the flap in place. Teasing one of his lock picks from his shirt pocket, Mycah began to unscrew the bolts using the flat end of the pick. His arms bent at an unnatural position, and his shoulders, already aching from the climb, creaked in displeasure. Sweat started to bead upon his forehead as the stuffy metal chute radiated his body heat back towards him.

I should've let Rayven go first. Made him do the dirty work.

Eventually the second screw loosened enough for Mycah to pry off the door. He tossed it through the opening and pulled himself through, flopping onto the closet floor like a trout slipping from a fishmonger's hands. Rayven followed with slightly more grace. They crept to the closet's exit. Outside, lit by the warm glow of a single lamp, stretched Rain's private quarters. At the far end, hiding behind a closed door, lay her study.

Mycah tipped his head toward a hallway leading out of the bedroom. "Head to the sitting room. Make sure we're alone, then keep an eye on the main entrance."

Rayven shook his head slightly. "We should stick together."

"We need a lookout," said Mycah. "And since I'm the better lockpick, that leaves you. Go. I'll get you as soon as I'm done."

Rayven fixed him with a steely glare that silently voiced his displeasure. Mycah thought he might refuse, but after a tense moment, Rayven muttered a hasty 'very well' and glided off down the corridor. Mycah rolled his eyes.

Mycah quietly tiptoed over plush rugs that littered the Stormqueen's bedroom on his way to the study. Easing the door open, he found a room filled to the brim with mysterious objects. At one end of the study, two obsidian carvings of naked enchantresses bookended a desk overflowing with metal orbs and old books held together by tattered bindings. Stacks of paper had commandeered the corners, and a journal covered with a tight, illegible script lounged in the middle of it all. Other items coaxed at Mycah's periphery, but his eyes had found their prize—the Staff of the Vernal Equinox, on display in a horizontal glass case.

This, however, was no ordinary display case. Thick, blown glass panes reinforced every couple inches with steel bars as fat as Jerud's fingers encircled the staff. At the center of the case gleamed a block of steel marred only by a small keyhole that poked out of its middle.

Mycah kneeled before the case and inspected the lock. It was of the pin and tumbler variety but masterfully built, with a narrow keyway and at least seven pins. Such a lock would present a challenge for the best lockpicks, but My-cah prided himself on being even better than the best.

Removing the picks from his shirt pocket, Mycah spread them reverently out before him on the ground. He took a deep breath and flexed his fingers. Grabbing a tor-sion wrench in one hand and a hook pick in the other, he cleared his mind and let his hands go to work.

Despite the lock's complexity, not an ounce of worry or doubt clouded his mind. It had always been like this on every lock he'd ever coaxed open. Man and mechanism merged. He became one with the lock. The tools were ex-tensions of his own hands, and through them his fingers danced over the pins. He felt and prodded. Hook pick be-came diamond pick and diamond pick became saw rake. Each tool manipulated the lock precisely when needed. All sense of time escaped him as he worked.

The lock surrendered with a click. Replacing his tools within his pocket, Mycah stood up and cautiously opened the case.

As he stood there with his hands hovering over the knobby staff, Mycah couldn't help but recall Jerud's insistent warnings. A single bead of sweat collected at his temple. Was there a hidden trap? An alarm that would sound if he stole the staff?

"God," whispered Mycah. "Please don't let this thing be cursed."

Holding his breath, he lifted the staff from its perch. After holding it for a couple of seconds, he let out a relieved sigh.

And heard a cry.

"Intruder!"

CHAPTER FOUR

A Sudden
Change of Plans

Mycah spun at the sound. A uniformed guard stood at the entrance to the bedroom.

"Intruder!" The guard drew his sword.

Blast! Where the Hell was Rayven? Why hadn't he called out? Mycah felt for his weapons but found nothing. He'd left them in the laundry basket.

The Stormguard ran toward him, sword held high and ready to strike. Mycah reacted instinctively. Lunging out of the study, he swung the staff in a sweeping arc and cracked the guard on his elbow with a sickening crunch. With a cry of pain, the guard released his sword while simultaneously pulling free his hand cannon with his good arm. Both hands clutching the staff, Mycah stepped into the Stormguard and swung hard to the right, smashing the guard's wrist into a nearby dresser. The guard grunted. His gun misfired with a deafening blast. Pinning the guard against the dresser with the staff, Mycah brought a swift knee into the man's groin.

As the man slumped to the ground in pain, distant shouts and pounding footsteps alerted Mycah from behind. Rayven was still nowhere to be seen. Either the man had been captured or he'd already fled. Running to the closet, Mycah rammed the staff downward into the laundry chute only for it to jam with a hand's length protruding from the chute. Mycah franticly swiveled the staff about trying to get it into the opening. He heard shouts right outside the closet now. Desperately, he pushed hard in the middle of the staff, bending it just enough for it to slip through the hatch and down the shaft.

As two hulking guards rounded the corner, Mycah slipped his feet into the hatch and arched his body into the shaft. Two blasts ripped into the chute barely a hand's breath above his head as he slid into the darkness. His shoulders pinched to minimize contact with the walls, Mycah sped down the shaft and plunged into the linen cart below. Shouts and curses echoed down from above as he fumbled about in the linens for the staff. Finding it wrapped in a bedsheet's cold embrace, he wrestled it loose and vaulted out of the cart.

Mycah wiped a hand across his sweaty brow. His plan was shot to Hell, and he had to act fast. His frock coat and weapons beckoned from the cart's depths. He could try to don the guard's costume and sneak out of the palace, but the sentries had already been alerted. Sneaking the staff out under his garb would be a virtual impossibility. But what other choice did he have?

Mycah snapped on the belt, snatched the coat, and sprinted to the exit. He threw open the door and popped his head out only to hear more shouts echoing down the hall—from both ends no less. Mycah swore under his breath. How in the blazes had the guards been alerted so fast?

A blast foreshadowed a musket ball that ricocheted past his face. Mycah pulled back and slammed the door shut, dead-bolting it from the interior. Pulling his sword from its sheath, he rammed the blade into the door frame and bent the blade to the side. Taking his frock coat, he fed a sleeve through the saber's hilt and around the door handle, hastily tying it off in a knot. Sounds of pounding fists and a rattling deadbolt followed Mycah as he retreated into the laundry room.

Mycah desperately surveyed the room. He had a minute, maybe two, before the Stormguards broke through his makeshift barricade. Multiple laundry chutes led up to various servants' quarters, but Mycah doubted he could make it halfway up a shaft before the guards broke in and shot him from below. Besides the door and the laundry chutes, no other exits existed. Except for…

Running to the side of the room, Mycah upended a laundry cart and hopped on top. He seized the grate covering an air vent and pulled franticly, but it was bolted tightly onto the wall. Looking about for a tool, Mycah's hand came to rest upon the hand cannon looped upon his belt. He drew the weapon and held it to one corner of the grate.

"Here goes nothing." Mycah squeezed his eyes shut as he pulled the trigger.

A wave of pain rippled down his arm as shards of mortar and metal exploded from the wall. Mycah coughed as he peered through the resulting chalky haze, ignoring a loud ringing that pealed through his ears. The blast had torn a hole in one corner of the grate. Wedging the staff into the hole, he pried the cover loose, tossed the staff into the vent, and plunged in afterward.

Compared to the laundry chute, the air duct seemed spacious—though just as dark and far hotter. Sweat oozed from Mycah's pores as he crawled forward, staff clutched in his right hand. By the faint glow behind him, Mycah spotted an intersection of several ducts ahead. Feeling about with his free hand, he found a small duct open above him, but it was far too narrow for him to enter. To his left and right, the main duct stretched into complete and total darkness.

As Mycah pondered which way to go, he wondered how everything had gone to Hell so fast. After so much planning, surveillance, and preparation—so many nights spent rehearsing every detail of the heist—how was it he now found himself stuck in a blistering air vent in total darkness with furious, bloodthirsty guards hot on his trail? How had the guard in Rain's quarters gotten past Rayven? Why was he there at all? There was no reason for anyone to have entered the Stormqueen's inner sanctum during her winter jubilee. Had the others been discovered, too? He fiercely hoped that Jerud was safe, at least. He wasn't sure he could forgive himself if anything happened to the old bear due to an error on his part.

Mycah shook his head. No sense in worrying. Right now he needed to make a decision and fast. He tried to think. Despite having studied the palace blueprints, he had no knowledge of the vent system or where it led. Even if he did have a light by which to guide him, he'd be lost as soon as he turned a corner. His sight would be useless. He'd have to depend upon other senses.

Shutting tight his eyes, Mycah focused on the other clues his body provided him. He could hear the hammering and yelling of the guards as they forced their way into the laundry room. The smells of hard steel and mildew worked their way into his nostrils. He sensed the vibrations of the pounding behind him, and felt the warm air of the vent waft over his matted, sweaty locks.

The heat. That's the key.

Mycah turned to his left and crawled toward the source of the hot air as quickly as the duct would allow. The heat would lead him directly to the boiler room, and from there Mycah could easily work his way through the kitchens and out the way he came. With any luck, he could outrun the Stormguards and slip over the palace walls before being caught.

The heat intensified as he pulled himself through the passage. Sweat poured from his face as he plodded along methodically, twist after turn. His hands felt like hotcakes on a griddle. Faster and faster he urged himself into the heart of the blaze.

His sweaty palms slipped on an opening he hadn't sensed. Opening his eyes—had they been closed this entire time?—Mycah glanced through a gaping hole into a blazing inferno of hot coals. He pulled back, shielding his eyes from the intense heat that radiated up from below. The vent opened into a massive central furnace, sealed tight except for a hatch through which servants could shovel charcoal.

The hatch however was shut, and it glowed a dull red. It would melt his bones like butter if he were foolish enough to try and force it open.

Even out of a direct line of sight of the fire, the blaze was overpowering. Mycah felt his energy draining rapidly. He had to act fast before he succumbed to the heat.

"Help!" he screamed. "Help! Open the door! Please! For the love of God open the door!"

Over the crackle of the burning coals, Mycah heard shouts of distress. They were followed shortly by the clanking of an iron pole and the creak of an oxidized hinge.

"Hullo?" called a voice.

Gritting his teeth, Mycah pitched himself forward into the furnace, somersaulting onto the searing coals. His boots sizzled, and sparks flew as leather met charcoal. He dove forward with all his might through the hatch, bowling over the terrified stoker who'd opened the door. The stoker crumpled into a pile, panicked and dazed. Mycah patted his face and arms, shocked he remained intact and unseared.

A second soot-covered worker loomed over him, shovel lifted in the air and ready to strike.

"By the moons, man," said the worker. "How in blazes did you—"

"The stairs?" Mycah stumbled to his feet and looked around the room franticly. "Where are the stairs?"

Confused, the worker pointed toward the far wall. Mycah ran.

"Wait. Stop!"

Mycah ignored the man and flew up the steps like a hawk on an updraft. Up the stairwell and out the door he went, his feet propelling him as he burst through the door to the kitchens.

A sense of order had been restored, and chefs and scullions bustled about in a controlled haste. At the sound of Mycah's pounding footsteps, a few heads turned his way, and eyebrows began to rise.

Mycah must've looked as if he'd been to Hell and back. His top hat and coat had long been discarded. Sweat slicked his hair and plastered his shirt to his skin. Soot likely darkened his face. Clutching the staff, he likely resembled a madman more than a palace guard, and yet people generally obeyed those who projected an air of authority.

"Out of my way." Mycah raced across the kitchen floor, shoving a sous chef who wandered into his path. "There's an intruder in the palace who came this way. Call the guards. Tell them to follow me to the back exit. Quickly now. GO!"

Chefs and assistants alike leapt aside to avoid his wrath, dropping pans and utensils in shock. Several hurried off down the corridor in search of more guards. Mycah smiled.

Like clockwork.

After exiting the kitchens, Mycah ran as hard as he could. But instead of heading to the loading area where the pastry cart was parked, he veered into a long corridor he and Rayven had passed while entering. If his memory of the palace blueprints served him correctly, the corridor merged into a breezeway that led to the gardens. As he ran, Mycah felt a surge of adrenaline course through his body. This was it! Despite everything he was going to make it after all! All that remained was to meet Jerud and Two-Foot Pete at the south wall and escape with the staff.

As he neared the merger of the corridors, a shadowy blur spun out from around a corner and clotheslined him with a vicious blow. Mycah's feet flew out from underneath him while the stranger's arm threw him to the ground. His head hit the marble floor with a bone-crunching crack.

Pain arced through him, pounding into his skull like nails. Bile rose in his throat, and his eyesight blurred. Through the haze, a distorted vision of a stranger danced about before coalescing into a figure with jet-black hair.

"Rayven?" whispered Mycah.

His vision faded to black.

CHAPTER FIVE

The Deal

Rayven. The traitorous son of a bitch. Because of Rayven, the guards must've known Mycah was inside Rain's private chambers. Because of Rayven, they'd known he would try to escape through the laundry room. And it was snake-faced, backstabbing Rayven himself who assaulted him just feet from the palace's exterior.

Mycah fumed as he sat on a cold stone floor. His circumstances didn't allow him many luxuries, but time he possessed in excess. He spent it thinking, pondering, and fuming about Rayven.

When he awoke, Mycah had found himself lying on his back in a small cell. His head roared with pain, and he'd promptly emptied his belly onto the floor in a fit of nausea. Mycah wasn't sure how long he'd lain there. Hours? Days? Perhaps longer? He'd been relieved of his trusty pocket watch, and a lack of windows prevented him from tracking the passage of time.

At first, the pain prevented Mycah from doing much of anything. The smallest motions caused him to writhe in agony—as if stinging nettles were being driven into the base of his skull one by one—and so Mycah remained motionless. Humiliating as it was, he couldn't even gather the strength to rise and crouch in a corner to empty his bowels. He soiled himself where he lay. He constantly faded in and out of sleep. When awake, he prayed for sleep to return to make the pain subside. After a dozen sleep cycles, the searing fire at the base of his skull ebbed to a dull ache, and Mycah became aware of two new companions—hunger and thirst.

While the fire in his head raged, his body had rejected even the notion of food, but as soon as the pain abated Mycah's stomach roared to life and staged a vocal protest. Mycah knew hunger well from his days living on the streets of Guildean, but thirst was another matter. His mouth felt as dry as a kiln.

Gathering his strength, Mycah had felt about the room searching for an entrance. His fingers traced along rough-hewn stone walls before finally sliding onto jagged wood. Pounding on the door, Mycah had hoarsely cried for water, praying that someone would answer his call. A splinter in his palm was his only response. Eventually, sleep eventually overtook him once more.

Luckily, Mycah's captors hadn't completely forgotten him. When Mycah awoke, he again returned to the door, intent upon calling for aid until his voice failed him. In the process he nearly knocked over a cup and plate that had been set just inside it.

Water! And food! He drained the contents of the cup in two long draughts then attacked the plate of food like a starved mongrel. The gruel tasted horrid, like millet mixed with chalk, and yet he licked the plate clean.

Throughout the process, Mycah felt no shame. He was surprised how quickly he surrendered his dignity when faced with death and starvation. With an influx of food energy to his system, Mycah pounded at the door and called for more. Despite his best efforts, no one came.

Every time when he awoke, Mycah found more of the same vile mush and a cup of water by the door, and every time after eating, Mycah would pound on the door. With each passing of the cycle, he poured less and less energy into his cries for help. Despair set in. Mycah considered himself an optimist, and yet it was difficult to view his current predicament with anything but pessimism.

Mycah feared death. He supposed most others did as well. He always assumed life—no matter how difficult or sorrowful or wretched—would be preferable to the alternative. However with each passing cycle, he became less and less sure. Would he be locked away indefinitely? Would he ever again see the light of day? Ever hear the voice of a friend? Would he ever feel a cool breeze upon his face or the warmth of a roaring fire upon his outstretched hands? Would life be worth living if he could never have or feel these things again? He no longer remained certain.

Nonetheless, the thought of losing his will to live still terrified him. Mycah supposed that if nothing else, his fear alone indicated his continued desire to live. That and the constant grumbling of his stomach.

And so Mycah passed the time as best he could, thinking about his past and the future he'd dreamt for himself. He thought about his friends, Jerud especially. And he thought about Rayven and his treachery.

He couldn't stop obsessing over the man. His aloofness and lack of conversation should've been indications of malfeasance. In Mycah's experience, traitors rarely drew too close to those they planned to betray. And he should've known better! He'd worked with his fair share of turncoats in the past. Perhaps he'd been too focused on the mission, too caught up in the idea of perpetrating the ultimate heist to see what was plainly displayed before him.

Everything about Rayven infuriated him. The way his eyes spoke in lieu of his mouth. The way his footfalls pattered far louder than they should. The way his keys jingled at his side.

Loud footfalls? Keys?

The click of a key turning in a lock startled Mycah out of his reverie. The footfalls and keys were real, not some product of his imagination! Terror filled him as he realized that perhaps his day of reckoning had finally arrived.

The door creaked open and a pale flickering light entered the cell, though after so many days of total darkness it seemed as if the burning radiance of God himself shone through the door.

A grizzled, bare-chested jailor loomed in the opening. In a rasp reminiscent of a razor drawn across a leather strap he spoke.

"Stormqueen Rain demands your presence. Come."

Mycah's voice creaked with displeasure after an extended period of dormancy. "What's to be done with me?"

"Come, or be removed by force," said the jailor.

Mycah gingerly rose to his feet. Shielding his eyes from the light, he stumbled into the passageway. After being imprisoned for so long in such a small space, even walking presented a challenge. Before Mycah could gather his bearings, two muscular guardsmen dressed in Rain's familiar ultramarine and yellow uniforms seized him by the arms and began dragging him down the hall. The guards carried Mycah past other cells resembling his own, past an open gate, and into the hallway beyond.

As they half dragged, half carried him, Mycah rapidly absorbed what he could of his surroundings. The narrow halls were lined with dark gray basalt and appeared carved directly from the stone. On and on they went, passing branching corridors and locked doors of weathered oak.

Mycah had assumed he was being held in the Stormqueen's palace, and yet the further the guards took him the more convinced he became this was someplace altogether different. None of the corridors matched his memory of the palace's blueprints. Moisture oozed from the walls. Whatever this place was it lay far underground, and if it was part of the palace, it was far older and more primitive than any part he'd seen.

The guards turned into an open doorway and carried Mycah into darkness, descending a gentle slope. Mycah's skin prickled in the chill air and a dripping sound rippled out before him. The guard's clattering footfalls changed to splashes. Was this some sort of cavern?

The guards stopped and dropped him. Dark, frigid waters swallowed him whole. Rising to the surface and gasping for air, he thrashed about, wiping the hair out of his eyes as he tried to still his chattering teeth.

The taller of the two Stormguards pushed forward a bar of soap with his foot. "Clean yourself, worm. Your odor is offensive."

The cold water sent a chill running down his spine, but Mycah knew better than to argue. The sooner he complied, the sooner he'd be allowed out. He stripped off his soiled clothes, grabbed the soap, and began to scrub furiously. Filth sloughed off his body. Despite the cold, Mycah welcomed the bath as it afforded him an opportunity to drink and rehydrate as well.

As he cleaned, the shorter of the two guards retrieved a parcel from a wooden stool propped up in a corner. When he returned, he unceremoniously dumped the bundle onto the soggy ground at his feet.

"Enough with the scrubbing," rumbled the tall guard. "Put on these clothes. Now. Before I make you."

Mycah emerged from the pool naked and shivering. Bending over, he sifted through the bundle. It contained only a simple cotton shift and matching breeches. A towel with which to dry himself would've been nice, but he supposed it didn't really matter. The clothes were already soaked from their encounter with the floor.

As he dressed, Mycah quickly considered his options. He could try to fight the guards, but the pair seemed alert, well rested, and well fed, whereas he could barely muster the strength to still his own shivering. Besides, each guard outweighed him by at least half his own body weight, and the taller of the pair towered over him by a hand's-breadth.

Fighting wasn't an option but neither was running. Mycah didn't trust his legs to carry him back out into the hall much less outrun a man. Not to mention Mycah had no idea where he was. Silence and obedience remained the only real options, but they were options with promise.

The jailor had mentioned that Rain herself had asked to meet with him, and the simple fact he was being given a bath and a change of clothes gave him hope. Perhaps a deal to avoid a premature death could be struck.

Once dressed, the two guards again seized him by the arms, carried him into the hall, and resumed their journey. As their boots clacked rhythmically on the stone floor, the grade of the floor began to slope upward, and the walls no longer sparkled with moisture. After several turns, the guards stopped in front of a heavy wrought iron door. While the shorter of the two guards reached for the hooped handle, the taller guard rammed a forearm into Mycah's throat and shoved him to the wall, knocking the breath from his lungs.

"Johnah? What are you doing?" asked the shorter guard.

The tall guard pressed his face close to Mycah's, looking him square in the eyes. "You listen and you listen good. I don't know why Queen Rain wants to see you, and I don't care. If it were up to me, I'd let you rot in that cell o' yours forever, wallowing in your own filth. Luckily for you I ain't in charge. That said, if you give the Queen any lip or even look at her funny, I'll gut you like a God-damned fish. Got me?"

Mycah could tell from the man's eyes he meant every word he said. He tried to nod in acknowledgement, but the man's thick forearm pinned his head to the wall. Not until his partner's hand rested upon his shoulder did he pull away.

Mycah sucked in some breath.

"Easy now, Johnah," said the shorter guard. "Nothing's to happen to him until Queen Rain meets him. You know that."

"I know, Sten," said Johnah. "Just making sure this worm knows his place."

Tugging open the door, the guards ushered Mycah into a circular room of moderate size, though being devoid of any furniture it seemed larger than it was. Oil lanterns flickered within, and two braziers flanking a wooden doorway at the far end of the room radiated heat. Mycah felt it cut through his soaked garb and envelop his body, helping still his chattering teeth.

The guards dumped him roughly in the center of the room.

"Kneel and wait," said Sten. He and Johnah took up position behind him.

Barely a moment had passed before the iron door opened, and two more guards led forth a man similarly dressed in a thin cotton shift and pants.

Jerud! By the moons but he looked bad! Sunken cheeks drooped under dull eyes, and tangles matted his beard. He'd lost weight, which he needed, but starvation was far from a healthy dieting technique. The beatings, of which Jerud had endured several, couldn't have helped. Mycah had held out hope that Jerud and the others had escaped, but apparently such hopes were idle fancy.

The two new guards deposited Jerud at Mycah's right with similar instructions to kneel.

"Good to see you, old friend," Mycah said.

"You too, lad," said Jerud. "I thought I'd lost you—"

A swift boot to Mycah's backside caused him to cry out in pain, as did Jerud following a boot to his ribs.

"Silence," said Johnah. "Speak only when spoken to."

Mycah peered at Jerud in silence. Though a dull sheen coated his eyes, behind it hid a silent sparkle Mycah hadn't seen at first glance. So. His old friend hadn't given up hope after all. With the two of them reunited, Mycah's spirits lifted. Perhaps all would turn out right in the end after all.

The door swung open and two more uniformed Stormguards entered. After them glided a diminutive figure dressed from crown to toe in a flowing maroon gown, head wrapped in a matching veil so that only a set of eyes peeked out. And what eyes they were. Piercing blues flecked with gray that stretched like midnight wells, holding a wealth of information hidden in their watery depths.

Stormqueen Rain.

Strange that when Mycah recalled the rite of spring he remembered the Stormqueen as a grand, imposing figure even at a distance when in person she barely stood tall enough to reach his own chin.

She glanced at him as she entered the room. Her eyes radiated power and demanded respect. Perhaps Mycah recalled Rain's aura more than her actual stature.

Behind the Stormqueen strode an unassuming gentleman of advanced years. A full crop of hair topped his head, but the color had faded long ago as it had from his close-cropped beard. Inconspicuous as he was, the man carried an air of wisdom and self-assurance lacking in most men. Mycah assumed he must be a sort of chamberlain, though he couldn't be sure.

Last but not least entered the traitor himself—Rayven, dressed in his familiar black attire. He sported a saber at his side in addition to the bow at his back, and in a notable exception to his minimalistic color palette, blue and yellow chevrons alternately adorned his narrow shoulders. Barely affording Mycah and Jerud more than a passing glance, he casually propped himself up against the far wall.

Rain positioned herself between the braziers and stared at the captives in front of her. Mycah felt a bead of sweat develop at his temple under the woman's all-consuming gaze. By the moons but the woman had piercing eyes! In a barmaid, Mycah would've found them mysterious and appealing, but Rain used them like weapons, boring into Mycah's brain to discern his innermost wants and desires. Was she working some sort of magic upon him? Mycah averted his eyes to the floor in a vain hope that breaking eye contact could prevent a spell from taking effect.

When Rain finally spoke, her voice flowed melodiously like chimes dancing upon a cool autumn breeze. Mycah couldn't help but lift his eyes and gaze upon the harmonious enchantress. Yes, if she were a barmaid, Mycah would find her very appealing indeed.

"First, I must commend you. No one has ever so much as tried to steal a loaf of bread from me, and yet you were audacious enough to break into my residence, impersonate my private guard, and try to steal the staff through which I call forth spring itself. And you very nearly succeeded. If not for the fickle loyalty of your compatriot over there, I'd find myself lacking my greatest prize."

Mycah glanced at Rayven, rage boiling under his composed exterior. How could the man just stand there, so calm and indifferent? Did he make a habit of ruining the lives of others to improve his station? Mycah wanted to charge the traitor and pummel him with a flurry of vicious blows, but his environs made that far from the best choice of action.

"You." Rain gestured to Jerud. "What's your name?"

"Jerud. Jerud Beyfield... uh... my liege."

"And you," said Rain, addressing Mycah. "What's yours?"

"Mycah Cuthbert... milady." How did one address a Stormqueen anyway?

"So Master Cuthbert. Master Bayfield." Rain nodded toward each of them in turn. "I find myself faced with a choice. Having never dealt with thieves before I find that I'm not entirely sure what to do with you. I suppose I could have you executed and be done with it. That would be the simple solution. It's the solution my chamberlain has advised of me. But it seems a waste to simply dispose of individuals with your unique skill sets.

"As it happens, I require the services of ones such as yourselves. Individuals skilled in the art of retrieval, shall we say. There's an artifact of great importance I require. It's not currently in my possession. I'd like you to remedy that. If you're able to deliver this artifact to me, I believe I could find it within my heart to stay your execution. So I offer you a choice. You may obtain said artifact for me— possibly perishing in the attempt—or you may choose the swift release of death now. Which is it?"

Jerud turned to Mycah, his eyebrows raised in appeal. "Seems like an easy choice, lad. What do you say?"

Perform another job or face execution. It seemed an easy choice. Too easy. There was certainly a catch, but a catch of any kind struck Mycah as preferable to certain death.

"I think I've got at least one more adventure in me," said Mycah.

Turning to the Stormqueen, Mycah responded. "Very well. We accept. We'll do our best to steal anything you want."

"Good," she said. "Are you a religious man, Master Cuthbert?"

The question caught Mycah off guard. "Uhh... yes. I suppose so. What does that have to do with anything?"

A twinkle gleamed in the Stormqueen's eyes, and Mycah swore she smiled underneath her veil.

"Because," Rain said, "I'd like you to steal something from God himself."

CHAPTER SIX

Genesis Retold

Mycah's jaw dropped. What did she mean by that? Was it possible? Was it a joke? Mycah couldn't imagine this powerful Stormqueen, this steely-eyed enchantress, would dangle death in his face only to joke about stealing from God.

"I'm... afraid I don't understand," said Mycah.

"Are you familiar with the story of Genesis?" said Rain.

"The creation narrative?" said Mycah. "Yes. I suppose so."

"Tell it to me then. In your own words."

"Milady, aren't you familiar with it?" asked Mycah. "Jerud's more pious than me. He could tell the story better, I think."

"I'm familiar with the story, Master Cuthbert. I'd like you to tell it to me as you recall it. Be specific but brief."

Mycah tried to think back to his days in the orphanage when well-meaning pastors had attempted to beat virtue into him through biblical passages. Despite his best efforts to the contrary, he'd picked up a fair amount of knowledge. He just didn't revisit it very often.

"Um, well, let's see," said Mycah. "In the beginning, God created the Heavens and—"

"No, no," said Rain. "I'm not interested in recitations of scripture. Tell me the story in your own words."

Be brief but specific. Tell the story in your own words. Lift your chin, back straight.

Mycah almost expected the crack of a ruler across his backside at any moment.

Just tell the story, however you remember it.

How hard could it be? Pausing a moment to collect his thoughts, Mycah started over.

"So, at the beginning of creation, God created the world. On the first day he created light. And also time. At least that's what some would argue. On the second and third days he created the heavens and the lands and the seas. After that he created the plants and the animals, and finally on the sixth day, he created man in His own image. And after that he rested."

Mycah noticed Jerud shaking his head in silent consternation. To be fair, his version did miss some key points, but it mimicked the Church's version close enough. Jerud could go suck an egg if he didn't like it. He'd tried to convince Rain into letting him tell the story, after all.

"What happened after that?" asked Rain. "Tell me the second half of the story. The story of the Garden of Eden and the Fall of Man."

Mycah felt a little more confident in this part of the story. It had always resonated with him for some reason. Perhaps because it reminded him of his own flaws and his willingness to break the rules to take those things he most desired.

"So then," continued Mycah, "God created the Garden of Eden, the very birthplace of all life. He shaped a river to run through it to bring water, he planted fruit trees and vegetables to provide food for man, and he filled the garden with birds and beasts of all kinds. God placed man in the garden to tend it, and he instructed him to eat his fill from any tree in the garden so long as he didn't touch the tree of knowledge of good and evil. God then noticed that man was lonely, for the birds and the beasts didn't provide fit company for him. And so God created woman from man, and they were happy together."

Rain raised an eyebrow. "And so man and woman lived happily ever after with God in the garden?"

"No," said Mycah. "Of course not. The serpent that lived in the garden was cunning and deceitful. It spoke to the woman and convinced her God had only forbade man, not woman, from eating from the tree of knowledge. And so she ate from the tree and then she in turn convinced man to eat from it. When God found out what the two had done, he became furious. He cursed the land under their feet, causing the Garden of Eden to wither and die. Man and woman fled from the cursed garden, and have been forced to live outside it ever since."

The room quieted when Mycah finished recounting the tale.

Rain observed him intently. "Do you believe this story, Master Cuthbert?"

Mycah took a moment to consider. "No. Not really. Not as such anyway."

"Why not?"

"Well I've never met a talking snake for one thing. And I don't believe in curses either. I guess... I guess I thought it was just a story. A story to give people something to believe in and teach people lessons."

"So you think it's some sort of metaphor?"

"Yeah. I suppose I do."

Rain regarded Mycah with cool stare. "You're right to be skeptical. Parts of the story have been embellished. But for all intents and purposes the story is accurate. I assure you the Garden of Eden exists. God resides there still. And curses are very real."

"How could you possibly know that?" asked Jerud. He'd remained quiet during the exchange.

"I know many things," said Rain. "Things you couldn't begin to comprehend. Things that would make you question your existence. Things that could shake the foundations upon which our society stands. How I know these things is irrelevant to your purposes, however. What matters to the two of you is this: you'll travel to the cursed land of our creation, obtain an artifact I desire, and return it to my possession. Through your task, you'll be able to determine for yourselves the veracity of my words. But for now, we've little time to waste. Guards? Bring the prisoners and follow me."

Rain turned toward the wooden door as the guards seized Mycah and Jerud and hauled them to their feet. Out the door they marched, trailing Rain like cattle headed to slaughter.

"Mycah, I don't know about this," whispered Jerud. "Stealing from a Stormqueen is one thing, but if what she says is true—"

"We'll just have to go along with this for now," said Mycah. "Try to have a little faith."

"Poor choice of words, that..." said Jerud.

The guards ushered the captive pair into an ominous high-ceilinged room with walls of polished black stone. In the center of the room on a slightly raised dais lay chains and anklets that fastened to the floor. A circular drain surrounded the platform. The guards shoved Mycah and Jerud onto the dais, snapping the restraints into place.

Looking around, Mycah spotted a rack containing pincers, hammers, and wicked blades of various shapes and sizes. Another rack contained vials of mysterious liquids and jars containing preserved... organs? A smell of dried blood and entrails emanated from the drain and forced a gag from his throat.

"Hey, hey—wait now," said Mycah as the guards finished securing the restraints. "This really isn't necessary. We'll do whatever you want. Honest."

Rain stood erect at one end of the chamber, her chamberlain hidden in the shadows behind her.

"Guards, leave us," she said.

"My queen, are you certain?" asked Sten.

"Go. Lock the door behind you."

With a quick nod, the guards marched out of the chamber and shut the door. The clack of a deadbolt finalized their departure.

Rain slowly approached the pair.

A wave of panic swept over Mycah. "Milady. My queen. Please. There's no need to torture us. We'll do as you ask. We gave you our word."

"He speaks the truth," said Jerud. "There's no need for this. Truly."

"I'm not going to torture you," said Rain. "For the task I've set before you, I have need of a more lasting compulsion. While I do believe the sincerity of your desire to appease me, I fear that your desire may wane over time. Absence rarely does make the heart grow fonder, I find. As such, I've devised an alternative method to ensure your cooperation."

Somehow that response did nothing to assuage Mycah's fears.

"But first," Rain said, "there's something the two of you require from me. Information. The artifact I require is a tablet, for lack of a better word, about so big."

The Stormqueen motioned with her hands, indicating an object approximating the size of a book, perhaps a hand and a half tall, a hand wide, and several fingers thick.

"It'll appear to be made of molten steel, or perhaps opaque glass, but it'll be cool to the touch. It will not contain any distinguishing features, and other than the substance from which it's made, you'll likely find it quite unassuming. This is the object that I desire.

"Finding it, however, won't be an easy task. Your minds are likely filled with wondrous visions of the Garden of Eden, bathed in warmth and sunlight. Or perhaps you envision the Garden as a forsaken wasteland, swathed in darkness and death. Abandon your preconceptions now. You'll find that the Garden is far from anything you could envision. I suspect what you find there will shock and confuse you. It may test your faith. But I warn you:

the curse levied upon the Garden is real. Find the artifact and get out. Don't delay."

Mycah's mind brimmed with questions. "Wait... if the Garden's neither a paradise nor a wasteland, then what is it? And what do you mean by—"

"Silence. This is a discourse not a discussion."

Rain reached into the folds of her robe and extracted an oblong pebble. In the darkness of the torture chamber, Mycah couldn't see the stone clearly. At first it appeared black as night itself, perhaps made of obsidian, but then a shimmer would pass over its surface and the stone would become translucent with flecks of silver within it.

"Give me your hand," said the Stormqueen.

Hesitant but cowed, Mycah cupped his hands in front of him. Rain slipped the stone into his palms. Mycah didn't expect the stone to be cold as the Stormqueen had already warmed it with her flesh, and yet it felt odd. It was cool to the touch, but a faint signature of heat emanated from its center as if a spark burned within.

"You hold in your hands the key to reaching the tablet," Rain said. "I can see from your perplexed expression that you've gleaned it's no ordinary stone. You can feel the heat within. You'll find the closer you get to the tablet, the warmer the stone will feel. I don't believe it'll burn you, but I don't know for certain. I doubt it'll lead you to the tablet itself, but it should get you close enough for you to find it. Take care of it, as it's one of a kind."

Until now, Jerud had watched in pensive silence. "Where'd you get that? Is that stone from the Garden of Eden? If so it's a holy relic and should be returned to the Church."

Rain raised an eyebrow. "Oh, I wouldn't do that if I were you."

"Why not?"

"Good question. Master Crawford?"

The chamberlain emerged from the shadows and strode to the rack containing the mysterious vials. Rummaging through a drawer, he procured a small leather pouch and brought it to the Stormqueen. Rain opened the purse and dipped her index finger inside it. When she brought it out, the tip of her finger was covered in an ashen, chalky substance. As she extended her finger toward Jerud, the big man cringed.

"What are you doing?" Jerud asked.

"Hold still," said Rain. "This won't hurt."

With Jerud still hunched, the Stormqueen drew a simple symbol on the man's forehead. A slash of her finger downward, to the left, then up and to the right all in one smooth motion. Withdrawing her finger, she dipped it back into the purse and turned toward Mycah.

"It's clear your friend has an appropriate fear of the occult," said Rain as she painted Mycah's forehead. "You on the other hand are clearly a skeptic. Do you remember what you told me when I asked why you didn't believe in the story of Genesis?"

Mycah's forehead tingled as the chalky substance met his flesh. He yearned to rub it off, but his hands were tightly shackled at his waist. "I said that I thought it was just a fable."

"You also indicated that you don't believe in curses." Rain's eyes twinkled. "Let's see if I can change that."

Rain stepped backward. Raising her hands out to her sides, she closed her eyes and began to chant in a quiet, steady voice. The words flowed forth in an alien tongue. As she chanted, Mycah's forehead began to throb, and his mouth felt strangely parched. Looking over at Jerud, he noticed that the man looked pale, as if he might lose his lunch.

"Jerud... you doing alright?"

Jerud moaned. "Ugh... Mycah... I... don't feel good."

The Stormqueen's tone remained fixed, but the magnitude of her voice rose steadily. As she chanted, the throbbing in Mycah's forehead worsened growing from a dull ache to a stinging pain. Thousands of tiny pins stabbed at him from the nether. He closed his eyes and shook his head, trying to banish the biting sensation to no avail.

When he opened his eyes, Mycah panicked. The walls of the room were gone! Darkness crept in from the room's exterior, fully engulfing the chamberlain, the racks, and the floor. He could barely even distinguish Jerud through the deepening gloom.

A pool of pale light illuminated the Stormqueen, defying the darkness as shadows lapped hungrily at her shoes. A dense fog began to boil out from the stones at Mycah's feet, mixing with the darkness to form a black ooze that clung to his breeches like damp moss. The black fog spun around the Stormqueen's feet like an adder coiling about its prey, forming an ominous inky cyclone. As the mist churned it lifted Rain from the ground, levitating her several feet in the air.

Mycah tried to stay calm. He tried to convince himself his mind was playing tricks on him. But as the darkness crept in from the edges of his vision and dark ooze consumed his lower body, he found it harder and harder to maintain any rational shred of skepticism.

This was a horrible mistake.

Jerud had been right. Who knew what a Stormqueen was capable of? Just because she publicly exerted her powers for good, to usher in spring rains and summer rays, who knew how far her mastery of the preternatural extended? Could she see into his mind and read his thoughts? Could she track him down if he and Jerud tried to flee?

A fire raged through Mycah's head. His vision blurred and the outline of the Stormqueen danced in front of his eyes, alternatingly illuminated by the light and consumed by the black haze.

A flash of blood-red light burst forth from her form. A booming voice emanated out, crashing into Mycah's skull like breakers on a windswept shore. The voice spoke not in the melodious tones of the Stormqueen but instead in a sinister, inhumane rasp—like the voice of a demon unleashed from the pits of Hell. Mycah wasn't sure whether the voice spoke in words or merely in thoughts. The sound reverberated from everywhere and nowhere all at once.

"*Two souls shackled, two souls chained. Two souls bound by trust and pain. Let two souls separate become as one, tied together under blood-red sun. If one shall fall, its mate shall break, and if one shall die, the other shall I take. Till autumn's first moon shall the souls be tied, and through their task they must abide. Let success or failure decide the fate of these two souls now tied.*"

A bloodcurdling scream rent the air—the scream of a woman, not a demon. Mycah felt a breeze whip around his face, tugging at his hair and pulling him toward the Stormqueen. Rasping curses mingled with the Stormqueen's screams. The black ooze swirled and foamed, circling around the Stormqueen like a cyclone. With a grand *whoosh* the ooze disappeared into the eye of the cyclone, taking with it the ominous blood-red light and the sinister, rasping curses.

Mycah's eyes watered, and his head pounded in agony. He could barely see the Stormqueen as she descended to the floor, and he couldn't discern if the remaining shadows were in the room or only in his mind. Struggling against his own fears, he slipped into darkness.

CHAPTER SEVEN

Curses

Mycah's skiff rocked to and fro, adrift at sea. Clouds shrouded the night sky, and cold rain poured from the heavens. The boat kept filling with rainwater, and lacking a bucket or hat, Mycah furiously baled with his cupped hands. No matter how hard he baled, the boat continued to fill, its edge sinking dangerously close to the water line.

As the wind blew, huge swells rocked him back and forth, tilting the sinking craft and further threatening his safety. The wind intensified, driving sheets of salty spray into his mouth and nose. As he crested a swell, Mycah peered over the edge of his boat and gasped. Instead of deep blue depths, a murky black ooze swirled around the skiff. And something lurked within.

Mycah squinted into the murky water. Something—or someone—was slowly sinking into the abyss. A pale corpse.

His own corpse.

With a powerful heave, a giant swell pitched the boat sideways and cast him into the darkness.

Mycah awoke with a startled gasp, his heart racing. Jerud squatted before him with his hand upon his shoulder and a worried look plastered upon his grizzled face.

"You alright, lad? I kept trying to wake you, but you wouldn't stir."

Mycah gripped Jerud's shoulder and squeezed—partially out of concern, but partially to convince himself that he was well and truly awake. "Yeah, I'm fine... I think. How about you old man? I was worried about you for a while there."

Jerud gave one of his reassuring chuckles, though it seemed a little forced. "Right as rain, lad. Nothing a bath and a hot meal won't fix."

Right as rain?

Jerud couldn't have known about his dream, could he? It was probably just a coincidence—it was a common turn of phrase after all. And yet something nagged at him. Something about two souls becoming tied together. Were he and Jerud somehow linked? Mycah tried to remember exactly what had occurred, but his head throbbed and dark visions of a horrible rasping voice assaulted him. Mycah shuddered.

"Jerud, where are we?"

Mycah looked around. He felt his back pressed against something cold and hard, and the seat of his trousers was wet. Above him, rain pitter-pattered against a sagging awning. Mycah sniffed the air and was greeted by the distinctive aromas of garbage and urine.

"We're in an alley across from the Stormqueen's palace," said Jerud. "I came to as some of the Stormguards dragged us through the back entrance. They dumped us in the street and told us to get the blazes out of there. You were still out cold so I slung you over my shoulder and carried you here to get you out of the rain."

Mycah slowly rose to his feet, steadying himself against a brick wall as his world momentarily swayed in and out of focus. He shivered as a cool breeze blew past. The cotton shift that he still wore—which once again was soaked—did little to cut the chill air's bite. As the breeze picked up, he noticed a warm weight pressing against his chest. Feeling under his shirt, he found a small leather pouch looped on a thong around his neck. A modicum of heat emanated from within.

The stone.

Jerud, also dressed in a thin cotton shift, looked miserable. Goosebumps covered his forearms.

"How long were we imprisoned?" asked Mycah. "Any idea?"

"Not sure," said Jerud. "Two or three weeks I think."

"Seems cold for early spring."

"Yeah. It does at that."

Mycah wondered if their attempted heist of the staff had postponed the rite of spring festival. It shouldn't have. Rain got the staff back, after all.

"Look Jerud," said Mycah. "We need to talk. About what happened back there."

"Yeah, I know. But I'm freezing my ass off here. How are you? Can you walk?"

Mycah nodded. "I feel like I've been stampeded by a herd of oxen, but yeah, I'm fine."

"Good," said Jerud. "I know a place we can warm up. Let's get moving."

***

Mycah lounged in a big copper tub. Steam lazily rose from the water's surface, and heat soaked into his weary bones. Jerud lounged in the tub next to him—warm, wet and content despite the fact his bulk left little room in the tub for hot water.

"Ahh," said the big man. "Now this is more like it."

With nowhere else to go, they'd trudged through the cold rain back to Marta's inn. When Marta saw the two of them drag themselves through the front door teeth chattering, bedraggled, and wet, she burst into a frenzy. First she raged, cursing like a farmhand and smacking Jerud in the backside as she ordered her waitstaff to fetch hot water for a bath and her cooks to bring food from the kitchens. But despite her anger she was concerned—a mother hen fussing over her chicks. After they'd had eaten their fill— several bowls apiece of steaming lamb stew and thick slices of crusty bread—Marta sent them packing to the steam room to clean up.

"So tell me Jerud," said Mycah. "What's the deal with you and Marta anyhow?"

"What do you mean?"

"I mean how do you know her?"

"I already told you. I used to bounce here back in the day. That was before Marta owned the place. Back then she just worked here. We met and became friends, that's all."

"C'mon," said Mycah. "With the way she fussed over you when we arrived? There's more to it than that."

Jerud sighed and sunk deeper into the tub. "What do you wanna know?"

"Was there something special between the two of you?"

"We were close."

"How close?"

"Close enough," said Jerud. "Anything else you wanna know?"

"What'd she do before she became owner?" Mycah asked.

"She was a singer."

"Really?"

"Oh yeah." Jerud's eyes faded into the past. "She had the most beautiful voice I'd ever heard. She was a songbird, she was. And as pretty as a peacock, too. Back in those days, she was the resident act. Night in and night out. She was all The Black Swan needed. People flocked from all over town to hear her. She made bouncing a joy. Five nights a week I got to soak in that wondrous melody while I watched the door. It was a joy, I tell you. A real joy."

"So how'd you meet her?" asked Mycah.

"What do you mean, lad? I just told you how I met her."

"No. I mean how did you get to know her? Did you take her out? Buy her nice things?"

"Ahh." Jerud nodded. "Just talking to her was one of the most courageous acts I'd ever performed. Still ranks up there, I'd wager. Turns out she was real sweet though. Hard exterior but soft on the inside. Like a..."

"Crab?"

Jerud frowned. "I was going to say caramel. Anyway, we went out a few times."

"And?"

Jerud sighed and stared off into his tub. "I don't know lad. It just wasn't meant to be I suppose. Maybe I'll tell you the rest of the story some day, but not today alright? I got enough on my mind as it is."

"Yeah, sure," said Mycah.

The two of them sat in silence, soaking in their separate tubs. Marta must've meant a lot to Jerud. Mycah wasn't sure he'd ever seen the big fellow so somber—and over a woman no less.

After a while Mycah spoke up. "So. We need to talk. About… well, you know."

"I know we do, lad," said Jerud. "I'm just not sure I know what happened."

"I feel the same way. My head feels like it was stuffed full of cotton. Maybe we can make sense of everything if we talk it through?"

Jerud looked uncomfortable. "Sure. Might as well put everything out there I guess. Where do you wanna start?"

Good question. So much had happened since he and Jerud had just sat and talked. The botched heist, the imprisonment, Rain's tales of the creation of man—and then that last incident with the ooze and the demon voice and the pain in his skull. Perhaps he needed to get the most difficult question out of the way first.

"Do you think we're… cursed?"

"I… I don't know, lad." Jerud scratched his beard. "I wasn't lying when I said I felt fine. I'm a little sore to be sure, and some of my memories are hazy, but other than that I feel like myself. And yet what happened back there? That I remember well. The creeping darkness. The black fog. And that voice."

Jerud shuddered. "It was inside me, Mycah. Felt like a demon was wrestling me from within. I'm not sure, but... I think the Stormqueen made a pact with it. With a demon. I think she bartered for our souls."

As difficult as it was for him to admit, Jerud's thoughts echoed his own. Mycah had always been skeptical. He only believed what his senses told him were true—that the sky shone bright, water was wet, and ice was cold. If a man tried to sell him something he asked to see it first, and if a gift were offered for free he waited for the catch. He'd never believed in superstitions and curses. He'd never had reason to. Until now.

"That voice," said Mycah. "I remember it saying something about us being tied together. That if one of us falls, the other one would too."

"Yeah."

"Do you... think that means what it sounds like it means?"

"What I think," said Jerud, "is that we should keep an extra close eye on each other from now on. Understand?"

Jerud raised his eyebrows in a manner that demanded a response. Mycah nodded.

"Good. But that's not the part I'm most concerned about. From what I remember that... *whatever it was* said we've only got until the end of summer to steal that blasted artifact and get it to the Stormqueen."

Bits of the rasping chant drifted through Mycah's mind.

Until autumn's first moon shall the souls be tied.

"Yeah, that's how I heard it too," said Mycah. "Blast it, Jerud. That doesn't give us a lot of time. Maybe four or five months at best. And that's assuming we knew where in the blazes the Garden of Eden was!"

Mycah threw up his hands in exasperation. "Look at me. Here I am talking as if the Garden of Eden is real and we could just waltz over there if only we knew where to look. Maybe we should ask a damn priest. God, this is all totally insane."

Jerud's face hardened. "Look, Mycah. About the Garden..."

Mycah cast Jerud a dubious glance. "Don't tell me you believe Rain's story? I thought you were the religious one."

"I am," Jerud said. "I mean, I don't. Believe her story that is. Not exactly anyway. But I do believe in the Garden of Eden. Mycah... I think it's real."

"You're serious?"

"Yeah, I am." Jerud lifted himself from the copper tub and grabbed a nearby towel. "And I think I know someone who might be able to help us find it. C'mon. It's time we got moving. There's someone you should meet."

CHAPTER EIGHT

A Lesson
in Geography

Mycah followed Jerud into a side street. "Remind me again who it is we're looking for?"

"His name's Father Maple," said Jerud as he walked. "He's a religious historian. I want him to show you something."

A vendor hawking pastries from a cart yelled at them as they walked past.

"Something, eh? You're still being very vague about all this."

"And you're still being very impatient."

"I'm plenty patient," said Mycah. "I just like to know what I'm walking into. How do you even know this guy, anyway?"

Jerud sighed. "First, you're the antithesis of patient—"

"Jerud! I'm hurt you'd say such a thing."

"Shut up and listen," said Jerud. "Second, this isn't some guy. This is a man of God. So show a little respect. Now to answer your question—he used to give sermons at Saint

Mark's in the lower quarter when I was younger. So I've known him a long time. Good enough for you?"

"This better not be a waste of time," mumbled Mycah.

Jerud slipped into an alley and Mycah followed. Tall brick walls loomed over him, blocking out much of the sun. With his eyes trained on the skies, he nearly stepped on a mangy cur that whined piteously as he walked past. It looked at Mycah with sorrowful eyes.

"Hold on a sec, Jerud," said Mycah.

He turned and ran back to the alley's entrance. The pastry vendor gesticulated wildly, trying to draw the attention of a middle-aged woman in a rich fur coat. Mycah sidled along the cart's edge and pilfered a beef pasty before heading back into the alley.

He approached the dog and slipped him the pasty. "Here you go, boy."

The dog tore into the meat pie ravenously.

Jerud shook his head. "You're too soft sometimes, lad."

"Well, I couldn't very well let the poor dog starve, Jerud."

"You do remember our first encounter, don't you?"

Mycah had barely entered his teens. He'd been roaming the city streets—up to no good as always—when a buttery, cinnamon-laden sweet roll tickled his nostrils and tempted his desires. He nimbly swiped the sweet, but the pastry cart's owner possessed the eyes of an eagle. He nabbed Mycah before he could escape and began to yell for the watch. Mycah had thought he'd be sent to jail for sure when a kindly gentleman intervened. The big man had beseeched the cart owner to please let his son go. He showered the vendor with coin and assured him that his son would be punished severely. Once safely extracted from the situation, Jerud introduced himself. That would be only the first of many times Jerud saved his hide.

"That was a long time ago, Jerud. I've perfected my skills a little since then."

"Just be careful, ok?"

The pair walked in silence. Soon enough the alley spit them out into the Plaza of Miracles, an expansive square that fronted the Grand Cathedral of Guildean. Despite having visited the cathedral too many times to count, Mycah couldn't help but stare at the majesty of Guildean's central basilica. Two blocky towers stretched toward the heavens, valiantly defying gravity in an effort to come closer to God. The towers stretched so high that even halfway across the plaza Mycah had to crane his neck upward to see their peaks.

Down closer to eye level, the cathedral's façade loomed over the plaza. Ornate columns topped with decorative cornices and friezes depicting man's struggle against sin spanned the width of the church. In the middle of it all rested a colossal rose window crafted of vibrant stained glass. Panes of every pigment, from deep purples to fiery reds and pale blues, melded together in a perfect harmony of color that sparkled in the afternoon sun's rays.

Taken as a whole, the cathedral made Mycah feel extremely small and insignificant. Mycah supposed that was the goal in a way. The friezes and sculptures and stained glass served a real purpose, acting as a poor man's bible so any pilgrim that reached the cathedral's walls, no matter how uneducated, could understand the Church's teachings.

But the sheer size of the structure? That was a monument to God's glory and a reminder of man's own insignificance.

Mycah swallowed a lump in his throat as he gazed at the structure. If God truly did exist, surely his presence and judgment was stronger here than anywhere else in the world. Mycah had never burst into flames upon entering the cathedral on any of his prior visits, but there was always a first time for everything.

"Impressive, isn't it?" said Jerud.

"Yeah. Makes me feel like an ant," said Mycah. "I just hope that rose window isn't a giant magnifying glass for God's wrath."

"God knows our sins, Mycah, but I don't think he's gonna strike us down for visiting his house. As long as you stay true in here—" Jerud pointed to his heart. "Forgiveness can always be granted."

They ascended the porch's marble steps and strode into the cathedral's wide nave. As awe-inspiring as the cathedral appeared from the outside, the opulence of the interior far outstripped its exterior. Columns at Mycah's sides stretched far overhead. They culminated in arcades that crisscrossed and merged into optical illusions that gave the domed ceiling an appearance of upward curvature except at its apex.

Mycah wondered how high the structure actually stood. Six stories? Eight? Ten? Along the entire upper half of the cathedral, narrow stained glass windows rubbed shoulders with the columns, allowing in more light than any stone structure of this size had a reasonable right to expect.

Four or five dozen pews lined the sides of the nave with more in the aisles at the sides. At the far end of the cathedral, a golden altar shone in a beam of light from the heavens. At a pulpit on the left, a minister delivered a sermon to a crowd of several hundred. Such a crowd would've packed most churches to the gills, but here barely a quarter of the seats were filled. The minister's chanting voice echoed down the sides of the corridor, flowing past the end of the pews and out the cathedral's open double doors.

Jerud swiped at the crown of his head as if to remove a hat that wasn't there. "I was thinking, Mycah. Maybe we could take in a sermon since we're here and all?"

"I don't know, Jerud. It's been a long time since I attended one. I don't know if now's the right time."

Jerud looked conflicted, argumentative, and sheepish at the same time. He wrung his hands.

"Go on. Spit it out," said Mycah.

"Look lad, I've been trying to keep my composure. Lord knows I have. But it's been a tough day. Real tough. I could use some guidance, and not the sort Father Maple can provide. If you don't want to join me that's your choice, but I need a few moments."

Jerud lumbered over and took a seat on a pew in the back. Hunched over with his head tilted toward the floor in deference, he hardly looked like the Jerud Mycah knew—the eternally optimistic, jovial, bear of a man that always had an answer and never lost his cool.

He's really shaken. How had I not noticed that?

Mycah had always used Jerud as a shoulder to lean on, never thinking that the big man might sometimes need a shoulder in return. But Jerud was no different than any other man, and in the past day his beliefs had been tested. He needed support.

Mycah sat down on the pew next to his friend. He waited for the pastor to finish the sermon, letting Jerud silently voice his thoughts and prayers with his maker. When the pastor quieted and people began to rise from their seats, he clapped a hand to Jerud's shoulder.

"Jerud, you've always been there for me. You know I'll always return the favor. I don't know exactly what we've gotten ourselves into, but together we can get through it. Even if it means fighting to the end of the world and back."

Jerud lifted his head and gave Mycah a warm smile. "Thanks, lad. I know we'll get through this. Though we might be fighting to the *beginning* of the world and back."

The big man's smile grew in appreciation of his own wit.

"Hardy har. Come on. Let's find this friend of yours."

Squeezing past exiting churchgoers, Jerud led Mycah to the side of the cathedral and out a small door at the south end of the transept that opened into a well-manicured garden situated among the church grounds. Jerud pointed to a small building at the end of a gravel path.

"Far as I remember, Father Maple lives in that mission house over there. It's as good a place as any to start looking for him."

"I thought the priests lived in the cathedral," said Mycah.

"The archbishop's quarters are there, as well as some of the bishops' and archdeacons'. But Father Maple's a simple pastor. The only reason he's living here at all is so he can access the church's archives for his research."

"Isn't there enough space for him in the cathedral?"

Jerud chuckled. "You never did pay any attention when you were younger, did you? Do you have any idea how big this place is? Have you ever wandered the church grounds?"

Mycah shook his head. "No, but that cathedral is huge. Seems like you could house an army in there."

Jerud snorted. "As I said, there's barely enough space for the higher-ups. The rest of the clergy live in mission houses along with the cooks and gardeners and caretakers. And we haven't even talked about the Holy Guard. There's probably a dozen barracks on these grounds alone."

The two of them pressed into the mission house, and after Jerud gathered his bearings he led them downstairs into a communal bedchamber. A lone priest was changing linens.

"Excuse me, Father," said Jerud. "Have you seen Father Maple?"

"Not since the morn, child," replied the priest. "You should try the library. He's often there reading well into the night."

"Thank you, Father." Jerud bowed in respect. Heading back up the stairs, he turned to Mycah. "The library... should'a thought of that. Father Maple's a bit of a bookworm."

"Seems like you know him really well," said Mycah as they traipsed back across the gardens.

"He was a mentor to me of sorts. Taught me a lot about the true meaning of faith. Honestly, you could stand to spend some quality time with him. When this Stormqueen business is over and done with, I mean."

"Not going to happen Jerud…"

"Hey, just a suggestion."

The pair made their way back through the cathedral, past the choir, and out the east end. Their path led to a massive tower supported by flying buttresses. Guards liveried in white and grey uniforms stood silently at attention at the gates. The guards didn't bar entry, but their stern, steely demeanors spoke volumes. After stopping to ask an attendant for directions, they found themselves at the entrance to the great library.

While the cathedral itself was breathtaking in its grandeur, the library possessed a more humble magnificence. The circular room stood some twenty paces across, though it extended upward for several stories. From the inside it resembled a silo, but rather than holding wheat or millet, stacks of books and parchments lined its walls, tucked into every conceivable crevice. A staircase snaked its way around the interior of the tower, providing access to even the most remote shelves.

On the main floor, tables of thick, polished oak sat side by side, illuminated by candelabras with drooping candles. At one table, an old man with thinning hair and a grey beard hunched over a large tome. He pressed his eyes close to the page.

"Excuse me, Father Maple?" said Jerud.

The old man lifted his head and squinted in the general direction of the voice. He fumbled for his spectacles. Donning them, his eyes widened in surprise.

"Jerud? Is that you? Why—it's been years!"

"We were hoping for a moment of your time if that's alright."

"Why, of course. Of course. Please, have a seat."

Father Maple gestured to a pair of chairs. Mycah grimaced as he sat. Though the Church could afford to build the grandest structure in all of Guildean, seat cushions were apparently beyond their budget.

"So, what brings you here?" asked Father Maple. He swiveled his head from Jerud to Mycah to Jerud and back to Mycah. Blinking furiously, as if to banish cobwebs only he could see, he suddenly seemed aware of Mycah's presence. "Oh my. Forgive me. Where are my manners? Come, introduce me to your young friend, Jerud."

"This is Mycah Cuthbert, Father."

"Pleased to meet you," said Mycah.

"The pleasure is mine, child. And Jerud, it's truly a blessing to see you again. Now come. You must tell me what brings you here. Do you come to regale me with tales of adventure? Or perhaps a bawdy tale of the conquest of a young damsel?"

Jerud blushed. "Father, please! I would never do such a thing..."

Father Maple smiled, a warm gesture that fitted someone whose title evoked the concept of a gentle patriarch. "My memories betray you. The Jerud I remember would recount his exploits to me more often than not. In fact, I specifically remember one story where—"

"Ahem!" Jerud averted his eyes. "Yes, well, that was a long time ago Father."

"Jerud, there's no need for shame. You know I've never judged you. That burden lies solely with our Lord. Besides,

I always enjoyed your tales! You let me live vicariously through your stories, and for that I'll forever be grateful."

The color receded from Jerud's cheeks, if only marginally. "Thanks, Father. I think..."

"So what can I do for you?"

"Well," said Jerud. "My friend and I were hoping you could give us a bit of a... history lesson."

The Father's eyebrows rose. "History, eh? Well, I suppose I'm qualified. What exactly did you have in mind?"

"We were hoping you could tell us about the creation of man."

"You want me to recount Genesis?" Father Maple's eyebrows crept back down into a furrow. "That's gospel my son, not history. What is it you truly wish to know?"

"Well, my friend—" Jerud nodded toward Mycah. "He believes that the story of creation is, well... just a story. An allegory."

"Is that so?" Father Maple's bushy grey eyebrows rose back up. Mycah watched the brows, transfixed. The Father certainly knew how to use them to dramatic effect. "Well, I'm fairly certain you don't require a history lesson. What you need is a lesson in geography."

"Geography?" Mycah asked.

"Yes, geography," said the Father. "Wait here. I'll be right back."

As the old man rose from the table and wandered off into a stack of manuscripts, Mycah recalled a memory of a splintered wooden desk at which he used to sit and a ruler-wielding priest, eying him with distrust.

"You didn't tell me I was going to be sitting through a lecture!" hissed Mycah.

"Would you quit complaining?" said Jerud.

"There better not be a quiz after all this."

"You're incorrigible."

"In-whatible? What's that supposed to mean?"

"You'd know if you'd ever paid attention in class, now, wouldn't you?"

Father Maple returned with a large, tightly coiled parchment. He unfurled it onto the table revealing a meticulously crafted map.

"This," he said with a flourish, "is a map of our world, reconstructed to the best of our abilities. Many historians and cartographers have toiled to make it as accurate as possible, with information from many a traveler."

He pointed to the corner of the document. "Here's the legend. It contains the standard information one would expect of it. Information on how to decipher creeks from rivers, paths from roadways, that sort of thing. There's a scale as well, of course. But this map also distinguishes between villages, towns, and cities. The smallest of dots represents a modest village, whereas the largest of dots represents a grand metropolis such as ours."

Father Maple drew his finger to a large dot somewhat west of the map's center. "This is Guildean, host of the Grand Cathedral and our home." He then pointed to several other large dots to the north, east, and south. "This is Hemswich. Here are Loweshall and Grouton. All impressive cities in their own right. Mycah, my child, do you notice anything peculiar about them?"

Mycah gave Jerud a sullen glance. "I knew there would be a quiz."

"Not a quiz," said Father Maple. "Just an observation. Does anything stand out?"

"Those are the cities that house the other Stormqueens, aren't they?"

Father Maple cleared his throat. "Well, yes. But that's not what I was referring to. Look at the map, child. What do you see?"

Mycah stared at the map, feeling as if some obvious clue stared him in the face and his brain merely lacked the ability to decipher it.

"Well, they're all surrounded by smaller cities," he said.

"Correct, but there's more to it than that. Imagine a ring of finite width and place it on the map." The elderly father took two fingers and traced them in a circle, passing first through Guildean, then Hemswich, Loweshall, and Grouton. "Notice that a ring of the proper size passes through all four major cities, as well as numerous smaller towns and villages. Imagine now a larger ring, one that fits just outside the one I drew."

Again, Father Maple drew a ring on the map with his fingers. "As you can see, this ring intersects fewer cities. If we were to repeat the process, we'd continue to intersect fewer and fewer settlements until..."

Father Maple pointed at the edge of the map. "Until we reached the edge."

"The edge of the world?" asked Mycah. "You're not serious?"

"It is indeed the edge," said Father Maple. "Though not quite how you might imagine it. It's not a cliff that plunges off into eternity. Rather travelers tell of it as the edge of our world and the beginning of a new one. As one nears the edge, trees dissipate and birdsong fades into silence. Animals no longer roam the land. Grasses grow much farther than one might expect, but even they too eventually wither and die.

"After that, the world... changes. Men have spoken to me of things they've seen there. Primitive things. Trees who spread their leaves close to the ground like squatting giants. Herds of mysterious beasts who hide in the underbrush and attack at night. Insects larger than housecats. I don't know how much faith to put in these stories. I've never travelled there myself. However, one thing is certain." Father Maple stabbed his finger at the edge of the map again. "*This* is the edge of our world."

"So what does this all have to do with Genesis?" asked Mycah.

"Isn't it obvious by now, child? Look here." The father traced his fingers back to the center of the map. "What do you notice about this part of the map?"

"No cities?"

"Correct. Picture a set of rings emanating from the center of the map. If you will recall the first ring that I drew..." Father Maple retraced the circle with his index and middle fingers, the ring that ran through all the major cities, Guildean included. "This ring contains the greatest population density of all. If you extend farther toward the edges of the map, you find fewer people. And if you venture closer toward the center of the map, you also find fewer people." His index finger jabbed back to the center of the map. "And at the very center you find no cities, no towns, nothing. Care to hazard a guess why?"

"Wait," said Mycah. He rubbed his temple. "Are you saying that at the center of this map—right at the center of our world—*that's* the Garden of Eden?"

"Precisely!" Father Maple raised his index finger in triumph. "As you can see, a simple lesson in geography indicates that man was created at the center of our world and has been migrating outward ever since, thus proving Genesis. The fact that no settlements exist at the very center of our world is further proof of the veracity of the story of the fall of man. No one lives there because the curse levied upon the land by our Lord as punishment for man's original sin makes it inhospitable to this day!"

Mycah absentmindedly felt at the pouch that hung from his neck—the pouch that held the Stormqueen's stone. "So that's it? The Garden of Eden is just... sitting there?"

"Yes," replied the father. "Remarkable, isn't it?"

Mycah inspected the legend. "So this is the scale, right?"

He pinched his fingers to match the width of the bar, then shifted them back to the center of the map, making a quick measurement.

"Let's see... that's only about, say, three or four hundred leagues from here." His mind racing, Mycah did a bit of mental math. "We could probably get there in a month and a half, maybe—ooph!"

Jerud had remained quiet the entire lecture until Mycah's outburst, at which point he dug his elbow into Mycah side none too softly.

Father Maple's eyebrows furrowed once more, and the old pastor pursed his lips. "Say, Jerud. What's this all about, anyway?"

"Oh, uh... We were just curious, Father. Needed to settle a dispute between friends."

"Seems like an awful lot of trouble, coming all this way to see an old man to settle a dispute." Father Maple regarded them with newfound suspicion. "What are you planning?"

"Nothing. Honestly." Jerud motioned for Mycah to get up. "It's been wonderful to see you Father, and I wish we could stay, but—"

"Jerud, don't lie to me!" Father Maple's voice rose in displeasure. "I've known you for far too long to be brushed aside like excess chaff. The two of you are planning something, and I demand to know what it is."

Jerud gave Mycah a cold stare, admonishing him for letting their intentions slip. Mycah responded with a shrug of his shoulders.

Jerud sighed. "We're... planning a pilgrimage. To the Shrine of Repentance."

The tension drained from Father Maple's body. "My child, why didn't you say so? Many pilgrims visit the Shrine every year. It's a sign you've chosen to accept your sins and confess them before God. Why, Jerud... I'm proud of you. And you as well, child Mycah."

"Um, yes, uhh, thank you, Father," Jerud said, his eyes lowered to the floor. "But really, we must be going now—"

"Nonsense. It's late. You can't expect to begin your pilgrimage tonight. Stay with me and break a loaf of bread. We have so much to catch up on!"

"Father, thank you for the offer, but I insist. We must be going. I hope you understand."

Father Maple sighed. "Very well then. If you must. Blessed be thy journey child, and may you always find your way back into God's light."

The big man motioned Mycah to the exit. As they passed through the door, Mycah turned to Jerud. "What was that all about? What's the Shrine of Repentance?"

"Quiet," said Jerud. "I'll tell you later. Right now we need to get back to Marta's. We leave first thing in the morning."

CHAPTER NINE

The Burden of Knowledge

Father Maple tossed and turned in his bed. His hip pained him as it did every night, but it wasn't the reason sleep eluded him. Admitting defeat, he sat up, his hands fumbling over his nightstand as he tried to find his spectacles. As he slipped them on, he turned up the lantern at his bedside from a bare glimmer to a dull glow. He heard a rustle behind him.

"Is everything alright, father?"

"Yes, Brother Georgio. My mind is disinterested in sleep tonight it would seem. I'm going out for a walk. Please, go back to bed."

Father Maple crossed the room and retrieved his habit from a dresser. After donning it, he slid his feet into a pair of worn slippers and headed up the stairs from the communal bedroom out into the cathedral gardens.

The night was still young, and yet a cool breeze nipped at his heels. Father Maple shivered as the breeze swirled around his legs and into his habit. Nearly a month had passed since the spring equinox and yet winter doggedly refused to relinquish its grip upon the land. By the Lord's grace the winter snows had finally abated, and yet frost crusted the blades of grass at his feet most mornings.

As he strolled through the gardens, he rested a hand upon the trunk of a young elm. The tree's bark scuffed his fingers as he drew them downward along the trunk. Kneeling, he trailed his fingers to the sapling's roots and over the damp earth to the protruding shoot of a sprouting iris.

Tending the garden ranked amongst his favorite duties, and along with history it was one of his few true loves. Patting the soil at the base of the iris, he felt the strength of the earth flowing into the shoot. It was miraculous that a plant could flourish given such humble ingredients as earth, water, and sunlight, and yet all of life was a miracle. Every living thing—every man, woman, animal, and plant—was a testament to the power and grace of God.

While any new parent holding a squalling babe could attest to the miracle of life, people often forgot the simple plant and its role in existence. Without it, man would have no bread to pacify his rumbling belly, no fire to still his shaking hands, no thatch to shield him from the driving rains. Truly blessed was man for God had provided for him, knowing of his need for food and shelter. Father Maple prayed.

Gardening also provided Father Maple with an opportunity to gather his thoughts. While he could easily lose himself for days within the vagaries of history, library study was an intellectual pursuit, one that required the full attention of the mind. Gardening on the other hand was a toil of the flesh. It occupied the body while allowing the mind to rest. As such, gardening presented an ideal opportunity for thought and for prayer.

Tonight, Father Maple's mind required the calming influence of the budding flowers and blossoming trees. As blessed as he felt to have been given the opportunity to lay eyes upon Jerud once again, the meeting had left him with a bittersweet taste. Jerud had acted anxious and tense. While he had no reason to disbelieve Jerud's assertion that he and his friend planned to visit the Shrine of Repentance, Jerud's mannerisms seemed out of place. Those seeking the shrine exuded a sense of composure from finally accepting their sins in the face of God. Jerud, if anything, seemed afraid.

Had Jerud committed a deed so heinous that he feared the wrath of God in confession? Father Maple supposed it was possible, but Jerud of all people should know that their Lord in his ultimate wisdom was merciful. Regardless of his past, if he repented, God would forgive him.

Jerud's friend on the other hand did not seem prepared to repent either, but for different reasons. The child appeared self-assured, cocky, and skeptical. Those were hardly the personality traits of a man ready to face his maker. If anything, they were the traits of a man who actively fought against God. While Father Maple was tempted to attribute Mycah's behavior to the brashness of youth, the child had actively questioned gospel. Why then would he travel to the Shrine of Repentance? It didn't measure up.

Perhaps exercise would help clear his thoughts where gardening had failed. Rising from his knees, the father crossed the remainder of the gardens and entered the cathedral. Despite the hour, glowing lanterns still illuminated the altar, and several individuals hunched upon pews in silent prayer. Crossing the transept, Father Maple paced down the length of one aisle, crossed over, and returned along the aisle's pair. His feet carried him up a spiral staircase to a narrow hallway directly above the aisle he'd just traversed. As he walked, he noticed a light seeping from underneath a familiar door. He knocked.

"Come in."

Father Maple cracked the door. Bishop Waverly sat at his desk, quill in hand, penning a letter in a large flowing script. Candles flickered inconsistently by the bishop's brow, sending shadows dancing across the page. Father Maple preferred lanterns for their even illumination, but to each his own.

The bishop lifted his head. "Father Maple. What brings you here at this hour? Is something amiss?"

"My mind races unfettered, Bishop. I saw the light under your door and thought we might talk." He glanced at the half-written letter. "Am I interrupting?"

"Not at all, Father." The bishop returned his quill to an inkwell. "I'm always free to share in the troubles of a fellow brother. Please, have a seat."

Father Maple entered and lowered himself onto a stool. The hard wooden seat pressed against his rear unforgivingly, but his feet appreciated the respite.

"I had a visitor today, Bishop. An old friend whom I hadn't seen in some time."

"I'd suspect this would bring you joy, Father, and yet your visage says otherwise."

"It was a joy, Bishop, and I thank our Lord for blessing me with long-lost companionship. Yet I'm not sure the visit was a result of mere happenstance."

The bishop raised a thin eyebrow. "Go on."

Father Maple stroked his beard, trying to collect his thoughts. "My friend came to me today with a youth whom I hadn't met, finding me in the library at my studies. Jerud, my friend, claimed that the young lad Mycah was skeptical of Genesis. He asked if I could help convince him its veracity. Of course I obliged, showing the youth the map of our world and explaining to him the implications."

"And was he convinced?"

"I believe so," said Father Maple. "But I began to wonder as to the motives for their query. Upon my insistence, Jerud professed to a desire to visit the Shrine of Repentance."

"That's a noble venture, Father. What has you concerned?"

"Jerud's demeanor was at odds with his declaration. He appeared... worried. Confused. And the youth didn't appear repentant at all."

"So you believe the pair had ulterior plans?" asked Bishop Waverly.

Father Maple hesitated. "I believe they plan to visit the birthplace of man."

Bishop Waverly's eyelids narrowed. "That's a serious accusation. What makes you believe this?"

"I don't possess any firm evidence to support my misgivings," said Father Maple. "I suppose it's mostly a gut suspicion. Jerud's a kind soul but is often misguided. His profession isn't one supported by God or common law."

"What would possess them to attempt such a journey?"

"I don't know, Bishop. My interactions with them today were brief."

"I see." The bishop steepled his fingers and chewed on his bottom lip. "Well, even if your suspicions prove accurate they wouldn't be the first souls to have embarked upon such a pilgrimage. Nonetheless..."

The bishop turned his eyes to Father Maple. "Thank you for sharing this with me, Father. I'll pray upon your words and elevate your concerns to the necessary parties. But don't fret. The Watchers are ever vigilant. They will protect us."

Father Maple cringed. "Bishop, know that I consider Jerud a friend. It would pain me for him to come to harm—"

"Father, it's not for us to pass judgment. Their fate will be determined by our Lord."

"Certainly, bishop. But is it truly necessary to involve the Watchers?"

"They do their duty and no more," said Bishop Waverly. "If your friends prove innocent of your allegations, they have nothing to fear. Now if you could provide me a brief description of the pair?"

Father Maple described them as best he could as the bishop jotted notes on a fresh page.

"That'll do, Father," said the bishop. "Now if you'd excuse me? I must return to my letter."

"Absolutely, Bishop," said Father Maple. "May the Lord smile upon you this eve."

"As with you, Father."

Father Maple rose and exited the bishop's quarters, closing the door tightly behind him. As he wandered back down the hallway toward the stairs, his mind felt no more at ease than before. Had he made the right decision in sharing his concerns? He'd need to pray more on the matter in the morning, perhaps after some sleep. Assuming he could fall asleep at all.

***

Milky globe grasped in her hand, Rain leaned into an overstuffed sofa chair. She flicked the globe out to the tips of her digits, flipped her arm over, and flexed her hand in a fluid, practiced motion. The globe travelled up her forearm and halfway up her triceps before pausing momentarily.

Back down her arm it spun, picking up speed. As it reached her palm, she flicked it into her other hand, using its momentum to shoot it around and across the top of her chest. As the ball returned to her palm, she dipped her arm, cradling it on the back of her hand between the tendons of her second and third fingers.

To the outside observer, the globe's motions might've seemed unnatural, as if controlled by magic. In truth, anyone could control the globe in such a manner. It just took patience, perseverance, and a little showmanship.

Knuckles rapped at the door. Rain set the globe down and smoothed her robes with her hands. "Come in."

Master Crawford pushed his way into the room, carrying a tray laden with a steaming teakettle of fine blue porcelain and two small cups.

"I couldn't help but notice the lights on, Mistress," he said. "I thought perhaps a cup of tea might help you relax. It's chamomile, with a hint of honey."

Rain regarded her chamberlain warmly. "It's late, Master Crawford. Shouldn't you be asleep?"

"I could ask the same of you, Mistress." Master Crawford set the tray down and poured long draughts into each cup.

"Two cups?" asked Rain.

"To be honest, Mistress, I made the tea for myself. But when I saw the lights, I thought perhaps some company might be nice."

"Ahh, so the faithful chamberlain reveals his true priorities." Rain raised a brow. "So I suppose I'm just an afterthought?"

Master Crawford grinned. "Well, not entirely. I did pass by your quarters. The route from the kitchens to my room doesn't normally take me this way, you know."

Rain lifted a cup by its handle, blowing on the hot tea to cool it. "Either way, I appreciate the sentiment. So, what is it you wish to discuss, Master Crawford?"

"Discuss, Mistress? I spoke of nothing but tea."

Testing it, Rain pulled her lips back from the cup's brim. Master Crawford must've pulled the kettle off the fire moments before entering her quarters. She set the cup back on the platter.

"True. And yet you went out of your way to seek my company. Something is clearly on your mind."

The chamberlain sighed, fingers intertwined before him. "Can I be frank, Mistress?"

Rain examined her old friend. Dressed in a pair of pressed, twill pants and a crisp, white shirt, the man cut as dashing a figure now as he had so many years ago when they'd first met. She recalled their initial encounter. His handsomeness had caught her off guard, with his bright blue eyes and strong jaw line. Her voice had squeaked as she greeted him. Though barely more than a girl at the time, she was still a Stormqueen, and it would've been entirely improper for her emotions to get the best of her. As such, she'd focused and conducted herself in a manner befitting her station, though secretly she'd wished that duty wouldn't ultimately preclude more personal interactions.

Even now with his hair greyed and his brow creased from age, he still affected her strongly, though she couldn't be sure if it was his countenance or warm companionship that attracted her most now.

"Edward, we've known each other for nigh on thirty years. Just the two of us are here. I'd be upset if you weren't forthright with me."

Master Crawford lifted his own cup of tea from the platter and cupped it between his hands, letting the warmth soak into his palms.

"People are talking, Rain. Complaining about the persistent cold. Thus far, I've only heard murmurs of discontent—grumblings regarding a morning's frost or a chill wind. But people are noticing that winter hasn't entirely faded."

Rain rubbed the back of her knuckles, as she was prone to do when concerned. "Honestly, I was worried that people would take notice last spring after those few late frosts. But it's markedly more obvious this year, I fear. Perhaps not enough for people to become overtly concerned, but enough to create a dialogue."

"My sources don't bring me any reports of suspicion, mistress. Not yet. But I fear if the chill continues into the summer months, there may be unrest."

Rain sipped the tea to soothe her nerves. Edward was right. If she didn't fix the weather soon, people would rebel. But what could she do? Her powers were failing her, and she had no idea why. She'd tried to explain it to Edward—she confided in him more than anyone else—but try as he might, he couldn't understand. Her powers hovered in her subconscious like a sixth sense. While a man might lose his sight or his hearing in old age, a Stormqueen shouldn't lose her powers. At least, Rain hoped not.

Her time with the previous Stormqueen, Gale, had been short-lived. At the age of twelve, while visiting the Stormqueen's rite of spring festival with her family, Gale's guards had plucked her from the crowd, telling her afterwards the Stormqueen sensed a spark in her. What followed was a whirlwind of change. Frightened and confused, she'd been whisked away on a secret journey with Gale to the Garden of Eden, a place her upbringing had taught her to be blighted and cursed. The Stormqueen had tried to warn her regarding what they'd find there, but it wasn't until her arrival and subsequent metamorphosis that she started to understand the true dichotomy between magic and religion—a dichotomy the Church had spent eons trying to repress.

At the time Rain didn't understand Gale's urgency, but the Stormqueen's haste had been born of necessity. A cancer of the flesh devoured her from within, and within weeks of their departure from the Garden, Gale's spirit had departed the mortal world. Rain had learned much in her few weeks with the Stormqueen: the true history of their world, as well as Gale herself understood it, the subtleties of harnessing her powers, how to select new Stormqueens and train them in the art. But nothing Gale had ever mentioned explained her recent decline in powers.

Rain had racked her memory for some forgotten clue from her past that might help explain her condition. She'd pored over the journals of previous generations of Stormqueens. She'd even sent missives to the other Queens—vaguely worded so they wouldn't suspect her powers were fading—asking if they understood the mechanism of their magic. All routes were dead ends, and so she found herself in her current predicament.

"My instincts tell me spring is coming, Edward," said Rain. "But I don't know how many more seasons we can expect that to be the case. To be honest, I'm worried too."

Master Crawford lowered his eyes to his cup. He understood the severity of the situation as well as she did. After several long moments, he broke the silence.

"Rain, you know I'll support you in any endeavor, no matter how difficult or unpleasant. I don't mean to question your judgment, but given the gravity of the situation, was it wise to involve the two thieves?"

Rain took another sip from her cup. "Do you think it'll set a poor precedent, my letting them go?"

"No, it's not that," said Master Crawford. "It's simply that... well, how should I put this? If we had a barrel full of applicants, they'd be the dregs. They're common criminals. I have to think we could've found someone—anyone— more capable to send on this quest."

Rain sighed. "Look, Edward, all I know is this: the young man, Mycah, is intelligent, resourceful—"

"As well as deceitful, brazen, and naturally suspicious," interjected the chamberlain.

"All true, but useful qualities in the correct circum- stances. Edward, the young man orchestrated an elaborate burglary of one of my most visible possessions. He snuck onto my grounds without a single one of my staff alerted to his intentions, and even when cornered, he eluded my guards numerous times. And he would have escaped with the staff if not for Rayven."

"Yes, speaking of which," said Master Crawford. "I don't care for him either. His loyalty is even more suspect than that of Mycah and his friend."

"Which is why I'm not granting him free rein," said Rain. "He's being watched. But his loyalty lies with the highest bidder, and for now that's us."

"Well, I don't trust him. And I don't trust this Mycah or his friend either."

"Neither do I, Edward," said Rain. "But my resources are limited, and we must be discreet. We did our due dili- gence while the pair was imprisoned. All evidence points to either Mycah or Rayven as the best fit for this particular crusade, and now we have both in our service. I'm not sure if either will succeed, but they have a better chance than if I sent my own troops in their stead. How do you think the Church would react if we sent a full delegation to the Genesis site? Do you think they'd welcome us with open arms?"

"No, but—"

"You know the Church would be happy to see us fall. They've long desired to rid the world of our influence. And they're so lost in their idolatry that even the arch-bishop may have forgotten why they haven't already crushed us."

Rain feared this the most. The Church knew the secrets of the Genesis site as well as she did, but centuries of their own rigid dogma might've clouded their thoughts. What if the Church had forgotten the Stormqueens' true purpose—to keep the elements at bay? Without them, the encroaching cold would blanket the lands in eternal winter, and no amount of prayer would stop it. The Church had never done more than point fingers at her and yell, but what if they finally meant to fill their empty threats with action?

"I simply meant there are other options," said Master Crawford. "Other people who could have travelled in the thieves' place."

"Who? Me? I don't relish that option. Repeated exposure to that cursed place is probably what killed Gale."

"I meant me."

"Oh," said Rain. "No, Edward. Not you. I couldn't. Let the thieves suffer the blight instead."

"I understand." Edward reached for the kettle. "More tea?"

Looking down at her cup, Rain realized she'd drained the contents. "Um, yes, thank you."

Master Crawford filled her cup and topped off his as well. Steam rose from the tea, though this time when tested, Rain found it to be the proper temperature.

"Do you at least think the thieves believed your tale?" asked Edward as he replaced the kettle on the tray.

"About Genesis?"

"Yes."

"I'm uncertain," said Rain. "It's close enough to what they've been led to believe to sound credible."

"But what'll happen when they reach the site itself?"

"The same thing that happened to me. They'll be surprised, but their minds will find a way to reconcile their beliefs with reality."

"I hope you're right, mistress. And what of the, erm, *curse* you placed upon them?" Master Crawford gave Rain a questioning glance.

"Let's hope it serves its intended purpose. Otherwise we'll be entirely dependent upon Rayven, and that's not an option I particularly care for at the moment."

Edward placed his teacup on the tray. "Well, mistress, I can't be sure the tea helped with my insomnia, but I did cherish our conversation. Would you like me to return the tray to the kitchens, or should I leave the tea with you?"

"Better that you take it with you," said Rain, taking a long draught and handing the cup to her friend. "Otherwise I'll consume more than I should."

Master Crawford gathered the tray and gave a slight bow. "Sleep well, my Queen. I'll see you in the morn."

As Master Crawford turned toward the door, a thought crossed Rain's mind. "Edward... one more thing?"

"Mistress?"

"Any word on the financier for the burglary?"

"Not yet, mistress. We're still looking into it, but we've yet to find any leads. Whomever requisitioned it hid their tracks well."

"I see. Well, thank you, Edward. For the tea... and the company."

"My pleasure, mistress."

As the chamberlain turned and exited her quarters, Rain couldn't help but admire the man's hindquarters. Involuntarily, she blushed.

Now Rain, get your mind out of the gutter. You've known him far too long to be falling victim to idle fancy now.

Although, just before he turned to leave, she was almost certain she'd seen a spot of color in his cheeks as well. Perhaps the lighting had merely caught him askew. Oh well. A lady could always dream...

CHAPTER TEN

A Journey of 400 Leagues

Nestled deep within a cocoon of warm blankets, Mycah rested peacefully. Lusciously insulated by the covers, he felt as if he could sleep forever. Vaguely from a recessed corner of his mind he heard footsteps, and then a bright light assaulted his eyes.

"Morning, sunshine!" boomed Jerud's voice.

Mycah cracked an eyelid. Jerud stood in front of a set of newly parted drapes looking alert, awake, and refreshed.

"C'mon, lad. Up and at 'em," said the big man. "We've got a lot to do. Can't have you sleeping all day."

Mycah groaned. "Ugh. What time is it?"

"Almost seven."

"Oh, so we've barely got twelve hours of daylight left. Wouldn't want to waste it."

Mycah rolled onto his side to shield his eyes from the encroaching morning sun.

"You know, you're right," said Jerud. "Perhaps we should sleep in. It's not like we have some horrible curse eating away at our insides, threatening to kill us unless we travel halfway across the world and back before the end of summer. What's the rush?"

"Glad you're finally talking sense."

Jerud walked to the door. "Hey, if you want to sleep in, that's your choice. But if you're not downstairs in five, I'll be back. And I'll bring a bucket. Straight from the horse trough."

"Spoilsport..." mumbled Mycah.

The door closed and Jerud's heavy footsteps receded into silence. Mycah stretched and crawled out of bed. He felt as if he could sleep for a week, and yet Jerud seemed spry as a country hen. Was Mycah the only one who'd been imprisoned for weeks in a tiny cell with a hard stone floor and not a scrap of bedding to speak of? Given his demeanor, Jerud must have been imprisoned in the luxury dungeon. Or perhaps the man's bulk made even a bare stone floor comfortable.

Mycah threw on his clothes—generously donated by Marta the day before—and wandered down to the common room underneath, joining a handful of bleary-eyed patrons. Mycah tried to stifle a yawn. Getting up this early was simply unnatural. Mankind had invented drapery for a reason—it was his small way of exerting dominance over the sun's malicious plans.

As smells of the morning breakfast worked their way into his nostrils, Mycah's stomach grumbled in complaint. He and Jerud had arrived back from the cathedral after the kitchen had closed, so dinner had consisted of a few slices of cheese and an apple he'd pilfered from the larder. This morning's fare appeared to be porridge with dried fruits and nuts, but it was the fresh buttered bread that truly awakened his senses. With no serving girl in sight, Mycah peeked through the curtains to the kitchen. A pile of freshly baked loaves sat tantalizingly within reach.

Spotting no one, Mycah slipped inside and nabbed a loaf. Holding it up to his nose, he inhaled its aroma—a warm wholesome smell with a touch of sourness imparted by the yeast. Pressing his fingers into the loaf, he relished in the crackle of the crust.

"What do you think you're doing?"

Mycah lurched backward, the loaf nearly flying from his fingers. He juggled it several times before finally catching it and slipping it behind his back. Marta stood in the doorway with a raised eyebrow and hands on her hips.

"Sorry Marta," said Mycah. "I was just following my nose. It smelled so delicious you see and—"

"Breakfast is for my paying customers. Honestly, I don't even know why I bother with you and Jerud. As if a meal, a hot bath, a change of clothes, and place to stay weren't enough. Perhaps we'll just make a habit of this, yes? Why not? I doubt I've got anything better to do with my free coin than take in a pair of strays..."

"Um, well, yes, thank you for all of that," said Mycah as he slipped the loaf back to the top of the pile. "I really am grateful. Honest. And I'll be fine without the bread. One meal a day and I'm good to go. Jerud would probably keel over, but a skinny guy like me—"

Marta pressed her fingers to her temple. "You've already sunk your fingers into it. Just take it."

In the blink of an eye, the bread materialized in Mycah's grasp. He hastily tore off a hunk and stuffed it in his mouth.

"Ohh, wow... mmm... Mawrta, dis is gweat," Mycah said between mouthfuls. "Hmm... you could staat your own bakewy, honest!"

He swallowed. "Oh, by the way, have you seen Jerud?"

"He's out back. Go, before I pop a blood vessel."

Eyeing a bowl of porridge in the corner, Mycah forced himself around toward the exit. Best to leave with the bread and consider it a win. Though he'd pulled himself out of bed, he'd certainly dallied for more than five minutes, and he didn't have any interest in being doused with a bucket of trough water. Now that he thought of it, it was unlike Jerud to make a timed threat and then disappear. Jerud always kept his word, and he understood the need for punctuality. Propping open the back door, Mycah found the source of Jerud's delay.

"Hey, Mycah, look who I found," said Jerud. Standing next to the big man was none other than Two-Foot Pete.

"Pete!"

The lanky man rushed Mycah and enveloped him in a big hug. "By the moons, son, but it's good to see ya! I was just tellin' Jerud 'ere 'ow worried I'd been these past few weeks. I'd no idea what happened to you two. When the Stormguards came fer us at the wall, I barely got outta there with my own skin, I did!"

"An' Jerud," said Pete, turning to his portly friend. "I waited for ya, by the moons but I did. When you didn't come... well, it tore at my insides. Near made me sick, it did. I thought o' tryin' to go in after ya—the whole gang did, what was left of us anyways—but the Stormqueen locked that place down tighter than a virgin 'ore!"

"Pete! Watch your tongue with the lad."

"Sorry, but it's true," said Pete with a bob of his head toward Mycah.

Mycah shook his head. "C'mon, guys. I'm a grown man. You think I don't know what happens at Marta's after dark?"

"There's no need to be vulgar, that's all..." Jerud scratched his neck uncomfortably.

"So Pete," said Mycah. "Tell me—how'd you escape?"

"Just got lucky, I reckon," said Pete. "Me and Jerud was waitin' for ya at the wall, just as we planned. We was startin' to get a little worried—you was a few minutes late, an' Jerud knows you're a stickler for bein' punctual. That's when the Stormguards came fer us. Jerud was hollerin' at me fer me to go, so I shimmied up the grapeline an' over the wall. Then I just ran. I 'eard a few shots hit the pavin' stones behin' me, so I didn't look back. Honest, I'm not sure they even followed me."

"Yeah," said Jerud. "I tried to follow you, but let's just say I'm not as fast as I used to be. Didn't even make it halfway up the line before they got me."

Pete smirked. "You ain't never been fast in yer 'ole life, Jerud."

"I got the gift of brawn not briskness, you old spider you..."

"So what 'bout you, Mycah?" asked Pete. "What 'appened back there?"

"It was a set up," said Mycah. "The Stormguards busted into Rain's quarters just as I snagged the staff. I managed to slip them for a while, even if it did mean crawling into the bowels of hell itself."

Pete scrunched up his face. "Were the blueprints off? How deep does that there palace go?"

"I'm exaggerating a bit," said Mycah. "But I did end up escaping through the boiler room. Jumped out a furnace and half scared some poor stoker to death. Wasn't easy, but I'd finally lost the guards and was making a beeline for the exit when all of a sudden I got jumped by Rayven. That backstabbing bastard..."

Pete rubbed his chin. "So that's what 'appened. Rayven sold us out, huh? What a prat... We didn't know what to think when just the three of ya never showed up."

"So everyone else is safe, then?" asked Mycah.

"Yeah," said Pete. "We all managed to meet up afterward. Like I said, we thought 'bout tryin' to bust ya out, but that was just wishful thinkin', it was. Discretion won out over valor, ya might say. Anyways, we was all so worried 'bout the Stormqueen comin' after us that everybody kinda went their own way. I'm pretty sure the Wentons an' Red left town, an' everyone else went unnerground. 'Cept for Jim, but you know 'im—'e could pass ya on the street and ya'd never know it."

"Well I'm just glad no one else got hurt," said Jerud.

"Yeah, me too," said Mycah. "So how'd you know we were out, Pete?"

"I gots my ears to the ground, son. Came by soon as I got word, an' good thing too. Looks like I caught ya just in time."

"Yeah, uhh... something came up. We're gonna have to skip town for a while."

"I've already caught him up, lad," said Jerud. "I gave him the whole story while you were getting dressed. And stealing bread by the looks of it."

Mycah looked down at the loaf sheepishly. "Erm... Marta ok'd it. In a sense."

"Sordid stuff what that Stormqueen done." Pete shook his head in admonishment. "Sordid stuff indeed."

"Look Pete," said Mycah. "It's been great seeing you, but I think Jerud's going to strangle me if we don't get moving soon. Take care, alright?"

Pete smirked again. "Son, you don't think I got up an hour before dawn an' marched all the way down 'ere just for my health, do ya?"

"What do you mean?"

"An' I thought 'e was supposed to be the smart one." Pete gave Jerud a raised eyebrow.

Jerud chuckled.

"Wait... you're not planning on coming with us, are you?" asked Mycah.

"Give 'im a prize, Jerud!"

Jerud's chuckle turned into a guffaw.

"Seriously, Pete, this isn't your fight," said Mycah.

Pete's demeanor hardened. "Boy, don't even try an' tell me what I can an' can't be doin'. Me and Jerud go way back. WAY back, you 'ear me? If you think I'm just gonna sit around and rot while my buddy's in a fix, then you're dead wrong is what y'are! I'm comin', and that's that!"

Mycah was taken aback by the force of Pete's display. He glanced at Jerud who gave a slight shrug.

"Well... alright," said Mycah. "I won't stop you. But it's going to be a long journey. Honestly I don't know how Jerud's going to make it."

"Boy, I'm not that fat." Jerud pointed a thick finger in his direction.

Pete put his hands on his hips and looked back and forth between the pair, shaking his head. "What would the two of ya do without me. C'mon 'round to the front. I got something to show ya."

Pete headed into the alley leading to the front of The Swan. Mycah and Jerud followed. As he reached the main thoroughfare, Pete pirouetted and flourished his hands.

"Well, whadya think?"

Three young horses stood tethered to a post above the watering trough, saddled and ready for travel. The closest one whinnied when the trio approached.

"Pete, where'd you get these?" asked Jerud with a wary eye.

"Well I didn't pinch 'em if that's what you're askin'," said Pete. "Look, I know a guy. Saved 'is skin once. Popped by 'is place this mornin' an' told 'im I needed some steeds right quick. 'E wasn' 'appy about me showin' up out of the blue, but bless 'is heart, 'e obliged. They're ours as long as we need 'em, s'long as we return 'em when we're done."

Pete stepped to the one on the end. "I chose this piebald mare as mine. Name's Sophie. She's a sweet'eart."

Two-foot Pete stroked her muzzle and picked a slice of carrot from his pocket. Sophie tossed her head and nuzzled Pete's hand, gobbling up the treat with glee. "I've only 'ad 'er fer an hour an' already it feels like I've known 'er fer a year.

"The big sorrel geldin' there's Champ. I figured 'e'd be the right size for ya, Jerud. A man yer size needs a stout horse, an' my friend said Champ there's solid as a rock. 'E should be able to carry ya all day without tirin'."

"He's a handsome animal," said Jerud, offering his hand for the gelding to sniff.

"Finally, that young salt an' pepper mare on the end there's yours, Mycah. 'Er name's Applesnatch."

"Applesnatch?" Mycah asked. "What kind of name is that?"

"Well, let's just say ya should keep an eye on 'er when you're near any apple carts. Or fruit stands of any kind, most like. She's got fire. You'll love 'er!"

Mycah approached the animal with suspicion. Her salt-and-pepper coat glistened in the early morning light. She stood tall and proud, her withers coming up nearly to Mycah's chin, and her eyes shone bright and alert. However she seemed somehow... impatient? Her tail lay flat and still, and her ears swiveled back and forth, absorbing every rustle and creak from the street.

As Mycah neared, Applesnatch turned her head toward him. Intelligence shone in her eyes. Rather than merely gazing upon him, she studied him—determined if he presented a threat or merely an annoyance. Reaching his hand toward her slowly, she snorted and tossed her head. Her ears flattened and she stamped a front hoof menacingly upon the ground.

"Umm, Pete. I don't know about this one..."

"What's wrong with you, lad?" said Jerud. "I thought you liked animals."

"I like *some* animals. Dogs for instance. You give them a snack and a scratch and they love you forever. But horses? Horses are different. Horses are... malicious."

Applesnatch snorted.

"Does 'e always complain this much, Jerud?" Two-Foot Pete stroked his mare's mane and raised an eyebrow at Mycah. Was he smirking?

"Generally, yes." Jerud chuckled. "Might as well get used to it, Pete."

"Guys, I'm not kidding," said Mycah. "I'm genuinely concerned here. I think she might bite my face off..."

Applesnatch continued to leer at him. Mycah took a step back, afraid he might be within snapping range.

"Nonsense, lad," said Jerud. "Look at her! She's a fine beast. Just brash and bit cautious, that's all. Just like you. Why you two are a perfect match, I'd say."

Mycah took a closer look at Applesnatch. Despite her initial warning to him, she now stood poised, head held high. Her eyes rested firmly upon Mycah rather than flitting about. A nervous mare would've danced and kicked, trying to pull out of her tether. On the contrary, Applesnatch didn't appear nervous at all—just cagey and tentative.

Mycah supposed he couldn't blame the mare. After all, an hour prior she'd been separated from her owner and dragged across town into an unfamiliar situation. Now a strange human was eyeing her with mistrust.

If I were a horse, I'd probably be far worse tempered than she. I'd kick anyone who tried to touch me, not just stamp a foot.

Mycah gazed deep into her eyes. He didn't observe any malice there, just apprehension. Holding her gaze, he stepped forth and extended his hand once again. Apple-snatch whinnied softly and danced a few steps to the side.

"Easy, girl," said Mycah. "I'm not going to hurt you. I know we got off on the wrong foot, but I just want to be friends."

Taking two more steps forward, he placed his hand on her flank. Applesnatch kept one eye locked on him the entire time but didn't recoil from his touch. Mycah stroked her gently. Keeping his gaze, Applesnatch whin-nied in acknowledgement of Mycah's efforts before turn-ing her head away. Mycah breathed a sigh of relief.

"See. What did I tell you," said Jerud. "A perfect match."

"Well, I don't know about perfect." Mycah stepped up around the mare's face. "She seems a little hotheaded to me."

Applesnatch lifted her head and snorted, then pushed him hard with her muzzle. Mycah toppled forward. The next thing he knew, he found himself elbow deep in frigid trough water. Jerud and Pete started cackling uproari-ously. Jerud nearly doubled over in glee, holding his sides as his booming laugh echoed out. Mycah stood and shook his arms in a futile attempt to dry off.

"Yes, ha ha. Very funny." Mycah glared at Applesnatch. She glared right back, a twinkle in her eyes. *So that's how it was going to be, was it?*

"Oh, son," said Pete as he tried to catch his breath. "You don't 'ave much experience with 'orses, do ya?"

"What gave it away?" said Mycah.

"Look, this mare 'ere, she's a lot like a woman. Ya gotta treat 'er nice, be gentle with 'er, an' above all, watch whatcha say. If ya do that, she'll treat ya right, but if not..."

well Hell hath no fury like a woman scorned, they say. Same goes fer a good mare, I reckon."

"You're wasting your breath, Pete," said Jerud, red faced from laughter. "Mycah's got about as much experience with women as he does with horses."

"Now that's patently untrue and you know it," said Mycah. "I've wooed plenty of fine girls."

"Oh, yeah?" asked Jerud. "And how far did all that wooing get you?"

"I've had a few second dates..."

Jerud wandered over and patted Applesnatch on her crest. Oh, so it was fine if Jerud came over and scratched her, apparently? She might as well bat her eyes at the big man and be done with it.

"I'm not talking about dates, lad," said Jerud. "I'm talking about relationships—of which you've had precious few. You've got to create a bond of trust with an animal, like you would with a woman. You have to treat them with respect, and listen to them when they speak to you. Now Applesnatch might not be able to express exactly what she needs, but she'll make it obvious through her actions. That's what Pete's trying to get at. Feed her, water her, brush and curry her when needed. Give her encouragement and love, and she'll treat you right."

Mycah contorted his mug into something between a scowl and a grimace. "This is my 'I don't believe you' face."

Jerud threw up his hands. "You're impossible! I honestly don't know what you're complaining about. Pete picked out a great horse."

"She's ornery and difficult. How exactly is that great?"

"Have you ever wondered why you never getting anywhere with any of the girls you're off wooing?" asked Jerud.

"I assumed none of them could handle my disarming good looks." Mycah thought he saw Applesnatch roll her eyes. Could a horse even do that? Apparently she could.

"It's because you're not picking the right gal," said Jerud. "You're always pining after some delicate flower with a wounded heart in search of a knight in shining armor. Well guess what? That's not you. You need a strong, independent woman. Someone with a little backbone. Someone who's willing to put up with your nonsense and put you in your place when you need it."

"'E's right, Mycah," said Pete. "Heck, I don't even know ya that well, an' I can see that plain as day. Wouldn'a got ya Applesnatch if I didn't. But ya know what? My friend now, 'e's got a daughter, an'—"

"Alright, alright, enough," said Mycah. "How did this turn into a discussion about my love life? I thought we were talking about horses."

"See, you're still doing it," said Jerud. "You can't think of Applesnatch as a horse. You've got to think of her as a lady. Am I right, Pete?"

Pete nodded.

"You've got to be kidding me." Mycah pressed his fingers to his temples. "Look, don't we have a deity to go rob or something? I thought we were in a hurry."

Jerud and Pete looked at each other, shrugged, and began discussing necessities for the trip. Though Pete had appeared out of thin air with the horses, he hadn't brought any supplies other than saddles, blankets, and bridles. Jerud had cajoled supplies for Mycah and himself from Marta, but now they'd need additional provisions for Pete—not to mention the horses. Rations, a bedroll, canteen bags, feed for the horses in case they couldn't find enough forage—the list was extensive. Jerud could probably sweet talk Marta into parting with the additional necessities, assuming she could find them, but Mycah didn't envy him the task.

Jerud and Pete wandered inside to gather what they could. Mycah opted to stay with the horses. Sitting on the tethering post, he stared at Applesnatch. Then he remembered the bread.

He hopped off the post. Fishing in his coat, he extracted the remainder of his pilfered loaf. Standing just out of reach of her bite, he offered it up in his hand.

"So, um, look," he said. He couldn't believe he was talking to a horse. "I'm sorry for calling you hotheaded. And claiming you were going to eat my face. A peace offering?"

Applesnatch eyed him, then the bread, then him again. After considering the offer for a moment, she tossed her head and whinnied before snagging the remainder of the loaf and chewing upon it heartily.

Note to self—bring lots of snacks.

Mycah walked to the mare's flank and patted her. "Well, looks like we're going to get along after all, aren't we, gal?"

Applesnatch turned her head to look at Mycah. She tossed her mane nonchalantly, the equine equivalent of a shrug. Pete had been right. She was a fiery one. But at least she could be bribed, and that was a quality Mycah felt fully comfortable exploiting.

CHAPTER ELEVEN

First Steps

Mycah's stomach growled. Looking up at the sun, he surmised it was well past midday, and all he'd eaten since their departure from Guildean was a half loaf of bread. Pressing his knees into Applesnatch's flanks, he urged the mare up next to Jerud and Pete.

"Hey, you guys have any plans on stopping for a snack anytime soon?"

Jerud gave his head a shake. "Nope. If you're hungry, you can dig something out of your saddlebag. But I'd suggest you be frugal. Never know how long these rations are going to have to last us. And you sure aren't getting any of mine."

Mycah rummaged in the sack tied at his pommel. Finding some jerky, he tore off a chunk and popped it in his mouth. Though he found the smoky flavor appealing, its texture left something to be desired. Chewing methodically, he kept Applesnatch at a steady walk next to the others. The muted clopping of the horse's shoes on the packed earth road joined the buzzing of insects and the whisper of the wind. Together they formed a traveler's serenade, wafting across the cultivated fields that surrounded the city.

"So are we just going to ride in silence for a month and a half, or are we going to do anything to pass the time?"

Jerud swiveled his head in Mycah's direction. Since exiting Guildean, he and Pete had exchanged the occasional wisecrack, but otherwise they'd seemed completely content to ride in silence.

"What did you have in mind, lad?"

"We could talk."

"Alright. What do you want to talk about?"

"I don't know," said Mycah. "Anything. This is going to be a really long journey otherwise."

Jerud chuckled. "Mycah, sometimes I forget how little you've experienced. On a long journey, sometimes you just run out of things to talk about. Better get used to the silence."

"Yeah," said Mycah. "But this is our first day."

Jerud shrugged.

Mycah snapped his fingers. "Hey, I know. You said you were going to finish telling me that story about Marta at some point."

Pete's eyebrows shot up. Clearly the lanky man knew something he didn't.

Jerud gave him a calculating look. "Yeah... I don't remember saying that. I think there was a 'maybe' involved there."

"C'mon Jerud—"

"No. Just drop it." The big man's brow furrowed.

"Fine. Be that way." Mycah took another bite of jerky and chewed. "What about you Pete. I'm sure you've got some fun stories to share."

"Oh, sure son. 'Course I do." Pete seemed eager to fill the silence all of a sudden. Maybe it had something to do with Marta. "Whadya 'ave in mind?"

"Well, how'd you get that nickname, for starters? Two-Foot Pete? I mean really?"

Pete chuckled. "Oh, well that's a fun story, see. It all started with Jerud 'ere. Ain't that right, Jerud?"

Jerud stared ahead sourly.

"Ehh… right," said Pete. "Anyways, me and Jerud, we'd just met at the time. Maybe a few months prior, I reckon. And boy was that quite the interduction."

Pete waved his hand absently. "But anyways, that's a story fer another time. Now Jerud 'ere? 'E was workin' for a wealthy merchant of a, shall we say, less than honest disposition. 'E was runnin' a scam where 'e was skimmin' off the top o' all 'is transactions. Jerud was a bodyguard o' sorts for 'im. This merchant was lookin' to expand 'is operation. Lookin' to appropriate some goods that wasn't 'is. So Jerud brings me in on it. Figured I'd be a good fit fer the job, see?

"Now, you gotta realize that at the time, I went by the name o' Fleetfoot Pete, on accountin' of my nimble prancers."

"Ain't nobody ever called you that, Pete," said Jerud.

So the big man was paying attention, after all.

"Well," said Pete. "Let's just say it was a name I was tryin' out for a while—to see if it stuck."

Jerud rolled his eyes.

"Anyways, so Jerud brings me in, right? An' this merchant? 'E ain't from Guildean, so 'e talks real funny like. An' 'e acted like 'e didn't understand what we was saying either, like *we* was talkin' real funny or somethin'. Can you believe that?"

"Shocking." Mycah lifted his eyebrows. Pete didn't seem to catch the meaning of the gesture, or if he did he ignored it.

"So Jerud brings me over and says to the merchant, 'Ey, this is my buddy, the guy I told ya 'bout. An' so I says, Hey, howdy, name's Pete. Looks like ya got yourself a two 'fer. Cause it's me an' Jerud, right? But the guy acts all confused like. So 'e asks me, so you's a two-foot? An' I says, No, we's a two 'fer. An' he asks, But you's a two-foot? An' now I'm thinkin' this guy's slow or somethin'. So I tells him, Well yeah, I gots two feet, but my name's Pete. An' so he says, Two-foot Pete?

"Well Jerud over 'ere just about thunk that was the funniest darn thing 'e'd ever 'eard. I mean, 'e just 'bout busted a gut 'e was laughin' so 'ard. Just couldn't stop no matter how 'ard 'e tried. The merchant? 'Ell 'e just looked confused, an' I was getting miffed 'bout the whole thing anyhow. That made Jerud laugh all the harder. An' so that's that. Jerud liked it and it stuck, I guess. That's how I got my name."

Despite his sour mood, Jerud cracked a smile. "It was pretty funny, I've got to admit."

"That's it?" asked Mycah.

"Well, yeah," said Pete. "What was you expectin'?"

"I don't know," said Mycah. "I thought there'd be some grand adventure behind it. Like something where you had a foot stuck in a trap and by using both feet at the same time you were able to narrowly free yourself and avoid certain death. I guess I was hoping for something... amazing."

"Lad, that's not how nicknames work," said Jerud. The big man's pleasant demeanor seemed to be coming back. "Nicknames aren't earned through some act of valor. They're usually some dumb thing someone says that ends up sticking 'cause everyone else thought it was funny. Most people don't even like their nicknames at first. But if you own it, then it becomes a part of you. And you learn to love it. Ain't that right, Pete?"

Pete's brow furrowed. "Well, now that ya put it that way, I suppose it's true."

"But some people have cool nicknames," said Mycah. "What about that backstabber Rayven? He may be a son-of-a-bitch, but you've got to admit—he's got a pretty good name."

"I'm not so sure," said Jerud. "I'd bet good money somebody called him that 'cause he's creepy and he looks like a bird. I'd bet they were making fun of him. But the name stuck 'cause it was a good fit. That's the other key—a nickname's gotta fit."

"So you're telling me 'Two-Foot Pete' was the right fit?"

Pete and Jerud looked at each other. Pete shrugged. Jerud smiled.

"Yeah, I guess it was," said Jerud. "Who would've guessed?"

Mycah placed the last of the jerky in his mouth and chewed. Maybe Jerud had a point. Friends could bestow nicknames, but enemies could as well—assuming the name represented some universally evident truth. Mycah was almost glad he'd never earned a nickname himself, though he couldn't help but wonder what random event in his life could've inspired one.

With Jerud's humor restored, the remainder of the afternoon melted away under a steady barrage of shared tales. Jerud and Pete swapped stories of heists gone wrong and escapes made by the seat of their pants. Jerud told a few tales even Mycah hadn't heard before, and Pete regaled the both of them with a thoroughly unbelievable story involving a beautiful woman, the Count of Hemswich, a fire that destroyed an entire city block, and a pack of lost and confused wild mules. Even Mycah chimed in with a few stories of his own adventures, though Jerud was already familiar with all of those.

Eventually, the sun dipped below the horizon, and the trio found a relatively secluded pasture between two farms in which to set up camp. Jerud worked on starting a fire while Pete taught Mycah how to care for the animals. He showed him how to remove a saddle, then brushed Sophie's flanks and back and checked her hooves for pebbles. Once done, he had Mycah do the same for Applesnatch while he cared for Champ.

Even though the ride had gone smoothly, Mycah still harbored a hint of fear that Applesnatch would snap at him again. She let him work without complaint however, and once Mycah began brushing her, a transformation occurred. She warmed to him instantly, whinnying softly with each stroke of the brush. She even wiggled her rump as Mycah brought it over her haunches. Mycah found the entire process, though time consuming, was quite soothing, both to himself and to Applesnatch. As he worked the mare's flank, he caught himself smiling.

Having finished grooming the tall gelding, Pete stood and clapped Mycah on the shoulder. "Well, son. Looks like you've got the hang of it. I'll be seein' if Jerud needs any help with supper."

Pete turned toward the fire.

"Hey, Pete," said Mycah. "Before you go—"

Pete turned back toward Mycah.

"I just wanted to say thanks. For picking out Applesnatch. I think she's a fine animal. And a good match."

Pete bobbed his head. "Sure thing, son."

Mycah finished brushing Applesnatch and checked her hooves. With that completed, he dug through his saddlebags and found his bedroll. Jerud and Pete's chatter carried over from the clearing, as did aromas of the night's meal. His nose detected only rehydrated beef and beans, but after a day of eating bread and jerky the thought of any hot meal was enough to make him salivate. As Mycah stood to return to the fire, Applesnatch nuzzled her snout in between the crook of his arm and pushed him.

"Uhh… what is it girl? Are you hungry?" Mycah checked his coat pockets. "I'm all out of bread, and it doesn't look like I've got anything else you might want."

Applesnatch tossed her head and nuzzled him again.

"You're not scared, are you? I'll be right over there with Jerud and Pete."

Applesnatch rolled her eyes and rested her forehead against Mycah's chest.

"I, uhh…"

Mycah felt confused. What could this horse possibly want? Gingerly lifting an arm, he scratched the mare's head. Applesnatch pressed her head deeper into his chest, and so Mycah scratched with renewed vigor. After a moment, tossed her head and gave a hearty neigh.

"Well, I'll be," said Mycah. "You wanted to say goodnight."

Bedroll slung over his shoulder, he sauntered to the campfire and took a seat next to Jerud and Pete, who'd already helped themselves to the stew. Mycah ladled himself a bowl and dug into its meaty contents.

"So guess what?" said Mycah around a mouthful of beef and beans—and barley. His nose had missed that part. "That horse over there? She wanted a goodnight scratch. Can you believe it?"

Jerud raised both eyebrows and tilted his head knowingly. "So it looks like someone's finally having a little luck with the ladies, eh?"

Jerud and Pete chuckled. Mycah smirked and dove back into his stew. Normally he would've put up a stink, but the mare had grown on him. And it felt good to bond with a female—even if the female happened to be a horse.

After supper, Pete curled up in his sleep sack and promptly began to snore. Mycah couldn't blame him. His own eyelids weighed heavily, and Pete had risen far earlier than he had. Laying down on his bedroll, Mycah cradled his arms behind his head and stared up into the heavens. A cool evening breeze washed over him, but the heat from the fire radiated warmth onto his exposed cheeks, keeping him toasty. Jerud sat, legs drawn before him, staring into the fire.

"What's on your mind, Jerud?"

Jerud lifted his head and blinked several times. "Oh, I don't know, lad. Just... thinking about this whole ordeal, I guess."

"You mean our insane quest?"

Jerud nodded.

"I know what you mean. I've been trying not to think about it, honestly."

Jerud continued to stare into the fire. "I know, lad. Me too. But I can't help but worry. Not just about what we'll face—though I do worry about that—but what if we fail? I'm a pious man. You know that. What if I fall before I've had time to make my peace with God? And then there's the business with the Stormqueen summoning that *thing*— that creature from the depths of Hell. If it truly has a hold on us..."

Jerud grew quiet. "I'm frightened, lad."

Mycah propped himself up on one elbow. "Jerud, can I be honest with you?"

"Of course."

"I'm scared too. About, well... everything. About what the Stormqueen might do to us. About what we might find on this journey. And definitely about that blasted curse."

Mycah shuddered as he recalled the demon's voice. Yes, it was better not to think about it. Too late for that now, though.

"Do you know I've never left the city?" said Mycah. "This is as far as I've ever been. I have no idea what we're going to find out there, and it scares the daylights out of me! Now you know I've always been skeptical, and not just about religion. About magic. About history. About women! But there's one thing I know for sure. You and me? We're a good team. If we stick together, I know we can get through anything. Anything, Jerud. So let's make a pact. We push our fears to the side—at least until we get the Stormqueen to free us from her witchcraft. We stick together, and we get through this. Agreed?"

Mycah locked eyes with Jerud. After a pause, the big man nodded.

"Alright, Mycah. You have my word."

Jerud spit in his hand and extended it. Mycah grasped it with his free hand and squeezed.

"Now go on. Get some sleep, lad. You look like you need it."

"That I do, Jerud."

Mycah nestled into his bedroll, feeling strangely more secure. He knew he could trust Jerud—he always had—but it still felt right to swear upon their resolve. Mycah closed his eyes and pulled his blanket up to his nose. As sleep overtook him, he had a feeling that perhaps the journey wouldn't be quite as horrible as he'd envisioned.

CHAPTER TWELVE

A Welcome Respite

Rain poured down from the heavens, cool and unrelenting. Mycah pulled the brim of his floppy hat down as water dripped onto the base of his neck. He'd purchased the hat from a passing farmer to help keep the rain out of his eyes, but he'd long since abandoned any hope of staying dry. Every scrap of cloth upon him, from the tip of his shirt collar to the hem of his trousers, was utterly and completely soaked. His feet swam in his boots, and he had no doubt when he removed them he'd find toes resembling decades old prunes.

Things could be worse, however. At least they weren't walking.

Applesnatch's hooves squelched as they pulled free from the mud. Mycah thanked the moons once again that Pete had brought the horses. Walking along the mud-plastered roads would've slowed their journey to a crawl, not to mention introduced a budding family of blisters to his heels. Of course, riding also had its pitfalls. Applesnatch had turned irritable and snappy from the rain. She'd nearly bitten off one of his fingers the past day.

The rain had fallen unabated for over a week. As much as the sodden days of travel sapped his spirit, the nights were even more miserable. Several evenings ago, Jerud had convinced a farmer to let them sleep in his barn, but Mycah had scarcely seen a scrap of civilization since. He'd spent his last three nights on a soggy bedroll, hunched up under the drooping boughs of waterlogged pines.

Each night Mycah lay upon his bedroll for at least eight hours, but if he caught even half that much uninterrupted sleep he considered it a blessing. However, the rain wasn't the primary reason for his insomnia. Memories haunted his dreams. Memories of black, churning ooze and threats spoken in a rasping, gravelly voice. More than once he awoke in the middle of the night in a cold sweat, goose-bumps covering his arms. He'd tried to keep his fears hidden from Jerud—fearlessness was a part of their pact, after all—but he was fairly sure the others had heard his startled gasps.

At least with the onset of the constant showers, a balminess reminiscent of summer had finally replaced spring's lasting chill. Good thing, too. A week of soaking in frigid rains and Mycah might've turned around and ridden right back to Guildean, curse be damned. There he might die a horrible death, but at least he'd do so in a dry bed.

Jerud slumped forward in his saddle, a sodden brown cloak draped around his wide shoulders. Not once had he complained about the rain, unless you counted his grumbles concerning the lack of hot meals. Suppers had consisted of bits of jerky and handfuls of nuts since the onset of the storms, but jerky didn't stick to the ribs like a good pot of stewed beef and oats did.

Onward they plodded, through the rain and mud. Applesnatch's hooves slurped with each step, creating a rhythmic sound with four beats to a measure.

Slurpity-slurp, slurpity-slurp.

The rain beat against the brim of Mycah's hat, like tiny batons upon a drum.

Pitter-patter, slurpity-slurp, pitter-patter, slurpity-slurp.

The monotonous dissonance rattled around Mycah's head.

Is this your defense to protect your kingdom, God? Drench us? Drain us? Batter us with an awful cacophony of sloppy feet and musical hats? Are you trying to demoralize us? Make us turn back? Because it's certainly working...

"Anyone know any good travelling songs?" asked Mycah.

Jerud and Pete looked at him as if he'd lost his mind. Mycah pulled the brim of his hat down over his eyes to shield himself from their stares.

"Just trying to brighten the mood a little. At least I tried..."

With the sky grey and laden with clouds, Mycah couldn't discern the hour. The growing rumble from his belly indicated it was closer to evening than to midday. Just as Mycah resigned himself to another restless night of tossing and turning on a sodden mat, Applesnatch crested a hill and a beautiful sight presented itself. A small farming community sprawled lazily over the countryside barely half a league away.

"Oh, thank the moons!" said Mycah. "I was beginning to think we'd never see civilization again. Now we can finally get a hot meal and a roof over our heads. Assuming we're stopping, of course?"

Jerud, despite his constant insistence upon traveling until dark, for once seemed perfectly content to retire early.

"Lad, we'd be mad not to stop and dry off for the night." Jerud pointed ahead toward a cluster of buildings. At the center of the bunch stood a lone two-story house with rubble masonry walls and a thatched roof. "And we probably won't even have to spend the evening in a barn. I'd wager that's an inn."

"Oh, that'd be right nice, it would," said Pete. "A fire, a bed, an' a mug o' ale. A man forgets the simple pleasures o' life when 'e's on the road, but 'e does!"

"Just remember," said Jerud. "If anyone asks we're pilgrims headed to the Shrine of Repentance. No more, no less."

Jerud reminded them to play the part of the penitent pilgrims at every conceivable opportunity. Mycah sighed in exasperation. "Why else in the world would anyone travel along this God-forsaken road except to get to that blasted shrine?"

Jerud gave Mycah a reproachful look. "Poor choice of words, lad, considering we're traveling to a land that's actually been forsaken."

"Jerud I—"

"Just watch your mouth, Mycah. If you go about using the Lord's name in vain like that people will begin suspecting us for sure."

Though he hated to admit it, Jerud had a point. It seemed like the closer to the center of the world they travelled, the more pious and devout the folk became. Perhaps the stories of the Garden of Eden and God's curse carried more weight here due to simple proximity. Regardless of the reason, Mycah needed to keep his tongue in check otherwise he might find himself thrown back into the rain with no sympathy from either Pete or Jerud.

"If it means sleeping in a warm bed tonight then I can be as well-behaved as an altar boy."

Jerud grunted, unconvinced.

The three of them spurred their horses onward, eager to exit the rain. Despite the season, few farmers tended the fields—though who could blame them given the downpour. As they neared the village, Mycah spotted smoke curling from jutting chimneys and heard the pounding of a blacksmith's hammer over the steady plopping of the raindrops. Jerud led the way to the presumed inn, a building with a roughly hewn sign hanging depicting a pair of cupped hands filled with fruits and grains. Jerud guided his gelding into the stable next-door. Within it, a lone stable-boy shoveled hay into an empty stall. Seeing travelers, he ran to the front, snatched his cap from his head, and hooked his legs in an awkward bow.

"Evenin', sirs. Staying at the Lord's Bounty tonight?"

"That we will lad, if you've the space for us," said Jerud as he dismounted.

"Oh, certainly sirs, certainly. We've not too many travelers these days. Master Lorry'll find rooms for you, without a doubt."

The youth took Champ and Sophie's reins and led them to empty stalls. Through he needed a stool to aid him, he quickly unsaddled the two horses and draped dry towels across their backs. The young lad looked to be barely twelve, but he moved with an experienced efficiency. Likely the lad had been tending to mounts since before he could even reach their muzzles. The youth returned for Applesnatch as Mycah removed a few belongings from his saddlebags.

"Oh this one's a beauty, sirrah! What a fine coat she has. She's a spirited one, I'd wager."

Applesnatch nickered and nuzzled the youth's side.

Mycah raised an eyebrow. "Looks like you've got the magic touch. She's normally wary of strangers..."

The lad laughed. "Oh, I'm not so sure it's me, sirrah. Likely she smells the treats."

The youth stretched a hand into his vest pocket and removed a slice of apple, which Applesnatch greedily swiped with the speed of a hawk. The poor lad barely escaped with his fingers.

"Oh, right. I probably should have told you," said Mycah, feeling a mite sheepish. "Her name's Applesnatch."

The lad paled, but to his credit he recovered quickly. "Oh, um, not to worry. I've handled plenty a mare like this one. Why, I can't even blame her. I'm partial to those apples, myself. Come fresh from my uncle's farm, they do."

As the lad led the mare to a stall, Jerud slipped him a copper, causing him to shower the big fellow with thanks and bows. All the while, Applesnatch nibbled at his coat pocket unabashedly, fishing with her tongue for more apple slices. The horse knew no shame, but at least she lived up to her moniker.

"C'mon lad," said Jerud. "Let's get inside and find the fire."

Mycah followed Jerud and Pete out of the stable and into the inn. A half dozen round tables populated the common room, and a bar at the back provided additional seating. The few locals at the bar quieted and looked up from their mugs at their entrance, but a quick nod of Jerud's head assuaged any fears the local farmers might've harbored. They promptly returned to their ale and conversation.

A fire crackled merrily in a hearth at the side, a large cross dangling over the mantle. Hanging his sodden cloak on a peg by the door, Jerud stomped over to the fireplace and pulled up a chair. Following his lead, Mycah and Pete hung their coats and joined the big man by the hearth. Once seated, Mycah peeled off his boots, stripped his waterlogged socks, and propped his feet up by the fire. The warmth radiating from the flames felt divine. Steam rose from between his toes as his wrinkled feet stretched back to normal.

Once they'd settled, an aproned innkeep wandered over to greet them.

"Evening gents," he said with a modest bow. "Welcome to the Lord's Bounty. My name's Percival Lorry. Might I interest you in a pint of ale?"

"That sounds splendid, Master Lorry," answered Jerud. "Three mugs if you please."

Master Lorry exited to draw the beverages, and Mycah, Jerud, and Pete sat in quiet bliss, enjoying the toasty warmth of the hearth. Mycah considered stripping off more of his clothing but decided against it due to social conventions.

The innkeep returned with the drinks. He set them on a nearby table and drew up a chair. In many inns, such a move might be viewed as impolite, but given the size of the community, Mycah wasn't surprised Master Lorry wanted to get to know his tenants.

"So what brings you travelers to Leesvale? You're not from Portage or Greenwich else I wager I'd have met you prior."

Mycah took a sip of the beer. It was a red ale, bitter with strong hints of raspberry and winterleaf, but good. Mycah hadn't been sure what sort of drink would pass as ale in these parts. He'd half expected to swallow a mouthful of dirty dishwater, but apparently this innkeep took his brewing seriously.

"We're pilgrims, from Guildean," said Jerud. "I'm Jerud. This is Pete, and the young lad is Mycah. We're making our way to the Shrine of Repentance."

Master Lorry made the Lord's cross over his forehead and chest. "Blessed be thy travels, friends. I made the trip myself many seasons ago. Quite the journey, it is. Not just of the body, but of the soul. It's a fair trip from Guildean, though, I'd wager."

"That it is," muttered Mycah. "And it feels even longer when the skies open up on you for a week straight."

The innkeep pursed his lips. "Well, I suppose that the rain's made your travels difficult, friend, but it's been a boon to us. Rain's the lifeblood of every farming community, you know. Perhaps it's a boon for you as well. A difficult journey'll make the reward all the sweeter when you reach the shrine. Far be it from us to question the Lord's ways."

Mycah nearly objected before Jerud froze him with a watchful eye.

"Well said, Master Lorry," said Jerud. "Well said."

The innkeep clapped his hand to his thigh. "Well then, friends, am I to assume you'll be spending the night here? With the weather such as it is, I'd urge you to regardless of my own interests. I have quarters enough for the three of you, or you can share a room if you're looking to save some coin."

Jerud checked his purse. "I think we can afford a small luxury, just this once. We'll take separate quarters since you have them. And a hot meal would be a blessing."

Jerud handed the innkeep a silver Guilder and a few copper pennies. Master Lorry pocketed the coins after a brief inspection.

"My better half's cooking up a lamb shank and spring potatoes for tonight's supper. I'll bring out a few dishes once it's ready. And I'll snatch a loaf of the morning's bread for you while you wait."

Master Lorry returned to the bar to refill mugs that had started to want for attention. Mycah picked at his shirt, plucking damp segments away from his skin to help them dry. As he did so, his hand strayed to his chest and the stone that hung there, dangling from his neck in a tan leather pouch. His fingers probed its edges, feeling the weight within.

Slipping the thong over his head, he loosened the pouch's tie and slid the stone into his palm. He curled his fingers over it and closed his eyes, focusing on the warmth within. In his mind's eye, he could see the tiny fire burning at the stone's center, but it was faint and distant—virtually the same as when they'd left Guildean. Mycah executed the ritual every few days, testing the stone for any changes, but he'd yet to detect any.

When Mycah opened his eyes, he found Jerud peering at him. "Any change, lad?"

"Not that I can tell," said Mycah. "It's been over three weeks since we left, and this blasted stone feels exactly the same as it did when Rain gave it to us. I'm starting to wonder if it works at all."

"Well, no use worrying about it yet," said Jerud. "We know where we need to go, and we don't need any stone to tell us how to get there. Let's just hope it works when we get to the Garden."

"I hope you're right."

"Now, put it away before you lose it. You know it makes me nervous every time you take it out."

Mycah slipped the stone back into the pouch and over his head. "And you tell *me* not to worry…"

Jerud frowned and took a swig from his mug.

Master Lorry returned with a tray laden with steaming bowls and a crusty loaf of bread. "Seems like you gents arrived just in time. My wife just pulled the lamb from the braising pot. I poked it with a fork, and it's fall-off-the-bone tender."

Mycah accepted a bowl of the steaming meat and potato dish. Inhaling deeply, he detected hints of thyme and rosemary as well as fresh butter and cracked pepper. The fat that marbled the lamb shank appeared to have rendered perfectly, coating the meat and the potatoes alike. His stomach grumbled in anticipation, reminding him of how long it had been since he'd enjoyed a freshly cooked meal. Grabbing a spoon, Mycah dug in.

Master Lorry took a seat next to the hearth and extracted a long-stemmed pipe from the front pocket of his apron. He tapped the pipe bowl on the mantle to settle its contents, then using a set of large wrought iron tongs he carefully selected a burning ember from the fire and dropped in into the bowl. As the innkeeper puffed at the bit, the bowl glowed and dimmed. After a few seconds, a rich, white smoke began to waft up. Master Lorry leaned back in his chair, smoking lazily. The farmers at the bar joked and laughed, sharing tales as they drank their ale.

As Mycah gobbled his lamb, he couldn't help but marvel at the inn's tranquil atmosphere. Go to any bar in Guildean and you'd be sure to find patrons drinking and dicing, banging mugs and catcalling serving girls. Between the barmaids and the spirits, brawling never lagged far behind. If the Lord's Bounty had ever hosted a fight, Mycah surely couldn't tell. Not a single knife mark scarred the tables, nor did any shards of broken glass rest upon the floor.

Of course, who'd be brawling in a small town such as this? Based on what he'd seen on the ride in, Mycah guessed there were barely a hundred people who called Leesvale home. Judging by the camaraderie of the patrons at the bar and the demeanor of Master Lorry himself, folks here knew each other, trusted each other, and were at peace in their own tiny slices of life.

As he neared the bottom of his bowl, Mycah tore a hunk from the loaf and used it to mop up the fat and juices that lingered in his bowl's bowels. When he'd consumed every last morsel, he set the bowl down and belched.

"Oh, erm... excuse me," said Mycah, pressing a fist to his sternum.

Master Lorry puffed out a mouthful of smoke. "Not to worry, lad. Around here, that's a sign of appreciation. I'll let the missus know."

Mycah reached for his ale to wash down his meal. Now that the aromas of herbs and rendered fat no longer rose from the bowl, he became more aware of the innkeep's pipe.

Mycah wasn't a fan of the leaf. He found a man could become dependent upon it if he wasn't careful, and it was rumored to drive men mad if used to excess. Since most of the leaf smoked in Guildean smelled like a mix of tar and old leather, Mycah had never understood the draw of it, but Master Lorry's particular blend smelled fruity and clean—like crisp apples and morning dew. It was intoxicating.

"Pardon me, Master Lorry," said Mycah. "But that leaf you're smoking—I've never smelled anything quite like it."

Percival Lorry grinned. "I don't doubt it, my boy. This here is Leesvale White, the finest leaf this side of the Snowfells. Grown locally, of course, by my youngest sister's husband. Can't say I know his secret to perfecting it, and I wouldn't share it even if I did, but I have a suspicion. Care to know?"

Master Lorry leaned in close. "I think it's Leesvale it-self. The clean water, the fresh air... Why there's some-thing blessed about this place, I tell you."

The innkeep leaned back in his chair and continued to puff on his pipe. Clean air and water? Mycah doubted that alone could justify the scent. There must be some secret, some additive or... something. Not that it mattered. My-cah still had no interest in the stuff, but by the moons did it smell sweet!

Having finished their meals, Pete and Jerud sat back in their chairs, chatting softly and swigging their ale. Master Lorry's pipe burned low, the leaf mostly extinguished. Leaning forward, the innkeep tapped his pipe against the inside of the fireplace, dumping the ashes into the coals. He turned to the trio as he returned the pipe to his apron pocket.

"Well, friends, your rooms are ready. I can show you to them at your convenience. But before I go, I felt the need to share a warning."

The innkeeper pursed his lips and wrung his hands. Looking around, he made the Lord's cross once again. "Gents, I'm a God fearing man. Honest and true. I believe in the good in this world. But there's been rumors lately, of a... dark nature. Pilgrims who've been travelling the road to the Shrine... well lately some have gone missing. John Ashbald, who lives but two day's ride from here, he found some grisly remains in his fields. *Human* remains. Said they'd been picked clean. Not as if by scavengers, but something else..."

Master Lorry swallowed hard. "Sorry friends. Simply talking about these matters makes me uncomfortable."

The man felt for his pipe, then seemed to realize he'd just put it away. "There's more. Wish there wasn't but there is. Less than a fortnight ago, a group of pilgrims coming back from the shrine were attacked. Covered with vicious bites and festering wounds, they were. They told of creatures rising out of the ground itself, waylaying them in the dark of night. *Demons*, they said."

Mycah and Jerud locked eyes. An eerie silence developed, broken only by the crackle of the fire and the chatter of the patrons at the bar.

"Demons?" said Jerud, looking a little pale.

Master Lorry scratched the back of his neck, clearly distressed by the topic. "Look—I can't confirm the tales. They're just rumors as far as I know. I just felt that as a man of God it was my duty to share with you what I'd heard. I'm sure three strapping gents such as yourselves'll be fine, but be sure to keep your wits about you nonetheless."

The innkeeper got up and turned to leave. He hesitated. "I hope to see you on your way back, friends. God bless."

After the innkeeper had left, Mycah pulled his chair in close to Jerud and Pete's. "Jerud, you don't think this has anything to do with us, do you?"

Jerud's brow furrowed. "What do you mean, lad?"

"You know what I mean." Mycah glanced about and lowered his voice. "Do you think those demons have anything to do with us? With the curse, I mean."

Jerud responded harshly, but in a voice barely audible over the crackle of the fire. "Why in the world would a demon be out there terrorizing innocents? We're the ones who got cursed."

"I don't know," said Mycah. "Maybe whatever the Stormqueen summoned got free. Maybe it's following us. Keeping an eye on us."

Jerud frowned. "Let's not start jumping to wild conclusions. I haven't noticed anything out of the ordinary thus far. How about you, Pete? You're the one with outdoorsman experience."

"I ain't seen nothin' strange, Jerud," said Pete. "But there ain't no way fer me to know if we're being followed. Not if whoever's followin' keeps their distance."

"But what if there is a demon?" asked Mycah. "What if it's following us, and it wants us to fail so that it can have our souls."

His hand strayed once again to the pouch around his neck. "What if—"

Jerud shook his head angrily. "This is useless, lad. All you'll accomplish with that line of thinking is giving us both nightmares." The big man lurched from his seat. "I'm headed to bed. I'll see the two of you in the morning. Bright and early."

Jerud stormed off to his quarters. Mycah rubbed his brow in confusion. "What's gotten into him?"

"Look, son," said Pete. "Don't joke with Jerud 'bout that sort o' thing. 'E gets worked up 'bout it. You o' all people should know."

"But I wasn't joking," said Mycah. "I'm concerned. Can't you see?"

Pete drained the last of his ale and set down the mug. "That's not what I mean an' you knows it. Jerud's worried, too, but 'e don't like to show it. So don't put 'im in a spot where 'e's forced to, get it?"

Pete grabbed his boots. "I'll see ya in the mornin', son."

Mycah sat alone in front of the fire, his remaining ale warming between his hands. Jerud's reaction seemed a little unwarranted, but he could've broached the subject a little more delicately. And there was their pact to not show fear—which Mycah was finding extremely difficult to follow. But who could blame him for wanting to share his concerns? The idea of some creature out there stalking them terrified him.

As he stared into the fire, Mycah began to think the rain had been the least of their worries.

CHAPTER THIRTEEN

Guardian Angels and Demons

Rayven's horse plodded forth, its footfalls muted by the damp earth. Rayven hunched forward in his saddle, his jet-black hair hanging limply, sticking to the collar of his coat. The rain had finally slowed around midday, turning into an intermittent drizzle. His clothes were soaked. Rayven barely noticed.

Often those drenched by rain cursed it just as those dependent upon it blessed it, but how could one either praise or condemn the weather? Rain was an inanimate force of nature, neither good nor evil. Allowing oneself to be angered or frustrated by it would be like allowing oneself to be infuriated by a rock or a blade of grass. It was foolish. Unfortunately, destiny conspired to force him into the company of fools.

"By the moons, but I can't wait to be out of these damned sodden clothes," said Johnah. "Feels like a fortnight since I've felt a good fire upon my face."

"Tell me about it," said Sten. "I think I could drink for a week just on the water in my boots."

Even now that the rain had abated, the Stormqueen's guards continued their incessant yammering. *Wretched fools.* And they were supposed to be the capable ones. The Stormqueen had sent him to follow Mycah and his fat friend Jerud to ensure they fulfilled their end of the bargain—but rather than send him alone Rain had forced him to babysit the two guardsmen. Of course, she didn't see it that way. The guards' intended purpose was to ensure Rayven acted in accordance with the Stormqueen's wishes, but they were fooling themselves if they thought they held the reins to the journey.

Oh, certainly the pair seemed confident. Muscles rippled under their shirts, and their skills with blades left little to be desired. Rayven couldn't compete with them in honest combat, but Rayven didn't believe in doing most anything honorably. Had he wished it, he would've slit their throats in the night with nary a peep from either one. For now, however, it served Rayven's interests to keep them alive and well. They were a useful if annoying resource, and he'd fall out of the Stormqueen's graces should he return having lost the two of them to some tragic accident.

Rayven had never envisioned himself in the position he now occupied—a position of permanence and wealth. How things had changed. Stability had replaced uncertainty, but unfortunately freedom had been replaced with subservience. Though coin had always drawn him like a moth to flame, so had adventure and mystery enthralled him—two qualities his current journey sorely lacked. If he and his buffoonish escort didn't encounter some measure of excitement soon, he might be forced to manufacture some simply to keep from losing his edge.

"This blade grows dull from neglect. My kingdom for a worthy whetstone."

The guards quieted and stared at him in confusion, like cattle trying to decipher the inner machinations of a deity. The words were the first to emanate from his lips in over a day, though likely that only partially explained their blank stares.

"Uhh... what?" said Johnah. "Did you lose your whetstone? Hell, I've got one if you need one."

Rayven met the large man's eyes with disdain. And they wondered why he didn't bother to talk to them.

"I'm not sure what good a whetstone will do you," said Sten. "Unless you plan to sharpen your bow."

Rayven briefly considered elucidating the finer points of his metaphor but quickly discarded the idea. What was the use? He'd just receive more vacant stares for his efforts.

Johnah and Sten ignored him and returned to their banter. "So where the Hell is this Leesvale, anyway?" asked Johnah. "Shouldn't we have gotten there by now?"

"The map had it a good eight leagues from where we camped," said Sten. "I'm sure we'll find it soon enough."

"We'd better. This damned weather is making me crazy as a loon!"

Again with the condemnation of the elements. Would it ever stop? Perhaps Rayven should've murdered the guards in their sleep after all—or at least the tall, annoying one, Johnah. What little time the man didn't spend spouting obscenities he spent boasting and flexing. He clearly viewed himself as the pinnacle of virile masculinity, complete with a total disregard for scholarly pursuits. The shorter one, Sten, repulsed him slightly less. At least he paused to give some thought to his verbiage before it spewed from his mouth. Of course, if he murdered one the other would have to join him as a simple matter of prudency…

The horses crested a small hill revealing a farming community.

"Hot damn, there it is!" said Johnah. "Looks like there's an inn and everything. Race you to it?"

Sten eyed Johnah and Rayven. "Let's take our time shall we? Won't take more than a few minutes to get there at this pace. And we wouldn't want to arouse any suspicions by riding into town like banshees."

Johnah frowned and mumbled something about sucking eggs, but he kept his horse at a steady trot. The trio passed by fields of waist high wheat separated by muddy brown furrows. Closer to the village, orchards of blossoming apple and cherry trees ruined an otherwise perfectly grey day. No more than a few hundred yards from the inn, fat raindrops began to once again batter them from the heavens.

"Oh damn it all," said Johnah. "You bastards can enjoy the rain, if you like. I'm getting out of here."

The heavily muscled man snapped his horse's reins and sped off toward the hostel. Sten sighed and gave Rayven a calculating glance.

"I trust you can make your way to the inn unsupervised?"

Rayven snorted.

"I'll take that as a yes." Sten spurred his horse toward the inn after Johnah.

As the two guardsmen's horses galloped off, Rayven kept his horse at an even walk, the raindrops splattering over his head and shoulders. If possible, he'd have slowed his horse further to give himself a longer respite from the louts. Unfortunately, the beast could only walk so slowly, and it seemed eager to be out of the rain as well.

Casually steering his mount into the inn's stable, Rayven slid from his saddle, snatched a pack from his animal's backside, and tossed his reins to a sunny-faced, over-eager youth.

"Evening sirrah, staying at the Lord's—"

The child's voice faded as Rayven walked away in silence. He slipped in through the front of the inn. The guards were warming their hands by the fire, talking to an unassuming man of middle years whose garb and demeanor identified him as the proprietor. Other than Johnah, Sten, and the innkeep, a few simple farmhands joked and chatted at the bar. None of them represented even the mildest of threats. His pack in hand, he glided to the opposite corner of the common room and descended upon a secluded booth.

Eventually the innkeeper made his way over.

"Evening sir," he said, looking Rayven over. His wet jacket hung limply over his thin frame, and his hair obscured much of his face. "You look soaked. There's plenty of space by the fire if you like."

"I prefer the booth."

"Suit yourself. Your friends over there mentioned you'd be coming in soon."

"They're not my friends."

The innkeeper scratched his head. "Um, I see."

The man clearly didn't.

"Can I get you anything?" he asked.

"Sustenance. And privacy."

The innkeep frowned and walked away, shaking his head ever so slightly. Rayven noticed the gesture, but it didn't upset him. He couldn't be bothered to engage in socially accepted civilities, and he certainly didn't expect the treatment from others. However, the innkeeper was a source of information—of which he had need—so he'd have to cover his disdain and engage the man in a more agreeable manner.

The innkeeper returned with a steaming bowl and a mug of rainwater, likely drawn from a horse trough. No matter. As the man set down the meal, Rayven lifted his head.

"Innkeep? A word, if I may."

"Yes?" said the innkeeper gruffly.

"Pardon my incivility. My travels have been trying. I shouldn't have been so... terse."

The innkeeper's brow furrowed, but his demeanor softened. "Well, I do suppose the weather can get to a man. No bother, traveler. I just like to be on speaking terms with my patrons, that's all."

"Understandable." Rayven sniffed the bowl. It contained a meat, a starch, and a vegetable. It would provide adequate nourishment. "If I might ask you a question?"

"Shoot," said the innkeep.

"Did you by chance encounter a party of three travelers recently? One young, one lanky, and one rotund?"

The innkeeper's eyes narrowed. "Why, yes, they passed through here. Left just this morning. Why? What business do you have with those pilgrims?"

Rayven dropped his head back down. "No business, innkeep." He lowered his voice. "Not yet."

The innkeeper scratched his arm nervously. "Now, look here traveler. I'm not sure what's afoot, but those pilgrims seemed like honest folk to me. If you've got an issue with them, I'm sure you can come to some sort of arrangement."

Rayven lifted his head and met the innkeeper's gaze. "You misunderstand. To the pilgrims, I'm no threat. Rather, I'm their guardian angel."

***

Mycah warmed his hands by the roaring fire. Jerud had stayed true to his word, waking him at the crack of dawn and forcing him out from under the inn's roof and back into the driving rain. Luckily, the deluge had slowed around midday, turning into a steady drizzle. For a moment in the midafternoon, it appeared that heavier rains would return, but instead they petered out and soon stopped altogether. The skies remained overcast, threatening the rain's return, but thus far Mycah's luck had held.

When the day's light started to fade, they found a secluded glade in which to set up camp. The lack of precipitation had given Mycah a glimmer of hope that they might be able to start a fire, but a week's worth of rains had soaked the underbrush to its core. Luckily, Pete—the crafty old bloke that he was—had thought ahead. In his pack he'd wrapped a small bundle of kindling in an old waterskin, keeping it dry throughout the day. By dragging a shard of flint across his dagger, a spark ignited and caught it in the tinder. Holding the bundle in his hands, Pete gently blew upon it, stoking the blaze, and placed it upon an over-turned stone. Ever so slowly, he added damp leaves and brush, creating a steamy haze. Soon enough, a roaring fire grew out of the kindling, burning hot enough to brush off any attempts to smother it with damp firewood.

A roaring fire meant warm feet, a dry bedroll, and real supper. Though the memory of Master Lorry's lamb shanks lingered fresh in his mind, Mycah was more than happy to eat a steaming bowl of Jerud's beef, bean, and barley stew. Over a week of cold, soggy rations had taught him to appreciate any hot meal.

Once he consumed his stew, Mycah unfurled his bed-roll by the fire. The lure of staying dry edged him closer, but fear of having his bedroll catch fire in the night kept him at a safe distance. Stretching out on the sack, he gazed into the inky blackness above.

The clouds still persisted, allowing not even the light of a single star to shine through. Mycah sighed. In Guildean, he'd rarely bothered to gaze into the heavens. Why would he? The very idea of it seemed mooncalfish. And yet since the beginning of their travels he'd found himself starting to admire the brilliant specks of light.

The moons often drew his attention even more strongly than did the stars. When all three of the moons shone proudly at the same time of night, it made for a spectacular sight, bathing the earth in a warm iridescent glow. With Pete's help, Mycah had learned to track the movement of certain stars across the sky, but as much as Pete swore by it, it didn't seem like a particularly useful skill. Rather than use the stars to navigate, why not simply bring along a map?

Mycah missed the stars, but least tonight they had a fire to warm them, and so there might be a chance for conversation. He turned to Jerud to chat only to find the big man snoozing away upon his bedroll. Pete remained up but was busy whittling some stick he'd found.

So much for that idea.

The fire smoldered. Mycah stirred. Nearby, Applesnatch nickered. What time was it? Had he fallen asleep? Through the dull glow of the fire's embers, Mycah could see Pete on his sleep sack.

The man sat up. "Did ya 'ear that?"

"Hear what?" asked Mycah, rubbing his eyes.

Applesnatch whinnied nervously.

"There it is again," said Pete.

"What?" said Mycah. "You mean Applesnatch?"

"No, I think I—"

Out of the darkness, a small leathery figure leapt toward Mycah. It landed on his chest, a twisted mass of feet, claws, and snapping jaws topped with bulbous eyes that dangled from the ends of wispy protruding stalks. The creature lunged for Mycah's neck. Mycah arched back, shrieking and flinging the abomination into the burning embers.

Chaos engulfed the camp. A mass of leathery creatures swarmed out of the surrounding darkness. The horses reared and screamed, kicking frantically to defend themselves as the little monstrosities snapped at their ankles. Jerud rose from his bedroll with a roar, hoisting a burning torch from the embers and swinging it about with wild abandon. Pete crouched in a defensive stance with his back to the fire, dagger held in one hand, pack in the other as a gladiator bearing a shield.

Knives twirling into his hands, Mycah slashed at two of the creatures as they dove toward him. He caught one in the neck and severed the eye stalk of the other. Behind him, the monster he'd tossed into the fire screeched in agony and kicked wildly, sending sparks and ash flying. Another abomination lunged at him from the side, latching onto his trousers with razor sharp claws. Pain seared through his leg as the claws bit into his thigh. Mycah bashed the thing with the butt of his knife, sending it to the ground confused and disoriented. Then another mass landed on him from behind. In a panic, Mycah spun and hurled the creature forward.

The burned body of the monster from the fire landed with a thud in the damp earth. In its jaws it clenched a pouch dangling from a torn leather thong. Mycah's hand shot to his neck. *The stone!* The creature had his stone! Mycah lunged toward the charred monster, but it sprung away with a speed that defied its haggard appearance. With the pouch still firmly grasped between its teeth, the creature sped off into the darkness.

"No!" shouted Mycah. He flung his knife in a desperate attempt to down the beast.

Around him, the creatures were fleeing as quickly as they'd appeared. Undoubtedly the monsters had planned to catch them unawares, but with the battle lost, they dispersed to find easier prey.

"Jerud! Pete!" Mycah yelled. "One of those things—it's got my pouch! The stone! We've got to go after it!"

"Calm down lad," bellowed Jerud. "Are you alright? Are you hurt?"

"Who cares!! We need to go after that stone, NOW!" Mycah turned to run into the woods.

Jerud's meaty hand clasped his shoulder, preventing him from escaping. "Lad, forget the stone. If we can get it back, we will, but right now we need to focus and take stock of our situation. Now, are you hurt?"

Mycah took a deep breath to calm his nerves, then felt about his person for injuries. Scratches on his neck and back stung, and claw marks lingered upon his thigh, but they appeared less serious than he'd initially thought.

"I think I'm alright. Just some scrapes. How about you, Jerud?"

The big man still grasped the burning torch in one hand. Blood dripped from a wound in his biceps, and though several jagged tears marred his shirt, he appeared to be in one piece.

"One of the beasts bit me in the arm, but I'll be fine. Pete?"

Pete hunched over by the fire, grasping his lower leg. "Oy. One o' 'em got me in the calf. By the moons, but it burns! 'Ow bad is it, Jerud?"

Jerud leaned over the lanky man and peered at his calf in the dim light of the glowing embers. "Can't quite tell, Pete. Looks like one of 'em slashed you." He prodded at the muscle with a thick finger, eliciting a grunt from Pete. "We'll bandage you up. You'll be fine. Just might have to stay off your feet for a few days."

"God damnit," said Pete. "Are the 'orses alright? Check their legs."

The two mares and the gelding were somehow still attached to their tethers, though all three of them danced about nervously. Applesnatch's eyes darted around wildly, her ears swiveling about as if on a pivot. Mycah spoke to her in a slow, soothing tone as he checked her for wounds.

"Applesnatch looks to be untouched, by some miracle," said Mycah. "I think Sophie's alright too, though she's got a few scratches."

"Yeah, same for Champ," said Jerud. "Looks like he crushed a few of the blighters underfoot. Good boy..." He patted the gelding approvingly.

Mycah returned to the center of camp. "Alright. Now that we've made sure everyone's alive, can we please go after the stone?"

Jerud shook his head as he walked to the fire pit. "Lad, think this through. It's pitch black, the horses are spooked, there's a horde of ravenous... well, *somethings*, for lack of a better word, out there, and we've got a casualty." Jerud started tossing logs and brush into the embers. "You want to go gallivanting off into the night after those things? Why, that's about the dumbest idea I've ever heard. What we need to do is build this fire back up and post a watch. In the morning once it's light, we'll figure out how to get that artifact back."

"Look, I get what you're saying," said Mycah. "But by morning that thing could be halfway to the Garden. We'll never find it."

"I wouldn't be so sure o' that, son," said Pete with a grimace. "Now I don't know what them beasties were. I'll be damned if they wasn't those demons that innkeep was talking 'bout. But them things bled and died. Those're beasts, not ghosts. An' beasts can be tracked."

"Yeah," said Jerud. "A pack of things that size is sure to leave a trail. We'll be able to find where they went."

"The one with the stone got burned in the fire," added Mycah. "I threw my knife at it."

"Did you hit it?"

"Not sure." Mycah picked up a burning log and thrust it into the darkness, surveying the carnage. "My knife seems to be gone in any case."

"Must've stuck it then," said Jerud. "For all you know it's bleeding out as we speak. With any luck we'll find it less than a league from here."

With the fire built back to a hearty blaze, Jerud rummaged through the packs and found strips of cloth for bandages. He helped Pete clean and dress his wound then went after his own. Mycah stooped to one of the dead creatures and poked it with the tip of his remaining knife.

"What in God's name do you think these things are?"

Jerud looked up from his bandaging. "Well, like Pete said, they sure aren't demons. Beyond that..."

"What?"

"You ever heard the story about the Jabberwocks?"

"Of course," said Mycah. "But that's an old wives' tale to scare children."

"Is it?" asked Jerud. "I'm not so sure anymore. At this point, I wouldn't be surprised if a dragon accosted us tomorrow."

Mycah wanted to argue, but he had no logical argument against what Jerud had just said. Could he be right? If Jabberwocks existed, why not dragons? And for that matter, why not demons? A chill ran down his spine at the thought.

"Well, don't just stand around there, lad," said Jerud. "Hoist those carcasses into a pile. They're creeping me out with those eyestalks of theirs. I'll torch 'em if I can get a good enough fire going. When you're done, try to get some rest. I'll take first watch."

Rest? Mycah would be lucky to fall asleep at all. As he begun the sickening task of piling the little leathery bodies, he couldn't help but feel it was going to be a very long night indeed.

CHAPTER FOURTEEN

The Den of Thieves

Mycah stumbled through the inky blackness. Thick acrid smoke choked his lungs and stung his eyes. His legs ached and his lungs burned for air. He yearned for release, but a singular thought carried him onward. *Run.* Mycah could no longer remember how long he'd been running. His entire memory seemed consumed by aching muscles and the never-ending darkness. *Run.* Mycah stumbled over something, whether a rock or his own feet he couldn't tell. He felt so tired. So very tired. If only he could rest, if only for a moment...

As he slowed, he heard a noise. A grating rasp, like the honing of a dull knife upon a grindstone. It echoed from behind filling him with dread. *Run.*

With a newfound energy born out of fear, Mycah ran as fast as he could. But the noise grew louder. Pain boiled through his legs and his lungs screamed as he pushed himself to the limit, and yet still the noise grew. When his body could withstand the torment no longer, he collapsed in a heap, panting desperately.

The noise vanished. Mycah peered into the inky darkness, his heart racing and sweat pouring from his face. For several moments, silence reigned. Then he heard a distinct *clack-clack*. First to his right, then to his left and behind him. The sounds reverberated from all around him now. *Clack-clack. Clack-clack.* At the edge of his vision through the smoky haze, Mycah saw a flash—a leathery foot with two hooked claws. *Clack-clack.*

Mycah awoke, screaming in terror. Sweat slicked his forehead and drenched his sleep sack. At his side, the embers of the campfire burned low, but smoke still rose from a pile of charred leathery corpses near the camp. The grisly work had nearly made Mycah lose his supper, but Jerud had insisted the devils be burned. Sleep had eluded him for some time after the grim task, but eventually exhaustion had won out and he'd drifted off. After such a nightmare, Mycah almost wished he'd stayed awake.

Beams of sunlight drifted through the treetops in the early morning—a welcome sight after so many days of storms. Perhaps for once they'd go a whole day of travel without rain.

"You doing alright?" Jerud stirred a pot of oats over the remainder of the campfire.

Mycah wiped his brow. "Yeah, just… had a bad dream is all. About those Jabberwocks."

Jerud nodded.

"You get any sleep at all?" Mycah asked.

Jerud shrugged. "A little. Enough." He tested the pot with his spoon. "Want some breakfast?"

Mycah glanced at the pile of charred corpses and swallowed a lump in his throat. "Um… not now, thanks. I'll eat something on the road."

Pete limped over from the horses which he'd readied for travel. "Well, don't let those oats go to waste. Spoon me a bowl, will ya Jerud?"

Pete awkwardly plopped into a sitting position on his bedroll.

"Shouldn't you be off your feet?" asked Mycah.

Pete snorted. "Ya sound just like Jerud. If I wanted to be babied, I'd go cryin' to my momma."

Jerud raised his eyebrows at Mycah and shrugged.

While the two older men ate, Mycah rolled up his sack and gathered his belongings. Rubbing sleep from his eyes, he shuffled over to Applesnatch to load his pack onto her back. Though her nervousness had left her, she seemed as alert as ever. She held her head high with her eyes wide and her ears perked. Had the horse slept at all? Mycah was pretty sure she could get by on much less sleep than he, but still. Perhaps Jerud should set Applesnatch as the watchman on future nights. Clearly her hearing was the best of the bunch—even better than Pete's, and that was saying something.

With his things squared away, Mycah returned to the campfire and took a seat. He glanced at Pete's leg. The man's calf was wrapped tight, the bandages bloodied but dry. Luckily for them they had the horses otherwise their travels would be halted for at least a week or two, no matter what Pete claimed. If it were Mycah that had suffered the injury, he had no doubt that even riding Applesnatch would be a challenge, but Pete seemed experienced enough on horseback that he could probably lead Sophie with his knees alone.

Thankfully, Jerud's wound seemed more of an annoyance than a disability. Mycah couldn't believe the little Jabberwocks had attacked the big man at all. It had been like ferrets trying to take down a fully-grown goat.

"Well, are you guys ready?" asked Mycah. "We've got a leathery monstrosity to catch, remember?"

Pete slurped the last of the oats off his spoon and waggled the utensil at him. "A few minutes 'ere or there ain't gonna make a mite o' difference, son. Chances are them Jabberwocks don't live far from 'ere, anyways. Most beasts o' prey don't stray more than a few leagues in any direction. If we can find 'em, we'll find 'em 'fore dusk."

"We'd better," said Mycah. "If we can't find that stone—"

"We'll find it," said Jerud. The man sounded more convinced than he looked.

Regardless of their assurances, Mycah's hopes had dropped about as low as a whipped dog's tail. Eons passed as the two older men finished packing their bags and readying their horses. Finally, they mounted up and set forth.

Pete rode in front, head bent down low searching for clues. At first, the demons' trail screamed out from under the trampled grass. However, the Jabberwocks had soon veered into the trees, at which point Mycah lost all ability to track the beasts. Pete reined his horse in and chewed his lip as he surveyed the forest floor. Mycah's hopes sunk even lower.

"Argh, this is impossible," said Mycah. "How in the world are we going to track these things?"

Pete looked back disapprovingly from the front. "Calm yerself, son. Trackin' takes time an' patience. But it ain't hard. Any fool can do it with the proper trainin'. 'Ere, lemme show ya. See 'ow the underbrush seems to part right there, an' 'en further along over there?"

Pete pointed out the locations.

"Um, yeah, I guess," said Mycah. What did he mean by 'any fool could do it,' anyway?

"Well, it's easier fer beasts the size o' those Jabberwocks to go 'round shrubs 'an over 'em. I'd wager they ran along those openin's." Pete urged his horse forward. "See? There's another break in the brush over there. That's a trail, son. Subtle, but it's there. Ya just gotta know what you're lookin' for."

Pete pointed out clues as he saw them—a drop of blood, a broken branch, a claw mark in the damp earth. As Pete pointed out the signs, Mycah realized that tracking, like thievery, was a fine art. In tracking, a hunter surveyed the situation and noted discrepancies, much like he would during a stakeout. Once Mycah applied himself and approached the process in the same way he'd approach a heist, his ability and confidence swelled.

"Hey, look there," said Mycah. "Down at the bottom of that tree. The bark's rubbed off. Even looks like there's a hint of char there. I think we're on the right track."

"Good eye, son," said Pete.

Jerud rode in the back, but even he nodded approvingly at Mycah's newfound ability. His spirits buoyed.

Shortly after noon, the trio passed a stream and started up a small hill. Pete lifted a hand and pulled his horse to a halt.

"What is it Pete?" asked Mycah. "Do you see something?"

"Not just somethin'," said Pete. "Somethin's. A whole lotta somethin's. Look there, an' there, an' there." Pete pointed out multiple spots. Some trampled leaves, claw marks in the mud by the stream, torn leaves and broken, weeping stems. "I think we're gettin' closer to these beasties' home. We should stay quiet, an' be alert."

Pete walked his mare up the hill. Mycah and Jerud followed. At the crest, the forest opened into a clearing. In it lay some mangled remains—one of the demons, its skin visibly charred.

"That's it," hissed Mycah. "That's the one."

Mycah spurred Applesnatch forward and hopped off the saddle. Kneeling down, he inspected the carcass, or what was left of it anyway. The creature had been picked clean. Bits of sinew and gristle stuck to the grass like a Hellish morning dew. Of the creature, only its bones and leathery skin remained. Scanning the glade, Mycah saw neither hide nor hair of the stone, nor any scrap of the pouch in which it had resided.

Mycah hung his head in defeat. "It's gone. The stone. The pouch... all of it."

Jerud pulled his horse alongside, the corner of his mouth turned down in disgust. "You're sure this was the one, lad?"

"It has to be. Look." Mycah lifted a patch of mangled skin from the forest floor with his knife. "See the burn marks? I don't think any of the other monsters fell in the fire."

"So the Jabberwocks eat their own," said Pete. "Smart move, burnin' 'em, 'en."

Jerud nodded in acknowledgment.

"Don't give up hope, Mycah," said Pete. "If this Jabberwock truly done stole yer stone, then one o' them others must've taken it. If we keep followin' their trail, we'll find it."

Mycah nodded glumly and returned to Applesnatch. The mare sensed his dejection and nuzzled him. Mycah gave her a quick pat as he hoisted himself back into the saddle.

Pete again took the lead, but this time Mycah trailed at the back of the pack, his heart no longer in the hunt. Jerud tried to cheer him up.

"Chin up, lad. It's not the end of the world. I'm sure we'll find the stone."

"And what if we don't?"

"Maybe we won't need it. Maybe the Stormqueen's artifact will present itself in some other way."

Mycah raised his eyebrows. "Oh yeah? How are we supposed to find a strange, mysterious artifact that we have only a vague description of without knowing where to look?"

Jerud shrugged. "We don't even know what the Garden will be like. Maybe the tablet will be right at the center on a pedestal or something."

The thought piqued Mycah's interest. It couldn't be that simple, could it? "That seems pretty darn far fetched, but regardless, I'm hoping that's not what we find."

"Why's that?" asked Jerud, his brow furrowing.

"Because that sounds like the most obvious trap I've ever heard of, that's way."

"Pipe down, ya blighters," said Pete. "I think I 'eard somethin'."

Up ahead, the forest thinned at the summit of another hill. Pete dismounted and limped forward, motioning for the others to follow. Dropping from his saddle, Mycah looped Applesnatch's reins around a tree branch and followed Pete, watching his step to make sure he avoided dry brush that would crackle underfoot. At the crest, Pete lay down and stared into a valley below.

"By the moons..." the lanky man muttered.

Mycah wormed his way in by Pete's side. He wasn't prone to using profanity, but this seemed like a proper time.

"Holy shit," he said.

Before them stretched a massive valley, completely stripped of trees, brush, and vegetation. A blend of soil, sand, and clay, mixed together and coagulated into reddish-brown globules, covered the ground. The earthy substance had been piled high into mounds that pockmarked the valley like goosebumps on a chilly forearm. Hundreds of the mounds dotted the valley, and from each mound roughly a dozen openings poked out, each about the size of one of the leathery monsters.

"Are those burrows?" said Mycah.

Jerud lay beside him slack-jawed. "Good Lord. There must be hundreds, maybe even thousands of those burrows. There can't possibly be that many Jabberwocks, can there?"

Mycah pinched his nose against the foul smell of carrion and decay that wafted from the hive. As he stared into the unholy morass of crudely built structures, something at the bottom of the valley flashed in the sunlight and caught his eye—a mound larger than the rest but without any obvious burrows and built of something besides the reddish earthy mixture. What was it?

"Guys, do you see that mound at the bottom there?" Mycah pointed it out. "Is that... garbage?"

"I just spotted it too," said Pete. "Looks like there's all kind o' junk in there. Weapons, clothes, bones, metal, rocks. Why them things is regular packrats, I reckon."

Mycah felt a surge of excitement. He forced his voice down to a whisper. "The stone! It's there, I'm sure of it. It's got to be."

"Now hold on, lad," said Jerud. "Maybe those Jabberwocks did take the stone, and maybe they threw it on that pile. But you can't honestly be considering going down there? It's suicide."

"Not necessarily," said Mycah. "Look. Hundreds upon hundreds of burrows and not a single Jabberwock in sight. Why? Those beasts attacked us in the middle of the night. They're nocturnal. They've got to be."

Mycah glanced at the sun. "It's just past noon. I bet they're sound asleep. We won't have a better chance to get the stone back than now. I can sneak down there and get it. I know I can."

"Damnit, Mycah, listen," said Jerud, grabbing Mycah by the arm. The man's use of blasphemy betrayed his intense concern. "If a single one of those things stirs, the whole hive'll wake. They'd tear you to shreds. Stone or no stone, you're not going down there. It's not worth it!"

Mycah's heart pounded furiously, fueled by a mixture of fear, adrenaline, and pure conviction. "Jerud... Do you remember the night we set out? I made a promise that I'd swallow my fear, stick with you, and see this thing through to the end. I've haven't done a very good job of that so far. I've been scared out of my wits half the time. But I meant every word I said. I'm not going to give up. We need the stone. You know that." He grasped Jerud's shoulder. "I can do this. You know I can."

Jerud pulled back his hand and wiped it across his face, cupping his jaw in his meaty palm. "Alright, son," he said after a moment. "But maybe Pete and I can set up some sort of diversion, get the Jabberwocks to—"

"No," said Mycah. "We're better off with them asleep. Plus I need to move now. Chances are this is as asleep as they'll ever be."

Jerud grimaced but nodded. Mycah stripped off his belt and withdrew his knife, removing anything that could clatter or make a noise. Taking a deep breath to still his shaking fingers, Mycah slipped off his shoes. He'd be better off without them. The last thing he wanted was a creaky sole bringing about his unfortunate demise.

"You're sure about this?" asked Jerud.

Mycah forced a smile. "Of course I am. It'll be just like the time I robbed the Guildean Museum of Cultural History. Except with larger rats. And more of them."

Swallowing his fear, Mycah channeled his inner ghost and sped down the hill. His feet danced over the loose soil, propelling him forward in silent, controlled bursts. Despite the unusual circumstances, Mycah found his body slipping into the role it knew best, that of cat burglar. Even with the full might of the noonday sun shining upon him, he became a shadow—ungraspable and indistinct. Like a jaguar of blackest night, he prowled from den to den. The garbage mound was his prey, and its demise was certain.

Approaching the pile of junk, Mycah surveyed it with an efficient purpose. His eyes flew back and forth across the mound hastily absorbing the contents as if scanning a document. A torn sleeve, a beaten pan, a jar, the bleached remains of a bird. *No, next.* A doll, a rusted knife, a weather-beaten boot, a chunk of marble. *No, next.* His neck swiveled right and left, his eyes straining to ensure no detail went overlooked.

He saw it. Half hidden under a moldy blanket, the familiar tan pouch peeked out, a broken thong dangling from its end. Watching his feet so as to avoid slicing a sole on an exposed blade, Mycah sprung up the mound and extracted the pouch. Within it, he could feel the smooth stone emanating a gentle warmth, but life as a thief had taught him to never assume one knew for certain the contents of a parcel. He loosened the bag's drawstring and peered inside. A translucent shimmer undulated over an inky black surface.

Mycah sighed. He tightened the pouch's drawstrings, tied a knot in the broken leather thong, and slipped it over his head. With a feline grace, he hopped to the loose soil underneath and raced up the hill.

As in any heist, the exit was crucial. Time was always scarce, and alarms could be raised at a moment's notice.

But this situation differed slightly. If caught, he wouldn't be imprisoned and tried but rather rent apart and consumed by a horde of razor-toothed monsters. Recalling the night's dream, his subconscious urged him to run, but Mycah forced his nerves down and maintained a swift, calculated pace.

Within moments, the mounds around him began to thin. Pete and Jerud's silhouettes poked out over the forest's edge. The relief in Jerud's face shone through, even at a distance.

As he neared the two men, the light of the midday sun waned. Mycah glanced up to see an elephantine hawk circling overhead. The beast was massive—so large it could've made a snack of one of the Jabberwocks had it wished. If the bird searched for a meal however it came at an inopportune moment as all the Jabberwocks remained asleep, a testament to Mycah's abilities.

The hawk cut loose with an ear-piercing shriek. As the cry echoed around the valley, Mycah felt a faint rumble—the rumble of a thousand tiny demons waking from a deep slumber.

In those precious few seconds, Mycah couldn't tell who screamed the loudest—Jerud, Pete, or his own subconscious.

"RUN!"

CHAPTER FIFTEEN

Rising Tensions

Perched upon the balcony overlooking her courtyard, Rain felt a cool breeze upon her cheeks. It whirled and played with tendrils of hair that had extricated themselves from her veil. The wind exhaled into her midnight blue gown, lifting the fabric and causing it to undulate with an unnatural verve.

The wind wasn't of her creation, but Rain appreciated it nonetheless. The dress, sheer though it was, trapped too much heat for her liking, and the cool breeze felt delectable as it pushed through its weave. The summer months often became unbearable when clad in layered robes, but duty forced her to adhere to certain standards of appearance. As much as she wished to don a pair of three-quarter length breeches and a chiffon blouse, such garb would detract from her image as an all-powerful enchantress.

While she enjoyed the cool breeze, it would only stoke the fires of rumor. Several weeks of warm weather and rain had soothed the scuttlebutt among peasants, but today's cool breeze would likely bring more raised eyebrows and whispered complaints. If the discontent were constrained to downturned lips and grumbles shared over mugs of ale that would be one thing, but unfortunately the problem had grown. Hardly a day passed that some raving lunatic didn't set up a makeshift dais made of an unused fruit crate and begin foretelling the end of days. Rain's informants brought news of them from around town, but often she could see them from her own balcony.

The presence of the criers was understandable. Winter's bite had persisted far into spring, and the unseasonable cool was an obvious target for attention-desperate madmen looking to draw a crowd. But with the onset of the warmth and rains, Rain had expected their preaching to cease. Few men possessed the conviction of spirit—or unbridled lunacy—to stand in the rain for hours on end preaching the end of days when crowds refused to gather and the few individuals that passed by scoffed in contempt. Yet the rhetoric had continued unabated for weeks in spite of the weather. If anything, the criers had redoubled their efforts.

The incessant preaching reeked of malfeasance, but what could she do? She couldn't exactly order her guards around town silencing the heralds. That would merely throw fuel on their fire. Nor could she seize one of the madmen and put him to the question. That would arouse the suspicions of the city watch, and relations with them were tenuous at best. Besides, from reports her guards brought the preachers truly seemed like isolated lunatics, indubitable in their beliefs and fervent in their delivery. So as difficult as it was, Rain ignored them. Any other approach would give credence to their claims, and Rain couldn't afford to have doubt spread through the populace like a plague.

But Rain couldn't believe the criers were a random occurrence. Someone knew, or at the very least suspected, that her powers failed her. But who? She'd only told Master Crawford of her plight, and she couldn't fathom his tongue wagging. So someone must've taken note of the weather, assumed her fragile, and begun to move against her.

While Rain pondered the identity of her mystery antagonist, she prepared for the worst. Gazing into the courtyard below, she studied the new recruits training under the watchful eye of her guard captain, Loren Farrier.

Her guards had worked their way into the city's underbelly like the roots of a gnarled oak, spreading word that the Stormqueen sought new blood for her ranks. Their efforts had brought in all sorts of applicants: street toughs, mercenaries, bodyguards, huntsmen, even miners and woodcutters. Rain had accepted the vast majority into her ranks, rejecting only those who seemed too headstrong or dimwitted to cultivate into proper guards. Though she hesitated to rely too much upon men of their caliber for protection, recent events indicated that retaining a greater standing force was wise.

Besides, Rain trusted her established guardsmen to oversee and govern the new recruits, especially Loren Farrier. If anyone could whip the disparate mob of brawlers and scrappers into a respectable fighting force it was him. Even from the balcony, Rain could hear the man shouting orders, running the men through fencing drills and group exercises.

Though the recruits knew how to fight, few of them knew how to fight as a team. Loren Farrier took it upon himself to teach them how to do so. The man wielded a riding crop as if it were an extension of his own arm. Today the group trained with halberds, and based on the crack of the riding crop and the cries of the combatants, the recruits would soon be expert halberdiers.

At the other side of the courtyard, more recruits trained in marksmanship with her guardsmen's signature long barreled muskets. Each shot that rang out over the plaza tugged at Rain's purse strings. Though sulfur and charcoal were plentiful, saltpeter was a treasured substance, making black powder expensive and difficult to obtain. While small amounts of saltpeter could be fabricated from animal dung or human waste, the process took time, and most animal waste became fertilizer for crops, besides. The only known saltpeter deposit of any real size lay at the north end of the Snowfells near the town of Craughhill. The miner's guild guarded it heavily. By all accounts, a fortress with walls thicker than a man's outstretched arms surrounded the mine. No one outside the miner's guild knew just how much saltpeter sat locked within the deposit, but the guild only released small quantities for sale at a time, at the very least perpetuating the notion of the material's scarcity.

Knuckles rapped on a hard surface behind her. Turning, Rain found Master Crawford standing at the foot of the balcony.

"Pardon, Mistress. Do you have a moment?"

Rain never tired of seeing the man's face, with his square jaw and handsome features. "For you, Master Crawford, always."

Rain gathered the folds of her gown and strode into the sitting room adjoining the balcony, settling herself into an overstuffed burgundy chaise.

"I have some documents that require your attention." The chamberlain handed her a sheaf of papers. "Orders for supplies, mostly, though there are some documents pertaining to changes in the quantity and frequency of patrols that also require your perusal."

Rain sifted through the papers, scanning the orders. The requisitions for additional supplies for the watch were expected: dyed cloth for uniforms, tanned leather for hats, boots, and belts, not to mention muskets, hand cannons, and sabers, and of course another hefty sum of black powder. Routine goods also made the list, but the quantities seemed outlandish. Three hundred bushels of wheat, two hundred of barley, three hundred pounds of salt beef. Bakers yeast, preserved beets, dried figs. The list went on and on.

Rain rubbed her brow. "Master Crawford, if I didn't know any better I'd think you were trying to beggar me."

"Apologies, Mistress," said the chamberlain. "The cost is high, but the increased volume of the watch dictates a need for supplies."

"I understand that, Master Crawford, but three hundred pounds of salt beef? We haven't recruited an entire army. Not yet."

"I felt it prudent to have several months reserves on hand, my Queen. Given the current... climate, shall we say."

Rain sighed. Emptying her treasury should've been the least of her worries, but she couldn't help but agonize over the extra expenses. She held the sheaf of papers back out for the chamberlain.

"Very well," she said. "Make the purchases. And the changes in the guard appear to be in order. So how are the new recruits progressing? I hope Captain Farrier isn't creating too many defections."

The corner of Master Crawford's lip curled upward. "Not too many, Mistress. The captain's hard but fair. The recruits see that, I think. Besides, there's food, pay, and a solid roof over their heads without any real threat of imminent action. Most of them are thankful for the mere opportunity to be here, and the captain quickly evicts any who aren't."

Rain played with the upholstery at the end of the chaise's arms. "And the question of crucial import—can these men be trusted in the event of a crisis?"

"No one can guess at the strength of a man's fortitude," said Master Crawford. "We won't know unless the situation presents itself. Let's hope it doesn't. I do know, however, that in a battle a man's conviction is buoyed by the demeanor of those around him, and I have the utmost confidence in our veteran guard. They'll ensure the new men don't disappoint."

"I pray you're right, both in their conviction and our need to determine it."

"A prayer, Mistress? That seems a mite disingenuous, coming from you."

Rain rolled her eyes. "You know what I mean Edward."

The chamberlain smiled and moved to depart.

"Before you leave, Edward... Any word on your investigation into the attempted burglary of the staff?"

Master Crawford frowned. "No, mistress. Whomever was behind it was extremely thorough in covering their tracks. The trail's run cold, I'm afraid."

Rain's fingers continued to tickle the upholstery, working at a loose string that peeked from the armrest. "I don't like it, Edward. Not one bit. Despite credible evidence, something tells me whomever is behind the botched burglary is also behind this wave of doomsayers. What are your thoughts?"

"If we ignore motive and only consider entities possessing the means with which to challenge you, then we narrow our list substantially. Either the Church, the city watch, one of the guilds, or your fellow Stormqueens wishes you ill, barring the influence of an unforeseen party. You know my suspicions already."

"Yes. I do." Rain snagged the loose string and yanked it from its home. "Perhaps you're right to amass supplies. I can't help but feel that a storm is brewing. A storm that I may be unable to control."

"Milady, no matter how terrible the squall, I have faith that you'll lead us through it unharmed." Master Crawford flashed a warm smile. "Now, regrettably, I must return to my other duties. Unless you have further need of me?"

Rain blushed under her veil. The man's unwavering confidence in her was reassuring. Potentially misplaced, but reassuring nonetheless.

"Nothing at the moment," she said. "Thank you, Master Crawford."

He gave a short bow and moved toward the door.

As he reached the exit, Rain called out. "Oh, Edward?"

"Yes, Mistress?"

Rain hesitated. "Perhaps later when you're not so busy... you could bring up some tea? For the two of us. It'd be nice to sit and chat for a while."

The warm smile returned to the man's face. "Of course, milady. I'd love to."

"Very well, then," said Rain. "I'll look forward to it."

As Master Crawford left, Rain considered. Had she been too forward? Would he misconstrue her invite for tea as something more? Was it, in fact, an invite for something more?

Don't be silly. The man's just being cordial. He's certainly not going to be making any advances on you of all people.

Regardless of how he felt, though, Rain was indeed looking forward to the tea. If nothing else, the upcoming pleasantry gave her something to think about other than the more pressing affairs of the world—like the young thief and his fat friend's quest upon whose backs so many lives rested.

CHAPTER SIXTEEN

Running Wild

A s the hawk's shriek echoed around the valley and Jerud and Pete's shouts rained down on him from
above, Mycah felt a tremor undulating through the loose
soil under his bare feet. Without looking back, he sprinted
up the last of the hill, his legs turning over faster and faster
like a water wheel met by a sudden flood. Jerud and Pete
flew through the forest ahead of him. Jerud half drug, half
carried Pete through the underbrush as he hopped toward
the horses on his one good leg, leaping over small shrubs
and debris with Jerud's aid.

As Mycah passed the forest's edge, he bent low and
grabbed his boots and belt in one smooth motion, never
slowing his stride. Behind him, the tremor was intensify-
ing. Again the hawk shrieked. An unholy screeching began, followed by the terrifying patter of the Jabberwocks'
clawed footsteps pounding the earth.

Mycah bounded through the trees, diving down the in-
cline with a wild abandon. Ahead, Jerud tossed Pete onto
his saddle and vaulted onto Champ's back with a powerful
leap.

"For the love of God, Mycah, run!" shouted Jerud. He ripped Champ's reins free from the tree and cracked them sharply, spurring the tall mount down the hill.

As Mycah neared Applesnatch, the mare's eyes widened in fear. She reared and screamed, pulling loose her reins with a sharp toss of her head. He could see the horse hesitate, considering whether to wait for him or simply flee in terror.

He was almost there.

"Applesnatch, wait!" yelled Mycah.

The mare turned to run. Half sprinting, half falling down the hill, Mycah lunged. Time slowed as he flew through the air. His boots and belt spun in a high arc, tossed in desperation. Applesnatch pushed off of her back legs, kicking leaves into the air. Mycah stretched for the saddle, his hands brushing the seat but failing to find a hold. As his hands slipped, he desperately grasped for anything. His palms burned as they slid upon stirrup leather, but he forced his fingers closed and hung on for dear life.

Applesnatch took off through the forest. Mycah clung to the leather strap as the stirrup bit into his palms. Rocks and brush pelted him with vigor. Branches slapped his face and arms. He bounced off roots and brambles as leaves and soil blew into his mouth and matted his hair.

Gritting his teeth, Mycah grasped the stirrup with both hands and pulled. The saddle shifted slightly around Applesnatch's flank but held. With his left arm looped around the stirrup leather, he reached up with his right. Fumbling for a hold, he grasped the saddle blanket and hoisted himself higher upon the mare's flank. One more heave sent him flopping onto Applesnatch's back like a beached trout.

Once there he became the horse's impromptu sparring partner with the saddle punching him in the midsection with each of the horse's footfalls. With one final breathless effort, Mycah pulled himself up and brought his leg over the mare's back.

Though finally seated, Mycah was far from in control. Applesnatch raced through the forest in fear, only partially aware of his presence. He hazarded a glance up the hill. Behind him a swarm of razor-clawed demons blanketed the forest floor, descending the slope in a living avalanche of leather and snapping jaws, trampling friend and foe alike in their heated pursuit. Hundreds, perhaps thousands, of the beasts ran. So many teeth. So many claws. Mycah saw himself, overrun, disappearing beneath the ravenous wave, his flesh torn from bone by thousands of jagged teeth. His heart lodged in his throat and the contents of his stomach threatened to expel themselves from his body. So many creatures. So hideous. So repugnant...

A thick, leafy branch whacked him in the skull, startling him out of his macabre reverie.

Don't look back. Don't even think about those things. Just flee.

Mycah turned around to find a burly oak converging on him. Applesnatch hurtled through it. Branches battered him, and bark ripped at his pant legs as they barreled past. He crouched low upon Applesnatch's back, pressing himself into the mare. In her wild flight, she seemed to have completely forgotten about him. Mycah let the mare head where she pleased, but truly he had little control over her path. Together they simply ran.

Trees flew past. Elms, maples, oaks, and sweetgums all whisked past in a blurry mess of green and brown. A breeze sluiced off Mycah's face, flowing through his hair and filling his shirt. The pounding of the mare's hooves merged with her forcefully exhaled breath, creating a steady rhythm. Through glades and over streams they galloped, man and beast merged into a single being with a singular purpose—to escape, live, and be free.

Time passed as they fled. Applesnatch never seemed to tire, her breath labored but steady. Mycah's extremities tingled with the lingering effects of adrenaline, both from the narrow escape from the Jabberwocks and the sheer thrill of the flight. Looking around, he saw nothing but an unfamiliar section of woods. Mycah pulled on the horse's reins, trying to slow the charging animal.

"Ho, there! Ho! Slow down there, girl."

At first, Mycah failed to capture Applesnatch's focus. He spent several minutes tugging on the reins and coaxing her to slow with softly spoken encouragements. Eventually, his efforts wormed their way into the beast's subconscious. She started to slow, first into a canter and then a trot as she took stock of her surroundings. Mycah also glanced around. Peering into the underbrush, he saw no evidence of the markings that he'd learned to associate with the Jabberwocks. He also saw no trails, footpaths, or signs of civilization of any kind and certainly no sign of Jerud and Pete. Forest extended as far as the eye could see.

Applesnatch's chest heaved between his legs as she caught her breath. Now that she'd finally slowed she seemed as alert as ever, ears perked and swiveling about. Mycah stroked the side of her neck to try to calm her.

"It's alright, girl. We made it... I think."

Applesnatch craned her neck to look back at him. Dressed as he was—no boots or belt, dirty, and matted with leaves—he probably resembled a fate-cursed beggar or a refugee from a war-torn land. The horse's gaze made him conscious of his own image. He brushed his pants and ran a hand through his tangled locks.

"You know I appreciate you saving my life and all," Mycah said as he stroked the horse's neck. "But maybe next time you could wait just a *little* longer before you take off running through the woods."

The mare frowned. Mycah had finally accepted she could roll her eyes, and now it turned out she could frown too? Next she'd be talking with her hooves.

"C'mon, I'm serious. If not for my cat-like reflexes, I never would've snagged your saddle."

Applesnatch rolled her eyes. Mycah grinned. Now that was the horse he'd learned to love. He patted her side.

"Well, girl, I've got to admit, I don't have the foggiest idea where we are. You have any ideas for finding Pete and Jerud?"

The mare stared at him in confusion. Aha! So he had finally stumped her! Perhaps she wasn't such a genius after all.

"I figured as much."

Mycah pursed his lips. What to do? Barring his boots and belt, all of his supplies still seemed to be strapped to Applesnatch's back, so that was a boon, at least. But how would they find his companions?

"Why don't we start by finding a stream or a pond or something. I could use a bath, and I have a feeling you could do with a drink. C'mon, girl. We'll figure something out."

***

Sometime in the late afternoon, they chanced upon a stream. Mycah stripped down and bathed while Applesnatch drank her fill. Even though Mycah hadn't exerted himself nearly as much as his mare, the stream's cool water felt deliciously refreshing upon his warm flesh. Taking a bar of soap from his saddlebags, he scrubbed the stink of the Jabberwocks off him, a fetid scent reminiscent of rotten meat and fresh droppings. Perhaps the stink only existed in his mind, and all Mycah washed away was dirt and sweat. Regardless, the act of washing banished the stench, replacing it with smells of perfume and tallow.

After he finished untangling his matted hair, he worked on scrubbing his clothes. The garments sorely needed a cleaning. Two solid weeks had passed since he'd given them a wash. They'd soaked in the rain not two days prior, but being doused in rainwater was a far cry from a thorough scrub. Soap grasped tightly in his fist, Mycah attacked the garments, laying them upon a shallow rock and scrubbing with vigor.

A spare set of clothes hid in his saddlebags. Those hadn't been washed in a fortnight either and probably smelled even fouler than his current attire. Spending well over a week in a rain-soaked saddlebag had a way of making things a mite musty, not to mention the smell of stale horse sweat that tended to permeate everything in those bags. Mycah considered washing them. If he went after them, he'd be forced to don wet clothes again—an unwelcome thought after so many days spent in the rain.

With the summer sun peeking through the trees and warming his backside, hygiene won out. The afternoon felt almost toasty, and his first set of clothes would be close to dry by the time the second set was washed, assuming he wrung them out properly first. Besides, Mycah had begun to formulate a plan to find Pete and Jerud, and it didn't involve using the remaining daylight hours. He'd wait until nightfall and travel northward toward the road using the tail of the Lupus constellation to guide him—he'd have to thank Pete later for teaching him that navigation trick. Admittedly, he could also use the position of the sun to reach the road, but Mycah suspected it would be just as easy to find Pete and Jerud at night.

Mycah knew Jerud well enough to expect what the big man would do in a situation such as this. Normally if separated, the two of them gathered at a predetermined location. Unfortunately one hadn't been set. That had been an oversight, but not one that they hadn't faced before. In such a case, the two of them generally found each other at the last place they'd both met. However, last night's camp had been overrun by the Jabberwocks, and Jerud, being the superstitious soul he was, would want to avoid that place at all costs—a sentiment Mycah shared. No, what Jerud would likely do is find a spot by the road on the way to the Shrine, sit his bulk down, and wait. He'd create some sort of signal to let Mycah know where he was. A fire, no doubt. With luck, Mycah would see the blaze half a league away. Should he somehow fail to find his friends tonight, he could always follow the smoke trail in the morning.

After another bout of furious scrubbing, Mycah hung his spare clothes to dry upon a low hanging oak branch. He patted the first set. Still damp. No bother. He found a sunny patch by the stream and stretched out, arms folded behind the back of his head. Nearby, Applesnatch nibbled at a leafy frond and peered at him quizzically.

"What? You act like you've never enjoyed a warm patch of sun before." Mycah scratched at an itch on his nose. "You know, you and me? We're not that different, really. We both enjoy the little things in life. A little sun, a nice bath, a bite of apple now and then…"

Applesnatch eyed him up and down as she continued to chew. With the horse staring at him, Mycah suddenly felt very aware of his nakedness.

Blasted horse! What was her problem?

Sitting up, Mycah shifted to a less exposed position. "Why are you looking at me like that? You're naked all the time and I don't ogle you!"

Applesnatch grinned and whinnied. Oh, so now the mare had resorted to catcalls? Blasted beast! Mycah got up, shuffled to the oak and donned his damp smallclothes.

This is ridiculous. Horses don't understand modesty… so why do I feel so blasted awkward right now?

Applesnatch continued to grin as she nibbled on tender summer shoots. Pete had certainly been right. Horses were like women—stubborn, infuriating, and awkward to be around. Of course, Applesnatch was also tender, caring, and as loyal as they came. She wasn't so bad, just difficult for Mycah to understand. *Just like women*, Jerud would probably say.

Once dressed, Mycah gathered his spare clothes and stuffed them back into his saddlebags.

"C'mon, girl," he said as he attached the bags to Apple-snatch's back. "Let's go find Jerud and Pete."

CHAPTER SEVENTEEN

The Shrine of Repentance

Finding Jerud and Pete turned out to be as simple as Mycah had hoped. He stumbled across the road as the last rays of sunlight disappeared behind the trees, and within a couple hours of travel, the glow of a roaring fire revealed itself. He found his two companions as right as rain—or close enough. Jerud's face had been creased with worry, but it brightened as soon as he caught sight of Mycah. The big man promptly crushed him in a hug that threatened to squeeze every ounce of breath from his lungs, but Mycah didn't complain. It felt good to see his lumbering friend safe.

Unfortunately, Pete aggravated his calf injury while trying to escape the Jabberwocks. The wound had reopened while fleeing to the horses. As pain lanced through his calf, he stumbled and strained the muscle, causing more trauma to already stressed tissue. Pete tried to downplay the severity of the injury, but he was limping badly. The man wouldn't be able to walk properly for at least a week.

Amazingly enough all the horses escaped unscathed. Not one sported so much as a cracked hoof. Good thing, too. With Pete hobbled, they'd have to rely on the horses to an even greater extent. Mycah again thanked the moons Pete had brought them, as without them they'd all be stewing in the stomachs of the little demons.

Jerud, absorbed in his thoughts, offered to tend to the fire throughout the night. Though the warm summer air had finally arrived, Mycah welcomed both the heat and the glow of the flames. It would help keep the Jabberwocks away.

Despite the day's traumatic events, Mycah slept as soundly as a babe that night. Between his physical exhaustion and relief at finding his friends unharmed, and with a hearty bowl of Jerud's beef and barley stew warming his ribs, sleep came easily.

In the morning, the trio broke camp bright and early, trying to put as much distance between themselves and the Jabberwock hive as possible. With the warm sun shining down, Mycah wished nothing more than to be able to stretch out upon a rock and soak in the sun's rays like a heat-hungry lizard, but the threat of the Jabberwocks kept them all moving, not to mention the threat of the Stormqueen's curse.

Blasted curse! Even the thought of it cast a dark cloud across an otherwise pristine sky. Mycah shook his head, trying to banish his encroaching grim thoughts.

Blessedly, the warm weather persisted for the next couple days, much to the delight of Mycah's feet. He'd really have to find a replacement pair of boots somewhere, but few traders traveled the road so near to the shrine. Pete had offered up his own boots, seeing as he was in no shape to walk himself, but unfortunately the lanky man's hooves dwarfed Mycah's. Worn upon his own feet, Pete's boots resembled clown shoes, and so Mycah went barefoot.

Near midmorning of the third day of travel, the party encountered a stone marker at the side of the road. Chiseled into it was a simple message, easily readable despite being weathered by wind and rain: *He who seeks Deliverance seeks the Shrine.* As midmorning became midday and midday became late afternoon, more and more markers intercepted their path, each bearing a different message. *The pilgrim's path is wrought with sin,* read one. *The penitent man kneels before God,* read another. As twilight's diffuse rays disappeared behind the trees, they encountered one that simply read: *The Shrine awaits.*

That night as they sat by the fire, a war of words erupted between Jerud and Pete. Jerud brought up a topic that had crossed Mycah's mind more than once over the past few days: Pete's health.

Jerud broached the topic gently, mentioning that none of them knew what lay before them in the Garden of Eden, what sort of terrain they might encounter or what sorts of pitfalls might obstruct them. He expressed concern that such a journey might be difficult for a horse. Jerud also mentioned how approaching the shrine on horseback might seem suspicious, as those humbled by God approached Him on foot, not borne by beasts of burden.

Pete stared at Jerud with a granite-like gaze. His hard stare spoke for him, but his silence lasted only so long. He began lambasting Jerud for questioning his health, claiming he could do anything that the journey required of him. With his fists clenched firmly at his sides, Jerud tried to stay calm. But Pete continued to push, and the big man grew testy. Soon the two of them were spewing curses and thinly veiled threats, Jerud in his big booming voice and Pete in his stern, grizzled one. Mycah had never seen an argument quite like it, certainly not any argument involving Jerud. He thought the pair might come to blows.

"Blast you Pete, you stubborn ox! This is our fight!" yelled Jerud.

"Ya otter-faced bastard! It's my fight too!" screamed Pete.

"Damnit, you thick-headed fool!" bellowed Jerud. "This curse rests upon me and Mycah alone! Blast it all, man!"

Thankfully, the argument never escalated into physical combat. It ended abruptly, with Pete agreeing to stay behind with the horses while Jerud and Mycah went ahead on foot. Pete's sudden reversal surprised Mycah, though it made sense. Pete knew he'd be a hindrance with his leg injured as it was. He simply wasn't willing to admit it—not without a fight. Under other circumstances, Pete likely never would've relented, but Jerud cared for Pete too deeply to let the man put himself in danger without good reason. As with many fights, the spark that lit the blaze blossomed out of concern not tension. Ultimately, Jerud's concern won out over Pete's displeasure.

In the morning, they set out into the woods north of the road to search for a spot where Pete could camp for a week or two. Within an hour, they found a suitable spot—a secluded rocky outcropping situated next to a stream where the horses could water. And the spot resided not ten minutes' ride from a meadow where the horses could forage.

Pete brusquely mumbled his goodbyes. The man might've ultimately agreed with Jerud, but that didn't mean he liked being left behind. A clap on the back and a 'see ya soon' comprised his entire exchange with Jerud. Mycah got nothing more than a nod.

Mycah's parting with Applesnatch was surprisingly more difficult. In just a few short weeks he'd formed an unexpected bond with the beast, and she with him, though the mare tried to hide it. As Mycah stroked her flank, she did her best to act aloof in the face of a difficult farewell.

"Take care of Pete, alright girl?" Mycah said. "He's pretty bummed out. I'm not sure he'll appreciate your usual brand of spunk."

The mare whinnied and looked off into the forest.

"And don't go running after me or anything, alright? I'll get by just fine without you."

Applesnatch, head still turned away, gave a derisive snort.

"C'mon… you know you might."

Applesnatch continued to stare off into the trees.

"I'm trying to say goodbye here. It'd be nice to get some sort of farewell, you know."

Applesnatch turned toward him and nuzzled him softly under the arm. She nickered once before returning to her watchful post. Mycah grinned. He'd miss the creature.

Hoisting his pack high on his back, Mycah set off back toward the road with Jerud in tow. The pair traveled in silence, though the forest sang with life. Birds chirped in the branches above as a warm breeze rustled through the forest canopy. Nearby, a brook babbled as it snaked its way over smooth, worn stones. Mycah's bare feet squelched in the damp leaves covering the forest floor.

Once they returned to the road, they set off toward the shrine. Dust soon caked Mycah's feet, and small bits of gravel bit his soles, keenly reminding him of his shoe situation.

"Any idea how far we are from the shrine?" asked Mycah.

"Not sure," said Jerud. "I'd wager we'll arrive today, though."

"I hope so." Mycah checked the sun overhead. Still midmorning. He wiggled his toes to loosen a clump of dirt stuck in between them. "So what's the plan, anyway? Once we get to the shrine, I mean."

"Well," said Jerud. "I'm going to visit the shrine itself. I plan on making my peace with God before we set out on the final leg of our journey. Might be nice for you do the same."

Mycah scratched the back of his neck. "Yeah, well, I suppose I could come with you, but I don't know if I'll be partaking in any soul searching."

Mycah never understood the point of confessionals. If God was all knowing and all seeing, couldn't someone confess their sins to God anywhere at any time? Why involve a priest? Or undertake a months-long journey to a shrine, for that matter?

Jerud shrugged. "A man's sins are between himself and God. If you don't think you're ready for it... well that's your choice to make. But visiting the shrine would help avoid suspicion."

Mycah raised his eyebrows. Jerud reminded him of an overbearing parent at times. "I guess I should rephrase my question. What's the plan after we visit the shrine?"

"We double back. Make like we're heading home. Once we're out of sight, we head into the woods and make our way toward the Garden. That should keep anyone from suspecting us of anything."

"Wouldn't it make more sense to skip the shrine altogether? Just head off into the woods now?"

Jerud gave Mycah a stern look. "I'm going to the shrine, lad."

"Just a thought..." said Mycah. Jerud could get testy when it came to his religion. "Well, hopefully I can acquire some boots there. This road is rubbing my feet raw."

"Don't expect to find any traders, lad," said Jerud. "This is a religious monument, not a thriving township. You'll be lucky to find anyone with a spare pair, I'd wager."

"I'll figure something out," said Mycah.

Jerud narrowed his eyes. "You're not going to steal anything, are you?"

"You know me, Jerud." Mycah grinned. "I'll be discreet."

Jerud sighed and shook his head.

Midmorning passed into midday. Not a single stone marker popped up along the path. Had the road any turns to speak of, Mycah would've sworn they'd taken a wrong one. Eventually, a curl of smoke above the treetops signaled civilization ahead.

As the road curved around a stand of maples, a small settlement came into view, nestled among the trees in a lush, green glade. After Jerud's dour speculation on the size of the community, Mycah expected to find no more than an altar and a few signposts, but a village rivaling the size of Leesvale greeted him.

Half a dozen log cabins squatted by the roadside—austere buildings that appeared to be made for function rather than form. Footpaths snaked their way to more cabins among the trees, the paths forking and intertwining like the tendrils of a spider's web. Off to his left, Mycah noted a carpenter's workbench. Fresh shavings that smelled of pine and sap covered it. To his right, a blacksmith's workshop lay silent, the fires cold. Hammers and tongs hung neatly in rows by the forge. Intermixed among the buildings were numerous small plots filled with summer vegetables: leafy field greens, wrinkled cucumbers, thick-tipped zucchinis, and fat, ripe tomatoes. Clucking chickens pecked at the ground, and a guinea hen dug for grubs between a pair of tomato plants.

However for everything the hamlet featured, certain things were obviously missing—the laughter of a child, for instance, or the swell of a woman's bosom. Only men tended the gardens, fetched water, and split logs for firewood. All were dressed in garments of purest white. Some, generally the elderly, wore heavy robes similar to those of priests at the cathedral in Guildean. Others wore tight fitting coats over starched shirts and pleated pants, all white and sparkling clean.

Pimple-faced youths mingled with men whose hair greyed at the temples. All of them moved with purpose and efficiency even when performing mundane chores such as sweeping or tilling soil, and all of them—at least all Mycah could see—were armed. A few carried nothing more than knives strapped to their belts. Others wore swords sheathed in banded baldrics, while others still had fierce-looking mauls hanging from belt loops at their hips, hammer claws peeking around their sides like watchful steel beaks.

"Watchers," said Jerud in hushed tones. "They call themselves the guardians of man. They watch the Shrine and protect the Garden of Eden. Be humble and respectful, and they'll treat you in kind."

A pair of Watchers stood outside the blacksmith's shop, conversing quietly. As Jerud and Mycah walked past, the Watchers bowed their heads without lowering their eyes. The gesture conveyed a modicum of goodwill without showing deference.

Mycah nodded in return as he spoke under his breath to Jerud. "They don't seem terribly congenial for being the guardians of man."

"They're not some bunch of hooligans dicing and drinking at a bar," said Jerud. "They're Watchers. Their mission is to guard the cursed land and protect those who would wander into it."

Mycah looked at the vicious arsenal of weapons carried by the Watchers. From a dark recess of his mind, he recalled the Stormqueen's torture room—the oozing blackness, the blood-red light, the voice like rocks being struck by lightning and shattered into a thousand shards. Could a sword or maul protect against a demon? Could a hammer blow to the head split a demon's skull as cleanly as a man's? Mycah's recollection of the demon was more ethereal than corporeal.

"Jerud, do you think demons can be killed?"

Jerud reacted as if smelling salts had been shoved under his nose. "Good Lord, lad—what kind of question is that?"

"I'm just wondering," mused Mycah. "All those weapons the Watchers carry—are they to keep things from getting out of the Garden or to keep people from getting in?"

Jerud's brow furrowed. "I'm not sure I follow. It's the same difference, isn't it? Either you keep the evil in or everyone else out."

"Just seems like a sword is of more use against a man than a demon..."

Though the paths between buildings snaked around drunkenly, the road passed through town as straight as an arrow. At the far end of the glade just past where the road ended a small building of white marble rose from the earth.

Neither a cathedral nor a tower nor a simple obelisk, the building was something in between. At its front, it resembled a church, though a simple one to be sure. An unpainted pine door stood in the building's windowless façade, which was perhaps a dozen paces wide and two stories tall. The building extended straight back, but its roof gradually curved upward like a wave cresting near a shore. At the far end the roof sharpened to a peak, pointing straight at the heavens.

Mycah gazed at the structure in awe. Though it towered over the modest log cabins scattered throughout town, the Grand Cathedral of Guildean surely dwarfed it. Yet it wasn't its size that captivated Mycah. The shrine's exterior lacked friezes or cornices or decorations of any kind, and not a single crevice marred its surface. Rather, the entire structure appeared chiseled from a giant slab of marble by God's own hand.

Mycah stared at the peak at the building's rear. How many hours had been spent polishing that peak to a pin-point? A man could skewer himself upon a piece of stone that sharp.

When they were a dozen paces from the monument's façade, Jerud stopped. His hands wrapped around the straps of his pack, the big man stared upward at the shrine. As the midday sun shone overhead and crickets chirped in the fields, Mycah afforded his friend a moment of silence.

"You know, lad," said Jerud after a long pause. "The Lord works in mysterious ways. I'm a man of God, but I never planned on making the pilgrimage out here. Never even gave it serious thought. Not sure why... Life always got in the way, I guess. Too many things to do. Skirts to chase. Saps to swindle.

"Doing what we do, it always gnawed at me. I knew thieving wasn't right, but I needed coin, and grifting came natural to me. I always assumed I'd make my peace with the Lord before I left this world, but now here, given the chance..."

Jerud sighed and stared off into the heavens. There was something odd about the man's eyes. They seemed... wet.

"Jerud... is something wrong?"

Jerud clapped Mycah on the shoulder with a meaty fist. "Look, lad. There's something I've been meaning to tell you. Something I've been thinking about a fair amount over these past few weeks. This is probably as good a time to say it as any." He looked Mycah square in the eyes. "This is going to be our last adventure together, lad."

"What? What are you talking about?" asked Mycah. What had gotten into the big fellow? "Don't go getting all morbid on me, Jerud. We're going to get through this just fine. We'll get back to Guildean. We'll get that Stormqueen to remove the curse, and—"

"No, no," said Jerud, shaking his head. "You misunderstand. I'm committed to this wild quest, trust me. It's just that... Well, I can't live my life as a thief anymore. Fate's led me here to this shrine. The Lord's trying to tell me something. I'm going to go in there and make my peace with Him for everything I've done and everything I plan to do on the remainder of this journey. But when we're done, I'm out. I'm going to live my life as an honest man, Mycah. I won't hold it against you if you keep on thieving."

Jerud chuckled. "Honestly, it'd almost be a shame if you stopped. You're one of the best I've ever seen. But I can't keep living my life opposite the Lord's plan."

Mycah's eyes had continued to widen throughout Jerud's revelation. Was this why Jerud had been so grumpy lately? Because he'd been struggling with this decision?

Mycah's tongue felt dry. "You're... serious, aren't you?"

"Yes, lad. I'm serious."

Thoughts raced through Mycah's head. Had Jerud thought this through? Of course he had. But what would he do without him? Jerud had been like a father to him for nigh on a decade. Feelings of disbelief and confusion mixed with betrayal. Memories of their exploits flashed through his mind: the thrilling theft from the Museum of Cultural History, the time Jerud fought off a pack of wild dogs with a pitchfork following a botched meat heist, Mycah's impersonation of the city watch when Jerud had nearly been arrested, all the time and effort that went into the robbery of the Stormqueen's palace and their subsequent incarceration. Their current quest. The campfire talks. The flight from the Jabberwocks. All leading up to this.

Mycah felt overwhelmed.

Jerud removed his hand from his shoulder. "Um, I know this is a lot to take in, lad." He fidgeted with his pack straps. "I'm going to go to the Shrine to pray. Maybe I'll see you in there?"

Mycah rubbed his forehead with his fingers. "Um... yeah. I mean maybe. I don't know. In a minute? I need to, um, do something. Find some boots, perhaps."

By the moons, but he was a mess! His thoughts darted about like a frantic waterbug.

"Yeah, of course. Take your time, lad."

Jerud approached the shrine and stepped inside, closing the door behind him. Mycah sat down at the side of the road. He folded his arms on his knees and rested his head upon them. His heart pounded and his stomach churned. The reality of Jerud's admission slowly set in.

No more adventures? No more heists? What would he do without the big man's guidance? Of course, Mycah was more than experienced enough to get by on his own. He'd been the one to mastermind all their recent robberies, including the theft of the Stormqueen's staff, but Jerud's contributions went beyond planning and execution. His reassuring chuckle, his broad grin, his consistent companionship. Without those, jobs would lose their sense of adventure and become, well... jobs.

Mycah tried to be rational. Jerud hadn't renounced their friendship, nor had he made any wild claims about leaving and never seeing him again. Clearly, they could still socialize, still drink and dice and laugh in the evenings, even if Jerud declined to take part in Mycah's less-than-legal schemes. Jerud had come to his decision after much soul searching. How could Mycah fault Jerud for following his heart—for accepting his own need to live a life free of guilt? Honestly, there wasn't anything to be upset about.

Then why do I still feel betrayed?

CHAPTER EIGHTEEN

New Boots

" Are you well, child?"

Mycah looked up to find a Watcher standing over him. The man held his broad shoulders erect and clasped his hands behind his back. Grey flecked the hair at his temples, but the remainder was a dark, rich brown, like a polished dresser of black walnut. His face showed the age of many seasons, but his watchful eyes shone bright. In those eyes Mycah saw wisdom, as well as concern and a hint of wariness.

"I, uhh…"

How to respond? A part of him desperately wanted to share his heavy heart with someone—anyone—even this man he'd just met, and yet he mustn't arouse any suspicions. How much had the man seen? Or heard for that matter?

"I, uh… lost my boots," Mycah said sheepishly.

The Watcher glanced at Mycah's feet. "Some would say that the pilgrim's journey is given meaning through adversity. That man's suffering reminds him of his sin and prepares him for his confession to God. Some would say that only through suffering can man truly understand the meaning of repentance."

"Yeah, well," said Mycah, "I've had my fair share of adversity and suffering lately. The boots are just the most recent bit of it."

The Watcher's eyes narrowed slightly, crow's feet extending from them as his penetrating gaze pierced Mycah's flesh. A bead of sweat began to form upon Mycah's brow.

"I see," said the Watcher after a lengthy pause. "Well, if a journey of suffering does indeed prepare one for confession, then it would appear you're ready. But repentance from sin is the Lord's domain, not man's. Man's purpose lies in the assistance of his fellow brother. Come, child."

The Watcher extended his hand. Mycah grasped it, and the tall man hoisted him to his feet. Wordlessly, the Watcher turned and headed toward a cluster of cabins. Mycah glanced toward the door to the shrine before following the Watcher.

"If you don't mind my asking, where are we going?"

"To try to find you some suitable footwear, of course," said the Watcher. "With any luck our storeroom will contain something your size."

"Oh, um, thanks… sir," said Mycah. Had the man introduced himself? How should he address this Watcher? "You know, I don't think I caught your name."

"I'm Knight Captain Orwell. And your name, child?"

"Mycah. So should I call you Captain?"

"My fellow Watchers call me Captain. The pilgrims generally call me Father. My mother called me Simon, and the Lord denotes me His child. All are acceptable. You decide which applies to you."

The Watcher continued to walk, straight backed, arms clasped behind his back. Apparently the Knight Captain enjoyed giving cryptic answers. In some strange way, the man reminded him of Rayven—not in his appearance by any means, but in the sense that everything he said seemed to contain a hidden message. Mycah would need to tread cautiously with him.

"So are you in charge around here?" Mycah asked.

The Knight Captain turned his head and raised an eyebrow a hair. "You're unfamiliar with our order?"

Mycah tried to recall what Jerud had told him. "You're Watchers. You watch over the shrine and protect the Garden of Eden, right?"

The Knight Captain stopped and lifted his gaze toward the heavens. *"In darkest night, the Watcher's eye is sharpest. In fiercest tempest, the Watcher's resolve is strongest. In the face of evil, the Watcher's faith is strongest. We are the Guardians of men. We are the protectors of the Garden."* The Captain shifted his gaze to Mycah. "That is our creed, child. Do you know what it means?"

Mycah rubbed at the nape of his neck. The man made him uncomfortable. "Well... no. Not entirely, I guess."

"You're familiar with the Fall of Man, I presume?"

"Yes, of course." Mycah recalled the Stormqueen and Father Maple's lectures. Hopefully this wasn't going to turn into another lesson in theology.

"When the Lord cast man out of the Garden, He cursed the land. The rivers boiled through the force of His wrath, His plants withered and died, and His gentle creatures transmuted into demonic beasts. To this day, His curse ravages the land. It is our sworn duty to protect man from the Lord's curse. We do so by protecting man from the Garden, and by protecting the Garden from man."

Mycah scratched his head. "Father, forgive me if this is a silly question, but why does the Garden need protection from man? Shouldn't we be worried about the demonic beasts and not vice versa?"

"I thought you said you were familiar with the Fall of Man, child?"

"I am." Mycah sighed. This was definitely turning into a lesson in theology. "At least I thought I was."

"Why did the Lord cast man out of the Garden?"

Mycah considered carefully. It wouldn't do to show his ignorance of gospel in front of this man. "For eating from the tree of knowledge."

"Precisely. Man's eating from the tree was the original sin, and by doing so man cursed himself to be subject to ignorance, suffering, and the dominion of death. And to be prone to sin for all of eternity."

"I'm not sure I follow. How does this tie back into the protection of the Garden?"

"Man's nature makes him ignorant and deceitful, and through ignorance and deceit man can cause great harm to himself and others. The tree of knowledge still resides in the Garden. Our true calling as Watchers is to prevent man from once again eating from the tree and incurring God's wrath. Truly, *that* is why we are the Guardians of men."

Captain Orwell turned and continued to walk, leading Mycah down a path lined with fresh pine mulch that smelled of damp earth and worms. Mycah had never considered that the tree of knowledge might still be alive and well. Hopefully the mysterious tablet the Stormqueen desired lay nowhere close to the tree.

Mycah made a mental note. *When in the Garden, don't eat any fruit. Or anything for that matter, just to be on the safe side.*

The Captain stopped in front of a cabin that looked the same as all the others. A guardsman at the door gave the Captain a deep bow of the head, similar to the ones Mycah and Jerud had received upon entering the village but slower and deeper—a nod that recognized authority and conveyed respect.

"Brother, if you please," said the Knight Captain as he motioned to the door.

"Certainly, Captain," said the Watcher, bringing a fist to his chest in salute.

The guardsman unlocked the door with a key that hung from a ring at his belt. He opened it and snapped back to his position of vigilance. The Knight Captain stepped into the cabin and Mycah followed.

Mycah instinctually surveyed the room. Two barred windows, each about as broad as a man's forearm, let in light from near the top of opposing walls. The guarded door presented the only entrance or exit. Had Mycah gone through with his plan of pilfering boots from the Watchers, he would've had better success stealing a pair right off a Watcher's own feet than trying to sneak into this storehouse. Thankfully, the Knight Captain seemed perfectly willing to simply give him a pair of boots. Amazingly, the idea of asking for them rather than stealing them had never crossed his mind. Perhaps a life of crime had jaded him regarding the goodwill of his fellow man.

Inside the cabin appeared even smaller than its outer dimensions suggested, most likely due to the sheer volume of supplies that packed its interior. Shelves and racks stuffed to the brim with all manner of non-perishable goods filled the room. There were supplies for soldiers, supplies for the home, trowels and shovels for gardening, needles and thread for sewing, whetstones for sharpening and hatchets for woodcutting. The items all lay in neat stacks, and small placards announced the contents from the front of each shelf.

"Wow," said Mycah. "Looks like you're prepared for just about anything."

"We try to be."

Mycah did notice one particular item missing from the storerooms. "Where do you store the guns? Do you have a separate armory?"

Captain Orwell shook his head. "Our order chooses to eschew the use of items forged through the fires of technology."

"Really? Why?"

"Because God created us as perfect beings in His own image. We believe that man is fully capable of defending himself through the strength of his own body."

"So you don't use guns at all?"

"Not merely guns, child. We eschew all technology, from muskets to pocket watches, and beyond that anything that degrades the perfection of man. You'll have noticed the lack of mounts here. The Lord blessed us with feet with which to walk, and so we walk. Speaking of which…"

The Knight Captain walked to a shelf at the far side of the room. "Just as I thought." He extended a hand and pulled out a pair of weathered boots. "These belonged to Father Carlton before he passed. They're worn, but the heel is sound. Come, child. Give these a try. I believe they're your size."

Mycah walked over and accepted the boots. Bending over, he tugged one onto his right foot. Surprisingly enough, it slipped on nicely. Mycah wiggled his toes and flexed his foot. His middle toe just barely reached the tip of the boot, and his heel felt secure. Mycah pulled on the shoe's mate and laced the pair.

Mycah stood and faced the Knight Captain. How should he thank the man? What was it that Jerud had said? *Be humble and respectful.* Well, that much seemed obvious.

"Thank you very much, kind Father," he said. "The boots fit perfectly. Um... clearly the Lord blesses me today."

Mycah almost grimaced at his own prose. He was overdoing it, and he knew it.

The Knight Captain's visage remained neutral. "The Lord brought you to me, but it's not His blessing that shrouds your feet. Today, my goodwill alone brings you good fortune. Remember that as you continue your journey."

The Captain extended one of his arms toward the door. "Now, my child, return to your companion, before your absence becomes worrisome to him."

"Of course." Mycah walked to the door and paused. "Thanks again, Father. For the boots, and the conversation."

The Knight Captain nodded in response.

Mycah walked back to the Shrine to find Jerud sitting outside the building, squatting upon his pack. The big man looked comical, like a fattened winter squirrel perched upon a sagging tree branch. Had Jerud already completed his confession? How long had he spent with the Knight Captain? Mycah thought only a quarter hour had passed, at most.

"There you are," said Jerud as he hopped to his feet. "When I stepped out and you were gone I got a mite worried, lad."

"You done already?" asked Mycah.

"Didn't take me long to make my peace. I'm a man of few words."

Mycah grinned. "You and I both know that's not true."

Jerud looked at the ground sheepishly. "Alright. You got me, lad. Like I said, I was worried. You seemed upset. Once I made my confession, I came right back out to see you. I... well, I wanted to apologize. I guess I could've broken the news to you a bit more gently. Look, just because I want out of the business doesn't mean I want you out of my life. You've got to know how much you mean to me, don't you?"

Mycah gripped Jerud's meaty arm and smiled. "It's alright, Jerud. I thought it over. I understand. I'm proud of you for following your heart."

Jerud's face brightened. "Really?"

"Really," Mycah said.

Jerud swallowed Mycah in a massive embrace. "Oh, lad, you don't know how glad I am to hear that. That means a lot coming from you, you know."

"Glad to hear it," squeaked Mycah. He tried to pat the big fellow's back from the confines of the bear hug.

Jerud released Mycah and took a step back. "So, what do you think? Want to make a quick visit to the Shrine?"

"You know what, I think I'm going to pass," said Mycah. "I'm not quite ready for it yet. I know we may never be back, but the way I see it I'll have a whole lot more to atone for in my future than you will. Might as well wait. And when I'm ready, I have a feeling God will listen, no matter where I do the confessing."

Jerud chuckled. "Yeah. You're probably right."

"Come on. We should get going. It's well past midday."

Jerud tossed his pack over his shoulders and tightened the straps. Just as he was ready to set out, he glanced at Mycah's feet. "Say... where'd you get the boots?"

Mycah grinned. "Interesting story, that. I'll tell you as we walk."

***

Knight Captain Orwell entered the dovecote and pulled closed the door behind him. From the outside, the building appeared to be nothing more than a simple barn, but a closer inspection revealed numerous clefts under the structure's front awning—holes just large enough for pigeons to pass through.

Inside the building, a large cage filled with chirping carrier pigeons lined the far wall. An elderly, spectacled man with wispy, white hair squinted into a leather-bound tome by the light of an unshuttered window. He raised his head at the creak of the door.

"Ahh, Captain Orwell, 'ow can I be of assistance this afternoon? D'you 'ave need of my messengers? I'm sure they'd be 'appy to stretch their wings on a day as fine as this."

"Not today, Brother Aldon. I have need of the missive from Guildean, the one that arrived two weeks ago."

"Of course." The spectacled man shuffled to a wooden container the size of a jewelry box. Undoing the latch, he flipped open the lid revealing row upon row of minute scrolls, each tightly rolled and tucked into a numbered compartment. Squinting through his spectacles, he scanned the rows meticulously. His eyes finally settled upon a tiny spool in the bottom left-hand corner.

Knight Captain Orwell watched the old man work. Grasping two pairs of steel tweezers, Brother Aldon carefully extracted the scroll. The elderly brother held the scroll's free end with one pair of tweezers. The other set he inserted into the scroll's center. He then pulled downward, delicately unfurling it. With a quick motion, he grasped the other end of the scroll with the second set of tweezers and transferred it to a reading stand underneath a magnifying lens.

Knight Captain Orwell nodded to himself in approval. Though his eyesight might be failing, Brother Aldon's hand remained steady. By the Lord's good grace, he might yet have a few more seasons of service ahead of him. Captain Orwell dearly hoped that would be the case. Not only was Brother Aldon the best pigeon fancier amongst the Watchers, but he was also a friend. Should the Lord decide to take the Brother, Captain Orwell would see him in the afterlife, of that he was certain. For now however, he preferred to keep the man in the mortal realm.

"Here y'are, Captain," said the old friar.

"Thank you, Brother."

Captain Orwell approached the reading stand. Peering into the magnifying lens, he saw a message written in a form of shorthand. To the untrained eye, the scroll appeared covered with complex scribbles, each symbol composed of a multitude of intersecting lines and markings. Some forms of shorthand emphasized speed of writing and as such were composed of varying forms of ellipses and lines that naturally flowed from the movement of the hand. Other forms of shorthand were ciphers, complex codes that required a key both to pen and to decipher. This was neither. Instead, this form of shorthand maximized information density. The small size of a pigeon's leg mandated that each iota of usable space on a transferred missive be used to its highest potential.

Captain Orwell had read the command when it arrived. Though he was confident in his recollection of it, he nonetheless wished to double-check a few key descriptions. In his experience, it was never wise to act in haste. Haste often led to mistakes, and mistakes generally led to regret. The Captain prided himself on his record and reputation, and he wasn't about to have any rash decisions tarnish them.

The Captain scanned the contents of the minuscule letter. The complex markings described in detail two individuals: a slender, brash, young man and a portly, barrel-chested veteran, both travelling together under the guise of pilgrims. The letter's instructions were quite clear. At the bottom of the small square of parchment an insignia burned into the page stood out like a sunflower amongst a field of dandelions—the mark of the archbishop of Guildean.

The Knight Captain straightened from his position over the magnifying lens. "Brother Aldon, thank you for your assistance. You may dispose of this message."

The brother bowed his head. "As y'wish, Captain."

Knight Captain Orwell exited the dovecote. With a purposeful step, he walked to a cluster of log cabins situated not far from the blacksmith's emporium. A group of Watchers stood in a circle, making idle conversation.

"First Lieutenant Armstrong," said Captain Orwell.

One of the Watchers straightened and brought a fist to his chest. "Captain?"

"Gather a party." The Captain's eyes narrowed. "I have a mission for you of the utmost importance."

CHAPTER NINETEEN

A Chance Encounter

A twig crunched underfoot, snapping with a pop. Mycah wiggled his toes happily. Though the woodland floor offered a gentler confrontation than the gravel road, he nonetheless thanked the moons for his new boots.

Overhead, late afternoon rays drifted through the forest canopy, reflecting off damp leaves to create shimmering sunlit patches. When the breeze blew and the leaves swayed, sunlight flashed through the forest's shroud—there one moment, gone the next. Mycah glanced behind him. He could've sworn he saw something. Was it the flashing sunlight or something else? He shook his head and turned to Jerud.

"So, Jerud, what do you think you'll do once we return to Guildean? Once this mess with the Stormqueen is all over with, I mean."

Jerud flashed a hearty smile. Though the big man's shoulders were broad enough to carry a mule deer, they'd sagged under the yoke of his choice to abandon a life of crime. Once Jerud revealed his intentions, the weight had lifted, and Mycah's acceptance and encouragement had further eased the burden. Now, Jerud seemed as chipper as a fledgling.

"I think I'll go back to The Black Swan," said Jerud. "If Marta'll have me, that is. Always liked working there. I figure I'm still hale and hearty enough to bounce. Who knows. Perhaps if I can get back into Marta's good graces, I'll be able to work my way up. Maybe help her run the place, if she's willing."

With Jerud so upbeat, Mycah sensed it was finally time to ask the question that had been bugging him for weeks. "So… you finally going to spill the beans about you two?"

Jerud snorted, but it was half-hearted—almost playful. "You're never going to let that go, are you?"

"Darn right I'm not! Not until I hear exactly what happened between the two of you."

Jerud shook his head. "I'll tell you, but you're not going to believe me."

Mycah hoisted his pack up higher onto his back as he walked. "Try me."

"Alright, here goes." Jerud took a deep breath. "Me and Marta? We went on more than just a few dates. In fact, we were… in love."

"I knew it!" said Mycah.

Jerud raised his eyebrow. "Do you want to hear the story or not?"

"Sorry. I'll clamp it." Mycah pinched his lips with his index finger and thumb.

"As I was saying, we were in love," said Jerud. "Madly in love, I might add. I didn't have much in those days— heck, I still don't—but what little I had, I spent on her. I bought her flowers. We ate at the finest restaurants the city had to offer. We even went to see the Guildean Phil-harmonic, though I didn't actually pay for those tickets. Don't ask."

Mycah tapped his lips and nodded.

"Marta was everything a man like me could've asked for. She was even willing to accept that I lived my life out-side the confines of common law. I would've done just about anything she asked of me. And then one day she posed me a question I was wholly unprepared for. She asked if I'd marry her."

Mycah's jaw dropped. "You're kidding?"

Jerud chuckled. "Yeah. That was pretty much my reac-tion, too. But no, she was serious. Looking back on it, I should've said yes—a hundred times yes. It's probably the best offer anyone's ever made me. Of course, my life would've turned out mighty different. Never would've met you, for one thing, and that would've been a shame. Trust me, lad, I cherish our relationship. Not the same way I cherished Marta, granted, but still.

"Anyway, to make a long story short I said no. Can't say why exactly. Guess I was the same as any other young man. Brash. Adventurous. Indecisive. And completely ig-norant of how good I had it. After that, well... Marta and I just parted ways. I couldn't work at the Swan anymore—not after that. So I focused on grifting, and that's how I met you."

Mycah let the story soak for a moment. "Of all the pos-sible stories, I never would've come up with that one."

Jerud shrugged.

"So what's your plan when we get back? Do you still love her? I've seen the way you look at her. Are you going to turn the tables after all these years and ask her to marry you?"

"Whoa, there, whoa," said Jerud. "Slow down, lad. For now I'm just hoping she'll let me work at the Swan. Perhaps she still harbors feelings for me—I hope she does— but I'll have to play things slow. See how things develop. Time has softened a lot of wounds, but you can't rush a relationship. That's something I learned a long time ago. The hard way, I might add. It's a lesson you should take to heart should you ever find yourself a girl."

"Oh brother," said Mycah. "Let's not turn this conversation onto me, now..."

"Just something to keep in mind," said Jerud.

As the afternoon turned into early twilight, Mycah tried to picture Jerud as a married man. A vision of him, aproned, barging his way through The Black Swan's kitchens formed in his mind. Admittedly, Jerud did have a few things going for him if marriage lay in wait. He was jovial and chatty—a trait that women seemed to love, especially old married women. He'd just renounced a life of crime to stay home and be civil. And the man had already let himself go. Mycah eyed Jerud's ample paunch. How did the old saying go? Fatten them up so they can't run away? Something like that. Marta wouldn't have much work to do in that department, that was for sure.

All in all, Mycah felt overjoyed for his big friend, but at the same time a sense of unease grew in his stomach. His neck burned and his feet itched. Something wasn't right. Was it jealousy? Fear of a future without Jerud by his side at every step and turn? No, that wasn't it. Something scratched at the corners of his mind, a feeling of restlessness and apprehension. Mycah glanced back once more. Had the sunlight just flashed again?

"Jerud," Mycah whispered. "Don't turn around. I think we're being followed."

Jerud's lower lip curled, but the big man's experience prevented him from displaying more than that small tell. "Are you sure?"

"No, I'm not positive," said Mycah. "But I've had a feeling for a while now."

Jerud muttered something under his breath. "I was afraid of this. I could've sworn I heard something a ways back. Let's just hope it's not the Watchers. You didn't say anything odd to that Knight Captain, did you?"

"No," said Mycah. "I told you about our conversation. If he had any suspicions, then I doubt it was from anything I said."

Jerud glanced into the darkening canopy. "Alright, look. Here's the plan. We keep walking just like we're doing. It's getting dark, so we'll use that to our advantage. Once the light's almost faded, I'll give the signal and we bolt to our right. There's a ridge we've been following, and a creek that way as well. I can hear it babbling every so often. We'll jump over the ridge and conceal ourselves in its shadow. It won't hide us for long, but with any luck it'll confuse our pursuers and give us an opportunity to strike."

Mycah rubbed at the stone around his neck. Touching it had become a nervous tick, and he found he played with it whenever anxiety gripped him. The stone's gentle heat soaked into his fingertips, but the intensity felt the same as it had the entire trip.

"Do you really think that's going to work?"

"If it's bandits, maybe. If it's Watchers..." Jerud grimaced. "Well, I guess it depends on how many of them there are."

"You're not being very reassuring," said Mycah.

"You got a better idea, lad?"

Mycah shook his head.

"Alright then." Jerud loosened a knife from a sheath at his side, and with the grace of a practiced cutpurse, he slipped the weapon into Mycah's grasp. "Take that. I know you lost yours to those Jabberwocks."

"What'll you use?"

"My fists if I have to. You need the knife more than me. Now just keep walking and act casual. When I run, you follow."

"Got it."

Mycah continued to walk, trying to act casual, but within his heart and mind raced. It was one thing to be engulfed in a fight and forced to react to survive—at that point instincts took over and either guided a man to victory or to his grave—but knowing that a fight was approaching was an entirely different matter.

Mycah ran through various scenarios in his head, trying to envision how he'd react in each case. What if the pursuers caught them before they found a hiding spot? Mycah could spin and throw a knife into a moving target at fifty paces, but he possessed only a single knife, and he suspected more than one man pursued them. What if they couldn't find a hiding spot once they reached the ridge? Should he climb a tree and dive on the pursuers from above? Would there be time for that? What if the attackers tried to surround him? Perhaps there would be sand by the creek, and he could throw it into their eyes to blind them.

Mycah shook his head to clear his thoughts.

Don't think about what's coming, just empty your mind and react, like you always do.

Though the sun had long since sunk behind the horizon, the dull gloom of twilight hung around stubbornly, like a lone reveler who refused to recognize the party around him had ended. It felt like ages had passed since he and Jerud decided upon a course of action. How much longer did Jerud plan on going? With the forest shrouding the sky, it would soon be so dark that Mycah might trip over a log and break his own neck. What an ignominious way to die that would be—slaughtered by a stump in the dark of night.

Jerud darted off to his right without a word like a thoroughbred blasting out of a starting gate, his powerful leg muscles propelling him with explosive force. Though startled by the man's initial burst, Mycah reacted quickly and bounded after him, his feet flying over the leaves with a rapid, measured stride. Mycah heard curses from behind, then the rattling of weapons and the pounding of feet.

Following Jerud, Mycah wove around saplings and ducked under branches that grasped for him in the gloom. Though Jerud's size limited his endurance, his strength and determination made him a formidable sprinter, and Mycah struggled to keep up, sucking breath back in long, forceful draughts. With adrenaline surging through his veins, his senses seemed amplified. He could hear his heart pounding, feel the blood rushing through his veins, and taste the sweat beading upon his lips.

Before him, Jerud leapt and sank into darkness. *The ridge.* Mycah followed suit, jumping as he reached the darkness and rolling when he hit the ground. Spinning around, he scanned the edge of the ridge for Jerud, but the blackness had swallowed him whole. Blast it! Where had the big man gone? The plan was for him to hide from the pursuers not from Mycah as well!

Crouched there in the darkness, something felt wrong. Mycah sniffed the air. A hint of smoke wormed its way into his nostrils, as well as the lingering smell of charred meat.

No time to dwell on it. Several figures poured over the edge of the ridge. The sky's fading light glimmered off drawn swords and revealed uniforms of purest white. *Watchers.* Five of them, by Mycah's count.

His heart skipped a beat. Five Watchers? He and Jerud were as good as dead.

Don't think, just react.

The one nearest Mycah pointed at him and shouted. "Betrayers of men! Stop!"

Jerud lurched out of the shadows with a roar, bringing a log as thick as a man's arm crashing into a Watcher's skull. Two Watchers spun toward Jerud while the other two lunged for Mycah.

A pair of swords flashed at him simultaneously. Mycah dodged to his left. The first sword stroke sliced harmlessly through the air. Bringing his knife up to his chest, he caught the second stroke squarely upon the knife's hilt. The force of the blow wrenched the knife from his grip and sent him reeling backward. Flailing, Mycah's foot caught upon a root, sending him tumbling onto his back with a thud.

In a panic, Mycah grasped at his side, desperately searching for something—anything—with which to defend himself. A splinter pricked him. A log! His fingers curled around an oddly warm chunk of wood that felt as if it had been split with an axe.

The Watcher who'd disarmed him stepped forward. He lifted his sword into the air. "In God's name!"

Mycah heard a growl. The Watcher hesitated, his sword held high.

A snarling beast lunged from the shadows. The Watcher cried in surprise as flashing jaws latched upon his throat. A hot liquid tasting of iron spurted across Mycah's face. The man's cry turned into a gurgle, soon replaced by the sickening sound of ripping flesh.

Good Lord, the tales were true! A cursed beast of the Garden is here to slay us all!

The second Watcher cursed and lifted his sword, but a javelin took the man in the chest. Dropping the sword, the Watcher staggered backward, slack jawed, hands clutching the haft of the spear as he tumbled over.

Mycah stared at the Watcher as he hit the earth with a thud. A javelin? Where had that come from? By the moons, were the cursed beasts armed?

Clutching the chunk of wood, Mycah hopped into a crouching position. In the darkness, he could barely make out Jerud's large frame struggling against that of another. A blur across the forest floor drew his eye, and something slammed into a tree.

With a vicious scream, another Watcher lurched from the shadows, swinging his sword in a wild arc. Mycah turned to face him, wielding his log like crude cudgel. Blood streamed from a gash in the Watcher's face. He screamed again, a bellow of rage and bloodlust, and raised his sword to strike. Mycah dove to the side and rolled, bringing his cudgel up to bash the man from behind, but the Watcher spun and turned his blow away with ease. Mycah kicked at the man's chest, but the Watcher danced back out of range. Mycah's momentum pitched him forward and he fell.

The Watcher pivoted and swung the sword around, aiming straight for Mycah's midsection. Halfway through the swing, a blade exploded from his chest. The Watcher dropped to his knees, blood streaming from his chest and mouth, soaking his white tunic. A shadowy hooded figure stood behind him, hands grasping the hilt of a wicked blade. With a well-planted boot to the back, the figure dislodged the weapon and pointed it at Mycah.

"Drop your weapon," said the figure in a husky voice.

Mycah released the cudgel.

"On your stomach. Don't even think about moving."

Mycah dropped to his knees. As he lay down, he peered forward, his eyes straining in the darkness, trying to discern his captor's identity. Though there was something odd about the figure's voice, the figure's stance and speech were undoubtedly human, not that of a monster found in tales told to misbehaving children. Who was this individual? Not a Watcher, clearly. Perhaps a hunter of the snarling beast?

"Look, I'll do as you say," Mycah stammered. "But there's some sort of beast out there. It took out one of those Watchers. Ripped his throat clean open. It's probably still nearby. In fact—" Mycah strained his ears. "I think I can hear it growling!"

"I'd hope so," said the figure. "Winny, you alright?"

Winny? The beast had a name, and it served the dark figure?

Two deep barks sounded from nearby, and then the low growling continued. The snarling beast... was a dog?

From the darkness, a voice called out. "Uhh, Mycah... you there?"

Mycah perked up. "Jerud?"

"I said don't move," said the figure, jabbing in Mycah's direction with the bloody blade. "And you," the figure called out into the darkness. "Shut up and don't move or Winny'll rip your throat out."

The figure hunched over the spot where Mycah had found his makeshift cudgel and produced a piece of flint from a pocket. Stabbing the sword in the ground, the figure struck the flint against the flat of the blade, creating a shower of sparks. After a few unsuccessful attempts, a spark finally caught in a small bundle of tinder. Slowly but surely, the fire grew, revealing a scene of carnage around them.

Five Watchers lay strewn about the small clearing, the three that had fallen near Mycah and two more near Jerud. Jerud's powerful blow to the first Watcher's head appeared to have broken the man's skull, as bits of bone peeked through his matted, bloody hair. Another lay sprawled on the ground near Jerud, his head twisted around at an unnatural angle. Already the man's face appeared puffy and pale. The scent of blood filled the air.

Mycah swallowed hard and shifted his gaze to the hooded figure. Under the light of the growing fire, Mycah saw a man wearing plain brown breeches and a fitted long-sleeved shirt of delicate grey wool partially covered by a heavy hooked cloak. The clothes were of fine construction and in good repair, though the pants were crusted with mud at the thighs.

The stranger rose. He was of medium height and build. The thin shirt revealed relatively broad shoulders but slender arms. The stranger stood tall and confident, with his chest puffed out in a display of bravado.

The stranger raised his hands and threw back the hood from his face. Mycah's eyes widened in surprise. Not *his* face, but *her* face!

From behind the shroud of the cloak's hood emerged a woman, her chestnut brown hair pulled tight in a ponytail at the crown of her head. Though her features were softer than a man's, her eyes, pale grey in color, were as hard as ice. She stared at Mycah with those eyes, a fierce fire burning within them.

"Who sent you here? How did you find me?" she demanded in her husky voice.

Mycah blinked, trying to process the questions. "Um, what?"

"Who sent you, damnit!"

"Well, the Stormqueen," said Mycah. "But—"

"The Stormqueen?" said the woman. That seemed to catch her completely off guard. "Which Stormqueen?"

"Rain, but listen—"

"No, you listen," she said angrily. "What does a Stormqueen want with me?"

"I don't know," said Mycah, starting to feel testy. "Who are you?"

"What do you mean, 'who am I'? Aren't you here for me?"

"Excuse me," cried Jerud. "But could you please sic this dog off of me?"

"No. Shut up!" yelled the woman. She turned back to Mycah. "You're telling me you're not here for me?"

"I don't even know who you are," said Mycah.

"THEN WHAT IN A MONKEY'S FLAMING REAR END WAS ALL THIS ABOUT?" The woman waved her arms about. She pressed a hand against her forehead. "Bloody Hell. This is a God-damned disaster..."

"Young lady, watch your tongue!" said Jerud. The dog's growling intensified.

"Excuse me?" said the woman. "I think you should be a little more worried about getting your throat ripped out than what words come out of my God-damned mouth!"

"Ok, everyone, calm down!" shouted Mycah, arms held up in appeal. "Maybe we all need to take a moment to figure out what's going on here."

"Yes, clearly," said the woman through gritted teeth. She pointed the sword at Mycah again. "You. Start talking. Who are you? Why are you here? Explain yourselves. And keep in mind that my blade has already tasted blood. Yours could feed its appetite next if I don't like your response."

Mycah gulped. Where to begin? And how much should he reveal? Who was this strange woman, anyway? "I'm Mycah. That's Jerud. The Stormqueen sent us, but not after you. In God's name, I swear it! I have no idea who you are."

The woman spat. "I care little for your oaths. If you're not here for me, then why?"

"We're... on a mission," said Mycah.

"What sort of mission?"

"Well, we're going to, um..." Mycah hesitated.

"Go on, spit it out."

Mycah sighed. "We're going to steal something. From... the Garden of Eden."

The woman snorted. "Hah. That's rich. Seriously, which son-of-a-bitch sent you? Was it Keralt?"

"Who?" Mycah was at a loss for words. The woman's eyes bore into him, full of rage and ferocity, but also determination. Something else resided there, too. Pain, perhaps—though whether of the body or the soul he couldn't tell.

"Bloody hell..." said the woman after a moment, her eyes losing some of their ferocity. She lowered her sword. "You're serious, aren't you?"

Mycah shrugged.

The woman laughed, this time catching Mycah off guard. "Hah! Ash and entrails! You two are crazy. Completely nuts! Don't you know that place is cursed?"

"Well, one good curse deserves another," mumbled Mycah under his breath.

"What was that?" asked the woman. Her eyes narrowed.

"Nothing," said Mycah, frowning. "Yes, we're aware it's cursed. Thanks for the insight."

"Yeah, well everyone's taught it's cursed, but it's different when you actually see it with your own eyes. Trust me, I've never been one to believe in fairy tales and curses, but there's something unnatural about that place. You don't want to go there."

"You've been there?" asked Mycah.

"Close enough," said the woman.

"Hey, look," called Jerud. "It's great that you're starting to get all chummy over there, but would you *please get this blasted dog off me?*"

The hardness returned to the woman's eyes. She paused, considering the request. "Alright, fine," she said as she sheathed her sword. "Winny, to me. But if either of you two try anything, and I mean *anything*, Winny'll rip your face off. She's as vicious as a Delovian saber cat and twice as mean."

The growling stopped. From the shadows near Jerud trotted a black and brown brindled mutt with a smushed face, strong jaw line, and a powerful musculature. She was a large dog, though not as large as Mycah had imagined her in the dark—perhaps two and a half feet at the shoulders. The dog held her head high as she trotted, her rump wiggling as she went.

Instead of heading for the woman, the dog approached Mycah. His heart skipped a beat seeing the large beast head straight toward him, but rather than attack him, the bitch came up and gave him a few delicate sniffs. Once acquainted with his scent, she circled and sat on her haunches next to him with a plop.

The woman blinked in confusion, her mouth open enough to catch flies. "Well that's... different."

"So... vicious as a Delovian saber cat, eh?" Mycah snaked out a hand and cautiously rested it upon the dog's shoulders, then moved it up to give her a good scratch between the ears. The dog closed her eyes and jutted her chin out ever so slightly, absorbing the scratches into her big, meaty head with a thin grin.

The woman shook her head. "I've never seen her react this way before. She normally greets men like she did that Watcher. With teeth and claws bared."

Jerud wandered over into the light of the fire, meaty hand massaging his neck. "Don't worry, lass. You don't need to convince me of the beast's ferocity."

As Jerud approached, Winny began to growl, a deep, rumbling sound that originated in her belly and reverberated through her chest. She bared her incisors.

"Whoa there, girl," said Jerud, taking a step back. "C'mon now, I thought we were past this."

The woman gave a satisfied nod. "That's more like it," she said as she sat down on a stump. "Winny, enough. You don't need to make him soil his pants."

Winny stopped her grumbling. Mycah stroked the dog's back and chuckled.

"Something funny there, lad?" asked Jerud.

"Oh, just remembering our introduction to Applesnatch," said Mycah. "You thought it was hilarious when she attacked me. Not so funny when the tables are turned, eh?"

"What the hell kind of a name for a dog is Applesnatch?" asked the woman.

"She's not a dog," said Mycah. "She's my horse. Actually—"

"Hey, lad," barked Jerud, snapping his fingers. "It's great that you're making friends with the nice lass and the dog who decided not to kill us, but we need to focus here. Those Watchers were after *us*. They knew we were here, and they meant business. Tomorrow, when this group fails to return to the shrine with us in tow, they'll get suspicious. And they'll find their way here, sure enough. When they see what happened here, they'll be out for blood."

Jerud turned to the woman. "Look miss, I appreciate you helping us out and all, but if I might offer you a piece of advice? Get as far away from here as possible. The Watchers don't yet know that you're involved, and I suggest you keep it that way. No need for you to get wrapped up in this mess. And God, what a mess it is." Jerud sighed as he looked around. "I'm gonna take care of these bodies. See if I can find some ditch to throw them into."

Jerud grabbed a brand from the fire and threw a lifeless Watcher body over his shoulder. He chose the one closest to the fire whose throat had been ripped open by Winny. The wound smiled at Mycah as Jerud tromped off into the woods. Mycah shuddered and turned back toward the fire.

The woman watched Jerud haul the Watcher off, then turned her eyes toward the fire, face a little pale. Clearly, the image of the corpse disturbed her. Apparently she wasn't made of quite as stern stuff as she pretended.

As the woman gazed into the fire, the heat of the flames seemed to rekindle the fire that burned deep within the woman's own eyes. Her cheeks reddened and she clenched her jaw. She stared as if the fire were leagues away.

"Are you alright?" asked Mycah.

"What?" The woman arose with a start.

"I said, are you alright?"

"Yeah… yeah, I'm fine." The woman continued to stare into the fire. "He's right you know. I need to leave. Now. Before they find me."

Her voice was distant, lost in a sea of thought—a sea churned by the fierce winds and crashing waves of a brewing storm. Was she talking about the Watchers or someone else?

The woman stood and turned from the light of the burning logs. "Winny, c'mon. Let's go."

"What, you're leaving? Now?" said Mycah. "It's pitch dark. The moons are waning, and under this thick canopy? You'll break a leg wandering through the forest."

The woman cast him a pained glance. "We're leaving. Winny?"

The dog whined and tilted her head.

"See?" said Mycah. "Your dog knows I speak the truth. You should at least stay until morning when you can see where you're going."

The woman stared at him, chewing her bottom lip, eyes still fierce. Mycah felt a bead of sweat develop under her firm gaze. Why was he trying to convince this woman to stay? She was ornery, dangerous, and clearly unnerved, and she'd tried to kill him and Jerud.

No. She saved you. You owe her your life.

"Jerud makes a mean beef, barley, and bean stew," Mycah said. "Why don't you stay and share a bowl. It would be the least we could do as thanks."

The woman's gaze shifted to Winny, who seemed perfectly content to sit and warm her haunches by the fire.

"Alright," she said, the fire once again leaving her eyes. "I guess me and Winny can stay for stew. We'll part ways in the morning. But don't think Winny or I are going to take our eyes off you! If you try anything—"

"Winny'll rip my face off, I know," said Mycah.

The woman glared as she sat back down on the stump. Mycah glanced at the dog. Winny seemed nonchalant—certainly not in the mood to do any more face ripping tonight.

The fire crackled. A light breeze tickled the forest canopy. Next to Mycah, Winny breathed noisily, sucking air in through her scrunched nose and releasing it through her wide mouth. Mycah and the woman sat in silence.

"So, I, uh... never caught your name," said Mycah.

The silence stretched. Mycah feared the woman hadn't heard him, but eventually she responded.

"Call me Cam."

***

Mycah, Jerud, and Cam sat around the fire, enjoying Jerud's signature camp stew. Having finished, Mycah let Winny lick his bowl, which prompted a derisive snort from Jerud. Meanwhile Cam, spoon in hand, dove into her third bowl of the hearty mixture.

Cam claimed to be a respectable hunter, but the way she attacked the stew made Mycah think otherwise. Either the woman hadn't eaten in days, or she had the appetite of a moose. Earlier when Mycah had asked Cam where her hunting bow was, Cam had replied that bows were for pansies and that real hunters took down their prey with a knife. He'd had a hard time arguing with that sort of logic, though he surmised that, pansies though they might be, bow hunters probably ate better than 'real hunters.'

Cam slurped her meal down, barely even taking time to chew between mouthfuls. Mycah recalled his time imprisoned by the Stormqueen when he'd attacked whatever foul pot of gruel that was placed before him with vigor. Was Cam that hungry, or did she lack manners? She polished off the last of the meal, setting the bowl and spoon down with a clatter. Mycah half expected her to belch in approval, but at least from that she refrained.

"Glad you enjoyed it," mumbled Jerud. He seemed displeased that Cam had stayed. Apparently he'd have been perfectly content to let the woman wander off in the middle of the night and possibly trip over a root and break her neck. Jerud normally bent over backward to make sure ladies were well taken care of, whether it be rushing to open doors or treating them to a meal on his coin, but something about Cam seemed to irk the big man. Probably her foul mouth. Jerud highly disliked blasphemers, and Cam being a woman seemed to make her swearing even less palatable.

Sensing that Cam had finished her meal, Winny shifted closer and began to lick her bowl. Paws gripping its sides, Winny's massive tongue mopped the bowl's bottom, lapping up any remaining traces of stew. Mycah checked the cooking pot that simmered over the coals. A tiny bit of stew remained.

"Anybody still hungry?" asked Mycah. Jerud shook his head. Cam seemed too full to move.

Mycah lifted the cauldron from the embers and doled the remaining stew into Winny's bowl. The dog attacked it with glee.

Mycah smiled. He could hardly believe this warm-hearted animal had killed a man just hours prior. Not only that, she'd saved his life. It was a sobering thought. Did he now owe a death boon to this dog? Or perhaps to her owner?

"Say, Cam," said Mycah. "Can I ask you something?"

"I don't know, can you?" said Cam. She leaned back against a stump, feet drawn up in front of her.

Mycah suppressed the urge to reply in a similarly snarky manner. He reminded himself that she and Winny had saved his life, and he should try to be polite. "Have you really been there? To the Garden, I mean?"

Cam's upper lip stuck out as she drew her tongue across her teeth. "You guys are really serious about going there, aren't you?"

"Yes."

Cam drew a knife from a leather sheath at her side. Mycah tensed at the gesture, but she withdrew a whet-stone from a pocket and began to draw the stone slowly across the knife's edge. Her fingers worked smoothly with a practiced precision that spoke of many hours spent honing blades. Her eyes stared at the fire as she worked, and her fingers moved independently. Perhaps Cam polished the blade to sooth her nerves, much like Mycah would twirl knives, or perhaps she did it as a visual reminder that she was armed and dangerous.

"When Winny and I first set out, we traveled through the woods. Stayed away from roads and settlements. It was easier that way, just the two of us. I didn't really know where I was heading, so we just kept going east. I'd heard stories about the Garden, but I'm not sure I ever really believed them."

Cam seemed to intentionally skirt about where she'd come from and why she'd left, but Mycah didn't press her. It didn't seem like the right time.

"Then one day, we hit it. I didn't notice it at first. The trees started to thin out, and I didn't think anything of it. But as we kept going, the forest started to change. The trees got shorter, stunted, like the life had been sucked out of them. The birds didn't chirp as much, and there was an eerie sense of stillness all around. Winny could tell something wasn't right, but I pushed on ahead. And then I saw it. I thought it was a deer. Then it turned around. The damn thing had two heads."

Cam shuddered. "Anyway, we turned back. Kept going till we got here. Didn't take too long for that eerie feeling to fade away. Been staying here ever since. Not a bad place to be, really. There's fish and game to be caught, and the odd berry to be picked."

Cam's fingers kept working the whetstone, drawing it back and forth across the blade. Mycah scratched his neck. So the curse was real. Mycah had never really believed in it. Even now he still harbored doubts. He probably would until he saw it with his own eyes.

"So that's as far as you got?" asked Mycah. "Never made it all the way to the Garden?"

Cam nodded.

"But you could show us how to get there?"

Cam looked up from the fire. "Now why the Hell would I do that?"

Jerud snorted. "We don't need her help, lad."

"Screw you, chubbs," said Cam, sitting up and brandishing her knife. "You'd be lucky to have my help."

"So you'll help then?" Mycah asked.

"I didn't say that," said Cam, settling back against the stump. "Why would I? I don't see what could possibly be in it for me."

"We have some coin. Not much, but a little."

Cam harrumphed.

"And you'd be welcome to share in more of our rations."

Cam raised an eyebrow. "How much of your rations?"

"As much as you need," said Mycah.

"LAD!" sputtered Jerud. "What are you—"

"I'll think about it," said Cam quickly. "But I'm not making any promises. And I'd only take you to the edge. If I take you at all, that is."

"Of course," said Mycah.

Jerud mumbled a curse.

Cam sheathed her knife and lay down upon the ground. Using her cloak as a pillow, she cuddled up next to Winny.

Mycah supposed he should turn in as well, but one more thing nagged at him. "Hey, Cam?"

An annoyed sigh came from beside Winny. "What?"

"Why did you save our lives? You could've just ignored us. Stayed hidden. I doubt the Watchers would have found you."

"Yeah, well, that was the plan."

Mycah raised an eyebrow. Not one to pull punches, this Cam. "So what changed?"

"Winny. She charged in like a God-damned banshee. Not sure why. I told her to stay put, and normally she listens. Guess she just liked you better than the Watchers."

"So I owe her my life then."

"Don't get any ideas. You owe us both. It's not like I sat around on my ass."

"I'll keep that in mind."

Cam snuggled into the cloak and soon began to snore. Before long, Winny had followed suit. The two of them worked in tandem, Winny making wheezing, snuffling grunts and Cam sounding like she was getting ready to hawk up a massive ball of spit. Mycah turned to Jerud to chat a bit before bed, but the big man had already lain down and had his back toward Mycah. Hopefully his mood would improve with a night's sleep.

Mycah nestled down onto his bedroll, closed his eyes, and let the duet of snores serenade him to sleep.

CHAPTER TWENTY

The Edge of Eden

When Mycah awoke, darkness still shrouded the camp. Only the barest glimmer of dawn's light trickled over the horizon and through the trees. Mycah rubbed his eyes and groaned. It was far too early to be waking up. He turned over onto his side, facing the remains of last night's fire. Beyond the burning embers, Cam and Winny were gone.

Mycah bolted upright. Jerud, usually the early riser, was sound asleep. He heard a noise from far off, something halfway between a grunt and snort. Was Cam in trouble? If so, where was Winny? Wouldn't she be busy ripping someone's face off?

Mycah hopped to his feet and snuck toward the noise. His bare feet pranced over the soft soil soundlessly. He heard another grunt, closer this time, followed by a thud and a rustling of feet. Peeking around a thick cluster of maples, he found Winny seated calmly, her powerful legs drawn up underneath her. The dog's tongue wagged languidly.

Despite his best efforts to remain silent, Winny's ears perked and her tongue disappeared back into her mouth. Her jowls rose as she swiveled her head to meet the noise. For a moment, Mycah thought she might pounce upon him and tear him to shreds, but Winny's face broke into a wide, panting grin and she turned back toward the clearing. Realizing he was holding his breath, Mycah exhaled. Even though he'd befriended her the night before, he still found himself intimidated by the hulking mastiff.

Crouching, Mycah sidled up next to Winny. With dawn approaching, he could just make out the scene in the clearing below. Cam wore her plain brown breeches from the night before but had removed her light grey woolen shirt. All that remained was an undyed brassiere that tightly hugged her small bosom. Over her shoulders hung a thick maple branch, as big around as a man's leg on the side where it had broken from its tree. Mycah guessed it weighed a good hundred pounds at least.

With the branch draped across her shoulders, Cam ran across the clearing at full speed. When she reached the other side, she unceremoniously dumped the branch to the ground at the base of a fallen oak. She hopped over the log, once, twice, and quickly now, ten times, twenty times by Mycah's count. She then returned to the hefty branch. Struggling with its weight, she wrestled it over her back and shoulders. With the load secured, she squatted down in place. Mycah counted another twenty repetitions. Once done, she sprinted back across the clearing, threw the branch to the ground and dropped to her stomach, where she pressed herself up off the forest floor and back down time and time again.

Mycah found his eyes lingering upon her body as she went through the routine. Sweat poured from her brow, soaking her hair and slicking her skin. Sharp lines divided her muscles, especially between her shoulder blades and at her abdomen, which protruded just a little and formed into a 'v' over her hips. Though her shoulders stuck out like spaulders, she was actually quite slender. Her muscles were tight and compact, not bulging and brawny like a man's. Her thin breeches clung to her thighs and hinted at powerful, long legs underneath.

She was certainly different than any of the girls he'd pursued in Guildean. Mycah had always found himself attracted to petite women—women who were slight of body with delicate features, owners of milky white skin and graceful arms, the sorts of women who had barely curved noses and soft batting eyes and whose lips pursed naughtily as if caught in a crime. Yet as he gazed upon Cam's partially exposed form in the clearing below, he found himself oddly captivated. There was something about her, a presence born out of power and grace that drew his eyes to her. His eyes fell to her small firm, bosom, tightly hugged by her brassiere. Of course, that was quite captivating as well.

Cam stopped and sat upon the fallen oak, panting. As she wiped the hair out of her eyes with a sweaty hand, she looked up. Her eyes paused upon Mycah, crouched by the cluster of maples next to Winny's powerful form.

"AHH!" she yelled. Cam fumbled for her woolen shirt that lay discarded upon the ground, trying to cover herself. "Where the Hell did you come from? Were you just sitting there, watching me?"

Mycah blinked. He realized he had, in fact, been sitting there ogling her without her knowledge. Women seemed to be fairly unforgiving of that sort of thing, even when fully clothed.

"No, it's not like that," Mycah stammered. "I heard a noise. You and Winny were gone. I thought you might be in trouble!"

Cam pulled the shirt over her chest, the fabric clinging to her skin. With her shirt rumpled and her hair askew, she seemed a sweaty mess. Where was the sense of presence Mycah had just witnessed, the power and the grace?

"So what," Cam said, walking toward Mycah. "You heard a noise, and when you got here and saw that nothing was wrong you just decided to stay and watch, like... like some God-damned creep?"

"No, I..." How could he respond without angering her? Honesty was probably the best bet. "I'd just never seen anyone doing those sorts of exercises. Certainly not a woman."

"Yeah, well, you should've said something. It's creepy as a one-eyed donkey, you watching me while I thought I was alone. And you!" Cam turned to Winny and brandished a finger. "Why didn't you let me know someone was here?"

Winny whined and tilted her head.

"Some use you are," Cam mumbled.

"Why were you doing all that stuff, anyway?" asked Mycah. "You know... if you don't mind my asking."

"You're a shining beacon of brilliance, aren't you," she said, wiping her face on her sleeve. "You must be a city rat."

"What makes you say that?" said Mycah.

"Look at you. You're soft and puny. Barely any muscle on you. I bet you couldn't even lift that log over there or run a league without stopping."

Mycah looked down at himself. He'd never considered himself puny, but his body type certainly veered more toward thin and wiry. "Now that's not really fair. I have a high metabolism. And running is one thing I'm pretty good at."

A look of disbelief cascaded across Cam's face. "Right. I'll believe that when I see it."

"You still didn't answer my question," said Mycah.

"Look, where I come from people work. They get their hands dirty. Carry their own weight. My father taught me that. You've got to be strong to survive." Her voice lowered. "Otherwise someone might try to take advantage of you. You've got to be strong. Got to be..."

Mycah raised an eyebrow. "So where are you from, anyway?"

Cam turned her head away. "None of your business."

Mycah thought he'd seen some of the fire back in her eyes. "Are all the women like you where you're from?"

"I said, NONE OF YOUR GOD-DAMNED BUSI-NESS!" Cam stormed off through the woods back toward the campsite.

Mycah glanced at Winny. Her eyes were wide, her head a touch low.

"What? Don't give me that look... I didn't say anything."

Winny exhaled loudly.

"Alright, fine. I'll go apologize. But I don't know what I did wrong."

Mycah trudged back toward the campsite, Winny in tow.

***

After Cam had eaten another hearty portion of their rations, they set out through the forest toward the Garden. Cam led the pack. She seemed intent upon jogging the entire way—whether as some sort of challenge to Mycah's earlier statement or not, he couldn't tell.

Winny trotted beside him as he ran. What seemed a decently paced jog to Mycah was apparently no more than a casual lope for the dog, who cherished the chance for a little exercise. Her tongue lolled to the side as she sucked air in noisily through her scrunched nose. For some reason Winny elected to stick close to Mycah, which annoyed Cam to no end. The woman kept looking back at her companion with pursed lips.

Soon enough the jogging came to a halt, but only because Jerud appeared to be on the verge of passing out. Mycah hid a grin behind his own labored breath. He thanked the moons it was Jerud rather than him that forced them to stop, as he'd never have heard the end of it from Cam. She seemed to gain pleasure from lording her athletic prowess over others.

"Is that all you've got, Chuckles?" asked Cam as she hopped from one foot to the other. Despite her early morning exertions, Cam bounced about, as energetic as a young pup. Must've been all the food she ate.

Jerud, bent over and gasping for breath, leaned against a gnarled oak for support. "The name's Jerud... not Chuckles... And some of us... aren't as young... and able-bodied... as we used to be."

Cam had taken to calling Jerud 'Chuckles' based on his icy demeanor toward her. Mycah found it hilarious. Jerud's throaty chuckle was one of his most endearing qualities, but he hadn't so much as cracked a smile since their encounter with Cam. Rather it seemed as if he'd been infected with a palsy that had paralyzed his face into a permanent frown and robbed him of all mirth in the process.

"Well, I guess I can slow down to a brisk walk," said Cam. "But don't expect to drag me to a crawl. If I'm going to take you to the edge of those damned cursed lands, then you'll just have to keep up, Chuckles."

Cam marched off ahead.

"What do you have against her, anyway?" asked Mycah, as he and Jerud followed at a distance.

Jerud looked like he'd swallowed a lemon. "Are you kidding me? She's vulgar and uncouth, she's got the mouth of a teenaged farmhand, she's clearly dangerous, possibly a little unhinged, she eats like a racehorse, and she has man shoulders."

Mycah raised his eyebrows. "Man shoulders? That's a little mean, don't you think?"

"Well you clearly wouldn't think so. You've been slobbering all over her since last night."

"What? Me?" Mycah was flabbergasted. "You don't think that I—I mean, c'mon... I'm not—I would never go for—"

"Oh really?" Now it was Jerud's turn to raise an eyebrow. "Then why did you ask her to lead the way last night when we clearly knew where we were going? Why the pleasant chatter over breakfast that you soaked up like a slice of day old bread despite her exhibiting all the eloquence of a hog sucking down a bucket of slop? Why the mooncalfish eyes upon her rear as we jogged?"

Mooncalfish eyes? Had he been staring at Cam's rump? It was rather shapely, he had to admit.

Mycah shook his head. "You've lost your stones, Jerud. She's not my type."

"Well that's for sure," said Jerud. "Trust me, when I told you you needed yourself a woman with some fire and a little backbone, I sure didn't mean someone like *that*." Jerud jerked his thumb toward Cam.

"Well don't go getting your feathers all ruffled. She'll be on her way soon enough. I figured it was the least we could do to share a meal and some conversation after she saved our lives and all."

Jerud grunted.

Mycah shook his head. The nerve of Jerud to insinuate he was drooling over Cam. He was just trying to be nice! What harm was there in showing a little compassion now and then? And what did Jerud mean by 'man shoulders?' Cam's shoulders were a little wide, to be sure, but not manly. But what did it matter? Man shoulders or not, he certainly wasn't interested in her. Not at all. Despite her shapely rump. And her chestnut brown hair and bright, grey eyes. No, not interested at all.

Winny, trotting halfway between Mycah and Cam, kept looking back as if sensing a rift. Mycah hopped forward a few steps and gave the dog a good scratch over the ears. Losing Cam he could deal with, but he was starting to become very fond of Winny. Perhaps once Jerud left for good, he'd adopt a mutt of his own as a permanent companion.

With Cam setting a brisk pace, they made better progress than Mycah expected, but by midafternoon Mycah started to get an itchy feeling upon his neck again. At first he thought the Watchers had already found and caught up to them, but Cam assured him Winny would've sensed people approaching long before any of them would've noticed. Then Mycah realized that his neck wasn't itchy, but rather warm. Sun shone through the canopy onto his head and shoulders. The trees were thinning.

Mycah used the skills Pete had taught him, searching the forest and looking for clues. The trees were definitely getting younger, their bark not as thick and rough as that of the ancient oaken sentinels that populated the forest even a day's travel back. Judging by their height, the oaks and maples here had seen only thirty or forty winters, but they looked healthy and supple. Mycah tugged on a thin, low hanging branch. It sprung back into place once released, undulating the way young, pliable wood was wont to doing.

Above him, leaves rustling in a warm summer breeze sang a solemn melody, lacking the trills and chirps of the regular choir of swallows and thrushes. Sprouting acorns left over from last year's autumn littered the forest floor, untouched by squirrels or rodents. Thankfully, the lack of critters also seemed to extend to nightmarish demons. No two-headed abomination had yet to rear its head—or heads, as the case may be.

The thinning of mature trees accelerated over the next few leagues. With more sun reaching through, small shrubs and grasses covered every inch of the forest floor, as well as saplings that were no more than a few years old. Barely a step passed that Mycah wasn't assaulted by some over-aggressive bush.

Cam unsheathed her sword and began hacking at overgrown shrubs and encroaching saplings. Winny, Mycah, and Jerud followed in single file to make the travel easier. Mycah longed for a blade with which to fight back against the underbrush, but Jerud's lone knife had broken in the fight with the Watchers. Little good the short knife would've done anyway. The brush was getting so thick that even a well-honed scythe would've had trouble chopping through it.

With a hearty thwack, Cam's sword cut through a swath of leafy young elms. Cam gasped. Mycah's heart leapt. What had she seen? One of the cursed demons? He rushed forth, burst through the opening Cam's sword had created, and found himself gasping in kind.

A massive valley stretched before him, filled with lush, green, knee high grass that swayed lazily in the afternoon breeze. Not a single tree or bush marred the grassy waves. The tree line ended sharply at his sides, extending as far as the eye could see. Off to the left, the tree line snaked its way to the base of a range of rocky mountains, individual hillocks of which extended into the valley itself. Off to the right, it ended abruptly at the edge of a large lake perhaps five leagues away. The valley sloped downward gently toward the lake and the edge of the barren peaks before funneling into a passageway between the lake's shore and the edge of the last rocky crag. Off in the distance near the base of the last hillock, Mycah thought he saw a glint of reflected light. Snow glittered atop the tips of the mountains, but there seemed to be none at the bases.

"Lord Almighty," mumbled Jerud. He made the Lord's cross with his thumb and forefinger.

Cam, mouth open, looked as perplexed as Mycah felt. If this indeed was the Garden of Eden, it certainly didn't look particularly cursed. In fact, other than the lack of trees it looked downright fertile.

"Um, Cam... Are you sure we're in the right place?" asked Mycah.

"What?" said Cam, blinking. "Oh, uh... Yeah, of course I'm sure. This is the way I came before. This has to be it."

"Really?" asked Mycah, spreading his hands out before him. "*This* is the cursed Garden that scared the beeswax out of you?"

Cam gritted her teeth. "I told you, I never made it all the way here. And I wasn't scared of this blasted Garden. I saw a beast with two God-damned heads!"

Mycah raised an eyebrow but remained silent. Cam seemed ready to sock him in the face if he questioned her bravery again.

Jerud rummaged through his pack, looking for a map. He pulled out a well-worn piece of parchment and carefully unfolded it. He mumbled as he looked it over, rubbing his chin.

"Should be here... took the road east from Guildean... through Benton and Leesvale... straight shot... but so much grass? Doesn't seem right... but the Watchers came for us... must be around here somewhere..."

Mycah's hand went to his neck. Closing his eyes, Mycah clasped the pouch that hung there. His eyes sprung open. He could feel the heat radiating from within! The signature was faint, but he no longer had to struggle to feel it.

"Jerud," he said. "This is the place. We're getting closer."

Jerud looked up from his map. "You're sure, lad?"

"Yes."

Cam glared at Mycah suspiciously. "What's that around your neck?"

"Nothing," said Mycah hastily. "Look, I guess this is where we part ways."

"Yeah, I guess so," said Cam. Winny whined.

"Jerud, have you got some rations and coin for Cam? We made a deal, and I intend to honor it."

Jerud harrumphed. "*You* made a deal." He slung off his pack and began to dig through it.

"Just some rations will do, Chuckles," said Cam. "Your coin won't do me much good where I'm headed."

"Fine by me," said Jerud. He tossed Cam a couple small parcels wrapped in canvas, the first one flat and tied with string, the next one a pouch tied off at the top that rattled as it flew through the air. Jerky and beans most likely, though maybe it was barley in the second one. Cam caught them with ease.

"Alright then," said Cam. She hesitated. "Um, well… good luck I guess, with whatever crazy mess you're getting yourselves into. C'mon Winny, let's go."

Cam turned around and headed back into the woods. Winny sat firmly on her haunches and whined, tilting her head.

Cam turned back around. "Winny, now." She pointed in the direction of the woods.

Winny rose to her feet, tail held low between her legs, but she only took a couple steps toward Cam before turning to look back at Mycah.

"Winny! I'm not going to ask again."

Winny hesitated. Cam stepped toward her and reached for the scruff of her neck. Winny crouched and sprang backward, bounding off into the grass, barking as she went.

"God damn it! What the Hell's gotten into her."

Winny stood in the grass, perhaps ten paces from Mycah's feet. She looked back toward the trio and barked three times—a loud, low, excited woof.

Mycah cracked a smile. "If I didn't know any better, I'd say she wanted to come along."

Cam looked like she'd swallowed a lemon. Mycah raised an eyebrow. He thought only Jerud knew how to make that face.

"This is ridiculous," Cam said. "Winny, here. NOW!"

Winny bowed low, her front paws splayed before her, and barked.

"Winny, come on." Cam threw her hands out to her sides.

Winny barked again and lay down in the grass.

Mycah felt an inexplicable warmth spread through his chest, not from the stone that hung from his neck but from within. He smiled.

"Well. Looks like Winny's made her choice."

Cam turned to Mycah. "We're not coming with you."

"She's not coming with us," echoed Jerud.

Mycah flashed Jerud his grin before turning to Cam. "Come on. You know the stories, the legends. You're telling me you're not even the slightest bit curious about what's down in that valley? Doesn't it interest you at all? Winny clearly wants to go. Why not tag along? Or are you scared of the curse?"

Cam clenched her jaw, blood rushing to her cheeks. "I'm not scared of any damn curse. I just don't have any reason to come with you. I have enough problems of my own to get mixed up with a couple of sorry-ass thieves, a Stormqueen, and a bunch of pissed off Watchers. Seriously, come on Winny. I'm not joking."

The dog barked again but didn't budge.

"Look," said Mycah. "All I'm saying is—"

"ARRGH! Shut up!" yelled Cam. She pulled out her sword in a smooth motion. Mycah and Jerud jumped back in alarm, but Cam pivoted toward the tree line and attacked a stand of young elms with a furious energy. Wood chips and leaves flew as she mercilessly chopped at the trees, screaming in frustration as she hacked away. After a minute she dropped the sword, panting and heaving, sweat beading at her brow.

Mycah looked at Jerud, mouth agape. The big man shrugged. Cam slowly bent over and picked up her sword, then sheathed it. Her back to Mycah, she spoke.

"Fine. I'll tag along. But only because of Winny. And if we all die a horrible, slow, lingering death, either at the hands of the Watchers or your Stormqueen or Keralt or God himself, know that I objected to this whole stinking, sodden, brain-addled sheep's taint of an endeavor."

"Um, noted," said Mycah.

And who's Keralt?

"Well then, what are you waiting for?" said Cam, heading off into the grass. "There's still daylight left. We should get moving."

***

Rayven plunged his finger into the damp earth and brought it to his tongue. The soil tasted tangy and tart with an aroma of fresh rain, pollen, and worms, but it possessed a distinctly metallic aftertaste. An aftertaste of blood.

Rayven stood and brushed his finger upon his pant leg. As he turned, he surveyed the area. The remains of a fire languished in the center of the clearing, and though someone had made a concerted effort to tidy up the campsite, all evidence pointed to a fight having taken place. The bodies would be nearby, undoubtedly.

"They were here," said Rayven, his voice flowing forth like the waters of a river finally released by spring's first thaw.

Johnah and Sten eyed him with suspicion.

"You sure?" asked Johnah.

Rayven leveled him with a cold stare. "If I'm unsure, I don't speak."

Johnah chewed his lip like a cow chewing cud. It was a look that rivaled his usual blank expression for best display of complete ineptitude. At least a glimmer of intelligence shone behind Sten's eyes, though it had nearly been extinguished by years of service in the Stormqueen's employ. Following commands, acquiescing, always responding to the demands of others before one's own needs—it had a way of dulling one's wits. Rayven would have to be keenly aware of his own mental faculties while accepting the Stormqueen's coin. The waste of his mind would be a tragedy far more terrible than the waste of one such as Sten's. Rayven glanced back at Johnah. He wasn't sure if toiling in the Stormqueen's employ had dulled that lout's wits, though perhaps being dropped on his head as a child had.

"No, I see it," said Sten. "Hard to tell exactly what happened. They cleaned up pretty well, but by the blood I'd say there were four, maybe five dead."

"Hell yes!" said Johnah, punching one fist into another. "Maybe we'll finally see some action. I wouldn't mind cracking some bandit skulls."

"No," said Sten, shaking his head. "This is bad, Johnah. This wasn't a bandit attack. This is Watcher territory. No bandit is stupid enough to hang out here. Either those thieves got themselves killed, or even worse, they killed a bunch of Watchers—in which case we've got ourselves a serious barrel of stink-all brewing."

Rayven nodded. Sten at least possessed a modicum of deductive ability. But only a modicum.

"The thieves survived. And they had assistance."

Sten turned his head toward Rayven. "And how do you figure that?"

Rayven considered drawing the answer out of Sten slowly, forcing him to think through the problem by providing clues that would guide him in the proper direction. But what would be the point? Whatever deductive skills the guard once had were likely flabby from disuse, like the muscles of a retired strongman. The thought reminded him of Jerud and subsequently of Mycah. At least the thieves had shown some creativity—even a little moxie at times. Rayven sighed.

"No trail exists heading back toward the road. Hence, they survived."

"Fair enough," said Sten. "But how do you know they had help?"

Rayven pointed to a spot near the remains of the campfire. "Paw prints."

Sten grunted and nodded. Johnah stuck his lower lip out, his brow furrowing as he attempted to work out the details. He looked like he might injure himself trying to form a coherent thought.

"So, what now?" asked Johnah.

"The Watchers'll be on their way," said Sten. "We don't want to be here when they arrive. We should leave. Seek out the thieves and get them out of this mess while we still can."

Rayven's eyes narrowed. "No. The equation has changed. An unknown variable exists. We'll watch and wait. If needed, we'll act. For now, we seek out the missing piece of the puzzle."

"Missing piece? What missing piece?"

Rayven headed off into the trees, leaving a confused pair in his wake. Buffoons, both of them—though what else did he expect? If neither had noticed the addition to the thieves' entourage, then neither would notice the subtraction either. He shook his head. At least he'd soon have some more appropriate, though most certainly more hostile, company.

CHAPTER TWENTY-ONE

A Garden Unlike
any Other

Mycah rubbed his eyes and tried to stifle a yawn as he trudged through the tall grass. He'd slept fitfully the night before, having dreamt of leathery winged demons with sharp teeth and clacking claws. They'd circled above him, stretching their talons toward the stone he carried upon his chest. Mycah had slapped their claws away, taking deep gouges on his arms as his did so, desperately trying to keep the stone out of the demons' clutches. As he furiously battled the encroaching monsters, the stone grew hotter and hotter and began to glow, turning from dull red to orange to bright yellow until it blazed as bright as the sun and seared his chest with a burning hiss. The grasses around him withered, dried, and burst into raging hot flames. As the light of the stone consumed the demons and grasslands and his own body in turn, Mycah felt only rapture, not pain.

Mycah shook his head. If the dream were a premonition about the Garden's curse, he'd yet to figure it out. But curse or no curse, there was something inherently eerie about the empty grasslands. No trees, deer, birds, squirrels, hares, or mice—nothing but tall, vibrant blades as far as the eye could see, waving and swaying in the wind.

They'd camped upon a patch of the lush turf and, lacking any firewood to burn, had eaten a cold supper. Mycah had tried to convince Jerud to light a torch from his pack, but the big man had insisted they save them for later, mumbling something about needing them to descend into Hell and back. Cam had mocked him for being scared of the dark.

Mycah frowned as he glanced back at Cam. Blasted woman! Scared of the dark? He'd never used those precise words. He'd simply expressed an adequate concern for what might be lurking in the darkness. Like, say, *ravenous demons*. Besides, it was clear that Cam was also on edge. For one thing, she'd foregone her morning exercise routine, citing a lack of branches or stumps or some such nonsense. While the excuse was plausible, Mycah suspected anxiety was the true culprit. Cam kept checking her sword to make sure it was still in its sheath—where would it have gone?—and every so often she'd give Winny a nervous pat on the back. Even Winny, who'd initially bounded up to several hundred paces in front of them through the tall grass, now stuck close, trotting stiffly between them.

Mycah led the way through the grassy vale, his fingers intermittently probing the pouch at his chest. It felt faintly warm, just as it had earlier in the day and the prior afternoon. Despite explaining to Jerud that the stone's warmth was hardly a precise indicator of direction, Jerud insisted

Mycah lead. The big man argued that even though the stone might be a poor indicator, it was the only one they possessed.

Given the stone wasn't being of much use, Mycah was forced to rely upon his gut, and so he headed toward the glint he'd seen past where the lake and the mountains nearly met. The glint had drawn his eyes the prior afternoon, and when he'd awoken in the morning he'd sworn he'd seen the sun once again reflect off something just past the last mountaintop. Lacking any other ideas, he'd headed straight for it, and no one had argued against him. After all, the only thing populating the massive valley was grass, so it made sense that the Garden, if it did exist, hid behind the long arms of the rocky mountain range.

As he marched, the mountains to his left approached like quiet sentinels. Mycah found himself staring at the hillsides. Like the valley the mountains were devoid of trees, instead covered by waves of knee-high grass and capped with rakish berets of sparkling white snow. Mycah had never really considered the close relationship between mountains and trees, but upon seeing the first without the latter, he found it was a disconcerting sight, like a hairless cat.

The sun soared high overhead as they neared the last hillock. Mycah paused and lifted his hand to shield his eyes. There it was again—the glint! He was sure he'd seen it this time. It had come from just over the hill in front of them.

Mycah grasped the pouch at his neck. It was definitely warmer. There was no doubt about it now.

"We're close," said Mycah. "I can feel it."

Cam eyed him suspiciously. "You still haven't elaborated on what that thing is."

"It's because I don't know what it is exactly," said Mycah as he drew his fingers back. "It's some stone the Stormqueen gave us. Lets me know where we're going. It gets warmer the closer we get to our target."

Cam laughed. "You've got to be kidding me. Seriously? It gets warmer? That's the oldest cliché in the book. Next you're going to tell me you've been leaving a trail of grain for us to follow when we leave."

"Look," said Jerud. "It doesn't matter what it is or how it works. If it leads us to what we're looking for, that's all that matters. Now let's keep moving. I don't know if this place is cursed or not, but it gives me the heebie jeebies, and I'd like to get in and get out as quickly as possible."

Jerud marched off ahead.

"What's up his bum?" asked Cam.

"I don't know. Jerud's always put a lot of faith in scripture. I'd wager this whole thing has him pretty spooked. I mean, you can't tell me you don't think this place is a little... off?"

Cam snorted. "Told you. I don't believe in curses."

Mycah rolled his eyes and hurried to catch up with Jerud.

As he skirted around the last of the foothills and into the passageway near the lake's shore, an unexpected vista rose before his eyes. The grassy valley extended far off into the distance, ringed to the west and north by the mountains and to the east by the expansive lake. The valley sloped gently downward, and in the center of it all stood a single, solitary peak of epic scope, both more bizarre and more majestic than any he'd ever seen.

The simple isolation of the mountain surprised him, but that was far from the only odd thing about it. The mountain loomed taller than any other in the surrounding range, and yet its proportions were all wrong. It seemed too wide at the base in one direction and not wide enough at the base in another. The peak rose up out of the earth at a slight tilt, its sides impossibly steep, and jagged crags stuck out near the top at unnatural angles like the quills of an angered porcupine. The mountain appeared as if it had been crushed by an immense power eons ago, leveling half of it and leaving the other half shying away in terror.

Hulking boulders and piles of lifeless rubble clawed at the structure's base like beggars pleading at the foot of a king, but grasses and vines also clung precariously to the mountain's cliff-like sides, giving it a living coat of greenery. As the sun shone on the colossal crag, light filtered into deep fissures and flashed off what appeared to be veins of pure silver. At the base of the mountain, a massive fissure nearly divided it in two, creating a yawning void of inky blackness that stretched into the bowels of the earth.

"The Garden..." said Jerud breathlessly. "I never thought I'd see the day."

"Garden? What Garden?" said Cam. "All I see is an old busted mountain."

Jerud's unblinking gaze focused on the enormous pinnacle before them. "No lass," he said, too awed to argue. "That's the Garden. Has to be. It's right in the ancient texts, right at the end of Genesis. *So the Lord God banished man from the Garden of Eden to work the ground from which he'd been taken. After He drove man out, He blasted the land with the full force of His might, leveling it and setting His curse upon it, to protect the tree of good and evil from man.* Just look at that mountain, of what's left of it. What power other than the Lord's could've done that?"

Cam seemed unconvinced. "I don't know, old man. I don't see why the Garden of Eden would be on a mountain."

"Not just any mountain," said Jerud with a far off look in his eyes. "The grandest mountain in all the lands. Can you just imagine it? How it must've looked before the Lord leveled it? It must've reached all the way to the heavens! Don't you see? It makes perfect sense. The Garden was the closest point to heaven upon God's green earth before He destroyed it. I reckon the tree of knowledge was right at the top."

Mycah rubbed his chin. "Maybe, Jerud, maybe... But the texts say God cursed the land to protect the tree. If you're right, then where's the tree now?"

Jerud stuck out a meaty finger, pointing it at the giant fissure. "What better way to protect the tree... than to send it to the pits of Hell?"

"You can't be serious?" said Cam.

Jerud turned toward the woman, his eyes harder than Mycah had ever seen them. "Take a look. There's nothing on that mountain but dirt and grass. Even if there were something up there, those slopes are far too steep for a mere mortal to climb. Whatever's left of the Garden is buried within. And that fissure is the only entrance."

"You're not actually suggesting..." Mycah's voice trailed off.

"I told you we might need those torches, lad." Jerud pulled himself into a proud stance. "I gave you my word that I'd stick with you through thick and thin, Mycah. You ready for this?"

Mycah swallowed, his mouth a little dry. "Yeah, Jerud, I'm ready."

As the words came out of his mouth, Mycah realized they were true. He was ready for whatever lay before them. In fact, he felt a strange sense of calmness, his mind overtaken by curiosity rather than foreboding. What was left of the Garden? What would he and Jerud find? What ancient secrets would they unearth? Assuming he survived both the Garden and the Stormqueen's curses, he'd have quite the story to tell.

Mycah turned to Cam. "So... you still in?"

Cam looked a little pale, as if her heart was having a hard time pumping blood to her face. "Damn it all to Hell... You guys are as crazy as weevils hopped up on turpentine, you know that?"

Mycah raised an eyebrow. "Um, you've said something to that effect before, yeah."

Cam hung her head and muttered another curse. Winny sat beside her and nuzzled her hand. Moments passed. Mycah was about to ask her if she was all right when she finally lifted her head. Her jaw was clenched and fire raged in her eyes. "Blast it all... Alright. Let's do this."

Mycah glanced at Jerud. The big man gave a solemn nod. Mycah peered down at Winny. She tilted her head and looked at him quizzically. Mycah lifted his head, took a deep breath, and set forth.

The sheer size of the mountain belied its proximity. The sun marched steadily toward the horizon as they approached the towering peak, sending long shadows looming across the grassland, extending like the fingers of the dead reaching for the souls of the living. The sun's rays glittered off the small faults that bestrewed the mountain, giving rise to a shower of sparkles that punctured the deepening shadows.

With the sun low in the sky, they neared the giant fissure. The yawning chasm stretched deep into the bowels of the earth. When observed from up close, the giant void seemed even more unnatural than before, as if it had been torn asunder by enormous hands. *Perhaps God's own hands?* The thought seemed absurd, yet how else would God have leveled the Garden if not by his own hand?

Jerud rummaged in his pack and withdrew three torches. Soaking the ends with lamp oil from a waterskin, he brought them to life with a fire steel and stuck them in the ground before him, one by one. As Jerud worked, Mycah slipped the pouch over his neck and loosened the drawstring. He slipped the Stormqueen's stone into his palm and closed his fingers around it. He could easily feel the heat now, warming his hand like a freshly boiled egg. He hoped it wouldn't get so hot as to burn him.

Once finished, Jerud grabbed a torch and rose. "I've got some extra rags and oil but probably only enough for tonight. Let's hope we can find what we need and get out before long."

Mycah and Cam each grasped burning brands. Winny, ears flat against her head, gave a nervous whine.

Jerud tilted his head toward Mycah's closed fist. "We're following you, lad."

"I still don't know how useful this stone is going to be," said Mycah. "If it comes down to choosing between paths, I'm not sure I'll know which one to take."

"Just follow your gut then, lad. If we take a wrong turn, we can always double back. Let's just hope that where we're going there's roads for mortal men."

Mycah nodded and turned toward the gaping void. With the light around them fading, he held his burning brand before him and stepped into the chasm.

At first, he felt as if he were stepping into a massive cave, one that would make a welcome den for a bear or saber cat, but the cave lacked the musk of a predator or the stench of decaying offal. Instead the cavern smelt sterile, like ancient bricks and hammered steel. A fine layer of rubble covered the floor, crunching under his feet as he walked. Even with three burning torches, the light from the brands quickly faded into the void, illuminating little other than their feet. Soon only a slit of light from the fissure's entrance was visible. Torch held high, Mycah strained his eyes, trying to make out any sort of feature from within the cavern.

Suddenly, he saw a glimmer—light from the torches dancing, playing, weaving through and around something in front of them. He headed toward it.

"Is that... *ice?*"

"Come on, really?" asked Cam. "You don't think Hell froze over do you?"

Jerud peered into the darkness. "I saw something too, lad. Could be ice. You never know. More than one theologian has hypothesized that the torments of Hell might consist of bitter frost as easily as burning flames." Jerud wiped his sweaty brow upon his sleeve. "Of course, doesn't feel too cold in here, does it?"

It didn't. The air felt warm and stuffy. Stale even. Mycah supposed it was preferable to the flesh-searing winds of damnation.

The dancing reflections grew closer. Soon the torches revealed a wall stretching into the blackness. Its surface was a dark, glossy, gunmetal grey, but it shone like a mirror. Gazing into it was like gazing into a still pond under the darkness of the crescent moons.

Hand still clutching the stone, Mycah held two fingers toward the gleaming surface. He half expected to see ripples extend from his fingertips as they touched, but instead they met a faintly cool, solid wall. Mycah pulled back his hand, leaving two greasy smudges on the otherwise pristine barrier.

"Well, this sure isn't what I was expecting," said Jerud.

"Yeah, me neither," said Mycah. "Why would there be a wall here?"

"Same reason there're walls anywhere else. To keep people out." Jerud pointed. "Look. There, to the left."

A dark patch in the wall... maybe an opening? Mycah crept forward.

"Looks like another fissure," he said, brandishing the flaming torch before him. "I think there's a path through. A corridor. Made of the same glassy stuff as this wall."

Crouching, Mycah squeezed through the opening. Cam came next, followed by Winny. Jerud huffed and wheezed as he attempted to squeeze his bulk through the crack.

"Can you fit?" asked Mycah.

"Urgh... gimme a sec lad. I'll make it..."

Jerud lurched through the opening, landing on the floor like a greased pig.

Cam chortled.

"Something funny there, lass?"

"Oh, nothing." Cam tried to suppress a snort. "Just that, you know, since gluttony is supposed to be a sin and all I thought it'd be a little easier for fat people to get into Hell."

Mycah couldn't help but crack a smile despite the situation. Jerud frowned and mumbled a number of unintelligible things. "Got big bones... can't help it if the years have added a few pounds... still strong as an ox... no respect nowadays..."

Perhaps it was his imagination, but Mycah thought the stone felt a touch warmer. "Come on," he said. "Let's keep moving."

At the first intersection of corridors, Mycah paused and stood with his eyes closed and his fist held out before him, trying to see if the stone would impart some grand wisdom that would reveal the proper path. It did nothing of the sort. Cam chuckled nervously and said he looked like a blind soothsayer. Given a total lack of cooperation on the stone's part, Mycah decided to head straight as long as possible. At least that would make finding their way out a little easier.

Soon they came across a door. It was set in the wall, recessed by the width of a couple fingers and solidly sealed.

No handholds, knobs, or locks of any kind marred its surface, and though there appeared to be faded markings painted upon it, age had rendered them illegible. The wall outside the door was similarly barren, though at the door's right a square of a dark grey, almost black, material rested ominously. It looked like broken glass. Webs of fine cracks littered its surface, but between the cracks a waxy material had seeped and congealed into hard, crystalline globules, like honey left sitting in a poorly sealed jar.

Mycah rubbed his forehead with the side of his fist. "This isn't right Jerud. Where are we? What is this place?"

The big man rubbed his chin, and his voice shook slightly as he spoke. "I don't know, lad."

"I mean, first we came here expecting to find the Garden of Eden. But this isn't a garden. It's not even above ground. How could anything possibly grow here? So maybe it turns out we're actually heading into the pits of Hell instead. But you can't tell me this is it! It's not like any Hell I've ever heard of. I mean, are there passageways in hell? And doors? Where's the fire and the brimstone? Where are we?"

"I DON'T KNOW, DAMN IT!" Jerud hung his head and wiped his hand slowly across his face. He looked exhausted. "I don't have the answers, lad. This isn't what I expected either, trust me."

Jerud sagged against the wall. "The Stormqueen knew this would happen. She warned us. Said the Garden was beyond what we could imagine. Well, here we are. I certainly didn't imagine this…"

Mycah looked at Jerud's slumped form. If this was hard to accept for him, he who'd been a skeptic his entire life, it must be soul-wrenching for someone as faithful as Jerud.

"Sorry for the outburst, big guy. Are you alright?"

Jerud sighed. "I'm confused, lad. Tired and confused. Not sure what to believe in or what to expect. Not to mention I feel a stomachache coming on. Probably got an ulcer from all this blasted worrying I've been doing."

Now that Jerud mentioned it, Mycah felt a little sluggish himself. Perhaps it was the stuffy air.

"I can't believe you two," said Cam. "Sitting here whining like you're upset we didn't waltz right into the blazing fires of Hell. I sure don't know what's going on here, but I'll take this spooky underground maze over a demon-infested hellhole any day, sure as a horse's hooves. So stop pussyfooting around and go find whatever the Hell you two are looking for!"

Winny make a sort of *aroo* sound as she yawned widely, as if unimpressed with the entire ordeal.

"I'm not upset, lass," said Jerud as he pulled himself off the wall. "Just conflicted."

As they walked they passed more intersections of corridors and more sealed doors, each with a similar dark grey square located at the side. Eventually the passage spit them out into a cavernous empty room. Here the metallic floor gave way to dirt—a bone-dry, crumbly soil that smelled of musty books. Not wishing to get lost within the expansive depths, Mycah hugged the side of the chamber, working his way around. Curved, basin-like protrusions stuck out from the wall at knee height at regular intervals, fashioned of the same glossy metallic substance that seemed to be everywhere. At the far end of the chamber, the smooth wall gave way to alcoves built into the wall itself, each large enough to fit a dozen men abreast. The alcoves, too, were largely empty except for lifeless, tentacle-like coils that protruded from holes in the wall like the spines of dead cattle picked clean by scavengers. Mycah thought he saw bleached bones protruding from the dirt in one of the stalls. He swallowed back a lump in his throat and moved on.

The next room featured more alcoves built into the walls, but they resembled display cases more than anything else. Most were partially covered by thick, cracked glass, while a fine mesh of some strong, flexible substance covered others. The remains of massive tanks lay discarded around the room alongside oblong vessels that seemed like they could've been used to store ale or lamp oil.

Jerud paused to rewrap and resoak the torches, which were burning a little low. While Cam wandered with Winny, Mycah walked over to a tank whose glass lining was still intact. With his fingernail, he tapped on the shell. A dull clink sounded out. The glass was thick, but the tank was empty, lifeless, and bare, just like everything else present.

Why were these objects here? And what were they? Mycah knelt down and sifted through the refuse. Debris of all kinds littered the floor: thin chips of glass that seemed to have come from dinnerware, scraps of paper that crumbled to dust under his fingertips, rusty metal shards and objects made of a substance both brittle and incredibly light. Mycah picked up a cylindrical object about half the length of his forearm and curled his fingers around it. It fit into his palm perfectly and felt as if it were some sort of tool, like the handle to a hammer or a carpenter's plane.

"Say Jerud," said Mycah nervously as he peered at the object in his hand. "How does the creation narrative go again?"

Jerud looked up from the torches. "What? What are you talking about, lad?"

"Genesis. The creation narrative. How does it go?"

"Mycah, I don't know what you're getting at exactly—"

"After God created the heavens and the lands and the seas, after he created the plants and the animals, then what?"

Jerud sighed. "*After God brought forth the living creatures, each according to their kind, and everything that creeps along the ground according to its kind, He said, 'Let us create man'—*"

"—'*in our image.*' Man was created in God's image." Mycah stood, handle still held tight in his fist. "But does the narrative say anything about *how* God created us?"

"He used his divine power."

"But what if it was more than that?" Turning to Jerud, Mycah felt a surge of understanding flow through his mind. Words poured out of him. "Man uses tools to craft the things he needs. Hammers, chisels, planes, augers. If man is crafted in God's image, then wouldn't it make sense that God crafted man using tools of his own?"

Mycah spread out his hands. "Look around us, Jerud. Don't you see what this all is? Tanks, pens, cages for animals. The last room we were in? I'd wager those alcoves were stalls, for cattle or horses! You remember what the Stormqueen said? She said the Garden existed, that is wasn't what we expected but that it *was* the land of our creation. Well this is it. This must be where God created man!"

Jerud took a deep breath. "Lad,—*if*—you're right, and that's a big if, that would mean God himself was once here, right here, in this very room."

Mycah's tongue scraped against the roof of his suddenly parched mouth. "Jerud, the Stormqueen also said that God still resided here. What if she's right? What if he's still here?"

Cam emitted a high-pitched squeal. Mycah grabbed a torch and whirled in her direction as several things happened at once. Dim blue lights streamed from slim crevices in the floor sending eerie shadows flickering across the ceiling. A faint humming sound began to emanate from all around. Winny barked furiously, alternating her deep powerful yelps with rumbling growls. Cam's sword rasped as it roared out of its sheath. And the stone in Mycah's hand pulsed.

Mycah and Jerud ran to join Cam and found her, sword drawn, standing in front of an open door.

"What happened?" asked Mycah.

"I don't know," said Cam. "I was looking at this thing." She gestured toward the dull grey protrusion next to the door, except it wasn't dull grey like the others. It shone a pale blue like the lights that gleamed through the ground. The square waxed and waned, first brighter and then fainter, but always the same pale blue. "I think my hand might've brushed against it, and the next thing I know this door whizzes open and all Hell breaks loose!"

"That's it?" said Jerud. "You just touched the square?"

"Yeah, I think so," said Cam.

"Well touch it again. See what happens."

"Are you crazy? Who knows what could happen! What if it blows my arm off?"

"I thought you said you weren't scared of anything."

"I said I wasn't scared of curses. I didn't say I wasn't—"

"Guys, guys," said Mycah. "The stone... it's pulsing now. Regularly. Cam, whatever you did, I think you awakened it."

It was true. The stone throbbed, not painfully or uncomfortably, but quite obviously.

Mycah stepped through the open door. Lights trailed along both sides of the passageway, leading in a singular direction. "Come on, let's follow the lights!"

Jerud snagged Mycah's arm. "Mycah, wait. It could be a trap."

Mycah held up his fist and uncurled his fingers. A faint orange light pulsated from the center of the stone, weaving around the swirls of midnight and reflecting off the flecks of silver that studded its depths.

"Jerud, we've got to follow the stone. And the stone is telling me this is the way to go. Now come on, both of you!"

Mycah jogged down the corridor, feeling a surge of adrenaline as he ran. What a stroke of luck that Cam had somehow found their path forward! Good thing he'd convinced her to come along. He'd have to rub that fact in Jerud's face later when the opportunity presented itself.

Despite the adrenaline, Mycah's muscles soon felt heavy, as though he'd run a league through wet sand. As he twisted around a corner, he was forced to slow into a steady trot. He half expected Cam to chide him with another sly remark about her superior physique, but surprisingly she also looked tired for once.

Through corridors and around corners Mycah went, always following the eerie blue lights that shone from the floor. Passing through an open archway, they encountered a dead end.

"Blast! What now?" said Mycah.

"Maybe Cam can feel up the wall and hope for another miracle," said Jerud.

"Now listen here—" growled Cam.

The doors of the archway behind them slammed shut. The humming Mycah had noticed earlier intensified.

"Oh, great. I told you this was a trap!" Jerud began to prod at the juncture of the doors.

"What the Hell did you say?" Cam shoved Jerud in the back. "'Feel up the wall'? What do you think I am, some sort of tramp?"

Jerud turned and straightened. "What in the world are you blathering about?"

"Do you have any idea how offensive that was?"

Mycah felt a tremor. "Um, guys—"

"Oh for crying out loud missy, get over yourself. We've got bigger things to worry about here."

"I don't have to take any guff from you, you giant sack of suet!"

"Oh, so it's time to hurl insults now, is it?"

The stone in Mycah's hand began to pulse rapidly, the heat filling his fist. "Guys—"

Winny growled, a low deep sound in the back of her throat.

"You better watch it, fat man. Winny'll rip your face off, and if she doesn't I might!"

"Oh, wonderful. Now I won't have to worry about starving to death in this God forsaken Hellhole. Instead I can just die a peaceful death after having my innards torn out by a savage bitch!"

The stone throbbed wildly. "GUYS!" yelled Mycah.

The doors burst open. Jerud, still leaning against them, toppled over and fell onto his rear with a thud.

The stone in Mycah's hand quit pulsating, instead emitting a steady, potent radiance. With his palm sweaty and starting to throb in its own right, he slipped the oblong stone back into the pouch around his neck.

Jerud stood up and dusted off his pants. "What in the blazes..."

Mycah looked around. What in the blazes, indeed.

CHAPTER TWENTY-TWO

The Tree of Knowledge

Rather than leading back to the corridor through which they'd entered, the doors opened into a mid-sized circular room with a domed ceiling like the top of an observatory. A raised dais circled the room's perimeter, with waist-high handrails at the edge. In front of them, perhaps a dozen steps led down to a flat circular expanse. At the other side of the room, another set of steps led to an archway like the one through which they'd entered. To Mycah's left and right, more steps led to corridors or stairs—he couldn't make out which in the darkness. Pale blue lights shone from the floor in two rows leading to a pedestal at the center of the room. Above the pedestal floated a perfect globe of what appeared to be liquid metal, levitating half a handspan in the air.

Cam gazed up and around at the glassy ceiling overhead. "Where are we?"

Winny sniffed nervously at the floor, stepping carefully and methodically forward.

285

"Looks like a solarium," said Jerud. "Except there's no sun." He pointed overhead. "Are those stars?"

Thankfully the wonder of the new environs had doused the fire between Cam and Jerud. Mycah looked up at the big man's insistence. The ceiling twinkled as if studded with thousands of far off stars, but it must've been an illusion. Unlike the night sky, the ceiling featured no clouds, no moons, no trace of dust or birds or insects—just faint flickering lights. Tens of thousands of them. The lights appeared to be impossibly far off, but they couldn't be stars. The constellations were all wrong.

The heat from the Stormqueen's stone seeped into Mycah's chest, causing his armpits to perspire and his neck to feel itchy. He wiped his sweaty palms upon his pants.

"Jerud, we're here. As soon as those doors opened the stone stopped pulsing. And now it's as hot as a coal. That tablet the Stormqueen sent us to get has got to be here." Mycah eyed the blue lights shining up from the floor. "And I bet I know where it is."

Mycah descended the steps to the circular expanse below and stared at the pedestal. The shimmering globe floated in the still air as if held there by nothing more than God's own will. Its surface was perfectly smooth, like a pool of molten steel pulled straight from a crucible. Mycah slowly approached the pedestal, each step sending reverberations around the empty chamber. As he neared the globe, he noticed that lights glowed faintly from the surface. Five ellipses, four in a line and one to the side, emitting a pale blue light.

"Be careful, lad. There's some powerful force in here. I can feel it in my bones."

Jerud's voice seemed far away. The closer Mycah came to the sphere, the more strongly it drew him toward it. He couldn't tear his eyes from the globe. The points of light seemed so familiar, so unique.

Like fingerprints.

He stretched out his hand, his fingers shaking in anticipation.

Jerud yelled. "Mycah, NO!"

But it was too late. Mycah pressed his fingertips into the glowing points, inhaled sharply and...

"Nothing happened," said Mycah.

Jerud was instantly at Mycah's side. "Really? Nothing at all?"

"No. Nothing."

"That's odd. I could've sworn I felt something deep in my chest, just as you stretched your hand out. Like a thickening of the air."

Mycah's eyebrows rose. "You felt it too?"

"Yeah. I was worried you might burst into flames." Jerud rubbed his chin with his meaty paw. "Here, let me try."

Jerud stretched out his hand, dangling it over the globe. After an instant of hesitation, he pressed his fingers into the glowing lights.

Jerud pulled his hand back and chewed on his lip. "You're right. Nothing."

Sweat poured from Mycah's brow and from underneath his shirt. "Well the tablet's got to be close. This stone is about to burn a hole in my chest."

"Look around," said Jerud. "Maybe we can find it lying around here somewhere."

Jerud waved his torch around looking for creases in the floors and walls, anywhere that something might be hidden. Mycah did the same, inspecting the base of the pedestal, looking for junctures, buttons, or marking. Unfortunately, the entire stand was seamless and perfect, fashioned from a single piece of the now-familiar glassy metallic substance.

Mycah scratched his head as he crouched beside the pedestal. His sweat was soaking through his shirt. Blasted stone! Where in the blazes could the tablet be? There didn't seem to be anywhere to hide the darned thing, and yet here the stone was, burning away like the fires of Hell! It would've been nice if the Stormqueen had given them a little more to go on. Hopefully her description of the tablet hadn't also been some abstract metaphor. But Mycah didn't think she'd do that to Jerud and him. It wouldn't serve her purposes if they came back empty handed.

Cam sauntered over, Winny at her side. She gestured at the ball. "So what is this thing, anyway?"

"I don't know," said Mycah. "I thought it would show us where the tablet is. But it doesn't seem to do anything."

Cam gazed into the sphere, her eyes lost in the depths of the shining globe. "There's something... powerful about it. A heaviness. Something that draws me in..."

Mycah nodded nonchalantly. "Yeah. Jerud and I both felt it too. Strange, huh?"

Cam pressed her fingers into the points of light. As she did so, Mycah felt a *whump* as a wave of pressurized air hit him in the chest, nearly knocking him over. Cam arched her back and screamed, a cry of pure agony streaming from between her lips, her hand shaking but riveted to the globe.

"Cam!" Mycah pounced up and reached to tear her away from the sphere as Winny barked frantically. He grasped Cam's arm.

***

Images and words. Just images and words. And yet so much more. More than letters, more than globs of paint, more than the passions and terrors and joys and sorrows represented within.

Stars screaming by, faster than an arrow, faster than a musket ball, faster than the rays of the sun and the dancing of the moons. Flickering points of light turned into rays of bright white brilliance. Streaking, streaming, shining. Here now, then gone, like the memories of a faded age. Such speed, such grace, such wonder. Such uncertainty.

Heavens.

An infinitesimal point, like a single snowflake in a blizzard. So far. So far and yet so close. An infinitesimal point, now larger than a man, larger than a mountain, larger even than the mind's own capacity to understand it. Soil, fertile and brown, falling between fingers, packed by generations of bare feet. Unyielding. Bearer of burdens. Water, flowing, falling from the sky, bringing life, washing away tears. So many tears.

Earth.

A blazing inferno, towering, consuming. Raging, uncontrolled, unbridled. Free. Deepest red, the color of blood. Steel, forged in flame, yet cold as death. Steel, flashing, slashing, taking. Always taking. And yet creating.

Structures of grandeur, of opulence, of decadence. Of power. Of deceit.

Fire. Metal.

A newborn babe, cradled in arms, arms of rapture, arms of joy. Giving, protecting, limiting, striking. Fists, raised in the air like flags, like weapons, like beacons of hope, like harbingers of death. Fear in a mother's eyes, a flash, a broken heap. Blood. Always blood. So much blood. And tears. Not enough tears to wash away the blood.

Man.

Vision. A vision of worlds, a vision of freedom, a vision of rebirth. Power, immense power, burning brighter than a million suns, pushing, prodding, soaring like a hawk. More metal. More anger. More blood. More joy. Cascades of joy, but also fear. Fear of the unknown. Fear of rebirth. Fear of God. Fear of man.

Fate. Faith.

Waiting. Endless waiting. Slumber, deep enough to soothe, deep enough to dull, deep enough to unravel. Memories lost. Lost to the void. An endless void. Endless waiting.

Faith.

Waiting. Endless waiting.

Faith.

Endless waiting.

Faith.

***

Mycah crashed to the floor. Above him he saw a figure. A man. Jerud. *Images.* His lips were moving. Creating sounds. *Words.* Many words.

"Mycah! Are you alright? Can you hear me? Are you alright?"

His head throbbed, not from pain, but from *density*. So many images. So many ideas. Mycah tried to recall them, but the throbbing only worsened. *So much blood.*

"Mycah! Can you hear me?"

"Yes, Jerud, I can hear you." Mycah clutched the side of his head.

"Are you alright?"

"I'm—" How could he respond to that? His brain felt as if it had been pressed through a fine sieve and reconstructed, piece by piece, memory by memory.

"I'm... fine. I think. What happened?"

Jerud rubbed at his eyes. Was he crying? "You grabbed Cam and screamed, frozen in place just like her. I didn't know what to do, lad, so I did the first thing that came to mind. I tackled the two of you using my pack as a shield."

"How long were we out?"

"What do you mean?"

"How long has it been?"

"I don't know. Seconds, maybe? It all just happened."

Mycah's eyes widened. Seconds? It had felt like years. Lifetimes. Generations.

Cam groaned and stirred. Winny was at her side, licking her face furiously. Mycah had never seen a dog so worried and yet so relieved.

Cam clutched her head. "Ugh... what was that? What happened?"

"You touched the globe and went rigid," said Mycah. "I tried to save you but... I failed, I guess. I don't remember. Jerud saved us. I think."

"Urgh…" said Cam. "My head. It feels… *packed*. Like a rucksack stuffed with too many clothes."

Mycah rubbed his temple. "Did you see… *visions?*"

Cam fixed her eyes upon him, mouth slightly open. "What did you see?"

"I saw…" Mycah tried to concentrate. But all he could see was—

"Jerud!" Mycah exclaimed. "Look, the pedestal!"

Near the base of the pedestal, where before the metal had lain smooth and seamless, a narrow mouth-like opening now yawned. Within it, a flat, tome-like object glimmered in the pale blue light.

Jerud crammed his meaty fingers into the opening and extracted a glossy, metallic slab—perhaps a hand by a hand and a half in size and two fingers thick, though grasped as it was in Jerud's gargantuan paws it may have been larger than it looked.

"The tablet," Mycah said breathlessly.

Cam was making odd expressions as she tried to stretch her face muscles. "Is that what you two are after?"

"It's got to be. It matches the Stormqueen's description exactly."

"Good," said Cam with a groan. "Then let's grab it and get the Hell out of here before I retch up whatever's left in my stomach. I think that sphere did a number on my bowels."

Mycah felt a little queasy himself, but the sensation of uneasiness had been nagging at him for some time now, certainly since before the incident with the globe. He also felt tired. Extremely tired. How late was it? It was impossible to tell from so deep within the mountain's underbelly, but Mycah would've guessed they'd entered only a few hours prior. The all-consuming fatigue in his muscles made it seem as if they'd been wandering the corridors for days. Perhaps his fatigue stemmed from the strange visions. *Endless waiting.*

Mycah stood and offered Cam a hand while Jerud stuffed the tablet in his backpack. Cam gingerly placed her hand in his. As Mycah pulled her up, he felt her callused palm press into his own, but his thumb slid across the smooth, delicate skin on the back of her hand. Cam's hand fit neatly in his, and despite the calluses it felt feminine— not at all what he expected from a woman of Cam's demeanor.

Mycah smiled. His hands were vital to his work, but he rarely noticed the hands of others. Yet here he stood, at the oddest of moments, taking notice of Cam's hand. A hand that felt somehow right.

Mycah looked up from their clasped hands and met Cam's gaze. Her pale grey eyes for once lacked fire. Instead they seemed deep and pensive but also guarded. Realizing that perhaps he'd held the grasp a little too long, he released Cam's hand and wiped his palm upon his pants.

"I, um, anyway," he said, looking around furtively.

"Right, um, yeah," said Cam as she scratched her neck and studied the floor. "Look, I, um... guess I should say thanks. For getting me out of... whatever that was. I guess we're even now."

Jerud snorted as he swung the backpack over his shoulders. "Hah. He didn't save you. I saved the both of you. If anything, we're even and Mycah owes both of us one apiece."

Winny whipped around and started to growl, her hackles rising stiffly.

Jerud threw his hands up. "Oh, come off it now. How could that possibly have been offensive? I was just speaking the truth, nothing more, nothing less."

"No," said Cam. "She's not mad at you. She wouldn't act that way."

Mycah noticed a faint drumming echoing from the corridors at his sides.

Cam drew her sword from her sheath. "Something's wrong."

The drumming sound intensified as figures dressed from head to toe in white began to pour into the room, swords gripped tightly before them. As they spotted Mycah and the others, a cry went up and they began to chant.

"In darkest night, the Watcher's eye is sharpest!"

"RUN!" yelled Mycah.

The first of the Watchers lunged toward Cam. A blur flew through the air, slamming him in the throat. Blood sprayed as Winny's teeth tore into the man's flesh.

"In fiercest tempest, the Watcher's resolve is strongest!"

A Watcher swung at Mycah, but Cam's sword deflected the blow and pushed the attacker back. Spinning, Cam whipped her blade around and brought it crashing into the man's neck. Blood spurted wildly from the wound. She slammed her fist into another Watcher's throat with a savage crunch, crushing the man's windpipe. At Mycah's right, Jerud swung his torch in a wide arc, bashing a Watcher in the face and setting his vestments aflame.

"In the face of evil, the Watcher's faith is strongest!"

"There's too many!" shouted Mycah. "They'll surround us! We can defend the room we arrived in!"

Grasping Cam's arm and Jerud's shirt, Mycah raced toward the room from whence they'd come. Jerud roared and spun his torch around, forcing the Watchers back. Cam lashed out with her sword and caught a man just above the knee, eliciting a cry of pain. Winny became a whirlwind of death, darting and dodging, ripping out throats and tearing through hamstrings.

"We are the Guardians of men!"

Mycah neared the double doors. With luck, perhaps the doors would snap shut again and spirit them away, far from the flashing blades of the Watchers. At the very least, the narrow archway would force the Watchers to attack one or two at a time. Mycah sprinted up the steps, Jerud at his flank. Just behind him ran Cam, as Winny barked and snapped viciously. The Watchers were closing in. There was so little time.

Then he heard a husky voice grunt in pain and surprise.

Mycah turned. A massive Watcher rivaling Jerud in size grasped Cam's sword arm tightly. Winny lunged and latched onto his arm, shaking with all her might, but the giant barely noticed, his eyes alight with a fierce bloodlust. The Watcher raised his sword.

Mycah didn't think. He merely reacted. Hurling his body down the steps, he slammed the massive Watcher square in the sternum with all his might, knocking him back.

Mycah's shoulder popped. The massive Watcher grunted. Cam yelled an obscenity.

"Mycah! Watch out!" yelled Jerud.

"We are the protectors of the Garden!"

Mycah felt a sharp pain explode through his skull and darkness consumed him.

CHAPTER TWENTY-THREE

Exodus from Eden

Cam collapsed into a snowdrift and vomited, but only bile splattered out. Everything else had been thrown up long ago.

Jerud crumpled in a heap next to her, his chest heaving, his face pale. Winny lagged behind, her tongue lolling like a side of beef left out to dry. When she caught up to them, she plopped onto her side in the snow, mouth open and panting heavily.

Cam clutched her stomach and grimaced as a spasm laced through her insides. Bloody Hell! At least the pain seemed to be abating. Her legs, however, felt like they were made of lead, and her lungs burned as if she'd inhaled a band of salamanders.

She glanced at Jerud. He lay upon his back, his arms thrown out to the sides as if waiting for vultures to come and pick the flesh from his bones. Snow crusted half his face, but he seemed not to notice. His eyes were unfocused and his breath heavy.

Cam pushed herself to her knees. "Come on. We're almost at the summit."

"Just go on. Leave me," gasped Jerud. "I can't go on. I feel like death."

With great effort, Cam lifted herself into a standing position. Over the top of the mountain, she could just make out the barest glimmer of dawn's first light.

"Let's go, Chuckles." She used the pet name she'd given him, but the moniker had lost some of its mirth in the past few hours.

"Leave me. I can't do it. I just can't."

Cam leered at his limp form. Jerud had clearly once been a formidable man. Legs as thick as tree trunks hid under his trousers, and his neck barely curved as it descended toward his shoulders. Many men sported broad chests and beefy arms, but it was rare to find a man with a thick neck. Those muscles took years of hard labor to develop, and they tended to stick with a man well into old age.

Of course, Jerud's rotund belly and sagging arms made it clear his best days were behind him. It was a shame really. Cam would've liked to see him in his prime. Nonetheless, Jerud's will was impressive. She'd expected him to give up long ago. At one point she actually thought his heart had given out and he'd passed, but the big man got up and kept moving after a short pause.

"Trust me," she said. "I'd have left you long ago if I wasn't worried about those Watchers tracking me after spotting your bloated corpse. Now get up. We've got to get over the summit before dawn."

Jerud groaned and rolled over, but get up he did, though agonizingly slowly. Cam patted Winny upon her rear to rouse her. The dog sucked in her tongue to hack up some phlegm before draping it out again. Poor girl. Her tongue nearly dragged in the snow.

Though Cam gave Jerud grief, they were all tired. *Unnaturally* tired. Their flight from the Watchers had drained what little energy they had left. Ever since she'd touched that metallic, God-forsaken, memory-altering sphere, events had seemed like little more than a blur. When the Watchers appeared, she'd acted on instinct, slashing with her blade and beating them off with her fists. When one of them grabbed her she thought the end had come. Until Mycah, the fool that he was, smashed into the ox-faced excuse for a Watcher and knocked her free. Blasted idiot! She hoped he was all right.

As Mycah got bashed from behind, Jerud had pulled her through the archway and into the small room. Winny had barreled in alongside them as the doors snapped shut, nearly nipping off the end of her tail. The room had trembled again and spit them out where they'd entered, whether through some dark magic or an act of God, who knew. Then their flight had begun. They raced through the corridors, twisting and turning where necessary. Twice they took wrong turns, but Winny remembered the proper path and redirected them before long. Through the room with the tanks and cages, through the empty cavern with the dirt floor, past the crack in the metal wall, through the giant fissure, and back out into the rolling grasslands they ran.

Panting, they'd paused under the darkness of the new moons and argued about what to do. Jerud had proposed trying to stage a rescue, but the bloated fool soon realized what a ridiculous idea that was. There had been at least two dozen Watchers, and they clearly knew their way about the damned metal prison better than she and Jerud did.

Cam refused to think of it as the Garden of Eden. If God did exist, the metal prison seemed about as God-forsaken a place as any she'd ever visited. Of course, she'd kept that thought to herself—Chuckles seemed to get fussier than a soggy alley cat anytime someone questioned his treasured beliefs. Cam wondered not for the first time if his brain had turned to fat along with his muscles.

Regardless, their only option had been to run. Fate had dealt them a lucky draw in that Lunaris, the greater moon, had already set, and the other two lesser moons were both waning. Night would cloak them until morning, but that gave them a scant few hours to disappear before the Watchers would be able to track them. Retracing their steps around the edge of the foothills and through the grass-filled valley would've meant certain death. The Watchers would've spotted them easier than an eagle spotting a hare in a freshly reaped field.

Their only hope had been to disappear into the mountains where the crags and crevices would hide them. From there, they could weasel their way back into the woods and give themselves a fighting chance at eluding the Watchers. As much as it pained her—and oddly enough it did pain her—they simply had to forget about Mycah and move on.

And so they ran. At first, Cam emptied her mind and let her body revel in the flight. There was nothing else in the world like the sheer rush of adrenaline that exploded through her muscles from physical exertion. Almost nothing could ruin the thrill of exercise, though Jerud had tried with his constant, labored wheezing.

Then the pain started. Her stomach had felt a little queasy ever since she'd touched the globe, but it wasn't until shortly after she began to run that the aches in her abdomen became significant. Cam knew her own body well enough to not dismiss the pain as cramps. This pain lingered deep within her belly, as if she'd eaten a meal that had been left out too long in the sun. After stopping to vomit, she'd thought perhaps the metal ball had bewitched her in some way, but Jerud paused to retch shortly thereafter, and from his retelling of the evening's events he'd never touched the globe. Even Winny heaved up the contents of her stomach onto the grass, and she possessed a stomach of steel. Cam had seen her swallow a festering, week-old pigeon carcass and survive it without so much as a loose stool the next day.

After pausing to retch a second time, Jerud had mumbled something about the Garden's curse, but Cam thought that was a load of bull droppings. As Cam had made very clear to them—over and over again, in Mycah's case—she absolutely, positively *did not* believe in curses. No matter how suited the evidence might seem...

Whatever caused the pains, it made for a Hellish night of travel. If she'd been alone with Winny, she could've toughed it out with barely more than a grimace, but having Jerud along for the adventure made the ordeal far worse. As much as Jerud annoyed the living donkey brains out of her, she couldn't very well leave the old man to die on the mountainside. It didn't seem right. So she drew on the memory of her father to channel her inner drill sergeant and slathered the man with insults to keep his pace from lagging.

"Move it, you sorry excuse for a Saladian slave monkey!"

"Keep your wide ass moving, you pathetic pile of muskrat dung!"

And of course, her own personal favorite. "I swear, if you don't hurry, Winny's gonna rip your face off, Chuckles!"

Of all the insults she hurled at him, it seemed the one that annoyed him the most was calling him Chuckles. Who knew why. All Cam knew was that the insults had somehow kept the giant, two-legged ox-cart known as Jerud moving, and it appeared they might even make it over the mountain's summit before sunrise.

With one last effort, Cam pulled herself over a ridge and stared down the slope of the mountain. Her legs burned and her hands ached from pulling herself across jagged slabs of granite and snow-covered boulders. Behind her, Jerud panted and heaved, sounding like a heifer with a case of black lung.

"I swear to God, lassy..." he gasped. "If we don't stop... right now... I'm just gonna... up and die on you. The Watchers be damned... I'll let the Lord take me himself."

Cam pointed to a rocky outcropping up ahead. "We can throw down our bedrolls over there. Those exposed rocks should protect us from prying eyes."

Jerud stumbled forward, too tired to nod.

Despite being as tired as she could ever remember, Cam slept fitfully. Perhaps it was the early morning sun that shone in her eyes. Perhaps it was the lingering pain in her stomach. Perhaps it was her fear of the Watchers overtaking and capturing them. Or perhaps it was the bleeding memories that had been crammed into her skull by that stupid ball of liquid steel. Cam dreamt of fire and metal, men fighting and women screaming, flashing lights and streaming colors. People, lost in time, endlessly waiting. And blood. Always blood.

Cam awoke in a cold sweat. She gazed into the cloudless sky. The sun had just passed its zenith. Not a long slumber nor particularly restful, but it would have to do.

Winny huddled next to her in a ball, eyes shut tight, her tail tucked under her feet. Cam peered over her at Jerud who was thrashing about, fighting dragons in his sleep.

Cam's stomach grumbled loudly. The stomach pains, now past, had left a giant void in her midsection screaming to be filled. She longed for scrambled eggs and toast, but there was little chance of feasting on that any time soon. Nonetheless, it would be worth keeping an eye out for unattended ptarmigan nests.

Cam hoisted herself up and approached Jerud. The big man mumbled and twitched, but his eyes remained closed.

"Come on old man, time to get up."

Jerud groaned and rolled onto his side, his fist clenched tight. Cam nudged him with her boot.

Jerud bolted upright, flailing about with his arms. "Grawah! Mycah! No!"

Cam jumped back, barely avoiding Jerud's swings. "Whoa! Settle down. It's just me."

Jerud sat there panting, a wild look in his eyes.

"Are you ok?" asked Cam.

"Um… yeah. I guess." Jerud peered overhead. "What time is it?"

"About half past noon, I think."

Jerud rubbed his brow with one hand and massaged his neck with the other. "Ugh. I feel like a rag that's been wrung out. At least my stomach's not screaming anymore."

Cam's stomach grumbled again. "Speak for yourself…"

"I was talking about the pains, lass. The curse must wear off after—"

Cam put a hand up. "Don't start with me. You know how I feel about curses."

"Whatever," Jerud grumbled.

Cam eyed his pack. "So… how about some breakfast before we go. I'm starving."

Jerud glared at her. "Food? Seriously? I just let my best friend get captured by Watchers while trespassing in the Holy land, and all you can think about is your stomach?"

"Jerud—"

"Do you have any idea what they'll do to him? Do you?" Jerud shook his head. "We've got to go back! We've got to spring him loose! Somehow. Maybe we can—"

"Jerud, we talked about this last night," said Cam. "Going after the Watchers in the open would be suicide. We need to get to the forest. Once there, maybe we can use the cover to our advantage. But right now we need to move."

Jerud looked ready to fight, but after a pause he sighed. His shoulders slumped. "You're right. Sorry I raised my voice. Let's go."

Cam hesitated. "I was serious about the food, though."

Jerud snorted as he stood. "And they call me the glutton..."

He rummaged through his pack and produced a few slivers of jerky and a couple hard biscuits. Grabbing half in a meaty fist, he held out the other half. Cam nearly lambasted him over the miserable offering, but she held her tongue. She'd been hard enough on the big fellow already, and the loss of his friend clearly hurt. Truthfully, she worried about Mycah too. She hoped they'd be able to free him once they reached the forest, but how?

Cam broke the biscuit in two and tossed half to Winny, who'd arisen and was stretching her back. Grabbing her things, she headed down the mountain's slope toward the tree line, sticking to rocky outcroppings and water-worn gullies to shelter them from prying eyes. The glimpses she caught of the valley bellow showed no signs of the Watchers, so they must've outpaced them through the night. That lifted Cam's spirits, but she continued to push forward as hard as she could. She knew firsthand how tenacious some pursuers could be, and she had no intention of being caught.

No, never again.

The sun arched across the sky as they marched, eventually sinking behind the mountaintop. As the day's light faded, Cam's stomach grumbled. The meager rations Jerud had passed out at noon had faded into a distant memory.

Winny trotted beside her, thick strings of drool trailing from her jowls. She looked up at the sound of Cam's stomach, ears perked and face full of hope.

Poor girl. She's likely starving.

Well, there was no sense in complaining to Jerud about it. The old meatbag had been about as talkative as a stone since leaving the mountain's summit. Cam wondered about him. He seemed to eat rather little considering how fat he was. Either he was sneaking tidbits on the side—a distinct possibility—or what her mother had said about one's metabolism slowing down with age was true. Cam pictured herself as an old maid, fat and slow from inactivity. She shuddered.

Cam emerged from the end of a barren gully and nearly stumbled into the forest. Nestled amongst the edge of foothills, the first trees stood no more than a couple hundred paces away.

"About time," said Cam. "Now maybe we can finally get a fire going and cook some... ACK!"

Jerud pulled her down roughly from behind into the tall grass at their feet.

"What the hell do you think you're—"

"Shh!" Jerud hissed. "Keep it down. I think I saw something."

"Um, yeah. I saw something too. *The forest.*"

"Don't be an idiot," said Jerud. "You know what I mean. Signs of life. I think there's someone out there." He poked his head up and stared into the trees.

Cam followed suit, poking her head up out of the grass, feeling like a groundhog searching for predators. She peered into the forest but saw nothing. She checked on Winny, who lay in the grass, feet extended to one side looking as if she hadn't a care in the world.

"This is silly," whispered Cam, as the wind picked up. "If there was someone out there, Winny surely would've—"

She paused in mid-sentence. The breeze carried with it scents of damp grass, pine needles, and gardenia blossoms, but also something else. A hint of smoke.

"Wait. I smell a fire," said Cam. "*Ox balls!* How did the Watchers beat us out of there?"

Jerud sniffed the air. "Doesn't make sense. No way the Watchers could've made it all the way around and through the valley that fast, and if they'd come over the mountains with us, we would've noticed them. They must've left a party waiting here in ambush, just in case. But they couldn't have assumed anyone would escape, and even if they did why would they camp out here? Doesn't make sense. Unless..."

Jerud rubbed his chin. "Unless they're not Watchers." He tilted his head toward Winny. "Can that dog keep quiet?"

"Seriously?" said Cam. "She's barely made a peep all day."

"I'll take that as a yes," said Jerud. "Come on. Let's go scout what we're up against. Just make sure that bitch of yours doesn't go barging in and give us away."

"Her name's Winny, you fetid sack of dung."

Jerud harrumphed and crept off through the grass. He moved with a silence and grace that belied his large size. Cam stared in amazement for a moment before hurrying to catch him. How did the big man move so quietly? Come to think of it, Mycah had made it clear from the start their goal was to steal something from the not-a-garden—she still refused to think of it as the Garden of Eden—but she'd never considered that he and Jerud might be professional thieves. As she watched Jerud glide through the grass, she realized he and Mycah must be pros. There wasn't any other way a man pushing three hundred pounds could be that good of a sneak without doing it for a living.

Jerud wormed his way around the underbrush and into the forest's outskirts. With a silent hand, he bent back a stand of young poplars to allow for a view into the forest. Crouching low behind him, Cam saw four men seated around a fire. Two were large, muscle-bound, and had the look of soldiers, but they wore uniforms of ultramarine and yellow. *Probably not Keralt's men, then.* The third was lean, sinewy, sported shoulder length black hair, and wore clothes the color of midnight. The fourth, a lanky man of middle age, had his back to the poplars and a bandage on his leg.

Throwing caution to the wind, Jerud pushed through the trees and into the clearing.

"YOU SON-OF-A-BITCH!" Jerud roared. "Came to finish the job, did you? Didn't ruin our lives well enough the first time? Well, let's have at it then!"

"Jerud. About time," said the thin man in black as he slowly lifted his eyes from the fire.

The lanky man at the fire jumped up and spun around. "Jerud? Saints be praised, it's you! I's been powerful worried, by the moons but I 'ave!"

The lanky man rushed Jerud and wrapped him in a huge embrace. The big guy seemed bewildered.

"Pete? What in blazes? What are you doing here? What is *he* doing here?" Jerud pointed a thick finger at the man in black. "In case you'd forgotten, that traitorous snake is the whole reason we're in this blasted mess!"

The man in black tsk-tsked. Jerud started to push the lanky man away, presumably to try and strangle the man in black with his bare fists. The two muscular soldiers stood up.

"Jerud, 'old on now," said Pete. "Trust me, I don't like that two-faced back-stabber any more 'an you do, by the moons but I don't. But 'e said ya was in trouble. Said the Watchers was after ya. Said ya'd need 'elp, an' given the circumstances, I was willin' to listen. 'E led me 'ere. Said if ya got out ya'd prolly come this way, so that's somethin' at least. Where's Mycah?"

Jerud spoke through clenched teeth. "Captured. The Watchers got him." He glanced at the man in black and the soldiers. "They got the tablet too."

Cam raised an eyebrow. That was a bold-faced lie! She'd seen Jerud pack the strange artifact into his backpack before the fight with the Watchers. He carried it as he spoke. What sort of game was he playing?

Pete swore. One of the soldiers, the larger of the two, spoke. "Damnit. Figures."

Figuring that she couldn't hide in the bushes forever, Cam stepped out from behind the poplars, her hand firmly placed upon her sword. Winny stalked along at her side, ears flat against her head and tail held low.

"Ahh," said the man in black. "The mysterious assailant appears with her trusty hound."

"Who are you?" said Cam.

"Who's that?" asked Pete.

"Pete, Cam. Cam, Pete. He's a friend," said Jerud. "That snake in the grass over there is Rayven. And if my memory serves me right, those two are Stormguards. Don't know their names. They didn't exactly introduce themselves when we first met."

"We were just following orders, big guy," said the shorter of the pair.

The taller one sneered. "Not to say that we didn't enjoy roughin' you up a bit, though."

Jerud clenched his jaw.

Cam turned to the one known as Rayven. Her hand tightened upon her sword. "What do you mean 'mysterious assailant?' Who are you? What do you know about me?"

Rayven tilted his nose up in the air as if he'd gotten a whiff of a fresh pile of manure. With a look of distaste plastered across his gaunt face, he flicked a hair back from his temple. "It appears my expectations exceeded reality. Pity."

"I asked you a question, mush for brains!" Cam said.

"Three," Rayven said as he stoked the fire with a stick. "You asked three."

Cam bared her teeth and snarled as she unsheathed her sword. What an arrogant creep! No wonder Jerud wanted to strangle this insufferable slug! She'd only spent a few moments in his company and already she was tempted to gut him.

The two soldiers put hands to weapons, but Rayven continued as if nothing had occurred. "You're the assailant who dispatched the Watchers. You're a woman. You have a hound. That much was obvious from prior evidence. I now also know that you prefer your right sword arm to your left, that you attempt to intimidate foes with ferocity to hide your fears, and that you're... ill-tempered. Does that suffice?"

Cam's mouth fell open. How in the world was she supposed to respond to that? She'd never been adept at winning wars of words. If only the creep had pulled a knife and rushed her like any self-respecting thug would do once provoked, she could've ended it simply.

"Alright now, settle down," said Pete. "No one need be gutted tonight, not if I can 'elp it. Now let's focus on the important thing at 'and 'ere. We need to figger out 'ow to spring Mycah loose!"

"And obtain the tablet," said Rayven.

"Blast it all man, don't ya 'ave a shred o' decency in ya?" spouted Pete. "Never mind. Don't answer that. We all know where yer loyalties lie."

Pete turned to Jerud. "Talk to me, bud. Whad'ya know 'bout Mycah? What 'appened to 'im? Got any ideas on 'ow to bust 'im out?"

Jerud sighed—a deep, tired sigh from the depths of his chest. "I don't know Pete. There's a lot of things I don't know right now."

Jerud wiped his face slowly with his meaty hand. "Lord, I'm tired. I feel like I could sleep for days."

"Ya doin' alright, Jerud?" asked Pete. "In all the commotion, guess I forgot to ask."

"I can't deal with this right now, Pete. I need rest. And food, too. Let's break camp and deal with this mess in the morning. Not much we can do for Mycah right now anyway."

Jerud turned to Rayven and the soldiers. "I'm going to set up my own camp with Pete. If any of you decide to drop by in the middle of the night, I'll assume that means you're itching for a fight. And I'll be *happy* to oblige. C'mon Pete."

Jerud turned to Cam. "You're free to join us if you like, but you're free to leave too. Your choice. Way I see it, this is our fight, not yours. Either way, I wouldn't recommend sticking too close to Rayven over there unless you fancy waking up with a knife between your ribs."

Cam sheathed her sword. Free to leave? Of course she was free to leave! She'd traveled with Mycah and Jerud entirely of her own free will! Perhaps hunger and, yes, even curiosity had played a part in her decision, but it was a decision freely made.

She thought of the past few madness-filled days—of the cursed lands, the metal prison, her visions, the Watchers. And of Mycah, blasted idiot! Mycah, the peeping tom. Mycah, stealer of Winny's affection. Mycah, ever cheerful, no matter how many times she deliberately spurned him.

Cam sighed. *Mycah.* Not for the first time, she hoped he was all right.

She forced a laugh. "Hah! You won't get rid of me that easily, Chuckles. You still owe me a few more meals before you and Mycah's debt's repaid. I'm sticking around. For now."

Pete raised an eyebrow. "Chuckles?"

Jerud raised a hand. "Don't ask."

CHAPTER TWENTY-FOUR

Crimes Against God and Man

Images and words. Just images and words. Except this time there were no words. Just images and sounds.

Bright lights, flickering, shining, streaming by with incredible speed. Stars. The soft patter of snowflakes falling, the drumming of rain, the silence of tears. *So many tears.* A fire, a fire to consume, a fire to forge. Crackling. Popping. Whispering. Arms, cradling a babe. Fists. A mother's cry, a flash, a sob. *Memories of a faded age.*

The pounding of footsteps. White robes. The bright flash of a swinging blade. The clash of metal on metal. A low growl. A spurt of red. The gurgle of a man drowning in his own blood. *Blood. Always blood. So much blood.*

Shouting, confusion, rage, panic, terror, concern. Cries of pain. More shouting. Familiar voices? Words?

"Mycah! Watch out!"

Now more stars, but far, far away, and moving so slowly. Barely moving. Green grass, waving. A warm breeze. Warmth? That was new. Footfalls, marching, clanking. More white robes.

Pain. Searing pain. And nausea. That was new too. Pungent vomit, metallic blood, the stench of bile. Smells? Tastes? *Memories of a faded age.* No, real memories. But faded, tattered, viewed from within a fog. Or perhaps not memories at all but events. Reality? What was reality?

Reality was pain and darkness.

***

Feelings. Sensations. Mycah could feel sensations, and he could distinguish their origins. He could feel a dull, throbbing pain. That came from his skull. He could feel a tightness, an emptiness. That came from his stomach. He could feel a dryness. That came from his mouth. A foul stench permeated the sensations, a stench of stale urine and dried bile. The sensations were real, not memories. Of that, he was certain.

Mycah's eyes fluttered open. The sun's rays shone down, filtering through layers of leaves before cascading upon his face. It was day—perhaps mid-afternoon. He groaned and heard a voice.

"Fetch the Knight Captain."

Mycah craned his neck to the side, taking in his surroundings. To one side, rusted nails held together planks of weather-beaten wood. At his other side, piles of goods stacked upon one another: sacks of grain, wooden crates, a fire-hardened barrel.

Mycah heard a bump and his entire body jostled. The barrel sloshed. Apparently, he was in the back of a cart, and the barrel contained, of all things, a liquid. Perhaps water.

"Water," Mycah croaked as he tried to make his tongue function. "Water."

No one seemed to hear him. Ignoring his headache, Mycah tried to raise himself into a seated position. The endeavor turned out to be more difficult than he'd imagined. He could barely maneuver in the cart's tight confines. His muscles also felt as if they'd been tenderized by an overzealous butcher. Was he sore from exertion, or had he been beaten? The part that made the simple task of sitting up the most difficult, however, was that his hands and feet—bare feet? where had his boots gone?—were clasped tightly with heavy chains. Given the state of his muscles, Mycah could barely lift his hands.

The cart creaked and dipped as someone hoisted themselves into the back. A man in a spotless white uniform seated himself next to Mycah on the head of the barrel. Grey flecked the man's rich, dark brown hair, and his face, though weathered, held eyes that shined. The eyes possessed wisdom and knowledge, but also something else. Sadness, perhaps?

"So child Mycah. We meet again."

"Water," croaked Mycah.

Knight Captain Orwell lifted his head and called out. "Brother Paulas! Fetch me a cup of water."

The Knight Captain sat beside him in silence, his eyes studying Mycah's face carefully. Eventually, the Captain rose and leaned over the edge of the cart. When he pulled back, he held a humble, wooden cup in his hands.

"Lift yourself, child, so you may drink."

Mycah summoned his energy and tried to sit. He very nearly fell back, but the Knight Captain's hand shot out.

He grasped the chains that bound his wrists and yanked, forcing him into a seated position. The Captain pressed the cup into his hands.

"Drink."

Mycah drank. The cool water flowed into his mouth and over his tongue, rehydrating pores as dry as the sun-bleached bones of the dead. Never had a drink tasted more refreshing in his entire life and never had one disappeared quite so quickly.

Mycah lowered the cup from his lips and held it out. "More. Please."

The Knight Captain took the cup. "You're not in a position to be making demands, child, even if they are laced with gratitudes."

Mycah looked down at his shackled hands and feet. Thick, wrought iron chains weighed heavily upon his arms, and an old, chunky padlock fastened the chains together. Mycah suppressed a smile. It was a simple warded lock, probably containing three or four wards based on the size of the keyway. The Watchers must've had no idea who he was if they thought such a pedestrian padlock would hold him! Mycah glanced at the cart bed at his side. The wooden planks were weathered and cracked. They'd easily yield an adequate splinter under the coaxing of his gentle touch.

Mycah wiggled his fingers, trying to banish a feeling of numbness that radiated down his fingertips and into his forearms. He'd need his fingers to be nimble for later. Best to keep his hands moving and his blood flowing.

Mycah noticed the Knight Commander staring at him, studying his every move like a general preparing for battle.

Clearly he'd been rendered a prisoner, but what exactly was his current situation? And what had happened since the battle? He was alive, that much was obvious, and despite his foul aroma and sore skull he seemed to be in one piece. Had the Knight Commander taken pity upon him for some reason? And where were Jerud and Cam? Were they prisoners as well? He needed answers, but he'd have to pick his questions carefully.

"I see," said Mycah. "Look, I'm not exactly sure how to proceed here. I've been a prisoner before, but... well, it's not important. Could I ask you a few questions?"

The Knight Captain raised an eyebrow. "Ever bold, I see, even in captivity. Not that I expected anything else based upon our prior encounter. Very well, child. I suppose you have some right to know your circumstances." The Knight Captain folded his arms. "You may ask, and I may or may not choose to answer."

"How long have I been out?"

"Unconscious? Just under three days."

"What happened to my boots?"

"*That* is your second question?"

"I considered asking it first. It's important to my understanding of the situation."

The Knight Captain blinked and his eyebrows lowered a hair. Mycah had clearly caught him off guard. The Captain paused, considering if this was one of the questions he should bother answering. "I had Brother Frederich remove them and return them to the store room."

"I thought they were a gift."

"They were."

"Then why did you take them back?"

"Your soul revealed itself to be unworthy of such a gift. When the opportunity presented itself, I had the boots returned so they might one day benefit a man who understands that regardless of what rests underneath the soles of his feet he must nevertheless kneel before God."

Even though the Knight Captain delivered the response in an even tone, Mycah detected an undercurrent of hostility.

"Very well, then. It's a shame, though. Those were good boots."

The Knight Captain sat forward and cupped his chin in his hand. "I know."

"So where are we?"

"On a cart, headed to Guildean."

"A horse drawn cart?"

"Correct."

"I thought you guys didn't believe in horses."

"How could we not believe in horses? There's one drawing this cart as we speak. I can see it from here."

Mycah raised his head and looked directly at the Knight Captain. His face remained impassive, neither amused nor angered by Mycah's line of questioning. Though the Captain revealed little emotion in the discourse, at least he was talking. That was something.

"Let me rephrase that. I thought you didn't believe in the use of horses for transportation."

"The Lord God created man in His image. To imply that the form of man is unsuited to travel would be an affront to God. So we walk."

"Then why am I in a cart?"

The Knight Captain tilted his head. "You've thus far shown little regard for the will of God. Why would this matter to you?"

Was the man mocking him? Or was this some logical extension of the man's theology that Mycah couldn't decipher?

"Never mind. So what happens when we reach Guildean?"

"You'll be tried as an apostate before the Archbishop and convicted for crimes against man and God. You'll likely be crucified and burned."

Mycah gulped. "What of Cam and Jerud?"

"Are those your conspirators? They'll likewise be tried, convicted, and put to death."

Mycah's heart sunk. "So you captured them, then?"

The Knight Captain paused. The moment of silence could've meant nothing, or perhaps it meant everything. The pause gave Mycah hope. Maybe Jerud and Cam had escaped.

"Their crimes are known. They'll be tried, convicted, and put to death."

Mycah raised an eyebrow. "You say I'll be tried. How can you be so sure I'll be found guilty of any crimes?"

The Knight Captain leaned back and recrossed his arms. "The evidence is irrefutable, child. Nine Watchers lay dead. Their blood is on your hands."

"I didn't kill any of them!" Mycah said defensively.

The Knight Captain's eyes hardened. "Whether or not they died by your hand is irrelevant. You were a party to their murder. That makes you complicit in the crime."

"Murder implies intent," said Mycah. "Our actions were in self-defense. Your men attacked us."

"They did so because you conspired to commit crimes against God."

Crimes against God? Mycah gave a muffled snort. What did that mean? Mycah thought he'd known what sort of journey he was undertaking, thought he'd known what obstacles lay before him and what risks he might face. He thought he'd find confirmations to stories of a long lost age. But in the heart of the strange metal castle he'd found more questions than answers. Though the Knight Captain claimed he'd been unconscious for three days, it felt as if he'd just left the site of the conflict. His mind hadn't yet had a chance to process what he'd seen— the peculiar environs, the snaking lights, the odd memories he'd never experienced himself. What exactly happened in the Garden? Could the Knight Captain explain?

Mycah cleared his throat. "Crimes against God? I suppose you mean visiting the Garden."

"That alone would be enough, yes. But you also committed the original sin—the most heinous crime against God of all. You ate from the tree of knowledge of good and evil."

"What?"

"Did I stutter, child?"

"No, but..." Mycah's headache intensified as he tried to think. What was the Captain talking about? What tree? If not for the chains upon his arms he'd have pressed his fingers against his temples.

"You must be mistaken. Of all the bizarre stuff we found in that place, vegetation wasn't one of them. I think I'd know if I happened across the tree of knowledge."

"You, child, would probably be the last to know. You look but you don't observe."

Mycah scrunched his forehead in confusion. He thought he'd be able to extract answers from this man, yet instead he felt more confused than ever.

"Look," Mycah said in a low voice. "I know you're a man of God. You can probably recall scripture by rote. You of all people should realize that that place cannot be the Garden of Eden!"

"Ahh, so you wish to add heresy to your list of crimes? Very well then." The Captain steepled his fingers and leaned in. "Let's discuss theology, shall we?"

"Look, I don't know what that place is, but it's not the Garden of Eden. It can't be. For crying out loud, you've been there. How can you believe that's what it is?"

The Knight Captain took his time in responding. "You're familiar with the concept of metaphor?"

"Yes, of course I am," said Mycah, exasperated.

"Stories change in the telling, but that doesn't mean their words don't hold truth. Sometimes stories relate truth in a way that's easier to understand than is reality. You think scriptures hold untruths? No. Merely metaphor."

"But the Garden, the story of Genesis, it—"

"Describes things accurately," said the Knight Captain sternly. "You believe your experiences to be at odds with scripture, but reconsider Genesis. The passages describe a wondrous Garden filled with trees and beasts and all the birds of the Heavens, but the passages only describe the Garden prior to the Lord's curse, not after. Pray tell, child... did you notice any beasts during your journey to the Garden?"

"No."

"Any birds?"

"No."

"Any trees?"

"No, but you said—"

"I am speaking in the literal sense," said the Knight Captain. "And the answer is no. You did not. The Lord's curse devastated the land. Changed it, transformed it. Consumed it. Surely you noticed the curse? The corruption that welled within you, gnawing at you from the inside? Growing with each passing moment you spent there?"

"I'm... not sure," said Mycah. "I did notice... certain things. Fatigue. A headache. Nausea. Some stomach pain perhaps."

"So you noticed, then. The longer one stays, the worse the curse becomes. Vomiting, burns, sickness, confusion. Even death. The curse is a sobering reminder of God's greatness and of his wrath."

Mycah vaguely remembered vomiting as he stared into the stars. That would explain the stench of bile upon his shirt. He checked his arms for burns, fighting down a rising sense of panic. Was the curse still with him? If it was, would he know? He didn't feel sick at the moment, and his current sense of confusion seemed justified given the circumstances, but what if there was more to it than that?

Mycah shook his head to clear the morbid thoughts. "Look, maybe the curse is real. But I never ate from a tree, much less *the* tree."

The Knight Captain looked Mycah firmly in the eyes. "No? Do you not suffer from strange visions, memories which are not your own?"

Mycah's eyes widened. "How could you know that?"

"Because I know of your crime, child. You're tormented by knowledge not meant for the mortal mind. Knowledge of good and evil."

Mycah recalled the strange visions he'd experienced. Images of horrible things—raging fires, clashing metal, anger, tears, blood. *Blood. Always blood. So much blood.* But there had also been other things, wonderful things—bright lights, life and rebirth, grace, wonder, brilliance. Could the strange floating sphere, the globe of liquid metal, could it possibly be... the tree of knowledge?

"You're wrong," said Mycah, though his voice lacked conviction. "What I saw from that sphere... it wasn't scripture. Or metaphor. Those images, those memories? They were real. They happened. I don't know when or to whom, but to somebody. I know it. I can't explain how, but I know."

The Knight Captain shook his head. "You're still unwilling to see past the deception fueled by your own predispositions. You should dwell upon your actions and try to find the truth within. Perhaps if you accept your sins and profess them to the Lord your soul will burn less violently in the afterlife."

The Knight Captain stood. "Before I leave, however, I offer you a question. A final morsel for thought. Man's original downfall came about as a result of the deception of woman. How exactly did yours come about?"

"What do you mean? Are you talking about the sphere? I just touched it."

"Did you?"

Mycah recalled the scene. He'd reached out and touched the globe of his own free will, but nothing had happened. Neither had anything occurred when Jerud touched it. Only upon Cam's touch had the sphere sprung to life, and only upon his own interaction with Cam had the memories sprung forth.

"You're not suggesting that Cam..."

"It's as I suspected, then," said the Knight Captain. He turned to leave.

"Wait," said Mycah. "Before you go, I have a final question."

The Knight Captain tilted his head. "Yes?"

"If you're so certain of my guilt, why do I still live? Why haven't you killed me?"

"Child, Knight Captain of the Watchers I may be, but even I do not have the right to levy judgment for crimes such as those you've committed. That responsibility lies with our Lord alone."

The Knight Captain turned his head toward Mycah, fire burning in his eyes. In a hard voice, he continued.

"But be certain, child. You have the blood of nine of my men on your hands. When you're tried, the Lord will find you guilty, and you will be punished. If you recall when we first met I told you that only through suffering can man truly understand the meaning of repentance. Well rest assured, you will understand the meaning of suffering. I'm not sure if any amount of suffering can cleanse your soul, but by the Lord's grace, I intend to find out."

With that, the Knight Captain hopped off the end of the wagon. The commander's last words echoed in Mycah's head like a grim portent. How much suffering could he endure? He didn't know, but he had no intention of finding out. The Knight Captain's plans necessitated a speedy escape, but luckily escape was a specialty of his.

CHAPTER TWENTY-FIVE

A Nightmare Revisited

Cam sat upon a fallen log, hacking at the remains of a fallen oak branch with a heavy, wide-bladed knife. When she was a young girl, her father had taught her how to whittle. She could remember sitting upon his knee as he told her in his deep, gentle voice the subtle tricks of the art. For beginners like young Cam, her father had recommended pine. It was a soft wood and easily found, but pine also had its drawbacks. It didn't hold detail well, and one had to use a piece that was old and dry, as whittling a freshly fallen pine bough would quickly result in fingers sticky from sap.

Cam could remember her father's warm smile peeking at her out from his bushy beard. After producing a pocket knife from under his coat, his large hands had cupped hers and placed the knife in her palm. With his rough hands grasping hers, he'd guided her through the motions, cutting into a small block of pine and giving advice as he shepherded her through the process. Take it slow, no need to rush, he'd said. Remember to cut with the grain. Those cuts will peel away smoothly. Cuts made against the grain will resist and cause the wood to tear. Watch your thumbs. Remember to keep your knife sharp.

Together they'd worked, the block of pine melting under her father's steady guidance. At the end of the afternoon, what had started as a shapeless piece of wood had transformed into a small wooden dog, complete with perky ears and a wagging tongue. Cam had been overjoyed. She'd kept the dog figurine with her at all times that summer and slept with it under her pillow every night. One day, a day many years after that summer but a day many years past, she'd remembered the figurine and looked for it only to be unable to find it. She'd screamed at her mother. Where is it mother? Where's the dog that father made me? Her mother had claimed ignorance, told her she should've taken better care of it. To this day, Cam suspected her mother knew what had happened to it.

Cam felt a tear trickle down her cheek. She missed that dog. And she missed her father. Pulling her hand up from the oak branch, she wiped the tear away before anyone noticed.

Looking down at the mangled limb between her hands, she tried to think of what her father might've said. Use a smaller knife, perhaps, or keep your hand steady through the cuts. Both pieces of advice would've been appropriate—if she was trying to whittle. Today, she merely wished to hack at a branch with a knife.

Nearby, Winny barked at Applesnatch, trying to goad her into playing. Winny had met other horses before, but for some reason she'd instantly gravitated toward Applesnatch. Perhaps it had something to do with Winny's indecipherable fascination with Mycah. Odd how dogs could detect things that were completely invisible to people. From the moment they'd met, Winny had been certain Applesnatch belonged to Mycah. How, Cam hadn't the foggiest idea. Perhaps some scent of his lingered upon the mare.

To her credit, Applesnatch had suffered the dog's barking in peace. Though she seemed thoroughly uninterested in playing, at least she didn't nip at Winny's tail as Jerud's horse Champ had done. Cam couldn't help but crack a smile as she watched Winny's antics.

"Something amuses you?"

Cam nearly jumped out of her britches.

"Flying antelope balls, Rayven! What the hell are you doing creeping up on me like that?"

Rayven stood behind her, pale face impassive.

"Am I at fault for your inattentiveness?" he asked in an oily voice.

Cam had thought Rayven a creep upon first encounter, but it took her a while to realize just how right she'd been. Jerud, who'd seemed as stealthy as a panther when he'd glided through the valley's tall grass seeking out the forest camp, couldn't even hold a candle to Rayven's sneakiness. The man moved as silently as death itself. It was unsettling.

"Rayven..." Jerud ambled over from his perch on a nearby log. The way the big man spat out the name made it sound like an insult. "Did you make yourself useful? Find anything?"

"I found Mycah," said Rayven simply.

Pete, who'd been tending to the horses, joined the conversation. "So, where is 'e? 'Ow bad is it?"

"The Watchers head to Guildean. They have Mycah. With horses, we can reach them by nightfall."

"Well, great," said Pete, clapping his hands. "Let's get movin' 'en."

"Wait," said Rayven icily. "Four score Watchers guard the caravan."

"Four score? By the moons, man," said Pete. "Are ya sure?"

Rayven leveled him with a cold stare. "If I'm unsure, I don't speak. The Watchers are well armed. There are sentries. An assault is ill-advised."

Cam swallowed. Eighty armed men? What could their band of five do against that?

Jerud mumbled a curse and wiped his hand across his face. "This is bad. I didn't think there'd be so many. Chances are they'll be eager for blood, too." He sighed. "Anyone got any ideas?"

The Stormqueen's soldiers, who'd been introduced as Johnah and Sten, trailed Rayven as they usually did. The tall, mean-looking one spoke.

"Why don't we just rush on in there and bust some skulls? I could use a good fight."

Rayven turned and stared at the man with confusion. For a moment, he looked like he might speak, but instead he sighed and a murderous look of disgust passed across his face.

"Well, ain't it obvious?" said Pete. "We're thieves. We'll bust Mycah out."

"Yeah, but how?" asked Jerud, turning to Pete. "It's not like we have a lot of options, you know. Not like that one time you and me were in a bind outside Grouton. At least then we had some supplies. Rope, rifles, a cannon. Not to mention we had the high ground."

Apparently Jerud was referencing some long forgotten adventure that only Pete remembered. "True," said Pete. "But we's got a few things goin' for us. We got us the element o' surprise. An' we can exploit them Watcher's crazy ideals. We may not 'ave any rifles, but neither do they. An' at least we's got 'orses!"

"I don't know, Pete. I don't think we'll catch those Watchers off guard. They'll be ready for us. Mark my words, they will. And as far as the horses go, that won't help us much. Might help us get away, but it won't help us spring Mycah loose."

Pete rubbed his chin. The shorter Stormguard drew his tongue across his teeth in thought, while the taller Stormguard looked confused. Rayven seemed indifferent.

Cam snorted in disgust.

"Well you sure seem to give up easy," she said. "C'mon, think Chuckles! We've got to have something that can give us an edge."

"We ain't got much, lass," said Jerud as he paced back and forth. "No cannons. No rifles. Rayven's the only one with even a bow. We've got limited supplies. It's just the six of us and your dog against—"

Jerud's eyes widened and he stopped in his tracks. "That's it."

"What's it?" asked Cam.

"I've got it. I know how we can rescue Mycah. It's crazy. Completely, utterly, totally crazy, but I think it'll work."

"Well, go on, spill it," said Pete.

"You're not going to like it," said Jerud.

"Come on, Chuckles," said Cam. "What's your plan?"

"I'll tell you, but first answer me a question. How fast can Winny run?"

***

Mycah lay in the back of the cart, his fingers trailing over the rough wooden planks at his side. Two dozen campfires smoldered around him, but their dim glow barely illuminated the cart's interior. No matter. For this particular task, Mycah preferred the darkness.

His fingers worked independently, gliding over the grains in the wood and searching for irregularities. Irregularities signified weaknesses—weaknesses his fingernails could exploit. His index and middle fingers traced the edge of two grains that drew together. A section from a tree's core. Finding a small gap, Mycah dug his fingernails in and pried out. With a little effort, he coaxed a finger-length wooden shard from the plank. He poked it with his index finger. It came to a neat point, ideal for the work awaiting it. Perfect.

Sliding his hands down to his side, Mycah picked up another splinter he'd extracted earlier. It was roughly the same length as the one just plucked except the end was rounded and blunt. This splinter had required a little more effort. Originally, it had been much thicker, but he'd picked strips from the splinter's shaft piece by piece, fashioning it into a miniature cudgel. Mycah peered at the crude imitation of a skeleton key in the dim light. Not ideal, but it would do.

Grasping one splinter in each hand, Mycah attacked the padlock that fastened them together. His first attempt to free himself had involved just the crude skeleton key, but apparently whoever had crafted the padlock hadn't been a complete buffoon. Though it looked rudimentary, the lock actually contained a two lever system. Mycah had slid the skeleton key into the keyway, turned, and heard a click, but the lock hadn't released. Another lever needed to be pressed simultaneously—a lever hidden by numerous snaking wards within the lock. To bypass those, Mycah needed a second tool. A precise one.

With the sharp shard grasped in his right hand, Mycah closed his eyes and let his fingers do the work. The splinter became an extension of his hand—an extension of his own mind. It poked, it prodded, it tested, without conscious input, without direction. When the splinter met resistance and he heard the faint scrape of metal on metal, he turned the skeleton key. He heard a satisfying click.

Mycah smiled. It felt good to pick a lock. How long had it been since he'd pilfered the Stormqueen's staff? A couple months? Longer? It felt like ages. When the Stormqueen had roped him and Jerud into her quest, he'd assumed the theft of the tablet would've required a full assortment of his skills—sneaking, masquerading, lock picking, perhaps even a few lies. The retrieval of the tablet had required none of that. In fact, it hadn't involved any special skills at all, unless you considered Cam's gender a skill. But the Stormqueen couldn't have known that. Even though she seemed to possess untold knowledge about the Garden, there was no way the Stormqueen would've sent him and Jerud to retrieve the tablet if she'd known how ill-suited they were to the task. Would she?

Questions bounced around Mycah's mind like fireflies in a jar. Not just questions about the Stormqueen's motives but questions of all sorts. What was the Garden, really? Had it been formed and cursed by God's own hand? And had he really 'eaten' from the tree of knowledge as the Knight Captain insisted? His talk with Captain Orwell had only confused him more about the events that had transpired. He needed time to think about everything he'd absorbed, both literally and figuratively.

Mycah blinked away the thoughts. There'd be time for answers once he and Jerud returned to Guildean and confronted the Stormqueen. Assuming he could get away, and assuming he could find Jerud. Had he even escaped the Watcher's clutches? Mycah fiercely hoped the big man was all right.

Cam, too, for that matter. Odd that he felt so concerned about her seeing as he'd only known her for a few days, and she'd been a royal pain in the ass the entire time. Insufferable woman, with her constant jeering and boasting! To be fair, he did his own fair share of gibing and boasting, but it was funny when he did it! When Cam did it, it was just annoying. Nonetheless, Mycah felt responsible for her. He'd involved her in his and Jerud's affairs, and he needed to make sure she made it out in one piece. Of course, he first needed to extricate himself from his current predicament, and that was no trifle.

Mycah slipped his hands from their bonds, carefully laying the chains down one link at a time to avoid making noise. At this late hour, his guards would expect him to be asleep. Unnecessary clanking would arouse suspicion. Hunching low to keep his profile below the sides of the cart, he bent over and used his makeshift tools to unlock the padlock at his feet. With his hands free, the second padlock yielded in an instant. Ever so carefully, he crept to the edge of the cart and peered into the camp below.

Just beyond the cart, two guards were chatting in hushed tones, warming their hands by a fire. Mycah recognized one of them. Before dusk, the man had dragged him from the cart and punched him in the stomach several times before informing him he had fifteen seconds to urinate before being thrown back into the wagon. Apparently not all the Watchers possessed the same level of composure and forgiveness that the Knight Captain did. Mycah didn't recognize the other Watcher, but both guards seemed alert despite the late hour. Beyond them, scores of Watchers lay asleep upon bedrolls, and at least a dozen that Mycah could see stubbornly resisted the call of the night, tending fires, sharpening blades, or preparing meals for the morning.

Mycah stifled a curse. He hadn't realized just how many Watchers the camp held, and far too many of them remained awake. Not only that, but his cart sat square in the center of the Watcher camp. Regardless of the direction he chose, sneaking out would involve bypassing a multitude of sentries. Even if he were armed—which he wasn't—fighting his way out would have proved impossible. Flight was an option, but he doubted he could make it through the throng of Watchers without being subdued. Perhaps he could steal the horse that had drawn his cart.

Mycah peered to his side. Blast! The horse had been unhooked and put out to pasture for the night. While it likely would've been too slow to help in his escape, he might've provided a decent distraction at least.

Mycah tapped his skull. A distraction! That's what he needed! But it couldn't come from the cart. That would draw attention.

He slouched back down and considered the supplies loaded at his side. Perhaps something in the cart could be thrown to create a diversion or tossed into a fire to create an unexpected blaze. As he started to pick at a burlap sack's drawstrings, he heard several alarmed shouts alongside a familiar sound—a low, deep bark.

Mycah sprawled on the cart's baseboards instinctively to avoid being seen, pretending he was still chained. Nonetheless, curiosity forced him to crane his neck up to try to catch a glimpse of whatever was causing the commotion. More shouts and barking reached Mycah's ears. A black and brown blur crossed into his field of view, speeding through the camp, knocking down one of Mycah's guards as it barreled over a campfire. Hot coals sprayed everywhere, setting fire to several bedrolls.

Winny! Despite never having seen her run so fast, Mycah was sure the blur was her. But what in the world was she doing in the camp? Were Jerud and Cam mounting a rescue?

As confused thoughts raced through his head, the baseboards of the cart began to rattle. That's when the shouts of alarms turned into screams of pure terror.

All around him, he heard men shouting, boots stomping, and swords ringing as they were drawn from sheaths.

Winny's barking was swallowed by an unholy clamor that rose like a giant wave, an eerie amalgamation of hundreds of high-pitched screeches and the clatter of twice as many tiny feet. Tiny, *clawed* feet. Mycah knew the cacophony well.

Throwing caution to the wind, he bolted upright and absorbed the nightmarish scene unfolding before his eyes. Hundreds upon hundreds of Jabberwocks streamed from the darkness of night into the Watcher camp, hissing and screaming like banshees sent forth from the depths of Hell. The Watchers at the far end of camp were being overrun, torn to shreds under a blanket of razor-sharp teeth and flashing claws. Nearby, Watchers were mounting a hasty defense, linking in twos and threes, backs together to protect against the crazed monsters. Swords hacked into the ravenous beasts, sending leathery limbs flying and sour stinking blood spraying. Screams of men and beast alike filled the air.

Mycah peered to his side. His ill-tempered Watcher guard cleaved a lunging Jabberwock in twain with a powerful sword stroke. As his blade cleared through the last of its viscera, his eyes shifted and he locked onto Mycah. With a roar, he rushed the cart.

"Secure the prison...ARGH!"

The Watcher guard stumbled as an arrow sprouted from his chest. He gurgled something incomprehensible and fell to his knees. Another nearby Watcher turned upon hearing his cry, but before he could take two steps toward the cart an arrow slammed into his sternum. An arrow fletched with feathers of darkest night. What in the blazes was going on?

A growing thunder of hooves drew Mycah's attention. Swathed by the flickering flames of spreading fires, a statuesque hero with flowing hair and a gleaming sword spurred forth a salt-and-pepper steed. As the steed's churning legs carried it forward, the hero's sword swung down and sliced a Watcher square across the brow, bursting his head like an overripe melon. Never slowing, the steed barreled over hissing Jabberwocks and flew toward the cart, skidding to a halt in front of him. Mycah's eyes widened. The steed was Applesnatch and the hero none other than Cam!

"Get on!" screamed Cam.

Mycah jumped from the cart onto Applesnatch's back, unceremoniously smacking his tender man parts on the saddle as he landed.

"Uff," he groaned.

From behind, Mycah heard a roar and felt a whoosh of air as a massive steed carrying an even more massive man rushed by. Bellowing with all his might, Jerud careened through the camp, cracking Champ's reins as he cleared a path through the carnage.

"Yah!" yelled Cam, as she snapped Applesnatch's reins sharply.

The mare reared and lunged forth. Mycah grabbed Cam around the waist tightly with both arms, hanging on for dear life as the steed surged into the fray.

"Good timing," said Mycah, as they raced behind Jerud.

"Just remember," shouted Cam over the cries of the Watchers and the screeching of the Jabberwocks. "That's two you owe me now!"

Indeed. Mycah had barely known Cam a week and already she'd saved his life twice. Oh the indignity of being saved by a woman, and multiple times no less. He'd never hear the end of it from Pete and Jerud, though clearly Jerud had a hand in the rescue as well. As they raced out of the camp and into the darkness, Mycah tightened his grip around Cam's midsection, and for once Cam didn't complain.

***

Knight Captain Orwell bathed in the red-orange light of a raging fire, sword held tightly in his fist. Rage boiled within him like a hot summer tempest. Blood stained his pristine white uniform, both his own and that of the unholy demons. A gash upon his leg would require sutures. Other less serious wounds would heal on their own.

A carnage unlike any he'd ever known surrounded him. Hundreds of the foul smelling, leathery demons pockmarked the ruined camp, some dismembered, some hacked into pieces, some still twitching in the throes of death. At least a dozen of his men had joined the everlasting vigil of the dead, and thrice as many nursed injuries ranging from minor to severe.

And in the madness of it all his prisoner, the heretic Mycah, had escaped. Gone. Rescued by his heathen brethren during the demonic assault.

A young, rangy Watcher appeared at the Knight Captain's side, panting from exertion. "You asked to see me, Captain?"

"Brother Mason," said the Knight Captain in a firm voice, his eyes focused deep within the soul of the fire. "Gather two of your best fellow scouts and return to the

Shrine. Seek out Brother Aldon. Have him send a missive to the Archbishop of Guildean. Have it read as follows: 'Suspicions confirmed. Suspects found, one captured. Attacked by demons. Suspect escaped. Dark times afoot. Full force of the Watchers returns to Guildean.'"

The Knight Captain turned to the rangy youth. "Repeat it to me."

The young watcher gulped, but he recited the missive flawlessly.

"Good," said the Captain. "Once you've delivered the message, gather the remaining Watchers, every man with the strength left to wield a blade. Follow us to Guildean. Set a hard pace. Now leave. Godspeed, Brother."

The sentry sprinted off into the darkness, leaving the Knight Captain to his thoughts. Rage still coursed through his veins. With anger threatening to cloud his judgment, the Knight Captain did the only thing he knew could sooth him. He thrust his sword into the loose soil at his feet, knelt beside it, and prayed.

"Heavenly Father," he said in a voice barely above a whisper. "Forgive me, for I have failed you. You delivered the child of sin into my hands so I might bring him to face your judgment before all of mankind. You sent the demons here tonight to test the depth of my faith and the efficaciousness of my commission. In the latter I've failed you, for I let the heretic escape. But in the face of evil, the Watcher's faith is strongest, and Lord, my faith has never been stronger."

Knight Captain Orwell stared into the darkened heavens. "Lord, I am your servant, and I hear your will. I vow, by your light and your grace, that I will find the heathen and his brethren, and I will bring them to justice. If it takes the last breath of my mortal soul, I will deliver them to your gates by the strength of my own blade! *I swear it!*

Slowly rising from his knees, the Knight Captain pulled his sword from the earth and held it high. In a loud, carrying voice, he cried out.

"Watchers! Hear my voice, and speak with me our creed! *In darkest night, the Watcher's eye is sharpest!*"

Voices from all around joined the Knight Captain's, booming from the farthest depths of the camp.

"*In fiercest tempest, the Watcher's resolve is strongest! In the face of evil, the Watcher's faith is strongest! We are the Guardians of men! We are the protectors of the Garden!*"

"Come, Watchers!" yelled the Knight Captain. "We march! To Guildean!"

CHAPTER TWENTY-SIX

Concerning Confessions

Rain burst into Master Crawford's quarters, her magenta robes swirling around her in a cyclone of chiffon and georgette.

"Give me some good news, Edward. I'm in desperate need of some. How did the meeting with the Captain of the Watch go?"

Chamberlain Crawford rose from his desk, setting down a sheaf of papers atop an already hefty stack of documents. His brow was creased, and dark circles under his eyes spoke of restless nights.

"Poorly, I'm afraid. The Watch Captain was unwilling to pledge his support in a conflict. Even when I offered certain financial incentives for him and his men."

"Bah." Rain paced back and forth across the room. "You know what that means. The Watch has already been bought off. Our offer was likely a pittance compared to whatever they've already been supplied with."

"Probably so, Mistress," said Master Crawford. "If it's any consolation, the Watch seems unwilling to pick sides at all. If they were bribed, it was likely to ensure they wouldn't come to our aid, not to fight us."

"Little good that'll do. Should the Church take up arms against us, we stand little chance of putting up a meaningful resistance."

Rain pressed fingers to her throbbing temple. The Church. Of course it had been the Church. Master Crawford's men had finally unearthed the money trail drawing back from the attempted theft of her staff. The process had been laborious and time consuming. The trail had contained more twists and turns than a back alley in the Guildean slums. But ultimately it led to the source of the financing—the Grand Cathedral of Guildean.

She'd always suspected the Church, of course. What other entity possessed both the means and the motive to depose her? The arms of the Church were far reaching, and as for the motives of the Church leadership? Well suffice to say that a cross-shaped target had been affixed to her quite some time ago.

The power of the Stormqueens stood as an affront to the veracity of gospel. Nowhere in scripture did it mention that God had created powerful enchantresses capable of harnessing the winds and rains to do their bidding. Instead the scriptures preached that all men were equal and powerless before God, and all women were equal and even more powerless before both God and man. A Stormqueen's powers were reason enough for animosity, but that a woman wielded these powers created an offense too great to overlook.

Rain was certain the Church would've moved against her sooner if it felt it could afford to, but the Stormqueens were too well liked and too vital to the populace to be expendable. The peasants relied upon Rain and her fellow Stormqueens to usher in the seasons and bring drenching showers for their crops. An attack by the Church on a Stormqueen would've created a bloody uprising no one would've benefitted from.

But with the changing climate and the past winter's bitter cold, rumors had begun—rumors that Rain's power over the elements was slipping. The Church had paid careful heed to the whispers and decided the time to strike was nigh. Thus they'd commissioned the theft of her staff, a commission that had landed in the laps of the thieves Mycah and Jerud. Ultimately they'd failed, but the Church's die had been cast.

Never mind that the staff was a meaningless token. Most assumed Rain drew her power from it during her autumn and springtime rituals, but the staff was nothing more than an intricately carved piece of wood. Few souls in the world knew that her connection with the elements actually flowed through an innocuous ring she wore on the third digit of her left hand. Without that Rain would be crippled, but the staff? That she could live without.

Nonetheless, the Church viewed the staff as a symbol of power, and in that they were correct. If the theft of the staff had been successful, Rain would've been weakened in the eyes of the populace, and any subsequent fluctuations in the weather would've been pinned as stemming from her loss.

Despite the failure of the thieves to steal the staff, the Church had plunged forth unabated. They'd seeded the city with fanatical criers raving of the Stormqueen's failures. They'd bribed officials to publish edicts questioning the intensity of the summer rains. In addition, fires had spread through numerous wheat fields to the west of the city. Rumor had it that representatives of the Church had set the fires to drive up wheat prices and create illusions of scarcity, leading some to question the summer's crop yields. So many carefully placed schemes to make it seem Rain was losing her grip on the elements. That grip, once lost, would make her expendable.

Rain snorted. The irony of the situation wasn't lost on her. After sensing a blip in the weather patterns, the Church had pulled out all the stops to discredit her when instead they merely could've waited. She clenched her fist and tried to feel the connection through her ring. The power still lurked there, but it was fainter than she wished.

Rain shook her head. If the Church deposed her, what did they plan to do with her? Imprison her and force her to control the weather from the confines of a cell? Would they kill her and hope the rest of the Stormqueens could hold back the elements without her? They couldn't possibly intend to remove all the Stormqueens, could they? Without them, humanity would be buried under an unrelenting winter. Civilization would fall. The archbishop had to know that... didn't he?

Rain wilted into a hard-backed sofa at the side of Master Crawford's room. Edward preferred his sofas nice and firm. She liked hers overstuffed, personally, but this one would have to do. Rain sighed and rubbed her knuckles.

See? You're polar opposites. You'd never even be able to decide upon the furniture.

Edward stood nearby, concern showing in his eyes. As Rain gazed upon his broad shoulders, grey hair, and weathered features, part of her wished nothing more than to throw duty to the wind and give into temptation. But she didn't. She couldn't. Not yet.

Master Crawford sat down beside her. He stretched an arm out behind her on the sofa.

"Rain," he said, calling her by her name as he so rarely did. "These are trying times. Know that whatever happens, whatever trials await us, I'll always be by your side. I'll always be there for you. I just wanted you to know that."

Rain reached up and grasped Edward's fingers with her own. "Thank you, Edward. I appreciate that. More than you know."

And so they sat, hand in hand, waiting through the night. Waiting together.

***

The wind blew, bringing with it a coolness that seemed unnatural given the season. Mycah hunched closer to the campfire and rubbed his hands together, trying to banish the chill. The temperature of the evening air hinted that autumn had arrived, but Pete with his seemingly encyclopedic knowledge of the movements of the heavens insisted the autumnal equinox was still weeks away. Otherwise, he said, Lunaris would be visible coincident with Cheru and Ubim, and the tail of the Lupus constellation would be lower in the sky. Or at least he said something resembling that in Pete-speak.

Mycah supposed Pete must be right. If autumn had arrived, that would mean the Stormqueen's curse would've already come to fruition, and the dreaded demon would've taken possession of his and Jerud's souls. Since his heart still beat in his chest it must be summer, but blast it all if the chill in the air didn't seem a little unnatural.

Nearby, Cam sat on her backpack while Winny, curled up in a tight ball at her feet, soaked in the fire's warmth upon her brindled backside. She grasped a paring knife in her right hand and a piece of pine she'd whittled into a crude facsimile of a dog in her left. Virtually every night for the past two weeks she'd spent a couple hours whittling, each time creating a figurine of a dog, each time becoming frustrated with the result and throwing the carving away. Mycah had praised her ability with the knife, but Cam always mumbled something about the carvings looking like monkey nuts.

Cam's knife bit into her fourth attempt. Mycah peered at the figurine. It was impressive how much detail she put into it. The dog's tongue lolled to the side, and its ears perked happily. Cam's blade scraped at the dog's flank, adding texture to its fur.

"Is that supposed to be Winny?" asked Mycah.

Cam kept her head down as she dug the knife into the soft wood. "Does it look like Winny?"

A long snout protruded from the dog's face, and the fur seemed shaggier than that of Cam's trusty hound. "Um... no. Not really."

"Well there's your answer, then."

Mycah raised his eyebrows and blinked. Weeks after meeting her, she still remained a puzzle. He lifted his head and searched for Pete and Jerud in the darkness. The two grizzled veterans were tending to the horses, checking their hooves for debris, brushing them, and giving them food and water. The poor horses were drained, but so were they all.

The flight from the Watchers had been exhausting. The night of the escape they'd ridden the horses hard, through the dawn and well into mid-morning. Eventually, they'd been forced to slow, as the horses' lungs pumped like bellows and their mouths had begun to lather. Applesnatch had held up admirably considering she'd shouldered both himself and Cam. Of course Jerud outweighed the two of them put together, so it was no surprise Champ had labored the hardest of all.

At that point, they'd all dismounted and trotted with the horses until nightfall. With the threat of the Watchers looming over them, they'd slept only a few hours before waking early and repeating the entire process. Again they'd ridden in the morning, and again they'd dismounted and trotted with the horses until well after dark. The process became routine for several days until Mycah stumbled around like the walking dead from lack of sleep. He began to drift off and hallucinate during the morning rides, dreaming of Watchers and demons, Jabberwocks and cold, sterile gardens with plants made of metal. Though they all desperately needed sleep, Rayven had pushed them mercilessly onward, claiming the Watchers would be pushing just as hard to catch them.

Rayven. Seeing him ride out of the woods with Pete and a pair of beefy Stormguards as they fled the Watcher camp had been quite a shock. Jerud had explained the situation later of course, telling him Rayven had followed them since they'd set out upon their quest. The Stormqueen had sent him to keep watch on them. When Rayven and his crony guardsmen had noticed the Watchers following them into the Garden, they'd gone to recruit Pete and laid in waiting for him and Jerud. Instead they found Jerud and Cam, and eventually Jerud hatched the idea to lure the Jabberwocks into an attack on the Watcher camp as a diversion.

Mycah craned his head over to his left. In the distance he could see Rayven and the Stormguards sitting at their own campfire eating a hastily prepared supper. Despite the clear disdain Rayven showed for the guardsmen, he always made camp with them at night, never once joining Mycah, Cam, Jerud, and Pete at their fire. Perhaps prior to Mycah's rescue Jerud had made it clear he was unwelcome in their camp, or perhaps Cam had insulted him. Mycah certainly wouldn't put it past her—she seemed to have a knack for that sort of thing. Or perhaps Rayven simply understood that his presence upset them, so out of respect for their feelings he let them be.

Rayven? Feelings? Mycah shook his head. When he'd been imprisoned in the Stormqueen's dungeon, he'd fumed and raged and plotted unkind ways to extract revenge upon the bird man for his treachery. The very thought of Rayven had made hate swell up from the depths of his stomach, but when he'd finally seen him again all Mycah had felt was indifference. With all that had happened in the past couple months—the Stormqueen's curse, the Jabberwocks, the Watchers, the Garden—Rayven's treachery seemed a distant memory. Not that Mycah cared for the spooky black haired bastard, but he figured his assistance in his escape made them at least somewhat closer to equal.

Mycah turned his head to the fire, but after a few moments he turned away. Every time he stared into a fire now he saw visions. Visions of fire and metal, pain and fear, and blood. *Always blood. So much blood.* Better not to stare at fires for too long lest the visions return.

He'd tried to talk to Jerud about what they'd experienced at the heart of the Garden, but the big man seemed unwilling to discuss it. Every time Mycah brought up the subject, Jerud would frown and switch topics. Either that or simply say they should wait—wait until they'd met with the Stormqueen. When they exchanged the tablet and Rain freed them from the curse, then there'd be time for answers. Until then, all they could do was speculate, and what good was that?

Well the time for answers was almost nigh. After weeks of flight they sat camped in the same pasture in which he, Jerud, and Pete had spent their first night out of the city so many weeks ago. The city's farms sprouted around them, and not even a day's ride separated them from the city.

"I can't believe we're actually going to make it," mumbled Mycah.

"What was that?" asked Cam, lifting her head from her work.

"Oh, nothing," said Mycah.

Applesnatch whinnied, and he turned his head toward the horses. At least she seemed happy, despite having to share her saddle with multiple riders. Mycah was still surprised Applesnatch had let Cam ride her at all, but it seemed as if Cam, Applesnatch, and Winny had all formed an instant bond. Perhaps a hidden force existed that tied together females in unity against men, regardless of species.

Mycah eyed the woman across from him. The fire bathed her face in a warm, healthy glow, and a loose strand of hair hung lazily across her brow. Part of him wanted to reach out and tuck the strand back behind her ear, but Cam would bite his finger off if he tried.

"Cam, can I ask you a question?"

"Oh, no. Not again."

Mycah turned up his hands. "What do you mean, not again?"

Cam sighed as she looked up from her figurine. "Another question. Always so many questions with you. You're like a bottomless pit of curiosity."

"Is that a bad thing?"

"Just ask your question."

Mycah took a deep breath. "Why are you still here?"

Cam glared at him.

"It's not like that," said Mycah. "I'm not trying to get rid of you. It's just that..." Mycah paused. "Look, when we first met it seemed you had a lot on your mind, like maybe there was something serious going on. I asked you to come along with us to the Garden. I'm still not entirely sure why. Maybe I thought it would be better if we all tagged along. That it would be safer. But then there was all that craziness, and we touched that sphere, and the Watchers got me, and—"

Cam looked at him in confusion. "Are you going to make a point, eventually?"

"Ugh. This isn't coming out like I'd hoped." Mycah wiped his fingers through his hair. "All I want to say is, I don't know what's going to happen once we meet back up with the Stormqueen. I'd love to have you with us. But if there's something else you need to go deal with, either now or later, I'll understand."

Cam put down her paring knife and looked at the dog figurine between her hands. Twice she opened her mouth, but each time she stopped before words sprung from her lips. She stroked the side of the wooden dog with her thumb as the fire crackled merrily.

"My dad taught me to whittle when I was seven," said Cam after a long silence. "Made me a dog just like this the first day he sat me down. His was better than this. Mine's crap. His? The ears, the smile? They were more lifelike. More full of passion."

Mycah was about to open his mouth to ask Cam what she was talking about, but a tingling in the back of his mind stopped him. On more than one occasion, Marta had told him to shut up and listen, and Mycah had a suspicion this might be one of those instances.

"Dad taught me a lot of things. How to catch lizards. How to climb trees. How to start a fire. And how to fight. Always told me that a real man faces his foes head on, toe to toe, blade to blade. I think he always wanted a boy, but he got me instead.

"I was always good at fighting. Dad loved it, but mother hated it. Hated that I'd spend the summer afternoons beating on a scarecrow with a stick. Hated it even more when I graduated to a blade. Said it didn't befit a woman. Said it would get me into trouble. I guess that's one thing she was right about."

Cam breathed a deep, heartfelt sigh. "I always thought he'd be there for me, you know? Always thought he'd be there to stick up for me in front of mother. When I kicked a hole in the chicken coop, he told mother to calm down. When I knocked out Dean Thomas's front teeth, he said I was just sticking up for myself."

Mycah didn't, in fact, know what Cam was talking about, but he wasn't about to say so. Not now. Not when he noticed the faintest glimmer of something wet and shiny in the corner of Cam's eye.

"One day mother raged at me. Who knows why... And dad did nothing. *Nothing*. Said he didn't feel right. Said he was tired. Said he didn't have the strength. I yelled and screamed. I cursed him to his face. I was angry. Shouldn't have done that. Still can't believe how fast it took him. He seemed so full of life, and then..."

Cam paused. After a moment, she wiped at her eyes. Mycah said nothing.

"Afterward, mother told me I needed to change myself right quick, stop living out dad's idle fantasies. Clean my shit up. Maybe she didn't say that. She never swore. Whatever, it doesn't matter. I told her to go stuff it. She didn't take it well. So she tried to get rid of me. Thought she could just sell me to the highest bidder. As if I was going to stand for that. Me! Can you believe that?"

Mycah wasn't sure if he was supposed to answer, but luckily Cam just kept right on talking, her voice getting angrier.

"And wouldn't you know? It was that rat bastard Morgan Keralt that paid the bride price. Thought he could fix it so his sodden son could finally tie the knot, as if that would make everyone forget what a corpulent, abusive sack of dung he really was!"

Cam gritted her teeth. "No. Screw mother. She was wrong. Learning to use a blade didn't get me into trouble. It's the only thing that saved me from a life of Hell."

After that Cam stayed silent for a long time, staring into the fire, a mixture of rage, pain, and sadness glimmering in her watery eyes. So much time passed that Mycah feared there might be something wrong with her, but what could he possibly say to her after hearing all of that?

Finally, Cam forced out a sound halfway between a snort and a laugh. "Guess I never really answered your question, did I? Why I'm here? I don't really know. Guess I don't have anywhere else to go. Can't go home. Wouldn't want to, even if I could. Got no family left. No one I'd consider family, at least."

Mycah realized he'd been leaning in, listening to Cam's story with rapt attention. He leaned back and rubbed his hands in front of the fire to give them something to do.

"I'm an orphan, you know," he said, to break the silence. "Never had a mum or a dad. Heck, Jerud's the closest thing to family I've got. Sounds like maybe I didn't miss that much, though."

Cam lifted her eyes from the fire. "How come you never mentioned that?"

"What? About me being an orphan? Guess it never came up."

Cam's eyes had lost their fire. Now they looked tired. "No, Mycah, you did miss stuff growing up on your own. A lot of stuff. You just missed the good and the bad."

"Huh," said Mycah. "I guess you're right."

The crackling of the fire filled the void left by the end of their conversation. Cam picked up her paring knife and went back to work on the fur of her dog-shaped figurine. Mycah lay upon his bedroll, trying to sort through what Cam had shared with him.

"Oh... Mycah?"

He craned his head toward Cam. "Yeah?"

"It's Camilla."

"What?"

"When we first met. You asked for my name. I told you to call me Cam. But my name's Camilla."

Mycah let that soak in for a moment. "You know, I think I like Cam better."

"Good," said Cam with a stroke of her paring knife. "So do I."

Mycah settled back down and stared into the sky. He wasn't entirely sure what had just happened or why Cam had decided to share that with him, but it seemed Cam would be sticking around for a little bit longer. And strangely enough, he liked the sound of that.

**

Father Maple awoke early once again, his hip paining him as it did most nights. He was used to it. The Lord had blessed him with more than his fair share of years. It was only just that He extract a bit of a price for his happiness.

Soon enough, the ultimate price would be paid. Father Maple was ready for it, but at the same time he hoped he had some time left yet. The garden still needed his attention.

Thankfully, Brother Georgio had acclimated to his frequent bouts of insomnia. The friar didn't stir as he donned his habit and slippers and headed up the stairs.

A cool breeze stirred the folds of Father Maple's robes as he pushed into the cathedral gardens. Such a breeze seemed odd given the season, and yet who was he to question the Lord's plan? The Lord worked as He willed, and if the Lord willed a cool summer Father Maple would suffer it, though his weary bones preferred the heat.

The light of dawn had not yet begun to brighten the sky. Normally, Father Maple cherished the hour before dawn for prayer. The chirping of crickets and the caroling of songbirds melded with the scents of roses and soil and dew to create a perfect backdrop for meditation.

Today, however, would not be a morning for meditation. People milled about, rushing across the grounds, moving with a haste that belied the hour. A multitude of lights shone from the upper windows of the cathedral. His eyes strained toward the barracks where a swarm of grey and white uniforms buzzed around angrily. Over the past few weeks the numbers of the Holy Guard had swelled almost fivefold. He'd grown used to seeing the guardsmen training and rehearsing their formations in the afternoons, but to see them awake and active at this hour of the morning was certainly out of the ordinary.

Father Maple noticed a friendly face, that of Brother Aldemant, standing not twenty paces away, holding a lantern and gazing upon the sea of activity.

"Brother," said Father Maple. "Do you have any idea what this commotion is about?"

The Brother jumped, startled by the Father's voice. "Ahh, F-F-Father Maple," he said in a stuttering voice. "I've h-h-heard rumors only, from p-p-passing guardsmen, but they are g-g-grim rumors indeed."

Father Maple raised an eyebrow. "What sort of rumors?"

"Well," said the Brother. "It w-w-would appear there was some sort of m-m-missive, from the W-W-Watchers. They've been attacked, by d-d-d—"

"Take your time, brother."

Brother Aldemant swallowed. "d-d-*demons!*"

"What? You cannot be serious?"

"It g-g-gets worse," said the Brother. "Apparently, there is evidence that someone s-s-summoned the beasts and set them upon the W-W-Watchers. None other than the S-S-Stormqueen herself, they say. The Holy Guard now g-g-gathers to subdue her and bring her to j-j-justice. Father, I f-f-fear this may be the start of w-w-war."

CHAPTER TWENTY-SEVEN

To the Stormpalace!

Driven by a desire to free himself from under the Stormqueen's yoke, Mycah awoke early the following morning and helped Pete saddle the horses while Cam performed her usual early morning calisthenics.

Once mounted, the leagues between themselves and Guildean glided past under the steady hoofbeats of the horses. Jerud seemed lost in thought, perhaps anticipating the final moment of reckoning with the Stormqueen that awaited them. Cam, sitting behind Mycah in the saddle, seemed oddly quiet as well. Perhaps she regretted sharing as much as she had and today intended to make up for it by barely uttering a word. With Pete choosing to munch on a stalk of hay in lieu of talking, Rayven—who muttered two entire sentences during the morning—seemed downright chatty.

By midday Guildean had popped into view, marked prominently at its center by the gravity-defying spires of the Grand Cathedral. As they neared the city, Mycah's neck started to feel itchy. That only happened when something wasn't right, but glancing back at the path behind

359

them he noticed no sign of the Watchers. Nonetheless, his suspicions arose. The thoroughfare seemed oddly empty, and fewer vendors hawked their wares from the roadside than normal.

As they approached the city gates, Mycah reined in Applesnatch.

"I knew it," he murmured. "Something's up."

Rayven and the guardsmen pulled up beside him. The tall, thickheaded Stormguard known as Johnah spoke.

"What's the hold up? Let's get you scabs back to the Stormqueen."

Mycah pointed at the gates. "Don't you notice anything odd up ahead?"

Rayven gave a snort of derision, as if to imply that asking anything of Johnah was asking too much.

"No city watch at the gates," said Jerud, answering Mycah's question. "That's odd. I wonder if something's amiss."

In response, a low, booming rumble echoed out from deep within the city. A second and a third followed in close proximity.

"What the hell was that?" said Cam.

Jerud and Pete looked at each other. "Sounded like... cannons," said Jerud.

Sten, the shorter of the two Stormguards, who by Mycah's estimation had muttered almost as few words as Rayven the entire journey, trotted his horse forward and spoke in a low voice. "No... It can't be. Not already. Rain said there would be time. Damn it..."

Sten turned his horse to face them. His jaw was set firmly, and his demeanor had shifted. His appearance of aloofness had disappeared, replaced instead with a hardened visage.

"Alright, listen up. Those blasts came from the direction of the Stormpalace. Our queen may be at risk. You four." Sten gestured at Mycah, Cam, Jerud and Pete. "Keep your mounts close to mine. I'll lead the way. Johnah and Rayven, bring up the rear. Keep your eyes open for anything suspicious. If anyone challenges us, don't hesitate to use force. Now come on!"

Sten spurred his horse into the city, and Mycah had no choice but to kick Applesnatch into a gallop behind him. More booms echoed from the direction of the Stormpalace as they galloped through deserted streets at a breakneck pace. Questions rattled through his mind. Was the Stormqueen's palace under attack? If so, by who? Wouldn't the city guards have come to her aid? Was that why they weren't present at the city gates? And why were the streets so empty? Had people barricaded themselves indoors to keep themselves safe from attack?

As they careened around corners and through alleyways, a cold sweat began to drip from Mycah's brow. Throughout the entire journey, he'd concerned himself with what the Stormqueen would do should he and Jerud fail to retrieve her artifact, or worse yet, what would happen if her curse came to fruition. Never once had he considered a scenario where the Stormqueen might perish before him! What would happen then? Would the curse be broken? He held no particular affection for the Stormqueen, but she needed to survive long enough to remove the blasted curse once and for all!

Through the worker's quarter they galloped, past locked storefronts and abandoned carts laden with summer squashes and melons. A few urchins roamed the streets looking for fruits and bread to steal, but the sensible adults had locked themselves indoors. Only furtive glances from behind closed shutters hinted at their presence.

Sten turned northward and led them into a maze of side streets. They galloped across an empty brickyard and into a residential area canopied by clotheslines laden with shirts and billowing white sheets. Cannons boomed intermittently, but soon other sounds became clear as well—a dull roar, born from men screaming and cheering, and sharp cracks of musket fire. Sten pulled his horse to an abrupt stop near the end of a narrow alley.

The Stormguard vaulted from his horse and peered around the exposed bricks. Applesnatch pranced nervously in place as Sten surveyed the surroundings. Mycah tried to sooth her with a gentle hand, but the sounds of the cannons and the smoke in the air had her spooked.

Sten pulled back from the corner, shaking his head. "This is bad. There's a barricade about two blocks ahead. A good two more blocks separate us from the southeast edge of the Stormpalace, and there's a sea of grey and white between that barricade and the palace walls."

Johnah pushed his way to the front and took a look. "Bloody Hell. Those Holy Guards are crawling all over the place. Too much smoke to see what the Hell's going on. God damnit! What do we do now?"

The Holy Guard.

Mycah swallowed a lump in his throat. The Watchers must've sent word about him back to Guildean after discovering the link between him and the Stormqueen, and they'd decided to take action. The entire Church was likely searching for him, Jerud, and the damned tablet!

"We'll double back," said Sten. "Head to the Third Street bridge. There's a service tunnel underneath the cross street that services the aqueduct. One of the side tunnels can lead us toward the Stormpalace. As long as the Holy Guard don't have it covered, we should be able to work our way back into the palace."

Mycah recalled the blueprints of the Stormpalace he'd obtained ages ago. None of them had given any indication that alternate, underground entrances into the palace existed, otherwise he would've used them to gain entry to the Stormqueen's quarters. Then again, none of the blueprints had mentioned a secret underground dungeon beneath the Stormqueen's estate either. Come to think of it, the dungeons had been surprisingly wet. It only made sense they were somehow connected to Guildean's underground aqueduct.

"Hold on a sec," said Jerud. "You're telling me the Stormpalace is surrounded by hostile guardsmen, is actively being fired upon by cannons, and you want to break back in? You've lost your mind, man."

"Our duty is to protect the Stormqueen no matter the cost," said Sten. "And unless I'm mistaken, you have a certain interest in seeing her through this battle yourselves."

Jerud paled slightly in response.

"Now saddle up. There's little time."

Sten leapt into his saddle and urged his horse back down the narrow alley. A few minutes of furious galloping brought them to the foot of the Third Street bridge. A steep embankment led down to where the aqueduct emerged from the earth's depths. A rusted metal grate covered the aqueduct's exit, but a porthole to its right offered an entrance into the sewers.

Sten sprung from his saddle and slid down the embankment. Johnah hopped off after him. Another boom rattled the cobblestones, and Applesnatch pranced nervously.

Mycah paused. "Hey, Sten... what about the horses?"

"Leave them," he said as he pried the manhole from its opening using a dagger.

"But..." Mycah glanced at Applesnatch. Ever since the flight from the Jabberwocks, he'd felt a special connection with the mare. Leaving her with Pete the first time had been hard enough. Now he was supposed to abandon her in the street with a battle raging mere blocks away?

"I can't," said Mycah. "She's a friend."

"We don't have time for this," shouted Sten. "Just leave the damn beast and be done with it!"

The manhole clattered to the ground.

"Look, I don't like it either, lad," said Jerud as he dismounted. "But what choice do we have? You know as well as I do that we need to finish this business with the Stormqueen once and for all. Unless..."

He turned his head.

"Oh no," said Pete. "Not again. I already stayed behind once. I'm comin' this time!"

Mycah hopped to the ground. "We can't leave the horses Pete. They're almost family. Besides, what would you tell your friend if—"

Pete was starting to turn red. "No, damnit! Why me? Cam loves—"

"Cam doesn't know the city," said Jerud. "And me and Mycah have got to go—for obvious reasons."

"Well what about Rayven?"

Rayven sniffed.

"BAH!" said Pete. His face had turned the color of a beet. He sighed and dropped his voice. "Fine. I'll take the 'orses. But only ours, not the Stormqueen's. I can't 'andle more 'an three. An' Jerud?"

"Yeah?"

"If anything 'appens to ya, I'll 'ave yer hide fer breakfast. Y'understand me?"

Jerud and Pete clasped hands.

"Go to Marta's if you can, Pete," said Jerud, as he released his lanky friend's grip. "Make sure she's safe. We'll meet you there when this is all over with."

Mycah turned toward the porthole below. Sten and Johnah had already disappeared into the tunnels, and he hurried to catch up. Winny bounded down the embankment and disappeared into the tunnel with a powerful leap. Jerud had a harder time of it, trying not to fall down as he descended the steep slope. Rayven looked on disapprovingly from the street. Cam, beating Mycah to the grating, slid into the porthole first. As soon as she disappeared, Mycah swung his feet over the opening and dropped down.

His feet splashed into several inches of standing water. Mycah blinked as he tried to acclimate his eyes to the darkness of the tunnel. He should've brought a brand, but they'd exhausted their supply during their trek through the Garden. He ran his hands across the walls. They were rough, made of old stone—like the tunnels leading from the Stormqueen's dungeon.

With a grunt and a wheeze, Jerud squeezed through the porthole and plopped down behind them.

"Tight fit, eh there Chuckles?"

"None of your guff now, Cam," said Jerud as he straightened his pants. "I ain't in the mood."

Rayven dropped into the tunnel last, slipping into the water like a raindrop. His hands made a quick striking motion, and a blaze erupted from a small torch held in his right fist.

Rayven eyed Jerud with disdain. "While a storm drain is an enticing spot to congregate, perhaps we could move along?"

In the distance, Mycah heard feet splashing. Sten and Johnah already commanded a sizable lead.

"Sure," said Mycah. "Just pass up that torch and—"

"I'll lead," said Rayven as he slid to the front.

"Fine by me," mumbled Jerud. "I'd rather not have my back exposed to you anyway."

Rayven led them through the tunnels at a swift pace, following the splashing of the Stormguard's boots. Despite the darkness and the tight confines, Winny bounded back and forth through the water and barked happily.

"Could you please silence that animal?" said Rayven.

"She's just having some fun," said Cam. "Ever heard of it?"

Rayven glared at her from the front.

Mycah had a sudden thought. "Hey Rayven, I'd bet you're a cat person, aren't you?"

Rayven paused in mid step for a fraction of a second, but Mycah noticed it.

"What makes you say that?" said Rayven.

The fact that you're a giant ass?

"Oh, just a hunch is all," said Mycah.

They continued to follow the splashing. Deeper underground they ventured, into tunnels seemingly made eons ago with walls carved straight out of the bedrock. The tunnels didn't just look old—they smelled old, like the inside of a tomb. No plants could survive in such utter darkness, but water lingered around their feet, and life found a way to prevail. A tiny, albino lizard scurried out of Mycah's way as he ran past.

Mycah spotted a glow in the distance and heard banging and curses. Turning a final corner, he saw Johnah holding a small brand like Rayven had while Sten banged upon an ancient wrought iron door, yelling powerfully.

"Can you hear me? Open up! In the name of the Queen!"

Rayven rested his forehead upon steepled fingers. "A locked door. Brilliant."

Sten turned. "Oh, save your contempt for once. Of course it's locked. I was hoping someone might be around to open it, but I've got a plan. You." He pointed at Mycah. "You've got nimble fingers if I recall. Work your magic."

Mycah stepped to the front of the throng and squatted in front of the door's keyhole. A wide keyway stared at him out of the thick iron, hinting at a pedestrian warded lock within.

"Should be easy," said Mycah. "As long as it's not dead bolted from the inside. Anyone got a wire or a thin dirk? Something like that?"

There were mumbles as individuals checked their pockets and backpacks. Rayven tossed Mycah an arrow with a field point. "Don't break it."

Mycah inserted the fine tip into the keyway. With a simple prod and poke of his fingers, he was rewarded with a satisfying click.

Sten wasted no time. He pressed his shoulder into the door and pushed. The door gave way, though the hinges protested loudly. Mycah barely had time to stand before the Stormguard had darted through the opening and into the hallway beyond.

"Hurry!" Sten shouted.

Mycah flipped the arrow back to Rayven and set off after him. Rough-hewn walls of dark basalt sped by, interspersed by occasional dim lanterns or recessed doorframes tightly sealed with hardened, fire-treated oak. Mycah stepped in a puddle as he passed a room that looked suspiciously like the cavern in which he'd once been so unceremoniously tossed.

"Hard to believe we finally made it back here, eh Jerud?" said Mycah.

"Yeah," puffed Jerud. "But this ain't over yet, lad. Let's just focus on getting back to the Stormqueen."

Mycah swallowed as he thought of the curse and nodded in response.

Sten led them up a long corridor and into passages that seemed more familiar. As they passed a doorway Mycah was fairly sure led to the laundry room, two deafening booms sounded out from above followed by crashes that shook dust from the walls and caused the floor to tremble. Before they reached the stairwell to the house proper, more crashes and booms rattled the walls, but these explosions sounded different than those from the cannons. A whip-like crack was followed by the sound of stampeding horses.

Sten paused at the foot of the stairwell. "Thunder... Rain's fighting back. That means she's still alive. Come on!"

With a few furious strides, they burst from the stairwell into the grand foyer at the base of the palace's double curved stairways. Men in ultramarine and yellow uniforms rushed back and forth, some carrying rifles and halberds, some shouting orders in strained voices, others carrying buckets of water and wet blankets. Smoke choked the air.

Winny whined. "Stay close and you'll be fine, girl," said Cam reassuringly.

At the center of the madness a tall man with broad shoulders and a face carved from granite shouted at every man that passed by and whacked those that failed to acknowledge him with a riding crop that he wielded in his right hand. Sten ran toward him.

"Captain!" said Sten.

"Sten," said the broad shouldered man. "What in blazes are you doing here? Where have you been?"

"Secret mission. Queen's orders. Just made it back."

"Well you picked a fine time to arrive. In case you hadn't noticed, we're rather deep in the weeds here. And who the Hell are these blighters?"

Captain Loren waved his riding crop at Mycah and the gang.

"Servants of the Stormqueen. Look, we need to find Rain. Where is she?"

"Harrying the blasted Holy Guard with all of her might. Last I saw her she was on the balcony—what's left of it anyway."

"Thanks."

Sten turned to run up the stairwell.

"Sten!" shouted the Captain.

"Yes?"

The Captain lowered his voice. "This will not end well for us. I'm not sure how much longer I can rally the men. If I fear our lines are on the verge of being compromised, I'll come for the Queen. Be sure your business doesn't interfere with our escape."

Sten nodded and ran up the stairs. Mycah followed, as did everyone else. A bare minute or two of flight carried them straight into a scene out of legends of old.

CHAPTER TWENTY-EIGHT

The Price of Freedom

Stormqueen Rain, dressed in a billowing gown of daffodil yellow, stood in front of a gaping hole in the side of the Stormpalace. Outside, dark clouds swirled menacingly, bone dry and crackling with energy. Mycah felt the hairs on his arms stand on end, whether from wonder or static in the air he couldn't be sure.

With bricks and mortar crumbling around her and hot winds whipping through the chamber, Rain stood in the hole, arms raised to the heavens, gesturing wildly. With each pump of her fist or point of her finger, a sharp crack of lightning darted out from the swirling clouds, blasting the courtyard below. Men screamed and cursed, and chunks of dirt and stone exploded into the air with deadly ferocity.

Four men had barricaded themselves in the chamber with the Stormqueen. Three of them were gigantic brutes wearing double yellow sashes upon their uniforms—the Queen's private guard. The other Mycah recognized as the chamberlain who'd stood by the Stormqueen's side throughout their first encounter.

371

"My Queen," shouted Sten.

Rain whirled as a blast struck the side of the room, shredding what was left of the balcony and sending stone chips flying. Rain stumbled and backed away from the hole.

The private guardsmen stood, hands on their weapons.

"All is well," said the Stormqueen, waving them down. "They're with us."

Rain ushered them into a back corner behind a make-shift barricade of dressers and sofas. "Sten," she said. "You've returned, and with the thieves. I'd begun to lose hope. Things haven't progressed as I'd hoped."

"Yes, my Queen. I can see that."

Rain turned to Mycah and Jerud, her face wrapped in a yellow veil of thin, almost sheer fabric. Mycah squinted at her face. He could almost make out her features. Almost.

"You survived," said Rain, eyeing Winny curiously. "And you brought others."

"You sound surprised," said Mycah.

"I am, but nonetheless pleased. But your return doesn't necessarily indicate success. Do you possess what I asked of you?"

"Yeah, we've got your tablet," said Mycah. "It wasn't easy, but we got it. Good thing we had Cam with us otherwise we'd all be out of luck."

Rain's eyes shifted to Cam. "What do you mean? This young woman discovered the tablet for you?"

Mycah shook his head. "No. We found it with that stone of yours. Sort of, anyway. But Cam allowed us to get it. It's a long story."

The Stormqueen's eyebrows rose. "Interesting…"

"What's interesting?" said Cam.

"Nothing. We can discuss it later. Show me the tablet."

"Jerud," said Mycah, nodding toward his big friend.

Jerud looped his pack from around his shoulder and set it down. The blood had drained from Jerud's face, and his hands shook as he loosened the drawstrings. From inside the pack, a metallic gleam shone through.

"We came through on our end of the deal, Mistress," said Jerud in a strained voice. "Now it's your turn. Release us from the curse."

Another boom shook the castle, sending dust swirling around Mycah's knees. Winny whined nervously.

"Regretfully, your timing is inopportune," said the Stormqueen. "Hand the tablet to Master Crawford. I'll release you from your burden once an opportunity presents itself."

Mycah felt rage rise within him. After everything they'd gone through—staving off the Jabberwocks, battling the Watchers, trekking through the cursed Garden—the Stormqueen was simply going to toss them to the curb like offal?

"NO!" shouted Mycah, surprising himself with the volume of his demand. "You'll do it now!"

Several of the Guardsmen, including Sten and Johnah, reached for their weapons.

"Watch your tone, kid," said Sten evenly.

"Young master," said the Stormqueen. "I appreciate your service, but as you can see I'm rather preoccupied at the moment."

Mycah gulped. "No," he said again, more steadily this time. "You'll do it now."

Mycah forced himself to take a step forward. He needed to do this. Not just for him, but for Jerud. "Do you have any idea what sort of Hell you've put us through? Not just me, but Jerud, and Pete, and Cam? We went to the ends of the earth for you. We fought off Watchers and demons for you. We rushed back here, pushed through sleepless nights and saddle sores for you. We ran through a sewer to get into a building that is *under attack by mortars* to get this tablet to you. And you're telling us to come back later? I don't think so. You owe it to us to keep up your end of the bargain. Free us once and for all from your damned curse!"

Mycah's chest rose and fell heavily. He'd barely drawn breath throughout his speech. The guardsmen eyed him like vultures eyeing a dying hare, but the Stormqueen remained silent.

"Very well," said Rain after a few moments. "If you wish it, I'll do it now."

"Um, Mistress," said the chamberlain from behind her. "Might I advise—"

"Not now, Edward." The Stormqueen closed her eyes and took a deep breath. She raised her hands, and a warm, dusty breeze began to swirl at Mycah's feet. Rain began to chant.

"*A journey made and prices* paid. *A burden carried and levied in* trade. *Two souls restless seek my fury to sate. Free them and return them their* fate. *Souls once tied and* bound *are now free to let their fates be* found."

The hot wind swirled tightly around Mycah's body and rose, whipping around his torso and blowing his hair askew before dissipating into nothingness.

"It is done," said the Stormqueen.

Jerud took a deep breath, as if he'd surfaced from an eternity spent underwater.

Mycah wiped sweat from his brow and brushed back his hair. "We're free?"

"Yes," said Rain. "Now the tablet, if you please."

Jerud reached his thick fingers and extracted the gleaming tablet.

Mycah closed his eyes and breathed deeply. He felt as if a massive weight had been lifted from his shoulders. So many months spent constantly worrying, awaking in a cold sweat from nightmares of the black-souled demon, fretting over the fates of himself and Jerud. All gone. Finally. And yet, he'd expected more. Expected to see the demon sent back to the fiery depths from which it had come. Expected to feel a warm sensation blossoming inside him, renewing what had once been shackled.

Mycah rubbed his chest. "You're sure the curse is lifted? I thought perhaps—"

"I tell you, it's done," said the Stormqueen, her eyes narrowing. "Now hand over the tablet."

Jerud extended his hand. The chamberlain reached to take it.

"Wait," said Mycah. "Not yet. I have questions that need to be answered. About the Garden. About—"

"ENOUGH! I don't have the time for this. Guards, take the—"

A devastating blast cut short the Stormqueen's words and knocked them all to their knees. Chips of mortar sprayed out from the walls, falling upon them in a shower. Dust swirled around Mycah, catching in his throat and making his eyes water. He coughed as he struggled to right himself.

"Jerud? Cam? Are you alright?" His voice sounded distant and watery, drowned out by a sharp ringing noise that seemed to emanate from the center of his skull. Somewhere nearby, Winny was barking nervously.

Jerud groaned and pushed himself up, the tablet still clutched in his fist. Cam struggled to her feet next to him, her hair and arms covered in a fine ivory-colored dust.

"Bloody Hell…" Cam said, clutching her head.

Mycah wiggled a finger in his ear to try to clear the ringing. As the pealing faded, other sounds replaced it. Mycah could distinguish the clang of blades and sharp cracks of musket fire, but they sounded muffled, as if heard through a thick, down pillow.

The chamberlain stooped next to the Stormqueen, brushing debris from her dress and helping her rise.

"Rain," he said. "It's time. We must go."

"Yes. Yes, you're right," said the Stormqueen, blinking in confusion. "But before we leave, I have one final surprise for our attackers. Give me a moment."

"Rain, please." The chamberlain's eyebrows creased and a sense of urgency infused his voice.

Rain ignored the man and stumbled to the gaping hole in the wall. She extended her arms and mumbled a spell. The skies rumbled in response. The winds picked up as the dark clouds swirled faster and faster, churning and picking up speed. Dry branches and leaves joined dust and debris in the hot, whirling cyclone, whipping around with destructive force. The air teemed with electricity. The hair upon Mycah's arms lifted up, and still the cyclone whirled faster. Mycah heard men outside scream.

A sharp crack of lightning burst from the darkest cloud at the center of the whirlwind, igniting the tower of swirling debris and creating a raging blaze that twisted and arched over a hundred feet into the air.

The Stormqueen turned from her perch. "Hah. Let them deal with that. Now, let's go. Guards, to my quarters. The rest of you, come with me. And don't lose that tablet!"

The Stormqueen's private guard drew their weapons and hurried off down the corridor, followed by the Stormqueen and her chamberlain.

Sten grabbed Mycah by the shoulder and shoved him toward the doorway. "You heard the Queen. Go!"

Mycah stumbled through the doorframe. Jerud lumbered behind him, stuffing the tablet back into his backpack, Cam at his side. Why were they heading to the Stormqueen's quarters? Shouldn't they head back to the basement and into the sewers? At least that would provide an escape route. If they were caught in the Stormqueen's quarters, they'd be as good as dead.

Mycah coughed in the persistent dust and turned to Sten. "Look, if you want to make a last stand with the Stormqueen, that's fine by me, but I'd like to get the Hell out of here if that's alright!"

Sten shoved him again. "What do you think we're doing? There's a secret passageway in Mistress Rain's quarters that leads to the dungeons. Now go!"

Mycah groaned as he ran. A secret passage? Really? If he made it out of this fiasco alive, he was going to flay the bumbling fool who'd provided him the blueprints to the Stormqueen's estate.

The sounds of fighting seemed close now. Gunshots and cries echoed up from the stairs. As they ran, the captain that Sten had encountered earlier stumbled around a corner, a couple guardsmen at his back. Blood streamed from a gash above his left eyebrow, and he smelled of sweat and black powder.

"Mistress," he said, panting. "We've been breached. We must retreat."

"Acknowledged, Captain Farrier," said the Stormqueen as she ran past. "Come."

A musket ball whizzed down the corridor, smacking into the ceiling with a crack. Mycah ducked and ran, following the Stormqueen as she burst into her quarters. Shouts and screams followed, very close now.

"Guards, secure the doors!" shouted Rain. She headed toward a large bookshelf on the far wall.

Two of the massive members of the private guard each grabbed one side of the double doors to Rain's quarters and swung them shut. As they did so, Mycah noticed a swarm of Holy Guardsmen charging down the corridor toward them. Several sharp blasts split the air. Two musket balls crashed into the heavy oaken doors, sending splinters flying. Another whizzed through the crack of the closing doors and landed with a wet crunch.

The Stormqueen cried out in pain and crumpled to the ground, clutching her back.

"RAIN!" The chamberlain dove to her and threw his arms around her shoulders.

"Secure the doors! Secure the doors!" yelled Captain Farrier as he rushed to the Stormqueen's side.

The private guard threw their weight behind the closed doors. Moments later, the doors swelled inward under the weight on an oncoming rush. Shouts and threats poured in, muffled but distinct. The thwack of an axe blade hacking into one of the oaken doors pulled Mycah's attention momentarily, but the Stormqueen's sobbing cries drew it back.

"Rain? Rain? Talk to me, please!" said the chamberlain.

The Stormqueen was sobbing. "Oh Gods, Edward, it hurts." A red stain was spreading across the small of her back, causing the thin yellow robes to stick to her skin.

"Come, mistress," said the Chamberlain. "We must press on. Can you make it to the passageway?"

Another crash behind him. The sound of blades biting into wood.

The Stormqueen gave a cry of pain. Her arms were shaking. "Edward. I... I can't feel my legs. *I can't feel my legs!*"

"Then I will carry you my Queen," said the chamberlain. He swallowed her up in his arms and stood. The Stormqueen's robes, so often billowing seductively, now hung limply from her tiny body.

The chamberlain's eyes twinkled with tears. "Captain Farrier, her ring. Take it. Open the passageway."

The captain nodded, silent. Gently, he removed a gleaming metallic ring from the Stormqueen's left hand.

Behind Mycah, there were more thwacks, more snaps as wood splintered. Shouts could be heard more clearly now. One of the private guardsmen cursed in pain. Winny barked fearfully.

The guard captain stepped to a grand bookcase nestled against the far wall. Searching with his right hand, he found a small indent in the wall and placed the ring within it. With a click and a whirr, the bookshelf shifted forward and slid to the side, revealing a stairwell that descended into the darkness.

A splintering crash forced Mycah to look back. One of the bulky guardsmen stumbled as one of the doors gave way, blood seeping from under his garb. A dagger protruded from his midsection. Two Holy Guard stumbled through the gap, pushed through by the force of men behind them.

The first fell immediately, a black feather-fletched arrow sticking out from his throat. The second crumpled under two simultaneous cuts from the swords of Johnah and Sten.

"GO!" roared Johnah as he cut down another onrushing attacker. "This fight's mine!"

Sten nodded, a quick somber action that conveyed more than words possibly could.

As Mycah absorbed the scene, Cam's hand closed around his arm and pulled him toward the passageway. "Come on, you fool!"

The chamberlain had entered the secret passage. Behind Mycah, the Holy Guard screamed in a frenzy. More shots fired. A musket ball whizzed past Mycah's head.

"Go!" shouted Sten.

"YOU BASTARDS!" yelled Johnah.

Jerud grunted.

Captain Farrier waved them past.

Into the tunnel they went, down a long dark flight of stairs deep into the earth below. In the darkness, Mycah's eyes failed him. He could hear the rattle of Cam's sword, Winny's panting, the clatter of footsteps, and distant, receding sounds of battle. Rather than trying to think, he merely followed. Now was the time for flight, not thought.

Eventually the stairs reached a landing. A dim lantern revealed various paths. Without hesitation, Master Crawford chose one and headed forth. Mycah could hear the Stormqueen's moans and sobs over the clatter of footsteps as they ran through another damp tunnel carved from dark stone.

Jerud grunted from behind. "Mycah, lad..."

"What is it?"

"I'm... not feeling so good lad."

"Come on, Chuckles. Pull it together," said Cam. "I know you've got reserves. Remember our flight from the Watchers? Don't make me yell."

Jerud grunted in response, but his breath was labored. Pained even.

As no one had brought a brand, they travelled in total darkness, following the sorrowful cries of the Stormqueen and the splashing of the chamberlain's boots. Mycah lost track of time. His legs ached and his stomach grumbled when finally a spot of light appeared in the distance.

Following the chamberlain, Mycah blinked repeatedly when he emerged out of a large pipe into a soggy patch of marshland overgrown with weeds. It looked like an abandoned irrigation ditch. Overhead, the sky burned crimson in the muted light of dusk. Hours had passed during the journey. Mycah craned his neck. Just over the mound of earth at his back, he could see the spire of the Great Cathedral of Guildean rising in the west.

"Well, Jerud, I don't know how we did it, but we did it," said Mycah. "We beat the curse. We escaped. We're free... Jerud?"

Mycah thought the big man had been right behind him. He turned to face the last few people emerging from the tunnel. Cam and Winny emerged, then Rayven, and finally Sten.

"Where's Jerud?" said Mycah.

Sten turned. "What do you mean? He was right here. He must be lagging behind."

Mycah called down the tunnel. "Jerud?"

There was no response.

"JERUD?" called Mycah again. Again, nothing.

Mycah ran back into the tunnel, trying to fight a rising panic. Where could he have gone? How could he have lost him?

As he ran back down the tunnel, he heard a weak sound. "Mycah..."

His eyes still adjusting back to the dim light of the tunnel, he spotted Jerud, sitting in the tunnel. One hand rested at his side, the other over his belly.

A wave of relief swept over him. "Jerud. You gave me a scare there. I thought we'd lost you."

Jerud chuckled softly, but his heart seemed not to be in it. "Can't lose me that easy, lad. Not quite." He coughed and grimaced.

Mycah knelt down by the big man. "Are you alright? What's wrong? You really that out of shape?"

Jerud grinned. "I never much cared for running." He coughed again. "Come on lad, gimme a hand."

Jerud extended the hand at his side, and Mycah pulled him up. Jerud draped the arm around Mycah's shoulders and the two slowly headed toward the tunnel's exit.

"What a journey, eh lad?" said Jerud.

"Yeah, I know," said Mycah. "Hard to believe we really made it back in one piece. Of course, it's not totally over. I still intend to get some answers out of the Stormqueen, assuming she survives."

Jerud groaned. "No lad. I think this is it. You can seek your answers if you like, but I made my peace with God at the Shrine. Now that we're free from the curse, well... I think it might be the end for me."

Mycah felt a pang of sadness. Jerud had mentioned this would be their last adventure together. He'd tried not to think about it too much, as the end always seemed too far out of sight. Yet here they were, finally at the end of the journey.

"We had a good run, though, didn't we, kid?" asked Jerud as they approached the tunnel's exit.

"Yeah, of course we did, Jerud," said Mycah.

Jerud's arm still draped around his shoulders, Mycah stepped back into the light. The rest of the party had moved on ahead, but Cam and Winny remained behind. At the sound of their footsteps, Cam turned. Her eyes widened and her mouth fell open.

"Jerud! *Shit!*"

"What?" said Mycah. He followed Cam's eyes to Jerud's stomach. His off hand was pressed tightly to his abdomen.

Blood slicked his hand and drenched the bottom of his shirt.

Mycah couldn't believe what he was seeing. "Jerud? What—?"

"Tried to tell you, lad. In the tunnel," said Jerud with a wheeze. "They got me. Hit me right as we headed into that passageway." Jerud grunted and lifted his hand, revealing a round puncture in his stomach half a hand in from his side. "Here, help me sit."

Cam rushed over and took Jerud's other arm. Between the two of them, they helped him over to the side of the embankment onto a relatively dry patch of soil. Mycah knelt down next to Jerud in a daze. Words flashed through his mind.

Blood. Always blood. So much blood.

"It's not that bad," stammered Mycah. "We'll get you to a doctor. You'll be fine. Cam, go get help."

"You're a bad liar," said Jerud with a smile as Cam rushed off. "A great thief, but a lousy liar."

Mycah forced a smile. "Honestly, Jerud. You'll be fine. You've had worse. Hurry Cam!"

Jerud grimaced and held his side. When the pain subsided, he waited a few moments before continuing to talk.

"I meant it you know. What I said at the Shrine. That this was going to be our last adventure. Never thought it would end quite like this though. Thought for sure we'd fail before we even got to the Garden. Marta's going to be furious with me."

Despite his best efforts, tears were starting to well in Mycah's eyes.

"It was glorious though, wasn't it lad? The Garden? Never dreamed I'd see it. Not proud of what we did there, to be honest, but the Lord'll forgive me. He already did. Back at the Shrine where I made my peace.

"Not sure Marta'll see it that way. You'll have to go to her for me, lad. Tell her I loved her. That I always loved her. And that I'm sorry for being such an ass. Tell Pete I'm sorry too. He'll never forgive me. Oh well. He can hassle me in the afterlife, I suppose."

Jerud suppressed a twinge.

"Jerud..." Mycah's voice trailed off. His heart stuck in his throat. There was so much he wanted to say, so much he wanted to share with Jerud. His best friend. His *only* friend.

"Jerud..."

"It's alright, lad. You don't need to say anything, just listen. There's a few things I want to tell you. Some things you probably already know, but I guess I never said. I know you never had a family. Lord knows I was never close with mine, and I never had a chance to start my own. Well, I've always... I've always thought of you as a son. To me. My son.

"You've helped me in more ways than you know, lad. Who knows where I would've ended up without you. Not to say we didn't get into our fair share of jams, but you know what I mean. My life was better with you in it. A warmer place. A brighter place. I'm proud of you, lad. I'm proud of you."

Mycah could no longer prevent it. Tears streamed down his face, dripping from his cheeks and onto the ground below. With a trembling hand, he reached out and grasped Jerud's meaty fist.

"Jerud, I..."

Jerud tightened his hold on Mycah's hand.

"I love you, Mycah."

"I love you too, Jerud." Mycah's tears fell upon their clasped hands. Through watery eyes, Mycah could see that Jerud, too, was crying.

Cam rushed back over the encampment. Seeing their tears, she hesitated. "I... uh, I think Sten has some experience as a combat medic. He's on his way. I'm... uh... gonna go look for some bandages." She rushed off again.

Jerud released Mycah's hand and wiped his face to dry his tears. "One more thing, lad. I know I gave you a hard time about Cam, but honestly, she's not so bad. Treat her well. Don't make the same mistake I did."

Mycah wiped his cheeks on his sleeve. "What? What are you talking about?"

"Come, lad. I see the way you look at her. The way you rile each other up. There's something there. I know you well enough to know that. And it's obvious she needs a friend in this world. Take care of her. And remember, you still owe her your hide twice."

Mycah nodded, not worried in the least about Cam. There'd be time for her later.

Jerud grunted again and grimaced. "Come Mycah, sit with me." He patted the ground next to him. "Let's watch this sunset. It's breathtaking, isn't it?"

Mycah sat and looked into the heavens. "Yes, Jerud. It is. It certainly is."

Sten came but Jerud waved him off. Mycah wanted to argue, but in his heart, he knew that he and Jerud's journey—both the Stormqueen's quest and their journey together in life—was finally coming to a close. As the light faded, he and Jerud just sat. Together, they watched the sunset one last time.

CHAPTER TWENTY-NINE

Revelations

Mycah felt tired. Incredibly tired. Not physically tired like after a long run or a day's hike. Not sleepy either, though truth be told he hadn't slept well, but mentally tired. Emotionally exhausted.

He took a deep breath to try and fill the gaping hole in his chest with a mouthful of air. It didn't help. At least his eyes, made puffy and bloodshot from grieving, had started to feel normal again. Mycah felt as if he should still be crying, but try as he might no more tears would come. Apparently all the liquid sorrow locked up deep within his soul had already been shed.

At least Jerud's suffering had been short lived. With Mycah's aid, Jerud had used the last of his strength to move into the nearby woods where the Stormqueen's men were gathering. Once upon his bedroll, he grasped Mycah's hand in his own and spent hours revisiting old adventures from his youth. As his strength faded, he fell into a restless slumber, mumbling phrases under his breath in a soft tongue and occasionally twitching in a spasm. As the night drew on, his breathing slowed and his muscles stilled.

In the wee morning hours, the life finally left him. Mycah had cried under the light of the moons, and as silent tears cascaded down his cheeks, he said a final goodbye to his best friend.

With Sten's help, he and Cam buried Jerud in the morning, making a simple cairn for him in the woods out of stones from a nearby creek bed. Mycah said a few words, but more out of custom than out of any need to express his own emotions. As far as he was concerned, the only one who really needed to know his emotions was Jerud, and he'd already bared his heart with his old friend before his passing. Besides, with only Cam and Sten in attendance it seemed silly to make a big speech. Perhaps if Marta and Pete had been there he might've had motivation to say something more memorable.

Mycah sighed. He still didn't know how he was going to break the news to Marta and Pete. Both would take it in stride, of course—each in their own way. Pete would curse and stomp and scream, but once the news settled in, he'd go and grieve on his own. Marta would likely listen to the news stone-faced and never mention her sorrow to anyone. Instead she'd hold on to her misery and bury it deep within her heart where only she knew how to find it. Poor Marta. There'd be no happily-ever-after for her and Jerud after all.

Mycah picked at a plate of scrambled eggs long ago gone cold. Cam sat nearby, whittling another piece of pine into a figure—not of a dog, but of a man. At first glance, the figurine looked a little like Jerud, sporting broad shoulders and an aura of burliness, but the figurine lacked Jerud's overall girth and featured wild bushy hair. Winny sat at Cam's feet, tail low and ears drooping. The poor girl knew something was wrong but couldn't quite figure out what.

In the distance, the Stormqueen's men had gathered in the forest and set up a hasty camp, complete with tents, cooking fires, and guard stations. Stormguards continued to arrive throughout the night and into the morning. Mycah estimated that the force now numbered well over a hundred. Clearly the Stormqueen had established a fall back point here in case of attack, and the surviving men— or at least those still loyal to her—had amassed awaiting orders.

And orders they received aplenty. Captain Farrier wasted no time in organizing the men and splitting them into teams: some to strike camp, to scout, to guard, to forage, and others split apart for specialty services like field surgeons to help tend the wounded. Mycah noticed Sten moving amongst the injured. His skills were limited, but he administered sutures with a deft hand, and he knew the proper poultices to administer to those in need.

Rayven roamed the camp's edge like a restless panther wandering between kills. Mycah thought he noticed him glancing in his direction more than once, as if debating whether he should come say something in the wake of Jerud's passing, but he kept his distance. Mycah gritted his teeth. He couldn't help but remember that without Rayven's treachery he'd still be in possession of his best friend.

Mycah stuck a forkful of greasy eggs in his mouth and chewed. His stomach growled with hunger, but he didn't feel like eating. Unfortunately, the eggs did as little to fill the void within him as did the deep breaths he kept taking.

Mycah sighed again. What was he going to do without Jerud? It wasn't so much that he needed the big man to help him with heists, or even to provide companionship, though he would sorely miss that. It was that Jerud had always provided direction. If Mycah had a question, Jerud always knew how to guide him to find an answer. Now Mycah had dozens of questions and no answers, and the thing he needed most was direction. What would he do? Where would he go? Mycah supposed the answers to those questions were closely tied to what he believed in, and at the moment, Mycah wasn't sure what he *could* believe in.

The crunch of leaves caused Mycah to raise his head. The Stormqueen's chamberlain, Master Crawford, approached.

"Do you mind if I sit?" asked the chamberlain, waving toward the log which Mycah sat upon.

"Suit yourself," said Mycah.

With a quiet groan, the chamberlain bent down and sat upon the log. Now that Mycah studied him from up close, the signs of age were evident upon his face. In those moments when he'd lifted the Stormqueen and carried her to safety, he'd seemed young and vibrant. Now in the full light of day and without adrenaline flowing through his veins, the man looked impossibly tired—almost as tired as Mycah felt.

"I'm sorry about your friend, young man," said the chamberlain. "He seemed a noble fellow."

Mycah nodded. "Thanks. He was."

"On behalf of the Stormqueen, I wanted to thank you."

"For what?"

"For fulfilling your end of the bargain, among other things."

Mycah harrumphed. "Not like we had much of a choice."

The chamberlain raised an eyebrow. "I suppose you didn't. But you prevailed where others would've failed. And that deserves recognition."

"He had help, you know," said Cam, looking up from her carving.

"While I'm not yet fully aware of your role in this quest," said Master Crawford, "your assistance is acknowledged and appreciated. The Stormqueen gives you her thanks as well."

Cam snorted and went back to her carving.

Mycah rubbed his thumb across the back of his hand. "How is the Stormqueen, by the way?"

Master Crawford wiped a hand across his chin, now covered with a day's worth of grey stubble. "Her condition is stable. She'll live. But her faculties may forever be compromised. A musket ball lodged itself at the base of her spine and cracked several vertebrae. Currently she had no feeling in her legs. I fear she may never walk again."

Under most circumstances, Mycah would've felt saddened to hear such news, even regarding a woman for whom he didn't feel much compassion. But Jerud's passing lingered fresh in his mind. He only had enough room in his heart for so much sorrow.

"Sorry to hear that," said Mycah.

Master Crawford pursed his lips. "I've known Rain a long time, young master. She's a strong woman, and she'll find a way to thrive despite any obstacles that stand in her way. I have faith in her."

Cam's knife scraped across her figurine, filling the air with a scent of pine.

"I still can't believe she actually went down that easy," said Mycah. "I figured she'd have some ward of protection or something. I guess guns are the great equalizer, aren't they? Neither Jerud's strength nor the Stormqueen's power could stand up to the force of a simple bullet."

"The Stormqueen is a powerful woman, to be sure, but she's ultimately just that—a woman like any other. Her fate will be no different than any of ours. You'd be wise to remember that."

The chamberlain clasped his hands before him. Cam continued to scrape her knife against the pine.

"Look, Master... Cuthbert, was it?"

"Just Mycah is fine."

"Very well, Mycah. I spoke to Rain early this morning while she was awake and lucid. She feels very strongly about the loss of your friend, and she knows you seek answers. As payment for your services, she's instructed me to answer any questions you might have, and I'll do my best to follow her instructions. However, before I answer anything, I must have your word that you'll not use any information I divulge against her or any of her followers."

Master Crawford turned to Cam. "As you also journeyed to the Garden, you may also partake in the questions. But I'll need an oath from you as well."

Cam's knife scraped to a halt against the wood. She put down the carving.

Mycah turned to the chamberlain. "Why would we agree to that?"

"Because you seek the truth, and this is your one chance to uncover it." The chamberlain met his eyes. "Not that it truly matters. The things I relate to you will likely seem so outlandish that you'll have a hard time believing them yourselves, much less convincing others of their veracity."

Mycah narrowed his eyes. He'd experienced much over the past few months. What could possibly sound outlandish given what he'd already seen and heard?

"What if we have questions you can't answer? What if I seek knowledge that only the Stormqueen possesses?"

Master Crawford lifted both eyebrows. "Young man, I've been the Stormqueen's confidant for over thirty years. Anything she knows, I know. I'm more than capable of answering your questions. Now, do you give me your word?"

Mycah took a deep breath. Could it be so easy? Ask and ye shall receive? Mycah stared into the chamberlain's eyes. Not a hint of malice or deception hid there.

"Very well," said Mycah after a pause. "You have my word."

"And you, Miss Cam?"

"Yeah, sure," said Cam, shrugging. "Why not?"

"My lady, please. I require a firm affirmation."

"Fine," said Cam. She too looked him in the eyes. "I give you my word."

Master Crawford nodded in acceptance. "Very well then. Ask away."

"Alright," said Mycah. "Let's start with what Jerud sacrificed his life to bring to you. The tablet. What is it, and why does the Stormqueen want it?"

"The tablet is a reservoir of information—information Rain believes will help her reverse the tide that's causing her powers to weaken."

Mycah lifted an eyebrow. "She's losing her powers? I thought that was just a rumor started by some farmers."

"Most rumors have a basis in fact, I'm afraid. Rain noticed her powers faltering nigh on three winters ago. You may have noticed certain *oddities* this year. Winter lingering longer than expected, cold snaps in the spring and summer, rains falling out of season?"

Mycah had noticed. The cold spring rains when he'd been released from the Stormqueen's dungeon. The cool evening breezes that made Mycah think autumn had already arrived. Even this morning held an unnatural chill.

The chamberlain continued. "If Rain's unable to reverse the loss of her powers, I'm afraid winter's bite will continue to worsen. How dire the situation might become, I cannot say. But Rain is concerned, and that in turn concerns me."

"So, what," said Mycah. "Is the Stormqueen going to perform some magic on the tablet and suck new powers out of it?"

Master Crawford cracked a smile. "If only it were that easy, but alas, no. As I said, the tablet is merely a source of information. I don't know what it will reveal to her nor where it will send her to renew the source of her powers, if indeed it reveals that at all."

Mycah scratched his head. "I'm a little confused."

"I can see that," said the chamberlain. "Tell me, Master Mycah, have you ever considered how Stormqueens are able to control the elements?"

Was this going to turn into another lecture? Mycah hoped not. "No," said Mycah. "I assumed they were just born with the power. They're enchantresses, after all."

"Well, I suppose they are born with it," said Master Crawford. "But what if I told you that Stormqueens are, in fact, *not* enchantresses, but rather... how should I put this? Technicians? What if I told you that *magic*, as you see it, doesn't exist?"

"I'd say you have a very poor memory," said Mycah, starting to think that perhaps the chamberlain had lost his mind. "Just yesterday I saw her blast men with lightning bolts called down from the heavens and summon a towering cyclone of flame with her hands. If that's not magic then I don't know what is."

"I acknowledge yesterday's acts, but what I'm saying is that what you perceived as an act of magic was merely an act of technology."

"I don't get it. What's the difference?"

"To the untrained eye, none. But in actuality, the difference is quite substantial. Rain herself has no powers, other than the power to interact with said technology. On her left hand she wears a ring. You may have noticed it yesterday as we fled the palace. The ring allows her to interact with a machine deep beneath the Stormpalace, a machine that allows her to control the weather, a machine that started to fail three winters ago."

Mycah's head started to spin. This wasn't what he'd expected to hear at all. The Stormqueen's powers were controlled... by a machine?

"Wait," said Cam, looking incredulous. "So you're saying Rain has no powers at all? When you said she was a woman just like any other, you meant it? According to you, I'm just as powerful as the Stormqueen?"

"Well, that's an interesting question," said the chamberlain with a raised eyebrow. "It is not true that she's just a woman. There are certain... markers, shall we say, in her bloodline that allow her to interact with this technology. Not every woman has those. But from my limited understanding of what happened aboard the Genesis you may share that same bloodline."

"What?" said Cam. "What are you talking about?"

"You helped obtain the tablet where Mycah and Jerud could not, correct? From the version of the tale I've heard, I suspect you share the same bloodlines as Rain."

Cam's brow scrunched together. She gaped like a fish.

"Whoa, whoa, whoa," said Mycah. A thousand thoughts flew through his head in all directions. "Just back up a minute. You claim that Rain has no powers, that she can't control the weather after all, that it's all some strange mystical machine underground that does her bidding. But, come on man, she's clearly a witch! She cursed Jerud and me. She summoned a demon from the depths of Hell and made a pact with it to force us to do her bidding."

"Young master," said Master Crawford. "I'm afraid those were simple parlor tricks, performed while you languished under the effects of a severe hallucinogenic drug. There was no demon, nor was there ever a curse. I regret that deception, but we deemed it necessary."

Mycah sat, dumfounded. He tried to remember exactly what had happened in the Stormqueen's dungeon, but his recollection was fuzzy. Rain had applied some strange substance to his forehead before the conjuring—a substance that made his forehead tingle and his head hurt—but it was a component of the ritual. Wasn't it? It couldn't have been a simple drug, could it?

"But there... was a demon," stammered Mycah. "I saw it. It spoke."

"Your mind saw what it wanted to see."

"So when she freed us from the curse—"

"Rain merely swirled some winds around your feet," said the chamberlain. "Again, I apologize for the deception."

Mycah shook his head. "Next you'll tell me the curse over the Garden of Eden isn't real, either."

"No," said Master Crawford. "That curse is quite real, though it may not be a curse precisely."

"What do you mean?"

"There's an unseen power that lingers over the Genesis, a power that's existed a very long time, a power I don't understand well myself. I believe it's related to a terrible accident that occurred at the Genesis early in its days. This unseen power is real, however, and it is deadly. Victims fall ill from short exposures, and longer exposures inevitably result in death. The effects become worse the further one delves into the site. I suspect there's a singular point at the core of the Genesis that radiates some form of dark energy, an energy that works its way into a body and slowly kills like a festering wound."

"Sounds like a curse to me," said Mycah.

"Call it what you will. 'Curse' is as good a term as any, I suppose. But I don't believe the dark energy is magical in origin. Rather, I think its origin is also technological."

"Wait a second," said Cam, finally recovering enough to speak again. "I'll get back to this whole 'bloodlines' nonsense in a second. But you've said something several times now about 'the Genesis.' Aboard 'the Genesis.' At 'the Genesis.' Genesis is a story, not a place."

"Yeah, you're right," said Mycah, feeling a spark light in the recesses of his mind.

"Genesis is both a story *and* a place."

Mycah and Cam looked at each other and at the chamberlain in confusion.

Master Crawford took a deep breath. "The story of Genesis is just that. A story. An allegory. A tale contrived to depict a confusing, frightening event in a manner that's accessible to the common man. A symbolization of ideas and concepts. But taken literally, the story of Genesis is untrue."

"Look," said Mycah as he lifted his hands in appeal. "I've always been a bit skeptical. I admitted right from the start when the Stormqueen asked me that I thought Genesis was just a story. But I also didn't think there was an actual place where it all started, where we all came from. Now I've been there. I've seen it. So you can't tell me it's just a story. Besides, the Stormqueen said so herself. She said the Garden of Eden exists, and God lives there."

"The Garden of Eden, as you believe in it, *is* there," said Master Crawford. "And the powers that personify God are still there as well, just in a different form—one modified by allegory. Tell me, what did you find when you arrived at the Genesis? Did you find a Garden? Or did you find something different? A giant structure, made of metal, filled with oddities?"

"Admittedly, it wasn't what we expected—" said Mycah.

"That's an understatement," said Cam.

"—but we saw the remnants of fields, stalls, cages, tanks. Evidence of where God must've created us."

"That's not where we were created," said Master Crawford. "Rather, that's how we were delivered to this world."

"Huh?" Mycah felt more confused than ever.

"That structure's not a incubator of life, but a *vessel*. A transportation device. It brought us here from the heavens. Its name is the Genesis."

"So you're saying... it's a ship?" asked Mycah.

"Precisely. The story of Genesis, as told by the Church, was crafted in part to insulate us from the true tragedy of what happened—of the accident that resulted in the manifestation of the curse, as you prefer to call it. The creators of this story, who at the time were a vocal minority, created a story that resonated with people who were scared and frightened, a story that's persisted to this day. But this story wasn't crafted to soothe. It was crafted to reclaim power. The Church is quite influential and—as you might've noticed—it's a patriarchy, governed and ruled by men and men only."

"I noticed," said Cam.

"Genesis was crafted in part to vilify women, to heap distrust upon them and wrench power from their hands. Which brings me to your question, Miss Cam. Our ancestors came to this world aboard the Genesis, led by women. Powerful women, with specific bloodlines that allowed them to interact with advanced technologies—technologies that granted them immense power. I believe you share these bloodlines. Cam, given the proper training, you could become a Stormqueen."

"WHAT?" Cam stood, a look of shock plastered across her face. She stared at her callused hands in wonder. "You're got to be kidding me... So when I touched that weird metal sphere and those bleeding memories popped into my head, that happened because... because of some power within me?"

"No. Not because of a power, but because of your bloodlines," said the chamberlain. "You see, within our blood we all contain certain markers—identifying elements that make us who we are. We inherit these markers from our ancestors. If you have the same nose as your grandmother or the tenacity of your father, it's because of these markers.

"For as long as man has existed, these markers—borne through our blood—have been passed down generation to generation. But our ancestors, those that came here aboard the Genesis, knew of ways to modify and tailor them to grant themselves unique abilities. Specifically, the ability to control technologies with their minds. That's how Rain interacts with her ring and how she controls the weather."

Mycah couldn't believe what he was hearing. The Garden of Eden didn't exist? Man wasn't created on this world but rather brought here? And the tree of knowledge wasn't a tree but some strange metal ball aboard a ship that travelled to this land through the heavens, captained by a group of superhuman, mind-reading maidens? Was everything he'd been taught as a child a lie? And as if things couldn't become any crazier, the Stormqueen's chamberlain now seemed to think that Cam—broad-shouldered, sword-swinging, curse-spouting Cam of all people—was a Stormqueen in hiding?

Mycah took a deep breath. "Hold on a minute. Back up for just one second. Are you saying... are you saying God doesn't exist?"

"As to that, I cannot say," said Master Crawford. "Perhaps the Genesis brought us here from the heavens where God created us. Perhaps it brought us here from a different world, but that in itself doesn't disprove the existence of God. Whether or not God exists is a personal question and cannot be answered by our history. But the existence of Genesis does discredit the Church, and that's why they're so eager to destroy us."

Mycah sat in silence while Cam stood, staring at her hands in disbelief.

"It's much to take in, I understand," said Master Crawford as he stood. "Though you have no more reason to believe me than you do the teachings of the Church, I feel that your own experiences will lead you to the same inevitable conclusions I arrived at long ago, once I found out what you now know. Take your time. Reflect upon what you, personally, have experienced. If you have any questions, don't hesitate to ask myself or Rain."

With that, the elderly chamberlain turned and headed back toward camp. Cam sat back down on the stump. She picked up the figurine she'd been working on and stared at it, lost in thought.

Mycah felt as if his world had been turned upside down. The story Master Crawford had related seemed utterly ludicrous—preposterous even. But was it really so far fetched?

Everything the chamberlain had said about Genesis and the origins of man seemed oddly plausible. Was it really more preposterous to think that man had been created by an all-knowing, all-powerful, invisible deity upon the summit of a mountain at the dawn of time than to think that man had been brought here by a vessel that could traverse the heavens? Both scenarios seemed unlikely, yet either could be supported by the evidence he'd seen. Mycah recalled the map Father Maple had shown him and Jerud at the Grand Cathedral's library showing the density of human settlements radiating out from a central point in the world. Whether man was created or brought to the Genesis site, the map would still make sense either way.

Of the two options with which Mycah had been presented, the one offered by the Church was more comforting. The Church's perspective offered a kind, caring God, and firm answers to questions about life and death. The chamberlain's history of man did neither. Instead, it raised more questions.

With that said, there were certain irregularities that made him believe that perhaps the chamberlain's story might hold some truth. For one thing the Church's teachings clearly misrepresented the Garden of Eden. Admittedly, the scriptures didn't describe in detail the Garden after God's curse, as the Captain of the Watchers had stressed, but anyone would be hard pressed to reconcile the sight of the massive metal structure at the Genesis site with a flourishing garden or a floating metal ball that burned memories into one's skull with a fruit-bearing tree.

Perhaps the biggest reason Mycah felt inclined to believe the chamberlain was a personal one—the simple fact that terrible things happened despite the watchful gaze of a kind God. Jerud, for all his faults, was a kind and pious man. Should his untimely death be considered a kindness? A gift from God?

Of all the things Master Crawford had related, Mycah had the hardest time believing that magic, of all things, didn't exist. Whether the Stormqueen's powers arose from some machine hidden deep underground or from a mystical force that welled up within her own bosom, what difference did it make? If you couldn't explain something then it was as good as magic. Guns weren't magic because everyone knew they functioned via black powder, and people knew how to make black powder out of sulfur and charcoal and saltpeter. Perhaps if the Stormqueen could explain how to conjure flaming cyclones out of thin air, then perhaps he'd finally stop believing in magic, but until that day, to him magic was *quite* real.

Cam stroked her wooden carving. "You know, my dad always told me I was special. Always said there was something inside me that burned brighter than in anyone else. But a Stormqueen? I don't think that's what he meant."

"I'm glad Jerud wasn't around to hear all that," said Mycah. "It would've just riled him up. Eaten away at him. It's better he died believing what he did. At least that way he died at peace."

Cam lifted her head. "So you believe what the chamberlain said? About Genesis? About our origins? About... me?"

"I'm not sure what to believe, to be honest," said Mycah. "But I'm more inclined to believe what he said than not to believe it, if that makes any sense."

"Yeah," said Cam. "It does."

Winny whined and stretched, laying her head upon Cam's knees. Cam gave her a scratch between the ears.

"So what now?" asked Cam.

"Good question," said Mycah. He grabbed a stick from the forest floor and began to poke the earth with it. "If we're to believe the chamberlain, then there's more at stake than us trying to sort out our feelings over history and theology. It sounds like we could all be seriously screwed if the Stormqueen doesn't fix her powers. As for you? Well... I have no idea what to make of *you* anymore."

"Oh, that's very flattering. Thanks, you *ass*."

"What I mean is that if you're a Stormqueen, then maybe it'll be up to you to help sort out Rain's mess."

"I'm not a Stormqueen," said Cam. "And I'm not going to be a Stormqueen."

Mycah snapped his twig in half. "Regardless, I can't really go back to Guildean. Sounds like the Church would put my head on a pike if I tried." He sighed. "Guildean's the only home I've ever had. And now I've lost it. Guess that makes me homeless. Again."

"And that makes two of us," said Cam.

A breeze stirred the leaves overhead, and sounds of activity meandered over from the Stormqueen's camp.

"I suppose we could stay a while," suggested Mycah. "Not for long. Just for a bit. Admittedly, I'm curious about that whole 'mysterious underground machine that grants powers to control the weather' bit."

"Yeah," said Cam. "And it would be pretty sweet to learn how to blast lightning from my hands. Even though I'm not going to become a Stormqueen. Just might be nice in a fight, you know?"

"We'd still be on the run from the Church. And the Watchers," said Mycah.

"I've been on the run for months now. Wouldn't bother me. Or Winny."

"And at least there would be food. Looks like the Stormqueen's men are well stocked."

"You know me," said Cam, cracking a smile. "Food is definitely a plus."

Mycah nodded. "So... alright then. We'll stay, at least for now. And we see where this journey takes us."

"Alright. It's a deal. For now."

Cam stuck out her hand. Mycah reached over and clasped it, locking eyes with Cam. After a moment, Cam let go. She looked at the ground furtively, and after tucking a stray strand of hair behind her ear, she hastily picked up her paring knife and went back to her carving.

Mycah smiled as he pulled back his hand. He had so much to dwell upon, so much to consider. He needed time to sit and think, but there'd be time for thinking later. Plenty of time. For now, as the cool breeze wafted through his hair and the touch of Cam's hand lingered on his skin, and with a newly minted pact agreed upon, the future suddenly seemed a shade brighter. With all that had happened over the last day, he'd consider any small ray of sunshine a blessing, though whether that blessing came from God, or a Stormqueen, or merely the sun, he didn't know. The answer to that question would simply have to wait.

ABOUT THE AUTHOR

Alex P. Berg is a mystery, fantasy, and science fiction author, a scientist, and a heavy metal aficionado. Connect with him at www.alexpberg.com. If you'd like to be advised when new books are released, please sign up for his mailing list on his website. You will only be contacted when new books come out, your address will never be shared, and you can unsubscribe at any time.

Word of mouth is critical to author success. If you enjoyed this novel, please consider leaving a positive review on Amazon. Even if it's only a line or two, it would be a *huge* help. Thanks!